Looking For Henry Turner

Looking For Henry Turner

W.L. Liberman

Published 2016 by Creativia
ISBN: 978-1534938083
Cover art by Kat Kozbiel

1

Toronto 1960

Ying Hee Fong looked like an angel minus the wings. Whoever shot him did a good job. He couldn't have been deader if he'd lived then died again. Blood gushed from a jagged hole in his right temple, spilling into a sticky pool circling his head. He looked serene. Dark eyes stared into eternity, legs sprawled, arms thrown up over his shoulders. Just like a kid making angels in the snow. Except the snow melted, stripping bare the rotting garbage of a back alley in Chinatown.

Ying worked for John Fat Gai, a gambler and racketeer. John ran illegal poker games and craps in dingy rooms above chop suey joints and small food markets where, for a nickel, you could catch a disease and buy a rotting cabbage. Wherever you found a spare table, chairs, bootleg whiskey and suckers willing to throw their money away, the action never stopped. Ying dealt the cards, sometimes straight up. The dealers worked six shifts a week from 11 at night until six the following morning. They got Sundays off. None of them went to church. Like the others, Ying came off a boat owned by John who paid customs officials at Pier 21 in Halifax to look the other way. He arrived with a host of other bedraggled refugees toting a battered suitcase and not much else. His life and earnings belonged to John Fat Gai. Ying had made his deal but decided he couldn't live with it. We saw the result.

John found out Ying had been skimming the pot. Ying went into hiding; an impossibility in a city where dirty money counted, information came cheap and fear ruled above the law. In a city known as Toronto the Good.

Funny. I never seemed to see that side.

My kid brother, Eli, gambled, although calling what he did, gambling, never seemed right. He went to the card dens and lost all his money. Most of the games in town barred him because he liked to turn over tables and sock guys after some card shark cleaned him out. Lately, Eli had been playing in Chinatown. He owed John Fat Gai a wad of dough. Usually, when Eli found himself in trouble, he called on me to bail him out. Depending on the circumstances, I'd say yes or no.

This time, I didn't hesitate, knowing what would happen to Eli if he didn't have the scratch to pay the debt. Most guys who crossed John ended up dead. In the past year, six bodies had turned up. Four had come in as floaters, two in Lake Ontario, one in the Humber River and another in the Don River. The last two cadavers had missing ears, eyes and tongues. Another had been burnt to a crisp in a house fire. The sixth guy took a swan dive off the roof of the Imperial Theatre on Yonge Street. Landed on a brand new Ford Galaxie crushing the hood. All connected to John. Nothing proven. No arrests made. No witnesses. No one even chirped.

My partner, Birdie and I, paid a visit to John Fat Gai to see how we could straighten things out. I think he respected me. I almost arrested him once. He feared Birdie because of his size and volatile temperament. John told me and Birdie, in the nicest way, to find Ying pronto or we'd find parts of Eli's anatomy all over Chinatown. Ying had committed an unpardonable sin. He'd stolen from John. We found Ying. We just didn't count on him being dead.

"Think it was John?" Birdie's deep voice rumbled in his chest.

I shook my head and thought. The angel's wings lay still. "This doesn't look good for Eli," I said.

"Maybe he needs to take a vacation, somewhere nice and quiet and out of the way," Birdie replied.

I thought about that too.

"Better call Callaway."

Birdie nodded, returned to his full height of six feet seven inches and strode to the phone booth on the corner. I'd worked with Callaway in homicide. I thought about families and how much trouble they caused. Mine had given me nothing but grief ever since I could remember.

2

"My God is the one true God," Birdie said.

"Uh-huh," I murmured, not troubling to glance up from the sports pages of the *Toronto Telegram*. The Argos had been sniffing around Russ Jackson, maybe signing him as the new quarterback. That would be a coup, for a change. A different kind of miracle.

I took a scant second to think about my own religious situation. It was tough being a Jew because the Jew was born with a stain on his soul. We carried a helluva burden being God's chosen people. I wouldn't wish it on anybody. All that pressure.

We lounged around the offices of Gold Investigations waiting for something to happen. That's me, Mo Gold and my associate, Arthur Birdwell, aka, Birdie. We had a walk-up over a hardware store on King Street west of Bathurst, south side. The sign said, Discretion Assured. I'd spent 10 years in the military and another 10 on the force before I decided I'd had enough of idiots telling me what to do.

Birdie smiled, opening his face to the grace of the early morning light. Around the wastebasket he'd littered crumpled balls of paper. Birdie considered himself to be a basketball maven, heir to the Harlem Globetrotters, so go figure. Couldn't dunk the low one.

"Because he is a merciful God, full of forgiveness." He leaned his large frame toward me. "I may commit terrible sins every day of the week but come Sunday, I am washed away clean, ready to begin again."

"Doesn't the church frown on committed sinners?"

I noticed that Dick Shatto, the team's best halfback, might be out for a few weeks with a hamstring pull.

The smile never wavered.

"Yes, that is true," he replied. "But they never give up on us. There is always hope and as long as you have hope, there is the possibility of salvation."

"Is that important to you? This idea of salvation?"

"Very important." Birdie boomed. "How would I live with myself if I thought that some day I couldn't be saved, redeemed by God?"

"You think about this often?"

"All the time."

"During the War?"

"Especially during the War. It was the War that helped me see the light."

"But you didn't go to confession."

Birdie shrugged his massive shoulders and leaned back in the wicker chair choking squeaks and groans out of it. He nodded. The stubble on the top of his scalp glistened. Occasionally, an island lilt murmured out of his speech.

"No, too busy killing Germans but I prayed and asked forgiveness before I shot the next Kraut bastard and when the priest came round finally, I didn't hold back."

I laughed.

"You kept him in the confessional for an hour and a half. When you got out, there must have been 60 guys lined up behind you. Before the next guy in line could sing, I saw the priest sneak out the back and hit the latrine. You must have scared Jesus right out of him."

Birdie guffawed with me.

"Those were special times," he said.

"You got that right," I said. I looked at Birdie and also thought about the fact that having a black man for a partner would get me lynched in Alabama. Torontonians had prejudice in them but they wore it differently. It came through veiled sneers and whispers not burning crosses and hangings.

Birdie and I met on a massive troop ship, The Grey Ghost, just after it steamed out of Halifax Harbour in May, 1940. Fortunately, it didn't get torpedoed. It carried us and 9998 other green stiffs heading for the war via a stopover in England. We bunked below the water line and none of the other rookies wanted to share the cubicle where we'd slung our hammocks. That was fine by me. Shit faces. All of them. I got my own back when I earned my stripes. I boxed in the military—middle weight—good way to let off steam and get your own back from guys who'd stiffed you one way or another.

A light tap rattled the door. I barked at it. After a moment, it creaked open and an elderly black woman poked her head in. She wore a Sunday bonnet, one with a tie under her sharp chin. Her cloth coat appeared worn but well looked after, carefully brushed. She had on her good shoes, the ones she'd wear to church. That's the feeling I had. She'd been praying recently.

"Mr. Gold?"

"That's me. Mrs?" I stood up to show her I had some manners.

"Turner. Aida Turner." She glanced quickly at Birdie, then turned away and stared at the floor.

"My associate, Arthur Birdwell." Birdie smiled at her. "Won't you sit down Mrs. Turner?" I offered.

She nodded without saying anything else, and positioned herself in the half-wingback chair I put out for clients. Birdie perched himself on the credenza beside me, swinging one leg that brushed the floor with the sole of his size 17 brown leather brogue.

"What can we do for you Mrs. Turner?" I asked.

"I want you to find my son. He's missing."

"How long's he been gone?" I asked, lighting a Sweet Cap.

"Eight years," she said.

I paused. "That's a long time. What about the cops?"

"They don't care. They told me he run off and he's gone for good," she replied.

I nodded, taking in this bit of wisdom while I heard Birdie tsking under his breath. "They're probably right," I said. "Listen,

Mrs. Turner...we don't take missing persons cases...it's still a matter for the police."

Her back stiffened and she glared at me. "I told you. They gave up–they don't want nothing to do with it and I got to know what happened to my Henry–he's all I got, all I live for..."

"Why now, Mrs. Turner? After all, it's been eight years."

She nodded like she expected me to ask the question. She took a gulp of air and swallowed. "I've been poorly lately. Finally, I went to the doctor. They gave me some tests. Cancer, they said. I don't know how much time I got left and I want to see my son before I die. I want to know he's safe."

Birdie shot me a look and I knew what it meant. I never liked it when he did that. It was his "God will reward us" look and I'd seen it plenty of times in Europe. Me and Birdie. Fish out of water in the Royal Scots Regiment. A Jew and a black man. I was 18 and Birdie was 20. We'd seen plenty and I owed him my life more times than I could count so when he gave me the look, I knew I was stuck.

I shuffled my feet, cleared my throat, scuffed my shoes, sighed and crushed the Sweet Cap into the ashtray. Birdie didn't have a desk and didn't want one. He liked the idea of me being the front guy. Would make people feel more comfortable, he said. Just looking at him made clients nervous.

"We get $250 a week, Mrs. Turner."

She'd been off in her thoughts too but glanced up sharply at my voice.

"I've got a thousand dollars. Took me 10 years to save it but I got it and want to use it to find my Henry..." She fumbled in her plastic bag and I was thinking, what? A maid or a cleaner somewhere, working to save that kind of money, scrimping every week, putting a little bit by, knowing what she wanted to use it for. How could I say no to that? I didn't feel guilty about taking it, we had to eat too. Aida Turner pulled a wad of used, crumpled bills bound with an elastic band and slapped them down in front of me. I counted out $250 and handed the rest back to her.

"We'll get what's owed when we're done. One way or another. If I think we're getting nowhere after the first week, I'll tell you, Mrs. Turner. I won't string you along to take your money, okay?"

Aida Turner allowed herself a glimpse of a smile. "Okay. Thank you." She glanced again at Birdie who gave her his most benign expression.

I basked in the glow of so much mutual admiration that I was attempted to light another Sweet Cap, but stopped myself and fidgeted with a pen instead.

"Ah, Mrs. Turner, tell me about your son, Henry. What happened to him? Tell me everything you can remember, tell me who his friends were, his known associates, tell me where he worked, where he liked to go in the evenings, any women he may have known, everything and anything; all right?"

Aida Turner nodded and handed over a photograph. A pose typical of high school graduation–blanket lighting, artificial smile–but I saw a handsome, young man, thin moustache penciled on his upper lip, nice teeth, sweet-looking brown eyes.

"That's my Henry when he was 18. He'd be 32 now."

"Just fill in the details, please," I said.

Aida Turner told her story: "My Henry graduated from Harbord Collegiate in 1946, he was a bright boy, full of ideas. He wanted to do well, and wasn't afraid of hard work, no sir, he would put his back to it, whatever it was. But he wanted to make a few dollars, settle in and have a family. His father died when Henry was just six and it was a terrible blow to him, losing his father at that age. He missed his father so. I tried my best but it wasn't the same. A boy needs his father, you know, to show him things, take him places. My Henry never had that but I did my best, I always tried as hard as I could. He could have gone to university if we had the money, but I just couldn't afford it. Henry didn't resent it, he wasn't angry or anything just knew he'd have to make it up himself. Henry worked as a stock boy at the supermarket for a while, then he went to work for the city as a cleaner, the wages were good and the hours weren't bad, sometimes, he'd be cleaning the parks and cemeteries. He liked outdoor work, felt it made him strong and healthy, he didn't like being cooped up inside. Then when he heard that the new subway was being built and the wages were good, he applied and got taken on. And that was fine until he had the accident and hurt his back, hurt it bad. He was in hospital for six weeks. After he got out, he couldn't work on the subway anymore, it was too hard so Henry got a job as a chauffeur for a wealthy family and that's when the trouble started."

"What trouble is that?" I had been taking notes as she talked, trying to make sure I had all the pieces.

Aida Turner glanced downward and kept her head down.

"There was a daughter, younger than Henry. She was wild and carried on and Henry, he always thought the best of people. Then, in the spring of 1952–May the twelfth–Henry disappeared. They said he never showed up for work that day but I know that's not true. Something happened and no one will talk about it. They're hiding something. Been hiding it for eight years. I've got to know what happened to him. I need you to find him for me, Mr. Gold. Please. It's what I hope and pray for every day." She rummaged in her bag and pulled out a hanky, gave it a mighty blow, snuffled a bit and stuffed it back in.

"Did Henry live at home?" I asked.

"Yes, he did."

So, I was thinking, maybe a Mama's boy, maybe a little too repressed, a young man itching to bust out on his own get out from under her thumb. All of these thoughts ran through me but I didn't want to jump to any conclusions too quick.

"We'll need to see his room," Birdie said in his deep, cavernous voice but gentle-like, he didn't want to startle her. Aida Turner looked at him, her eyes wide and lips tight but she nodded.

"Does this mean you are taking the case for certain?"

I nodded at her.

"I guess it does, yeah. I wouldn't have taken your money otherwise, Mrs. Turner. In the meantime, write out everything you can remember about what happened, okay? Give us a list of all his friends and associates and any contact information you've got. And leave us your address and phone number. When would be a good time to take a look?"

"This evening will be fine, if you like. I get home from work around seven. Here's the address and phone number. I'll prepare the list for you this evening."

She picked up a pen from my desk and I slid a notepad across to her. She bent her head down concentrating on the writing. After several moments, she examined her work and set the pen down. I stood up and reached across the desk to shake her hand. Her strength surprised me, callused palm, sinewy fingers, hands that had done hard work for a long time. I could feel the broom and mop handles, sense the scrub brushes in those fingers.

"We'll see you this evening, Mrs. Turner, probably closer to eight o'clock, if that's all right."

She released my hand and clasped her handbag as she stood.

"That'll be fine," she said. "Goodbye." She nodded at Birdie who acknowledged her, then tugged at the door and left. I heard her footsteps echoing in the hall fading down the corridor leading to the staircase. The door went and the outside bell jangled and then silence.

"I know," I said. "Sucker for a sob story but you're worse than I am."

Just as Birdie opened his mouth to answer, the bell from the street door jangled again. Birdie was about to stand up from his perch on the credenza but sat back down, while I remained behind the desk. We heard a clattering of high heels on the stairs, it grew louder in the corridor, then the door burst open. A pretty, young, blonde woman in an Oleg Cassini tailored suit, with matching hat and gloves and shoes carrying the tiniest square handbag, appeared, breathless and panting from climbing the two sets of stairs. She had an attractive heave to her bosom. I looked some more. She was a dish–long, golden tresses falling about her shoulders, red lipstick applied well, startling blue eyes and if the suit had been a little snugger, I could've traced every curve and nuance of her body.

"That woman…that woman who was just here…what did she want?"

The eyes grew larger as we greeted her with utter silence. A silence that egged her on.

"Tell me, do you hear? I demand to know...."

I stood up slowly. "Take a load off first. Miss...?"

She looked at me, then at Birdie, then back at me again. I could tell she liked the idea that she could get what she wanted whenever she wanted it. She made a growling sound deep in her throat but sat down in a huff.

"Mrs. Lawson. Mrs. Alison Lawson."

The name seemed vaguely familiar and to appease her, I sat down too. Birdie remained where he was.

"Thank you, Mrs. Lawson," I said. "And your interest in the lady is...?"

"I hate the way you don't finish your sentences. Didn't you graduate from school?"

Together, Birdie and I guffawed.

"I graduated from several schools of all different types, Mrs. Lawson."

"I see," she said rummaging around in the tiny bag, although hunting and pecking would be more accurate. A tigress on the prowl. She removed a cigarette case, unsnapped it and placed a Dunhill between her ruby lips. I leaned over with a light, which she took, and she stared at me from under some awfully long lashes.

"You were saying?" I said and snapped the lighter closed, dropping it into my jacket pocket.

"Mrs. Turner works for me as a housemaid, well actually, she works for my parents but you can see I have a direct interest in what she does."

"Not if it's personal business, Mrs. Lawson," Birdie boomed not sparing the resonance. She gave him a withering look but needless to say, he didn't melt or flinch.

"Everything Aida does is my business. Everything."

"I'm sorry to disappoint you, Mrs. Lawson," I said. "Was there anything else we can do for you?"

She drew heavily on the cigarette, blew a plume of smoke and nodded.

"Yes, I'd like to hire you." I raised my eyebrows. "Things have gone missing lately, that's why I followed Aida. I suspect she might be the thief."

"What sort of things?" I asked.

"Money, a watch, a charm bracelet, that sort of thing."

"Valuable?"

"Well, the money was petty cash–a few dollars here and there, the watch and charm bracelet were given to me a long time ago and have sentimental value, their actual worth is minimal."

"How many servants do you have on staff, Mrs. Lawson?"

"Seven."

"How many live-in?"

"Just two–Aida and the cook. Aida has two evenings and Sundays off to go to church. She's a religious woman."

"Has Mrs. Turner been in your employ long?"

"Forever. Since I was a little girl. After I married, I convinced my parents to let me take her along, part-time. She spends two days a week with my mother. My husband had no objections."

"And yet you suspect her now, after all these years, of taking things of little real value?"

"I do."

"Yet, given the number of staff you have and likely other service people who come and go, you have quite a few people moving through your house, do you not?"

"Certainly. I can't keep track of everyone and then I'm not always at home. I do have a life of my own."

"Of course. I don't think we can help you, Mrs. Lawson. I suggest you call the police if you have some evidence and they will assist you free of charge," I said.

She leaned forward in her chair, arching her back, then stubbed her cigarette out in the ashtray.

"I don't want my husband to find out and we don't need the publicity. I want this done discreetly. I'll pay you a hundred dollars a day."

I paused, letting that sink in.

"That's very generous of you, Mrs. Lawson but beyond our normal fee for this sort of thing and besides, we have a client already. Perhaps I can refer you to someone else?"

"So, that's it."

"Pardon?"

"Her money is good but mine isn't?" She stood up abruptly. "You're making a big mistake. More than you'll ever know." Alison Lawson turned on her sharp, expensive heels and without glancing back, stalked out leaving the office door open. We heard her beating a tough, fast rhythm on the stairs.

Birdie raised his eyebrows at me. All I could do was shrug. A nutcase. We get them all the time. Most aren't as attractive as Alison Lawson, however.

3

John Fat Gai slurped noodles in his restaurant of the same name–Fat Gai's. Bang on the corner of Spadina and Dundas, prime real estate in Chinatown. Most people didn't know that Toronto had the largest Oriental population outside of mainland China. You think San Francisco has a thriving Chinatown? Forget it. Nothing compared to Toronto. All of this played right into John Fat Gai's hands, of course. More shopkeepers to buy his protection racket. More marks for his gambling tables. More addicts for the dope he peddled and the girls he pimped. Nothing but a sweet guy all in all. John the warlord with Chinatown as his kingdom.

John occupied the corner booth at the back. He sat facing the door so he could monitor who came in and who went out. A mirror hanging on the opposite wall helped him observe the foot traffic but it had been set at an angle so he didn't look into it directly. That was bad luck. I'd thrown a chair through it once but that was another story. Also bad luck.

Birdie and I pushed our way in. John's cronies sat packed around two wooden tables, laden with food. I spotted barbecued pork spare ribs, kung pao chicken and Shanghai noodles. The aroma hit me and my mouth watered. The high-pitched conversations halted midscreech as we stepped inside. John's goons wore snap-brim fedoras, padded jackets and high-waist, pleated trousers with snaps. Each man wore a shoulder holster and filled it with their weapon of choice, a nickel-plated .45 pistol. A dozen pairs of hostile eyes turned in our direction.

Just as a precaution, I packed my service piece. Birdie packed two, one under each arm and he kept a snub .38 down his right sock. Out of the corner of my eye, I noticed some legit patrons scurry away. Birdie scorched the room with his fiercest glare. John sat back in the leatherette booth eating calmly, set down his chop sticks, and sipped some green tea, all without looking up. My gaze flitted between the tables of silent gunmen and John, then back to the gunmen.

"Smells good in here," I said.

John smiled. Suddenly, everyone smiled. John beckoned and the animation returned. The gunmen continued attacking the platters in front of them.

"I certainly wouldn't mind some chop suey," Birdie said.

"We're not here to eat."

"Well, we could shoot somebody and then eat if that will make you feel better."

I paused and turned to him. "It might," I replied.

John sat there with an amused look on his face.

"Ah so, venerable gentleman. To what do I owe dis pleasure?" he trilled.

"Cut it out, John," I replied and Birdie tssked again.

John threw his head back and laughed. He had a slender throat, a clean-cut jaw and a clean upper lip. Unlike his gang, he remained bareheaded, his lank hair parted in the middle falling foppishly over the tops of his ears.

"Sorry," he said in the well-modulated tone of a BBC announcer. "Just my little joke." He'd grown up in London learning the family trade. After he'd gotten into a little trouble bribing some customs agents, John had been deported. He came to Toronto to settle and established a string of enterprises including this thriving restaurant.

John moved opium through a warren of warehouses all along the docklands. None of this proven, of course. He'd never been charged with anything serious, never had anything stick. John traced his lineage back to the Sung Dynasty around 1100 A.D., marking the rise of the merchant class in cities spread out across China. With the rise of the merchant class, greed, avarice and crime became engendered. In a way, John came by his criminality honestly.

I knew John to be a contented killer with an obsessive interest in spirituality. He believed in ghosts and evil demons frightened him. He wore a jade dragon pendant around his neck as a talisman. He carried a ring of jade coins to symbolize good fortune.

On the table in front of him, he spread out a handful of playing cards, all eights from each of the suits. Eight meant good luck. Festooned inside his house he'd planted bamboo, another means to ward off evil intentions. Each common room had aquariums stocked with fish as fish represented the means to overcome barriers in life. He ate peaches every day imported through his own trading company. The peach symbolized longevity and immortality.

I'd heard rumours that he slept with lights ablaze to deter the spirits from attacking him. He carried firecrackers in his pockets to ward them off. Every night, flares were lit outside his house. His guards patrolled the halls, corridors and elaborate grounds carrying burlap torches soaked in kerosene. I pictured them tripping and setting the joint on fire. Chinese hellfire. I'd bring the weenies and marshmallows. I think that's why Birdie spooked him. John thought Birdie represented a demon that had his number. We did nothing to discourage that notion.

Birdie and I slid into the booth opposite him. The goons moved to squeeze in beside us when Birdie gave them a look. They hesitated, looked at John, who, with that amused look, nodded slightly and they backed off. Then he barked something in Mandarin and the two disappeared.

"Ying's dead," I said.

"I know," John replied.

I took out a pack of Sweet Caps and offered them to John. He looked down and flinched. Only four in the pack. Four–symbol of death in

Chinese culture. He shook his head curtly. I put the pack away without taking one out.

A waiter set a tin pot of green tea before us, ceramic cups flipped over and steaming liquid poured out. I picked up the cup and sipped. Birdie took one sip and sucked the cup dry. Less than twenty seconds later, a plate of spring rolls appeared and some pork dumplings.

"Please," John said. "You are my guests." He scooped up the eights and slid them into his pocket.

We dug in. Had to admit the food was good–fresh and hot. Birdie could have downed the contents of each platter himself. Keeping him fed had been a problem in the Army. He lost over 50 pounds and always complained about being hungry. Never enough rations on hand.

"I don't like being used, John. Neither of us do."

John accepted this comment silently. If we'd been Chinese and had said this to him, he'd have had our throats slit and bodies dumped in the harbour.

"I understand," he replied. "Unfortunately, I didn't kill Ying."

I went for a spring roll. It crunched nicely between my molars.

Birdie shoveled three dumplings into his mouth.

"Why not?"

The two men hovering near by tensed, one muttered something I took to be a profanity but John shushed them with a gesture.

"Simple," John replied. "He took a great deal of my money and I want it back. If I was going to have him killed, the money had to be recovered first. It is still missing. I had every reason to keep him alive you see. As did you," he said to me. "This is a most unfortunate occurrence for your brother, unless you can pay his debt, of course."

I digested this along with the spring rolls. John wanted his cash, all of it. "Any ideas?"

John shrugged. "That is your business. For your brother's sake, I hope you come up with a solution quickly."

"You don't want to go to war with us, John," I said and held up four fingers.

"Agreed," he replied amiably but glanced at Birdie nervously and worried the dragon pendant. "Better for all of us if you find the money."

"How much is missing?" Birdie asked, pouring out more tea for the two of us.

John shifted in his seat, then drummed his slender fingers on the table. He drummed each hand ten times. I nodded.

"Okay, John. We'll keep looking."

Birdie grabbed the last two dumplings and spring roll, and downed another cup of green tea. We eased out of the booth. As we stood up, the tables of henchmen went silent. I nodded to John. "I'll let you know if we find out anything."

John smiled coldly. "Don't make me wait too long."

As we pushed through the tables and chairs and the inert, watchful bodies, John kept watch in the mirror. He spread the eights back on the table.

4

Aida Turner kept a two-bedroom flat on Symington Avenue not far from the Junction, a run-down crossroads of industrial wasteland mixed with dilapidated residences, a stone's throw from the barren emptiness of the railway lands. Earlier waves of immigration brought Ukrainians, Macedonians, Croatians, Serbs and Poles looking for a better life.

This section of the city had never seen good times. The bosses of the foundries, the mills and the wire factories liked to keep their workers close by. They felt they could get more out of them that way and they did, working them to death on land polluted with lead and iron. The stench from the tanning factories and meat packing plants lay like a thick, sour slab. Home to the largest stockyards in the country and I swore I could hear the cattle lowing in fear just as they were being slaughtered.

Fifty years ago, the district had such a serious drinking problem with the workingmen flooding the bars and taverns after their shifts that it voted to go dry after Prohibition. It remained dry ever since. The bars closed and Methodist churches took their place scraping some respectability out of the industrial waste that had been left behind.

Aida Turner's flat occupied the main floor of a row house at 263 Symington, above Bloor Street but below Dupont Avenue, light years away from Mrs. Lawson's residence, I guessed. At seven-thirty that evening, we paid her a visit. The flat looked small but cozy. She kept it spick and span. A chain-link fence and a well-oiled gate led to a recently swept walk up to the front door. The flat had a decent-sized living room and a faux fireplace, a working kitchen with fitted appliances, a threadbare but clean and well-maintained carpet in the living room, two small bedrooms at the back, the larger of the two was clearly Henry's. It overlooked a small garden. Compact, but neat, the grass raked, flower beds clean where roses and hydrangeas bloomed, a large sunflower perched on either side of the bed with some hosta filling in the blanks. A tiny oasis surrounded by rotting vegetation. I nodded my approval.

"Nice garden." I stood in her kitchen gazing out the back window. "I like a bit of gardening myself, find it relaxing, eases the strain of the day."

"Do you get many stressful days, Mr. Gold?"

I looked at her and smiled, like she was telling me that the stress of losing her son could not be equaled. "I've had my share—we both have–depends what's on the burner, if you know what I mean, Mrs. Turner."

"Or who," Birdie said and he gave me a look that told me what he was thinking. I knew because I thought the same thing–my father, a notorious gunsel and thief, currently incarcerated in the Don Jail. The old man had been a blight on my life ever since I could think. Ever since I had a conscious memory and that would make me maybe four or five years old. This time he'd been done for manslaughter and it looked like a life stretch. If he ever got out, he'd be old and decrepit.

"May we see Henry's room, please?"

She rose stiffly from the hard backed chair in which she'd been sitting. "It's through here."

Henry's room mirrored the rest of the place, neat and orderly. His clothes hung tidily in the closet, dresser drawers filled to the brim, two pairs of shoes, one brown, one black, perfectly polished and placed heel-to-toe on a rack. A high school yearbook lay on the side table. I took in photos of Henry in his football and track uniforms.

"He fit in there, Mrs. Turner?" I held up the yearbook.

She looked wistful for a moment. "Oh yes. Henry was always popular in school, he had a lot of friends and not all of them was colored neither. It just didn't seem to matter when it came to Henry, he was friendly with everybody."

"What were his prospects?"

"Like I told you, he always worked after school and after he finished, he didn't have any trouble finding jobs."

"Then he started working as a chauffeur for the Foster family..." Mrs. Turner nodded. I set the yearbook back on the dresser careful not to disturb any of the photographs or trophies. Two for track and field I noticed, so Henry had been a talented runner. "Do you work for a Mrs. Lawson presently?"

"I do," she replied. "And her parents too."

"Have you noticed anything going missing in the household? Nothing too valuable, knick knacks and such."

"No, I haven't noticed anything missing, Mr. Gold. Why do you ask me?"

I described the scene after she left the office. Aida Turner opened her eyes wide and then swallowed hard.

"I should have told you this but Mrs. Lawson is Alison Foster, the girl that Henry was supposed to be driving when he disappeared."

That got my attention. "You shouldn't have held back on that, Mrs. Turner." "I was going to say–it was, just–hard for me to get the words out."

"Why you still working for those people?" Birdie demanded.

Aida turned to him, imploring. "I might learn something, something that will tell me about Henry and where he is." Aida Turner shook her head and tears squeezed out of her eyes. "I'm willing to do anything to get my Henry back, Mr. Gold, even if it means working in that house until the rest of my days."

"Okay, Mrs. Turner. We'll need that list of names if you've got it."

While Aida Turner went into the living room to write out the list, Birdie and I poked around in Henry's room. I heard a distant knock on the front door, it opened and there came the murmur of voices, female voices. Company.

Birdie pulled out a dresser drawer. "Didn't take much stuff with him. These drawers are full."

I stopped. "You thinking that, maybe, he thought he wasn't going too far or for too long?"

"Well, if I was fixing to take off, I'd want my stuff with me, my good clothes. I wouldn't leave all this behind unless I be coming back."

I grinned. "Good point, Sherlock. Maybe something took young Henry by surprise, something he wasn't expecting."

We continued to search methodically but found nothing of consequence, no diary, no letters, no notes, no indication of his innermost thoughts. A few record albums–Nat King Cole, Johnny Mathis, John Coltrane, Cannonball Adderley, Satchmo–seemed like our boy Henry was a jazz fan. Birdie stared at the records. And I found a copy of Ralph Ellison's, *The Invisible Man.* I had read it but wondered what attracted Henry to it. The copy was dog-eared. I slipped the book into my pocket. Jazz and Ellison. Interesting.

"How many jazz clubs in town?" I asked. Big band was more my thing. I liked classical, opera and rockabilly too but I could never really dig jazz.

Birdie shrugged his massive shoulders.

"Only five or six good ones," he said with regret.

Downstairs, Aida Turner worked on the list and read it over. She perched on the sofa. A young black woman sat beside her. She gave me a hostile glare and fired another one, even hotter, at Birdie. We each took a chair.

"I write slow," she apologized. "This is my niece, Adele Rosewell."

"Miss Rosewell." Miss Rosewell didn't answer at first. She wallowed in anger or resentment.

She spoke in a well-modulated tone. "I told my auntie this is a crazy idea, hiring the likes of you."

"Adele." Aida Turner looked alarmed.

"I take it you don't approve?" I asked.

"That is the understatement of the decade, Mr–whatever your name is."

"Gold. Mo Gold. And my associate, Arthur Birdwell but call him, Birdie."

I said, "Do you have any idea where your cousin might be, Miss Rosewell?"

"Of course I don't," she said.

"Then what do you suggest? Don't you want to know what happened to Henry?"

She pressed her lips together.

"Naturally, I do. I just don't have the confidence that you or your associate, Mr. Bird Brain, can put my auntie's mind to rest."

I stood up and Birdie stood up with me. "Well, Miss Rosewell. That's fine. We'll happily return the dough Mrs. Turner gave us and be on our way."

Her expression changed, clouded. She hadn't expected it to be so easy.

Aida Turner had put down her pen. "Now Adele, I know you mean well but this is my business. I need to know what happened to Henry. And I think these gentlemen can find out for me. Goodness knows, the police haven't done anything these past eight years, now have they?"

"I don't want to see you get hurt," Adele replied.

"I've already been hurt," Aida Turner said. "There's nothing much more can hurt me now. I need the truth. That's the only thing that can help and if these men can deliver it, then it's worth double the price. Triple even." The pen resumed its scratching. "I'm sure these gentlemen would like a cup of tea, wouldn't you?"

"That would be swell, thank you." I liked a cup early in the evening. Reminded me of when I was a kid, before the rough times.

Adele rose from her perch stiffly, threw out another minesweeper of a glare. "Very well."

Then moved purposefully into the tiny kitchen. I took a look. Nice figure. Conservative skirt and jacket, well-cut. Sensible shoes with a bit of a heel. Muscular but nicely shaped calves. The rattling of crockery took on a shrill tone.

"Don't mind her," Aida Turner said. "She's just looking out for me. She and Henry were close. Adele has a good job. Works in a bank downtown. Graduated from university too."

"Maybe I should apply for a loan," I said.

"Now you," Aida Turner admonished.

"Mrs. Turner, did Henry keep a diary or ever write letters to anyone, have a notebook maybe?"

She looked at me sadly.

"No, not that I know of. Henry wasn't much for writing, he knew how to write, don't get me wrong but he just didn't express himself much, if you know what I mean."

"Quiet sort?"

"Sometimes," she replied. "But when he was happy, the words flew out of his mouth."

"And was he happy those last few days," I asked her.

Aida bit her lip, then shook her head.

"It's too far back," she said, "and so close."

"We need your help, Mrs. Turner. Was something bothering Henry those last few days?"

"I asked him what was wrong but he wouldn't say anything. Just smiled and put his arm around my shoulder and said not to worry, that everything would be fine." She buried her face in her hands. "I should have made him tell me but you can't make a grown man do anything he doesn't want to do. It was hard enough when he was six or seven but then, in the end I couldn't do anything to get him to tell me what was wrong."

"Don't blame yourself, Mrs. Turner," I said. "We'll find out for you."

Adele Rosewell brought in a tray stacked with tea things. I went over to help her but she ignored me. The tray thumped down and the crockery jumped. Some tea slurped out of the pot. Aida Turner suppressed a sad smile.

"How do you take it, Mr. Gold?" Adele asked.

"Just as it is–no sugar."

"And you?" she asked Birdie.

"White," he said. "Extra white." That got him a glare.

We all sat there awkwardly and sipped for a moment.

I held up the dog-eared copy of *The Invisible Man.* "Ever see this book before?"

"I know it was in Henry's room," Mrs. Turner replied

"Ever read it?"

"I'm not much for reading, Mr. Gold, except for the bible, of course."

"I read it," Adele said.

"And?"

"It's a masterpiece. I think he's a genius."

"So do I." Adele's eyes widened. She softened for a moment then caught herself and lowered her face into the teacup.

"Mind if I keep it?" I asked Aida Turner.

"No, I don't mind."

I knew what I wanted to say and I hated the thought of saying it.

"Mrs. Turner–I'd be derelict if I didn't mention this and I'm sorry to have to say it. But we," and I glanced at Birdie who frowned, "believe the likelihood is that something happened to your son and he's dead. I can't think of another way to put it."

She surprised me.

"Oh, Henry isn't dead, Mr. Gold. I'm sure of it."

"I'm not sure I understand."

She stood up. "I'll show you."

She moved like a woman with aches and pains but too proud to let them show. We heard her rummaging around in a closet. She returned holding a large, beat-up box. She set the box down on the coffee table.

"He leaves me things," she said with a smile.

"What sort of things?" Birdie asked her.

Aida reached into the box and pulled out some objects–a small doll without a head, a white rose made out of cloth, looked like it had been snipped from a dress or an ornamental pillow, fragments of letters, a pair of dice, a piece of copper wire.

"Where did you find these objects?"

"Why, outside my front door."

"How do you know they were from Henry?"

"I just know," she replied. "These things have some kind of meaning but I haven't been able to figure out what yet. I found two of them on my birthday." Adele Rosewell looked embarrassed but held her tongue. I could see she thought her aunt had lost touch with reality.

I examined each object carefully, then set it back in the box. With due respect for their preciousness.

"Thank you Mrs. Turner." I stood up. Birdie rose. "We'll keep you informed of our progress. Thank you for the tea. It was nice meeting you, Miss Rosewell."

Adele Rosewell nodded curtly but didn't say, likewise. Her mouth pinched tight as if she bit her tongue. I expected to see blood any second.

Aida Turner shook each of our hands firmly but imbued with an indescribable sadness. I loved and hated my work. The hope I saw in Aida's Turner face caused me pain and it would make me sick at heart to disappoint her. In my experience, however, disappointment was an all too common occurrence. But I thought, maybe this time it would be different. People didn't come to us because they were happy or even hopeful. Usually, they were scared or angry and needed to be doing something because doing nothing just wouldn't work for them. I knew it wouldn't work for me. Aida Turner's love for her son now became my burden, mine and Birdie's. I couldn't wait to get it off my back.

As we left the flat, the presence of Adele Rosewell stayed with me, even though I didn't want it to. Maybe the fear, even revulsion I saw in her eyes, the disapproval on her face, the hard lines of a sensual mouth, moved me. Birdie had already forgotten her but I couldn't shake her from my mind.

5

Birdie and I had some legwork to do, catching up with people, following a trail over eight years old. We stirred dead ashes in the grate of a fire that burned out long ago.

Holding Aida Turner's list, I got in the passenger side of the Chevy Biscayne, white paint job, red leather interior–a large, comfortable car with enough under the hood to keep me happy. Birdie slid in behind the wheel then fired the ignition. *The Invisible Man* pressed against my kidney.

I looked over the list that Aida Turner had written out so carefully in her neat hand and then took another peek at the graduation photo. The hint of a smile touched on Henry Turner's handsome face, an earnest expression, honest and sincere, almost guileless. I noted the strong jaw, the even white teeth–a good-looking kid and I thought about the young Alison Foster and her influence on him. Maybe she'd been one of those good-hearted souls who was color-blind and saw only a person's inner qualities? Maybe. But that wasn't the brash sex-bomb who'd sashayed into my office.

"Time to pay Mrs. Lawson a visit," I said.

"Now you're talkin'. Let's rattle her manicure." Birdie guffawed loud enough to make me roll the window down. After he subsided, he added, "Man, there's a lot going on there."

I had to agree.

Birdie pulled around the back of our building sluicing through the alleyway. There might have been two inches of clearance on either side. If you parked here, you had to have a ragtop or else, shinny out the window. Neither of us had put a nick on the Chevy yet and I wanted to keep it that way. Two parking bays sat between a dumpster and a rod iron staircase. I used my key on the back door and we pounded the stairs. We found visitors waiting for us on the landing outside the door, still rattling the knob.

"Hey," I said. "You'll crack the glass if you shake it any harder and it'll cost you eight bucks to have it fixed."

Detective Sergeant Roy Mason straightened up, frowned, and dropped his bony hand to his side. Inspector Harry Callaway snorted. He chewed on a toothpick, something he did regularly, ever since his wife forced him to give up cigars. Callaway was a large, smooth Irishman, with graying hair slicked back from his forehead, a lantern jaw and cold, blue eyes. He wore a grey suit to match his hair and fiddled with a grey fedora in his right hand, rotating it along the brim through his thick fingers. Roy Mason stood tall and skinny in a caved-in way. A taciturn man given to sniggering. I couldn't stand Mason, considered him to be the worst kind of cop. A prick who stepped on the face of the next guy to make himself look good. But Callaway was okay.

"Allow me," I said, shaking out a bunch of keys and fitted one into the lock. Callaway dropped into the half-wingback while Mason lounged in the corner watching. "What are you having?" I asked.

"The usual," Callaway replied.

I poured the two of us a belt of Canadian Club each. Birdie didn't drink much and I wouldn't give Mason spit if my life depended on it. We clinked water glasses.

"Slan," Callaway said.

"L'chaim," I replied.

Callaway hesitated, then took a sip of the Scotch. I sat behind the desk, Birdie rested in his usual spot on the credenza and swung his leg in a long arc. I could see it annoyed Mason to no end. I shook out a Sweet Cap, snapped my lighter and took a long drag.

Callaway ran a stubby forefinger around the glass rim. "Had a call," he said.

"Oh yeah? Good for you."

Callaway ignored me.

"A guy named, Lawson. Some big shot industrialist. He complained to me loud and long about the treatment of his wife by one Mo Gold. Wanted me to throw the book at you. I told him you hadn't broken any laws recently but since we were acquainted I'd have a quiet word. That seemed to pacify him for the moment. And that's why I'm here. So, humor me, Gold, and tell me a story, one that I'll like, all right?"

I laughed. "This is getting comical."

"Put me in the joke," Callaway replied and Mason sniggered. I shot him a look and he stopped.

"Mrs. Lawson," I began. "Young, beautiful, sexy, born rich, married rich and trouble from the tips of her toes to the tip of her nose and all those curves in-between. If I were her husband, I'd be on the floor barking if she blinked at me."

"Well," Callaway drawled. "Maybe that's just you." Birdie guffawed.

"Maybe."

So I filled him and Mason in on what happened, more or less. Told him I'd refused Alison Lawson's dough and that put the peeve into her and she must have run to hubby and complained about how rude I'd been when I'd been very polite, excessively polite in my opinion.

"She just doesn't like to hear the word "no," I said. "Probably the last time was when she threw Pablum at her nanny during snack time."

Callaway rolled more of my Scotch around his tongue.

"Think there's any proof to the pilfering beef?"

"Not a chance. I told her it was a matter for the police. She said they didn't want the unnecessary publicity and also didn't want her husband to be bothered with this. Said she wanted it to be handled discreetly. Offered us a hundred a day."

Callaway whistled. "That's pretty good scratch."

"We can't be bought. We have our principles, don't we Birdie?"

"I was thinking about a new suit I saw in the window of George Richards," Birdie boomed.

"There you go," I said. "We're incorruptible. Besides, I didn't like her attitude. So what are you going to tell the husband?"

Callaway yawned.

"Nothing to tell. I told him I'd look into it and that's what I did. End of story. I don't care for these big shots, either. They piss me off to tell the truth." Callaway glanced up at Mason, who, studiously, examined the hair on his skinny knuckles. Callaway cleared his throat and stood up reaching for the door. "What's this I hear about a stiff in Chinatown?"

"We tried calling you," Birdie said. "But you were off-duty."

"He was a card dealer, wasn't he?"

"That's right. Ying Hee Fong," I replied.

Callaway chewed his lip. "You guys found him?"

"Yeah."

"Why?"

"John Fat Gai was looking for him–said he was skimming the take from his table."

"That so?" Callaway chewed the toothpick for a while, then looked at Mason. "Roy, step out for a moment. I need a quiet word with these two."

Mason looked surprised and hurt but covered it fast. "But…" Callaway jerked his head, then turned away from him.

Mason left reluctantly pulling the door closed behind him, none too gently.

"The walls have ears," Callaway said. "You guys working for John Fat Gai?"

"He asked us to find Ying, that's all. And we did," I replied. I decided to keep my brother out of the picture for now.

"You kill him?" Callaway's voice went low, descending into a husky whisper.

I sighed, sat back in my chair and stubbed out the Sweet Cap.

"I'm surprised you'd ask me a question like that. You know me better. That's the way we found him. He was dead in the alley, all right?"

Callaway nodded and examined his fingernails for a while.

"He was one of my guys."

"What? A cop?"

Callaway shook his head. "A snitch. He was giving us good info on John Fat Gai's operations. There's at least half a dozen murders we figure John is good for."

"That's all? I think you're miscounting," I said.

Callaway slammed his meaty palm on my desk.

"We were making good progress until this. Now it's all gone to shit. Someone fingered Ying to John. Then he hires you two to find Ying? Ach…" And he swiped at the air raising a breeze. "It all stinks."

"Yeah. Maybe." I glanced at Birdie who'd remained stridently impassive. "What're you gonna do about it?"

Callaway glanced up at me sharply.

"That's just it, to the department, Ying's just another dead Chink in Chinatown. I kept this one to myself, no one else knew and he still took two slugs in the head."

"Maybe you talk in your sleep?"

Callaway smiled ruefully. "Yeah, maybe. You guys hear anything, I want to know about it first."

"Sure, sure, you got it, Callaway."

"Why you working for that gangster anyway?" Callaway asked.

I shrugged. "It's a job, nothing more, nothing less."

Callaway snorted. "I thought you had some scruples, Mo, what happened to 'em?"

"Well, it beats going hungry."

"Sure," Callaway replied but I heard the disappointment in his voice.

I looked over at Birdie who studied the polish on his shoe tops.

"Anything else?"

Callaway said, "The way I hear it, you'd be hard pressed to collect anything from John Fat Gai. Most of his associates end up dead."

"Funny," I said. "I heard the same thing but somehow I think John will come across for us. He likes us. We get along swell. Besides, we've got strong survival instincts and what with God on our side, well…" I shrugged.

"Sure you do," Callaway said. "If you find out anything interesting about John that you think I should know, you can reach me any time. I'll always take your call."

"We work odd hours."

Callaway glanced at his watch, it was going on ten p.m. Neither Birdie nor I made a move. "No kidding."

He sat back for a moment, grinding his teeth with gusto.

"This Mrs. Turner. She on the level?" he asked.

I said, "Why would she start to steal after all these years? And then, take items of little or no value? Doesn't add up."

The Irishman nodded. "I'm with you but still, I've got to take it seriously when we get a complaint from a prominent citizen."

"I understand completely," I said, thinking the Super must be breathing down his neck pretty hard. "We're gonna have to talk to Mrs. Lawson, just so you know."

"I ain't responsible for you," he said to me. "Or you," and swiveled toward Birdie who smiled at him.

"That's the last thing I want," Birdie said. "I report to me and to God, no one else."

Callaway rolled his eyes. "Where'd you get him, anyway?"

"I didn't–he got me–some foxhole in Holland I think it was. We had a few bodies piled up around us."

"Oh yeah, that. I forgot."

Callaway pushed himself out of the chair, stared nostalgically at the empty tumbler for a moment, then put on his fedora. Callaway had been in the Navy, a lieutenant commander and flew Corsairs. He had that roll when he walked as if the deck still heaved beneath him. At the door, he paused. "Remember, you find out anything about Ying, you let me know."

"Of course," I said.

"God bless," Birdie intoned and Callaway shot him a funny look. Then I shot Birdie a funny look but he remained oblivious.

After Callaway pulled the door behind him, I turned to Birdie. "Let's start with Aida's list. We can tackle Mrs. Lawson later. She's not going anywhere."

"What about Ying?"

"We'll start with his digs, see what we can find."

Birdie rose to his full height and gave me an evil grin.

"I haven't been to confession in a while. It's time to do something that might make me feel a little bit guilty."

"Time for Eli to take a little trip. Lay low until this mess blows over," I said.

"Think he'll take much convincing?"

"Leave it to me. C'mon, I'll drop you on the way."

6

I drove Birdie to the corner of King and Spadina where he hopped out and disappeared into the gloom. I kept going east on King Street through the centre of town, out the other side to the east end. Eli lived in a walk-up on Hamilton Street, a one-way rabbit warren of rickety attached houses built before the war that looked like they dated back to the Middle Ages.

The third floor. Naturally, he had to live on the third floor. I parked the Chevy and hoped not only the hubcaps but the wheels would still be on it when I returned. After the sixth set of stairs, I began to wheeze a little. Okay, more than a little. I took a moment to catch my breath then banged on his door. I knew he'd be home. I heard the radio playing some big band number. He didn't have any dough so finding a card game wouldn't work. He had markers all over town.

"Yeah, yeah," he said as the door swung open. He stood in the middle of the frame with his mouth open, a fag dangling from the corner of his lip. Every time I looked at him, it got me how closely he resembled the old man, Jake. Fired me up. The same loud mouth. The same stupid ducktail. The same cocky stance. I reared back and socked him one, knocked him back into the decrepit room he called home. He staggered backward, crashed against the wall and slid to the floor. He sat there stunned for a moment. Then he felt around his jaw line and squeezed out a grin.

"Nothing's changed," he said. "Hello Mo. Good to see you too. Come on in, why don't'cha?"

"Thanks. Don't mind if I do." I kicked the door closed behind me, reached under his bed and pulled a battered suitcase out from under it. I set it on the rumpled mattress, flipped the lid and started throwing whatever clothes I found within reach, into it. He watched me with an amused expression.

"You're taking a little trip."

"Am I? Where am I going? Somewhere nice, I hope."

"I hear Florida is lovely this time of year. Or maybe, Chicago. You might even want to try the west coast. Beautiful sunsets."

Eli pushed himself up. "You mind telling me what the hell is going on?"

"You're leaving town. Your little buddy, Ying, is dead. I figured the two of you worked together to skim the table."

That shocked him. He paled slightly.

"Ying? Gee, that's too bad. What happened?"

"Shot in the head. Brains splattered in a back alley in Chinatown. And if you don't get outta here, the same thing's going to happen to you," I snarled. I slammed the lid of the case shut.

"Who's got the money?"

Eli protested. "What money?"

I stalked over to him and yanked him up to his feet by the front of his shirt. I stuck my face close to his. "Don't get stupider. I'm talking about John's dough. The dough Ying skimmed."

"I had nothing to do with it, I swear it. Does it look like I got any money? Besides, I haven't had a game in days. Does that sound like me? You know if I had any cash it would be burning a hole in my pocket."

Eli talked a good game, just like Jake. I let go of his shirt. I wanted to believe him if only because he was my kid brother.

"We're wasting time. John's gunsels could be on their way over here any minute."

"What if I don't wanna go?" Full of bravado at the worst possible time. I wanted to smack him again.

"I'll take you to John Fat Gai myself and dump you right on his doorstep trussed up like a turkey, how's that sound? If you're going to commit suicide, I might as well give you a hand."

"You'd do that," he said.

"Try me."

Eli put his hands up. "Okay, okay. How long do I have to be gone?"

"Until I figure this mess out and let you know it's okay to come back. Although if I had my way, I'd like to see the back of you for good."

"Spoken in the true spirit of brotherhood," he sneered.

I grabbed him by the shoulders.

"You're not him, you understand. So don't even try. Why you'd even want to be like him is beyond me." I pushed him down hard. He sprawled over the suitcase.

"Jesus. You're in a mood. Okay, so I've got a little gambling problem. I can handle it."

"No you can't," I replied. "Here," I reached into my pocket and tossed him a wad. "There's 300 bucks. All I could spare on short notice. I'll drop you at the bus station and you grab the first one out of here. Once you settle somewhere, you let me know the address and I'll give you the all clear, understand?"

Eli eased himself off the bed and went to the coat stand.

"Yeah, sure I understand." He shrugged into a threadbare raincoat and picked a crumpled fedora from a nearby coat hook. "I'll be okay." It sounded to me like he tried to convince himself. He took a quick look around. "Let me grab my shaving kit." He disappeared into the toilet and re-emerged a moment later with a small, leather pouch. "Ready when you are, skipper." That was an old joke between us. When we were kids, we used to pretend we owned a yacht. I'd take the helm and Eli played first mate. Not much has changed.

I nodded. "Let's go, sailor."

Chinatown oozed steam and sweat and the sharp aroma of salt mixed with rotting garbage. The main drag, Spadina Avenue, teemed with life as pedestrians squeezed along the narrow sidewalks. Down the alleyways, coolies dumped and hosed out trashcans in the back of the fruit and vegetable markets. Kitchen boys took cigarette breaks in the humid air, their soiled whites turned gray in the yellow pools of light spilled out by the streetlamps. Away from the crowds and traffic, the streets stayed closed and dark, the narrow houses shut tight as a battered tin can.

Ying lived three doors down from the old synagogue on Beatrice Street in a ground floor apartment. It was just back of eleven when I pulled the Chevy up in front, coasting to the curb. I rolled down the window and lit a Sweet Cap staring at the front door. No lights. The place looked deserted. John Fat Gai owned the house and a dozen others up and down the street. He warehoused his workers and charged them exorbitant rents. Calling them workers seemed a sick joke, more like indentured slaves paying off their servitude over generations. The debts passed on like a malignant family heirloom. I didn't blame Ying for ripping John off, I might have done it myself in similar circumstances.

I flipped the stub out the window where it disappeared down a sewer grate. I checked my holster for reassurance, grabbed a torch from the glove box and got out of the Chevy, closing the door quietly. Peered up then down. Too many one-way streets in Chinatown. You could end up where you began facing in the wrong direction going nowhere.

The main entrance was communal and unlocked. The interior light had burnt out. I took a sniff and gagged, assaulted by the stale, waxy odor of peanut oil used and reused a hundred times. The walls sweated grease. Gut lurching, I switched on the torch and made my way to Ying's door–it opened to my touch. I unholstered the .45 and prodded the door open a crack, thinking that someone had gotten here ahead of me. Well, Ying had been dead for all of a day and he'd stolen something people wanted.

The narrow beam of the torch lit up a jumble sale. Ying's modest flat had been thoroughly done over and the perpetrator didn't seem too concerned about leaving a mess. I tutted under my breath. Ying may have been careless but not entirely stupid. He wouldn't have left John's cash hidden here. Didn't stop the intruder from ripping up floorboards and punching holes in the walls, just in case.

Like a lot of these older houses, the rooms were well-proportioned with high ceilings and large windows. Ying covered them over with a sheet. Well, his decorating taste didn't add up to much. The joint consisted of a room, a kitchen and a toilet. The living area comprised the one room. Against the far wall, Ying had shoved a single bed that had been dumped over. Opposite it–another single bed. Each mattress had been viciously slashed with the guts left hanging out.

Ying had a roommate and the lodger had a young child. A small crib lay flipped over on its side. An old coal fire stoked the flat. The rest of the furniture consisted of a rickety table and two chairs where they took their meals. That was it. No sofa, bookcases, end tables, bureaus or lamps.

A door opened to a small closet with some of Ying's clothes, a rumpled grey suit with the pockets ripped out, the sleeves slashed and the shoulders torn away. Not much of a legacy. I wasn't sentimental but I felt some pity for a guy living like this with practically nothing to show for it. I wondered what happened to the kid and presumably its mother. Sticking around didn't seem like an option not with John Fat Gai on the scene.

I shut the closet door and crouched down by a pile of debris in the middle of the floor and began sifting through the junk. My knees hurt and that told me I'd been kicked around a few too many times. Sifting through, I found a snapshot of a young Chinese girl taken with a cheap Brownie box camera. The photo had perforated edges but no date. She was pretty in a simple, unaffected way with a smooth complexion and long hair flowing down her shoulders. I pocketed the snap then trod carefully over to the kitchen area. The icebox screamed empty; a rancid slab of butter, half a bottle of butter milk, an orange and a piece of cheddar that would have been a challenge for a mouse with very sharp teeth. So, Ying wasn't a gourmet chef, no surprise.

I shut the door and the icebox began to hum. I turned toward the cabinets when a sap cracked me behind the ear. I sagged to my knees. I hadn't heard the guy come in and cross the floor. I grabbed on to the counter and tried to pull myself up and the sap cracked me again. I know I wheezed or gasped as the back of my head exploded in pain. Before hitting the floor, I pushed myself away from the counter and the sap whistled down my cheek thudding against my left shoulder. I fell on to my back and before he could bash my brains in, I brought the .45 level and squeezed off a shot. There came a yelp and a mighty curse.

"Son of a bitch!" a voice growled.

"There's another one coming your way," I hissed to the scrabbling of feet and hands. The guy made plenty of noise now as he beat a retreat slamming through the door. I heard his footsteps thudding on the landing. I lowered the gun and lay there panting, my head feeling like an egg with a thin shell. I blacked out.

The torch lay by my side. I still held the gun. He hadn't come back or I'd be in much worse shape. I worked my way up to my knees and grabbed the counter for leverage heaving up to my feet. But the world tilted and I had to steady myself for a minute. Bending over the sink, I ran the cold water over my handkerchief, wrung it out and pressed it to my throbbing head. I may have retched once or twice but managed to keep it off my suit jacket. Small mercies. When I could stand without falling over, I flicked the torch around. Seems like I winged him. I saw fresh streaks of blood on the dirty linoleum. Hope I shot him in the nuts, the bastard.

Suddenly, the room seemed a lot wider and reaching the other side required real effort but I made it in under an hour or two. Once outside, I closed the outer door behind me. I'd expected the cops to show up but apparently the sound of shots was familiar in that neighbourhood. I managed to square up and stagger to the Chevy looking like a mug who'd had too many. I fumbled with the keys and only dropped them twice. Once behind the wheel, I slumped back for a second and closed my eyes. I probed the back of my head and felt a hard boiled egg. The skin didn't feel broken and there wasn't any blood but the pain had spread down my neck into the shoulder. The guy had done a good job. I'm glad I returned the favor. I started the engine, put it in gear and drove slowly home, praying I hadn't emptied the trays of ice in my freezer.

7

"What's this guy's name again?" Birdie asked early the next morning. He'd noticed the lump on the back of my head and the wobbly way I moved, like an old man with a bad hip and two decrepit knees. He raised his eyebrows but didn't bother making a remark. I'm sure he guessed what had happened, that I'd been surprised by somebody at Ying's place. He seemed more embarrassed for me than anything else.

I placed the photo of the Chinese girl on the dash where he flicked a glance at it while I wheeled the Chevy to the east end.

"Leon. Leon Jackson. High school chum of Henry's. If it'll make you feel any better, I winged the other guy."

"That's reassuring," Birdie replied. "What's this Jackson do?"

"Drives a hack. I called the dispatch and they told me where to find him".

I drove east on Wellesley, watching as the street narrowed and turned from a busy commercial thoroughfare into a quieter residential area with neatly trimmed lawns, crisp flower beds and freshly painted fences. Like some deity had walled out the city and turned it into a pastoral garden. I turned south on Sherbourne. Rising like a shimmering blight on the landscape, I saw the turrets of St. Jamestown in the distance, warehouse for the poor, the depraved and most of those who'd plain run out of luck, where the junkies crawled into dark corners to die. Half a block down, I pulled into a taxi stand.

"Don't think they'll mind," I said. I took a moment to cast a scarce thought toward my father since we happened to be a stone's throw from the Don Jail, his current residence. My old man, that goniff, that hard-hearted crook, held a tight place in my heart for reasons I couldn't begin to fathom.

Ruby's Coffee Shop had put its best foot forward this morning. A guy in stained coveralls washed the scummy plateglass window; filthy from the chimneys blowing coal dust all over creation. Just inside the door stretched a long, Formica counter with cracked leather swivel stools and beyond, half a dozen moth-eaten, brown velveteen booths. A black man I took to be Leon Jackson sat in a booth at the back sipping coffee, dragging on a cigarette, scanning *The Racing Form.* I nudged Birdie, who turned heads as we walked through. Birdie cast a long shadow across his table.

"Leon Jackson?" I asked.

Jackson resembled a stocky fireplug in a leather vest and neat denim shirt rolled up to the elbows. His forearms bulged like he'd been used to doing something other than driving a cab, hammering concrete with a sledge maybe. Calluses coated his thick hands. He wore a closely shaved goatee and his front teeth reminded me of a crooked picket fence. "Maybe. Who wants to know?"

"Got your name from Aida Turner, man. Can we sit down?" Birdie asked him.

"Mrs. Turner?" Leon's face cleared. "You cops?"

I shook my head. "We're working for her, trying to find out what happened to Henry."

"Now," Birdie repeated. "Can we…?"

Meaning eluded Leon Jackson for a second, then he smiled, the crooked teeth beckoned. "Oh sure. Help yourself. You want coffee?" We nodded. "Hey Ruby," he hollered. "Two more coffees here for my friends."

"And a hard-boiled egg," I shouted, mimicking a favourite line from the Marx Brothers. Leon's face dropped, Ruby's brow knit and Birdie guffawed.

"Ignore him," Birdie said. "He has a strange sense of humour."

I shrugged. It came out before I could clamp down.

Leon looked at us with a sincere uncertainty.

"I feel bad for her, Mrs. Turner I mean."

"Meaning?" I asked him.

"Cause Henry, he ain't coming back, that's for sure."

Birdie always seemed bigger in close quarters and I thought if he filled his lungs with air, he'd send the table flying. "Why you say that?"

Ruby brought the coffees, setting them down carefully in front of us along with a metal container of cream and another for sugar. She watched me carefully making sure I didn't dump some sugar in my pocket or palm the tableware.

"There you go," she said.

"Thanks Ruby," Leon replied.

"Mmm-hmm."

And she went behind the counter again, picked up the cigarette she'd left in the ashtray and took a long pull, never taking her eyes off Birdie for a second.

"No, no, I didn't mean it that way," Leon stammered. "It's just that...if he hasn't come back by now, you know, then I just don't think he's ever going to, that's all. You see what I mean?" He kept a pencil behind his ear, for writing down fares.

"We just want to know more about Henry, that's all. What he was like, his habits, if he was seeing anyone, that sort of thing. What can you tell us, Leon?"

The coffee cup came up to lip level.

"Me and Henry, you know, didn't see each other much after we finished school. Kinda went our separate ways. He was working. I was working, never seemed like there was time to get together like we used to." He took another sip of the coffee. "It was a bad thing he done, running off like that and I tell you what, it surprised me too."

"Why's that, man?" Birdie asked him.

"'Cause Henry always played it straight, never stole or cheated, even at school. Most of the guys we went to school with cheated at somethin', you know, but not Henry. He didn't want to let his Momma down, he said, had to do it on his own, no matter what the obstacle, you know? Henry wanted to get a place for the two of them, so his Momma could take it easy, she worked so hard, he said. So, it don't make any sense him running off and then never to come back? Never to get in touch, not once? Uh-huh."

"He have any girls?" Birdie asked.

Leon smiled and nodded, showing his teeth.

"Yeah, well, he was crushing on a girl back then."

"You remember her name?" Birdie asked, sweet as pie.

"Her name's Rochelle Dodson," Leon replied.

"She a white girl?" I asked him. Leon shook his head. "Got an address or a phone number?"

"She's in a situation right now," Leon said. "Living with a big sonofabitch, works down at the docks, name of Steve. . . .Steve O'Rourke. . . ."

Leon patted his pockets before coming up with a frayed pad, pulled the pencil from behind his ear and wrote out the address and phone number. He ripped the sheet off the pad and slid it across to me. It was a place in the Junction, not far from where Aida Turner lived. A place where people who knew they were down on their luck, lived.

"She's got a couple of kids. This guy, Steve, he's a bad man, you know what I mean? A big mutha. . . not many men could take him. . . ." Then he glanced at Birdie. "Not many," he said as Birdie looked back.

"Hey Ruby," Birdie called. "More coffee over here, if you please."

Ruby snapped to, pulling her face out of the paper.

"Right away, master." And laughed full out. "Hard boiled egg," she muttered, then slapped her generous thigh.

8

Rochelle Dodson lived at the corner of Annette and Dundas and as soon as I saw the house, I began to feel sorry for her. A rotted, wood slat fence cordoned off a rutted yard leading up to a ramshackle structure. Grey laundry flapped in the dry wind, barely hanging on to a line that dipped dangerously low.

I knocked on the door and a slim, haggard-looking Negro woman with shockingly blonde hair opened it. A child in the house cried and a couple of others screamed and Rochelle Dodson looked as if she had enough of just about everything.

"I ain't buying anything," she said, though she regarded Birdie curiously, who gave her his best smile.

"We're not selling anything Rochelle. I'm Mo Gold and this is my associate, Arthur Birdwell." Birdie bowed to her slightly and Rochelle's eyebrows shot up. "We'd like to talk to you about Henry Turner. We're trying to find out what happened to him."

At the sound of Henry's name, Rochelle glanced behind her, pulled the door closed, then slumped down on the stoop.

"You looking for Henry?" she asked.

I nodded and gave her my most reassuring smile.

"I ain't got much time…my man is due home from work…Henry…things woulda been different…" And when she turned her head slightly I noticed the bruising along the jaw line. Because of her color and the way she applied her make-up, it wasn't easy to see but as she tilted her head from the shadows to look up at the sky, squinting in the sunlight, it seemed pretty clear what had happened. I glanced at Birdie. He'd seen it too.

"What did you mean? About Henry," I asked her.

Rochelle gave a sad, little laugh, almost a cry of despair choking out of her.

"I meant that life with Henry wouldn't have been this. He would have been a good provider. I would have kept my dignity. We would have had children but Henry wouldn't have wanted us to live in these kinds of circumstances, you know?" Her voice was high and sweet sounding tinged with bitter pain.

"This was a serious thing between you?" Birdie asked her.

Rochelle closed her eyes like she imagined it in her mind.

"Uh-huh," she said. "We were supposed to be married and then all of a sudden, he upped and disappeared. It made no sense, no sense at all," and Rochelle shook her head sadly, tears splashing down her cheeks.

"Were you in touch with Henry at that time?" I asked.

She looked at me defiantly, nostrils flaring.

"'Course I was, we saw each other every day, didn't we?"

"Just tell me what you remember."

She smoothed her cotton shift over her narrow thighs.

"We had plans," she said. "Such wonderful plans. We were going to get married in a church, the Baptist church where my parents went to services every Sunday. It was small but the chapel was very beautiful and the altar could make you cry out to Jesus when you saw it. Oh my, it was like a small piece of heaven right here on earth. But then Henry got a little funny about it."

"How so?' I glanced at Birdie.

"Well, all of a sudden, he wasn't sure about getting married in the Church, wasn't so keen on it. I asked him why and he said that the Church kept the black man down, didn't let the black man live up to his potential and that our lord Jesus was white and didn't represent the black man at all. And I said, what about His suffering and His anguish? Isn't that our suffering and anguish too? And he said, but what good will it do us just to suffer? When are we going to get past that? Half the time, I didn't know what he was talking about. I just wanted to get married in my mommy and daddy's church, that's all. Such a beautiful, restful place," she said in a dreamy kind of voice, a voice infused with fatigue, a voice that sounded as if she lay down for a minute, she'd never get up.

Birdie's face became strained and excited. Any talk of religion, no matter what, got into his blood.

"He turned away from Jesus?"

Rochelle squinted up at him.

"Yes, sir," was all she said in that sad tone.

"Did Henry talk about his plans at all?"

Rochelle shook her head.

"No, sir. I mean, Henry hadn't formally proposed or anything, like he didn't get down on his knees and ask me to marry him but we had this understanding, we just knew that we would be together and we started talking about marriage in a natural kind of way. Henry had saved enough money to buy us a small house in a good neighborhood, so we'd have a decent place to raise our kids," and as she said this, I noticed she turned her head away and looked at the street, not wanting to let the pain of her own misfortune encroach on her thoughts. She imagined what could have been there.

"Tell me about the days leading up to his disappearance. Did you notice anything unusual, anything strange that happened? Did he appear to act normal?"

Rochelle shuddered, "Henry did seem nervous, you know and I didn't see him as much, he kept on saying he was busy and couldn't get away. I was afraid... afraid that something had happened between us, something I didn't know about even and I asked him if he was unhappy with me. Oh no, baby, he said, it's not you, I'm just taking on some extra work to make us some more money, you know, so we can save up even more. And he looked different, sort of scared but tired too, you know that kind of tired that gets behind your eyes? And then the next thing I know, he's gone off, left without a word, not telling me anything, not saying goodbye. I went crazy, called everybody looking for him. He'd just disappeared…vanished…"

"No word from him since?" I asked.

Rochelle shook her head slowly, swiped at the tears with the back of her hand.

"I got to go," she said and jumped up disappearing inside, then slammed the door.

A large, hard-looking man, in work pants and undershirt strolled up the walk whistling under his breath. He carried a metal lunch box under his arm, had a scar above one eyebrow, a thin-lipped mouth below a wolfish face.

"What you sellin?" he spat.

"Nothing," I said. "She ain't buying. Just a waste of time. Don't worry, mister, you're wallet's safe here."

"Shove off." His lips twisted into a cruel grin.

I tipped my hat and moved down the walk with Birdie on my heels. I could feel the heat in him percolating through his veins, wanting to take a crack at the guy so badly the breath rattled in his cavernous chest. The suspicious brute followed us with his wolf eyes, making sure we skedaddled off his property, ensuring no one fleeced him out of a nickel. The guy seemed a lit firecracker with a slow burning fuse. He couldn't wait for it to go off. Birdie had his eyes closed, pinched with rage. The big man went inside and no sooner had the door slammed than I heard voices raised through the cracks, one a low-pitched growl, the other whiny and frightened.

Birdie took a step toward the gate but I put a hand out and caught his arm.

"Not your fight pardner, leave it be," I said.

Birdie gave me a cold look but finally eased off and I knew somehow it wasn't the end–that someone would pay down the line.

9

I'd parked the Chevy on Annette and we walked up the block towards it. Some kids played stickball in the street and that took me back; listening to the shouts and screams, the cries of disappointment and yells of triumph, the good-natured taunting and jeers. Thinking those days were over, I looked at the group and saw just kids, maybe nine or ten years of age, a mix of colors in them, some brown, some black, some white, thinking, they were just kids and didn't give a shit about anything but having a good time. Not thinking where they were headed, if they'd fail in life or would claw their way to some kind of a win. They just liked playing the game, knowing who had strength, who faltered and adjusted to that. I stopped. I took my time, appraising them. Birdie figured it out. He knew what I felt when I looked at those kids.

"You don't think her kids have much of a chance, do you?"

"Not much. Might call for one of your miracles."

Birdie grunted. "There ain't many to go around. We save'em for the rough times."

I nodded and went round the driver's side door with my key in hand. As I fumbled with the lock, I noticed a yellow Buick Roadmaster, two-toned, white-walled and showroom ready, parked half a dozen cars back. I squinted and could just make out a pair of hats perched on heads through the windscreen.

"Company," I murmured casually.

Birdie bent his head but didn't answer and I saw his right hand snake into the inside of his jacket as he came around the end of the car. I was about to open the door when I heard a powerful engine rev, then gun. I stepped toward the street. The Buick leapt forward jackrabbit style, tires screaming. The kids stopped their game and turned. The Buick lurched toward me, then screeched to a halt laying down a track in the asphalt. The front right tire came perilously close to my foot.

Birdie had one hand on the roof of the Chevy and in the other, his nickel-plated .45. I turned slowly and looked into the car. Two Oriental faces stared back at me. I felt nothing but their good will. They wore identical hats and identical gray suits, rumpled in the heat. The closest one said, "Mr. Fat Gai say we watch you. He looking for his money. You find it, you tell us, then we don't kill you."

I reached into my jacket pocket and saw them twitch, reaching for their weapons. "Relax," I said and pulled out a packet of Sweet Caps. I offered one through the window, the passenger reached out to pluck one from the pack. I grabbed his finger, twisted it over and mashed it against the doorframe. He yelped.

"Listen. Don't threaten me–ever. If I find any of John's property, it will be returned to him, minus our agreed commission, understand?" I glanced at the driver who listened and watched intently but hadn't moved. His buddy wore an inverted clown face oozing constipation but give the little creep credit, he didn't utter a peep and I knew how much pain this little trick caused.

"We are honorable men," I said to the driver, who smirked silently. "You tell John, I am his number four, you get me?"

I released the other guy's finger, tossed the cigarette on to his lap and turned away leaving my back exposed. The Buick tore down the street. A high-pitched curse blew back in a tunnel of air, something about my testicles shrinking into blueberries or maybe prunes. The kids watched them go and then re-started the game.

"Smooth," Birdie said, re-holstering the .45.

I grinned, shaking out a Sweet Cap putting it between my lips. "I knew you'd be impressed and you're a hard man to impress."

"I'm impressed by God," he boomed.

I sighed. "Don't start." I got in behind the wheel. I drove thoughtfully back to the office, the lump on the back of my head throbbed worse than a hangover.

I flipped through the mail. A packet had arrived from Callaway. It contained a mimeographed copy of the case notes from Henry Turner's disappearance. There wasn't much, just a few pages plus a statement Alison Foster, accompanied by her father said the scrawl, had given to the police a couple of days later. It added up to a missing person's report, sketchy and notable for its considerable lack of detail, not to mention, almost indecipherable penmanship.

This comprised the era before typewriters became mandated equipment. Cops had a choice. Since each bullpen only had one or two typewriters per floor, handwriting the reports seemed easier. And fudge the details in Egyptian hieroglyphics if so desired. I know. I'd done it myself on numerous occasions. The only difference being, that my handwriting resembled legitimate cuneiform, a sacred code interpreted only by me. I couldn't even make out the signature of the attending officer, even if I wanted to follow it up. What a perfect way to run an inept bureaucracy. No one could blame anyone for anything since the reports had been documented in black and white and open to any translation on the open market.

"Got anything on tomorrow?" I asked him.

Birdie looked up, riffled the pages of his bible, then slipped it back inside his breast pocket. "Nope."

"Good," I said. "Let's rattle the cage of a gilded bird."

Birdie smiled.

"I thought you were going to say, ruffle a few feathers."

"Am I that obvious? Please. Give me some credit."

He frowned for a moment. Birdie had a face like rubber, he could pull it inside out and back again. "I'm fresh out."

"Liar," I replied affably.

He pointed a meaty forefinger. I was the only one who could get away with that and we both knew it. The worst thing to be called in Birdie's book. It meant that you'd lost sight of god and Birdie's vision had always measured a perfect twenty-twenty. He waggled the forefinger in front of my nose and showed me some teeth.

10

I had a weakness for a well-turned out ankle and Adele Rosewell had the prettiest set I'd seen in a long time. Ankles and how she used them said a lot about a woman, in my opinion. A shapely pair of gams could be ruined by plump, ungainly ankles. When those delicate bones disappeared into flesh, it became a sacrilegious occurrence. I told myself that Adele Rosewell could fill in a lot of the blanks about Henry Turner. Self-delusion was one of my specialties. I liked women, always did, just never had much luck with them.

I grabbed an open meter on Queen Street not far from the red-faced façade of City Hall. I took it, leaning up against the side of the Chevy pulling on a Sweet Cap gazing at the street's reflection in a magnificent plate glass window, a sliver of the majesty of one of the new skyscrapers thrown up by a cartel of crooks that had greased the palms of the local planning committee. They made my old man look like a saint.

A ray of sun blasted out from a cloud and the entire street scene came to life on the screen of the gigantic glass surface–a translucent ice rink in the air. A two-tone Buick Roadmaster sat parked across the street and appeared then disappeared with the flow of traffic. I squinted up into the sky and could have sworn the building waggled in the light breeze.

The Montreal Bank and Trust occupied the ground floor where Adele Rosewell worked as an assistant loans officer. I checked my watch–almost noon and I figured she had to come out sometime. A traffic cop came to check out my parking status so I pumped a nickel into the meter, flicked the lever and was rewarded with a full hour of leisure. The cop touched the brim of his cap as he swaggered off in search of fresh game.

As I turned back, I spotted her coming through the main doors bobbing in a throng of the newly released who looked as if they hadn't felt the sun on their faces in years. She tried to hide herself behind a pair of round sunglasses the size of dinner plates but she didn't fool me. The outfit today came grey and tailored, the ankles trimmed to the wind, sailed along beautifully.

I ground out the butt and straightened up. She stopped suddenly and a guy behind her bumped into her back, excused himself but gave her an exasperated look before stepping around. I couldn't see her eyes behind the dark dishes but figured she gazed in my direction.

"What are you looking at?" she demanded.

"Ankles," I muttered.

"What?" Clearly, this was not the answer she was expecting.

"I'm a sucker for ankles. Yours are of a superior variety."

"Is that so?" Perhaps there was the hint of a smile, a twitch at the corners.

"Buy you lunch, Miss Rosewell?"

"I don't have time for lunch."

"How about a cup of coffee?"

"I've only got thirty minutes," she said.

I nodded and gestured for her to take the lead. You see, I could read women pretty well. She didn't hesitate.

Adele Rosewell led me to a tiny café off Wellington called The Cosmopolitan. She commandeered a table at the back, away from the windows. I followed behind so I could continue to observe a pair of perfect fibulas make music in the air. I knew the place. In another life, it had been owned by a good citizen named Pinky Zukerman, an erstwhile associate of Jake Gold.

In those days, it had a chrome counter and leather banquettes and was an active place where graft and corruption opened as easily as a jar of pickles. Its proximity to city hall yielded convenience and opportunity. Fat cats of all stripes used to take a cup of Joe here and lie about the contracts on offer. Pinky had died at least ten years earlier. He'd been five years into a fraud beef at Kingston pen when his heart, never the most reliable instrument, coughed its last on the greasy food and overheated atmosphere in the prison laundry. They'd found him stuffed behind one of the industrial washers with a shiv buried in the folds of his work shirt. Those in the know assumed one of Pinky's deals had come back to haunt him in a terminal manner. I looked around the place. The chrome and leather had disappeared. Rod iron and checkered tablecloths had taken their place.

"You like your privacy," I said.

She settled herself into the rattan seat and removed the glasses giving me the once over. "I need to be aware of the company I keep," she said.

I ordered two coffees and a Danish for me since I felt peckish.

"Prying eyes?"

"Something like that." She paused. "Where's your gargantuan friend?"

I shrugged. "In church probably." Her eyebrows went up. "Birdie is a very religious man, Miss Rosewell, and he takes his faith seriously."

"Well, Mr. Gold, life is indeed full of surprises and I see you've had one yourself." She gestured to the lump I was nursing.

"Yes, it is and yes I have."

"What do you want to know?"

"You deal with customers like this?"

"Like how?"

"With a curt, business-like manner."

"I'm a professional so I do professional when I'm at work. I'm not there to be anyone's mama, you understand?"

"What about when you're not at work?"

"That's off-limits and besides, you'll never know."

"You've got something against the Jews?"

Her face hardened. "I never said that."

"White men, then?"

"I thought you wanted to talk about Henry. Is this all just a joke to you, Mr. Gold?" The undercurrent of anger felt alive.

"I did and do. Relax. I know when to be serious, Miss Rosewell and I do take my work seriously. What can you tell me about him, Miss Rosewell and I want the unedited version, okay? I don't want to hear about Henry the choir boy, if you get what I mean."

"You think all colored people are up to no good?"

"Now who's being touchy? I just want the full dimension. If I don't know him, I can't understand him. If I can't understand him, then how the hell can I find him?"

"I think you are a strange man, Mr. Gold. How *will* you find Henry?"

"I don't know… yet. And I'm sure you didn't mean that in a negative context." I glanced at my watch. "I think we're down to 27 minutes."

She sat back and shook her head. Her hair had been straightened and had auburn highlights. "Ask your questions," she sighed.

"Okay. What do you think happened to Henry?"

"I don't know. I've been asking myself that question for eight years."

"When your aunt first told us of Henry's disappearance, experience suggested to me he was dead. Sorry to be so blunt but that is usually the case."

"And now, Mr. Gold? Do you still believe that?"

I hesitated.

"It's still the most likely possibility but I have to wonder how and why that would happen. Was he involved in something dangerous? Did he owe the wrong people money? Did he have a quick temper? Would he have gotten into a fight with someone?"

Adele shook her head.

"Henry would never get involved in anything illegal or dangerous knowingly. He just wasn't made that way."

"I think that's the point, Miss Rosewell. Something happened to him maybe where he couldn't help it. Didn't see the danger of the situation."

"I can't think of a thing like that. Henry always stuck to the straight and narrow, always did the right thing."

"Maybe his sense of righteousness got him into trouble?"

Confusion swam into her luminous eyes. "How so?"

"Maybe, he was the kind of guy who charged into a situation without thinking. Being the good Samaritan." I smiled grimly. "Rescuing the damsel in distress."

"Do you believe my Auntie could be right? That Henry is hiding somewhere?"

I hesitated. False hope is a powerful trap.

"I have no reason to believe it one way or the other. There's no evidence yet to suggest he's dead or alive. Only the absence of time suggests he is dead."

"But he could still be alive. It is possible," she said.

"I found your Aunt's conviction surprising. Sometimes, instincts can be very powerful. It is strange for people just to disappear completely without leaving a trace. At some point in the past eight years, some indication that Henry was no longer with us should have come to light."

"So you think he's hiding somewhere?"

"It's only a possibility. I'm willing to expand my thinking on that score."

"And if he's hiding somewhere, could it be near by?"

"I don't know, really. It all needs a much closer look."

Adele took a sip of her coffee.

"I guess I never really figured that was a possibility. Like you, I thought he'd had an accident or something terrible had happened to him and he wasn't coming back."

"Well, could be his mind snapped and he's just out of his head," I said. "But from what you and your aunt said, Henry seemed to be pretty level-headed."

"Things like that just don't happen," she replied. "Not to people like Henry."

"You know a Rochelle Dodson?" I asked.

In a dainty way, she drained her coffee cup. Meanwhile, I had wolfed down the Danish, then wiped the apple smear from my chin. She didn't blink but I felt her disapproval. "Certainly, what of her?"

"She seemed to think that she and Henry were an item. To the extent that they were supposed to get hitched even though there'd been no formal proposal; on Henry's part, that is."

"I wouldn't know about that." And her voice took on a frosty tone.

"You didn't approve?"

"Well, I think Henry could have done better for himself, if that's what you're asking. She's nice enough, I suppose but I think she might be somewhat delusional."

"So, she was making it up?"

"Maybe she was. Do you think Rochelle's got something to do with Henry disappearing?"

"Have you seen the man she's living with?"

"No."

"Well, a Wildebeest is better looking and he'd scare the fringes off Roy Rogers' rawhide elbows plus he's got the temper of a constipated bear. Word is, he likes to use his fists."

Her eyes widened. "On her?" I nodded. "Children?"

"They've got a small herd, so who knows?"

"Oh, I do feel sorry for her." I half-believed her. She didn't emote like a Sarah Bernhardt but she didn't come off like a Freezee either. "So, you think this man…?"

"It's one possibility to check out, that's all. He seems like the possessive type." "I see."

I sniffed the air. The pungent smell of ground coffee. "It's an angle, that's all. So, you have no ideas on that score?"

"No, I don't." She glanced at her wrist. "I really must go. My boss places a lot of emphasis on punctuality."

"I bet."

"It's not that bad."

"Well, maybe we can pick this up another time."

"Only if you have more questions about Henry."

"Naturally. What else would I have questions about?"

I paid the bill and walked her back to the glass enclosed tomb known as a bank. We said our goodbyes and she shook my hand in a brisk manner, then took those fabulous ankles away from me not hesitating or glancing back, not even once. That hurt. Then I thought, a Jew and a shicksa, a black shicksa yet. Can't happen. Not in this lifetime. Which is why it almost made sense. The world, I told myself, was made up of infinite possibilities but maybe not my world.

11

"What do you think happened to Henry Turner?" I asked Birdie. We headed to the Foster's place. They had a swanky address: 56 Burnside Drive. Birdie was one of the most thoughtful, intelligent men I'd ever met, which is why he didn't say much. He knew better.

As usual, Birdie took his time answering and that told me he really didn't want to say. "Not sure," he said finally.

"You think he's dead?"

Birdie shrugged. "No body anywhere."

"I'm sure they were counting on that," I said. I didn't elaborate on the who. That was what we were supposed to be finding out.

The Fosters house on Burnside Drive stood at least 60 feet back from the curb. It boasted a wide, sweeping drive with a small roundabout, an imposing three-story building fronted with faux stone and pillars where plaster lions posed snarling.

"Nice digs," I said.

Birdie snorted. "Five or six families could live here, easy."

I parked behind a maroon Caddy convertible; you could do shish kebab on those fins. Birdie and I went to the door and I rang the bell. A long moment later, the bell echoed throughout the house, a Negro houseman opened the door.

I said hello, as politely as I could and handed him my card. The man took it and read the fine print several times, then slammed the door in our faces. I removed my hat and sighed. A moment later, the door opened and the houseman beckoned us in.

"This way," he said, studiously ignoring Birdie. "Mr. Foster is on the terrace having his breakfast. You may join him there, gentlemen." And he eyed Birdie suspiciously, who, in turn, stared back until the houseman twitched and backed away.

We strode through an expansive living room. It had a well-manicured wool carpet and heavy brocaded furniture. Then we entered a library with stuffy looking leather wing-backed chairs and built-in oak bookshelves that ran from the floor up to the ceiling and all around leaving only gaps for the windows.

The houseman slid open a glass door and we stepped on to a patio that overlooked a sculptured lawn, a sparkling pool and flowerbeds bursting with color. Some people knew how to live. Others just have the means to and I figured that the Fosters had a lot of the latter.

A thickset man with iron-grey hair sat with his back to us. He hunched over a glass table.

"Mr. Foster?"

Without turning around, the man waved to us like he summoned a waiter or barman at his club. Exchanging looks, Birdie and I walked around the table where we could face him square on.

Dickson Foster shoveled eggs and toast into his face while slurping coffee. He had a wide head and jaw that jutted out defiantly. A thick rib of bone subbed in for a brow and his face remained hitched into a permanent scowl. You could dredge Lake Ontario and fill the trench between his eyes and cross the bridge of his nose. Small, grey eyes and like the rest of him, filled with suspicion. He looked us up and down but didn't invite us to sit or offer a cup of coffee but kept us standing while he continued to eat. He had dressed casually in slacks and a blue cotton shirt, open at the throat. His skin resembled the color of brick. On his feet, he wore a ragged pair of slippers.

"What do you want?" he barked and flicked his eyes over Birdie, then looked down at his plate. Nothing appeared to come between Mr. Foster and his grub. Unless he wanted it to.

"We're looking into the disappearance of Henry Turner," I said.

Foster hesitated for a second, then kept eating. Finally, he finished up by swabbing the plate with the last shred of toast and bit down on it hard.

"I don't know anything about that." He sucked back the dregs of his coffee. He jangled a bell that sat on the table tray. "One day he was here and then he wasn't. Just took off. Disappeared. Didn't even have the courtesy to give notice."

"You sure about that?" Birdie asked.

Foster glared at him. "Perfectly sure."

"Can you tell us about the last few days he was here, Mr. Foster?" I asked.

"You're asking a helluvalot, mister. That was eight years ago. I don't have much to do with the hired help," he replied without hesitation and I marveled at how practiced some were who spoke with such pure arrogance

"Even so. Henry Turner was your private chauffeur. He drove you, your wife and your daughter, didn't he?"

Foster glared at us in turn. "That's what chauffeurs do, in case you weren't aware."

"Uh-huh," I replied coolly. I shook out a Sweet Cap and lit it, taking my time, blowing a thin stream of smoke, somewhat in Foster's general direction.

"I don't care for your manners," Foster said.

"That makes two of us," I replied. "But the fact is, Henry Turner used to work for you and he disappeared while he was in your employ. One night he was driving your daughter and the next thing anyone knew, he was gone. Your daughter, Alison, I believe, had been picked up by the cops around that time, maybe even the night Henry disappeared. I think the charge was joyriding. That's no big deal. Lots of rich kids have nothing better to do than terrorize the streets in their Daddy's cars. Lots of them get picked up by the cops too. Usually, they get a slap on the bum and get sent back to mommy and daddy. Sometimes, but not always, booze is involved. Anyway, your daughter came home safely and no one has heard from Henry since. Any thoughts on that?"

Foster laughed harshly just as the houseman hurried over and cleared up the table. No one moved. Foster waited until the servant had taken the breakfast things back into the house and closed the patio door behind him.

"Okay, so, you think you're a tough guy, do you? You and your friend both. I resent your implications about my daughter."

I took a pull on the fag. "I've met your daughter, Mr. Foster."

The chair scraped on the patio stones as he tried to stand up but managed it awkwardly catching his foot on one of the legs. His brick complexion had turned puce. The back of the chair thwacked the stones hard. Foster yelled a little bit. He had spittle in the corners of his mouth. Bits of egg and toast flew out. I felt like taking cover.

"Now you look here. You think you can barge into my home and talk to me this way?"

I wanted to point out we had been announced and allowed to enter but Foster didn't seem in the mood to listen. He shook a forefinger at my nose.

"One phone call from me and I can have your license pulled, you get it? I could crush the pair of you–like that." A dramatic snap of the fingers, a bit weak, in my opinion. "But I'm not going to. You know why?"

I shrugged. Birdie remained impassive.

"Because of Henry's mother, Mrs. Turner, that's why. She's a God-fearing, church-going woman and I know she's been torn apart since her son disappeared. I'm a deacon myself and for that reason, I'm not going to just kick you outta here."

"Go on," I said.

Foster looked a bit exhausted from the tirade. He picked up the chair and set it upright, then sat down gratefully.

"You sure know how to get a fella riled up, Gold."

"You look like you've had plenty of practice," I replied.

Foster wheezed and it took me a moment to figure out he was laughing.

"Maybe you're right about that."

"You were saying, Mr. Foster?"

He rubbed a paw along his grizzled jaw line.

"My daughter did get picked up for joyriding around that time. As it turned out, my wife and I were away–Palm Springs–some resort out there, can't remember the name–Rancho something. Alison called me. Explained she'd gotten into a little trouble. I called Henry to go pick her up. Then I called the stationhouse and got it all squared away. The next day, we flew home. But by then, Henry Turner had left. But when he didn't show up by the next day, I spoke to Mrs. Turner and she said he hadn't been home. I advised her then to call the police, which I believe, she did."

"You know anything about some items gone missing from your daughter's house, Mr. Foster?"

Now, he really looked flummoxed. "You've lost me."

"Your daughter, Mrs. Lawson, came to our office earlier. She wanted to hire us. Said some items had gone missing and accused Mrs. Turner of stealing them."

"Mrs. Turner? I don't believe it. Why would she? That doesn't make any sense at all, does it?"

"No, it doesn't," I agreed. "Any idea why your daughter might want to put Mrs. Turner in the frame for it?"

"I can't think of any reason and that's the God's honest truth." He looked from me to Birdie and back again. "Now, is there anything else I can help you boys with?"

I shrugged.

"Not for the moment, Mr. Foster but I'm sure we'll be speaking again."

The lines around his throat tightened a bit.

"Listen, I'd like to know what happened to Henry, too. For his mother's sake. She doesn't deserve to suffer like this. Like I said, she's a God-fearing woman and deserves better. I hope you do find Henry for her just so she can ease her mind."

"You think Henry's dead?"

Foster's eyes went stony.

"I just don't know, Mr. Gold. These are things better left in the hands of God."

That seemed to cap a wonderful morning.

"We'll see ourselves out, Mr. Foster."

12

I told Callaway we'd be taking a crack at Foster's daughter and that's what we did. Fresh from talking to the old man whetted my appetite for strange encounters. It didn't take long to get there.

Alison Lawson lived in a fine, Tudor-style mansion in the Rosedale district of the city, an area so gentrified, it might have been airlifted direct from Scarsdale.

When I rang the bell, I heard it gong deeply inside. A pretty maid in a cute uniform opened the door.

"Can I help you gentlemen?" she asked us demurely.

"We're looking for Mrs. Lawson."

"Who shall I say is calling?" she asked and glanced boldly at Birdie. He had that effect on most people, especially women. From over her aproned shoulder, I spotted Alison Lawson who had emerged from somewhere else in the house. I took in a large foyer with marble floors and entrances leading off from there.

Alison Lawson stopped suddenly, put a hand instinctively to her throat, then having made a decision, carried on walking toward us, having pulled herself together in record time.

"It's all right, Essie," she said. "I'll talk to these gentlemen."

Essie bobbed her head then scurried off.

"Please, come in." We stepped inside. Birdie bowed his head getting in the door. "This way."

And she led us through to a drawing room, plenty of thick carpeting and big, comfy chairs to sink into and a large couch that'd hold ten, large-boned people easily. She must have hired her mother's decorator.

Birdie and I parked ourselves on the couch. Alison Lawson, perched on a wingback chair, her body taut. She opened a silver cigarette box on a marble side table and lit up with a lighter in the shape of a knight. The flame came out of the visor. I thought it was very cute.

"We just had a conversation with your father, Mrs. Lawson."

She exhaled heavily. "What did you talk to him about?"

"We chatted about Henry Turner."

Alison Lawson froze for a moment paling slightly but brought herself under control. Coolly, she blew out a stream of smoke before replying.

"What did happen to Henry?"

I exchanged a quick glance with Birdie who sat impassively looking directly at her. He did this to unnerve her. He had a way of unnerving a lot of people.

"I was hoping you could tell me. After all, you had to be one of the last people to see him before he disappeared."

She held the smoldering cigarette rigidly, her right hand stiff, braced with her left clamped on her wrist.

"Was I?" she asked.

Birdie snorted like an elephant snuffling through its trunk. Alison Lawson didn't break her pose, nothing cracked. She could have been a marble statue smoking a cigarette.

"Well, yes, you were and what's more you know that, so why play these silly games with us, Mrs. Lawson when there are serious things to discuss?"

She smiled coyly. "I like playing games."

"Evidently," I replied. "Like accusing Aida Turner of stealing when she didn't. Just another, what? Amusement for you?"

Her smooth brow creased for a moment. "But things have gone missing, Mr. Gold. I wouldn't have come to you otherwise."

I sighed. "The night before Henry Turner disappeared, you were out joyriding with some of your friends. You were pulled over by the cops and taken downtown. Your parents were at some retreat in Palm Springs. They sent Henry to bail you out. Feel free to pick the story up from there."

She mashed the half-smoked cigarette out in an onyx ashtray heavy enough to take a man's head off. "I think I'm tired of this game, now."

"Lady, answer the question," Birdie growled.

"Or what? You're going to punish me? How exciting." And her eyes went cold and her lips pencil thin.

"Maybe I'll just put you over my knee," Birdie said.

"Ooohh, that sounds like fun," she cooed and I got the impression we were dealing with something a little different here. "And I'll have you charged with assault."

"Just tell us what happened, Mrs. Lawson and we'll get out of your way. I'm sure you have a lot of things to do today and so do we," I said, conscious of the fact that we were getting nowhere with her.

"All right." And she smiled prettily. "I was out having some fun, that's all. Things got a little bit out of hand as they often do. My boyfriend at the time, Harvey Troyer, had taken his parents' car and he didn't have a license. We were young and stupid. He didn't really know how to drive. He thought he did but it's not the same thing, is it?"

"No, it isn't," I said, just to sound agreeable.

"The police officer who stopped the car was particularly unpleasant. And when Harvey threatened to have his badge–his father was a judge but he's retired now–well, the officer got nasty. He had the car impounded and we were driven down to the station and suddenly, the evening wasn't much fun anymore. We sat in a dingy, smelly little room for a few hours and then finally, Henry showed up. I was cross with him, I'll admit. I demanded to know what took him so long and he told me he'd been waiting outside in the corridor for the longest time. The police wanted to make us suffer, I suppose. I couldn't wait to get out of there. Henry drove me home and that's the last time I saw him. And it's also the last time I saw Harvey Troyer too, the stupid idiot."

"How many in the car with you?" I asked.

"There were four of us."

"I'll need their names."

She patted her hair. "Well, Harvey Troyer, the fink, I've already mentioned. And then there was Gayle Sorenson and her boyfriend at the time, Rance Callaway."

The name gave me a jolt. "Did you say, Callaway?"

Alison Lawson smiled as sweetly as a cobra. "That's right, I did."

"Anything between you and Turner?" Birdie boomed.

She turned her attention to him. "Certainly not," she replied coolly. "I liked Henry but not in that way. Besides, that would have been asking for more trouble than even I would have liked. I'm not going to deny that I liked a bit of adventure in those days. Now, I'm just an old married woman."

"What's going on?" an assured but quizzical voice said. I looked up and saw a tall, blonde man with wide shoulders and carefully manicured hair wearing a Tip Top Tailors custom made suit that probably set him back 300 bucks. He stared at us with a puzzled expression on his clean, smooth face. "Who are you?"

Alison Lawson looked up and smiled at her husband. "Oh darling, we're just exploring some of my sordid little past."

Before he could respond, the housemaid appeared with a dry martini on a silver tray. After he lifted the glass and put it to his lips, he murmured, "Thank you, Essie." She did a little curtsy then scurried off. He drank a bit deeper. It wasn't even noon yet.

"Ahh, needed that. What part of your sordid past is being examined exactly?" he asked his wife.

Birdie jumped in first. "We've been asking your wife about Henry Turner."

Mr. Lawson wrinkled his smooth brow. I put him in his late 30's, just about old enough to have seen active service during the war. He took another glug of the martini. This seemed to enlighten him.

"Ah yes, the missing chauffeur. Poor fellow."

"Did you know Henry Turner, Mr. Lawson?" I asked him.

Lawson smiled, "Sorry, before my time, I'm afraid. Alison and I have only been married a couple of years. I'd heard about him, of course." He turned to his wife. "Are these the two you were telling me about earlier, darling?" She looked up at him, made a pouty face and nodded. His expression hardened. "Right. In that case, I'm going to have to ask you two to leave my house or I'll call the police. You've no right to be here and I don't think a second complaint will go down too well, do you?"

I shook out a Sweet Cap and took my time lighting it, then grinned at him through the smoke. "That must have been a damn good martini, Mr. Lawson."

He looked at me uncertainly.

"Yes, Essie knows how to make them. By following my instructions, of course."

"Of course," I allowed and laughed, not pleasantly. "I guess you needed that to stiffen your resolve."

"Now look here…"

"It's okay. I've seen plenty of guys like you, Lawson. Guys who have it handed to them on a silver plate. Guys who think they're tough and think that just because they have a position in society they can treat other people like dirt."

Lawson paled. She bared her fangs.

"Reginald. Are you going to let him speak to you like that?" Her tone could have minced diamonds. Lawson glanced at his wife uncertainly then back to me.

"I want you men out of my house," Lawson said. He went over to the phone where it rested on a mahogany side table. Even the phone was pampered.

"Mr. Lawson," I began, "we're investigating the disappearance of Henry Turner and…."

"I don't give a damn…"

"…we'll continue to investigate his disappearance no matter where it leads or who we need to question. You can call the big boys downtown all you like but that's not going to change. I hope you get my drift."

Lawson's pale face reddened then went florid.

"Out," he yelled. "Before I do something drastic." He glanced at Birdie who sighed and shifted his weight. "Er, I mean, don't come back here or I'll have you arrested on the spot."

"Don't think so," I said. I took a deep drag and exhaled slowly.

"What?" Lawson was stunned. Alison Lawson shot daggers at her husband, her expression porcelain.

"Maybe you know something about Henry Turner and maybe you don't but your wife does."

"You leave my wife out of this."

"As soon as she comes clean, we will."

"Why you… you…." He sputtered. "You, dirty… miserable… filthy… "

I cut him off.

"We're going to find out what happened to Henry Turner, Lawson and there's nothing you can do to stop us."

I nodded at Birdie who kept his eyes fixed on the Lawsons and it wasn't a friendly look. I doffed my hat and we strode across the foyer clicking our heels in unison.

"Oughtta be a song and dance team," Birdie said. "Putting on the jive."

I wasn't sure if he was referring to the Lawsons or the two of us.

13

From my vantage point behind the wheel, I surveyed the sweeping driveway, the breadth of the front lawn, the splendor of the house and knew secrets had been bottled up inside.

"Well, we've stirred up the hornet's nest," I said. "Guess we'll be hearing from Callaway any time now."

Birdie grunted and stared out the window.

"There was a big estate near where I grew up," he said. "Looked like this. Manicured grounds, nice orchids in the garden. I remember thinking how pretty they were. The owner was a sonofabitch too."

"White man?"

"Uh-huh."

"We're not all bad."

"So you say."

"I do say."

Birdie turned to look at me. "How you planning on getting out?" Lawson had parked close behind my Chevy and I was a nose back of his wife's Caddy.

"I was thinking of driving out over the lawn. What do you think?"

"I think that's a good idea. Don't miss the roses over there."

"Sure thing," I replied, putting the car in gear.

I made certain to leave deep ruts in the grass. It was a little bumpy but navigable. As I came around and headed down the driveway, I glanced in the rear view mirror. Thought I saw a set of curious eyes staring out from the living room, then a swish of curtains. I liked to think the Lawsons went at each other tooth and nail back in their comfy living room after we left. Would have been fun to watch too. I realized I wanted to smash the Lawsons, that I hated who and what they represented. Smugness, arrogance and money. I wanted to drive my fist through it. Birdie saw the expression on my face.

"Don't lose the plot," he said.

The Flit Construction Company had won the contract for extending the Queen Elizabeth Way highway westward expanding it to six lanes so traffic could float in and out of the city bypassing the residential streets. The Queen Elizabeth Way or QEW first opened in 1939 just as the war commenced, beginning life as a four-lane that went right into St. Catharines–smooth sailing all the way.

Building roads meant big business and took big money and Mr. Flit had both. Henry Flit Senior now served the back end of a five-year stretch for bribery. Apparently, some inspectors and city planners received anonymous contributions to their retirement funds and these payments formed a trail back to Mr. Flit who didn't deny it. He didn't deny it because he took the rap for his kid whose guilt had been cast-iron. The empire carried on under the sure hand of Henry Flit Junior. The Flit contracts had been maintained since the schedules lagged and the province needed to have these roads pasted down pronto. Tons of automobiles itched to cruise this new super highway. Flit came up for parole in the fall, for good behaviour, meaning he didn't kill anybody while inside. I'd heard he'd had a fairly easy ride. Money can buy a lot of things in prison. I don't think Flit Junior had put the champagne on ice just yet.

It was easy to spot the site. Dust churned up and spiraled into the air visible for miles. I turned the Chevy onto a slip road and pulled up behind a half-ton Ford pick-up. I'd seen battered tins cans with fewer dents. Concrete pylons separated the old highway from the new section. As we stepped out, Birdie became annoyed as he watched dust settle on his new Sy Sperling jacket, a 56 tall. I was a 40 regular and could buy off the rack. Most of the activity took place a few hundred yards ahead with twin jackhammers roaring and a backhoe stepping in to scoop up the crackling mess, spewing its load into the back of a monstrous dump truck. The site office consisted of a mobile home towed to a new location every other day as machines split the ground open, metal beams laid down, forms built and concrete poured–all at a manic pace. Like the old days of the railroad laying miles of track every day to meet the quota set by the bosses. Same thing with the roads I reckoned. A young stud wearing a hard hat, kerchief pushed below his chin, sleeveless tunic, blackened Levis and scuffed boots, leaned up against a concrete barrier sucking on a fag. A blue eagle tattoo etched into each bunched bicep darkened by the sun.

"Looking for Frankie Deans," I yelled above the roar of the Caterpillar grinding away. The young guy cupped his ear, nodded, then pointed toward the site office set back on a grassy verge away from the noise and the dust.

"Up yonder," he said, then took another pull while he glanced casually at Birdie who continued to pat and swat with hands the size of sauce pans, flicking specks off his lapels.

I nodded my thanks and we headed toward the trailer stepping over metal railings, dodging madmen with wheelbarrows. A beefy, brick-colored guy with a tan line below his eyebrows sat at a rickety card table with his hard hat off sweating over a blueprint jawing on a field telephone. Limpid blue eyes followed our progress as we approached even though his mouth kept moving. We stopped in front of him. Birdie cast a long shadow. The guy dropped the phone into its rickety cradle.

"Say, could you stand right there all day?" he asked in a languid voice then gave us a lazy grin. Birdie stepped away letting the light hit him right between the eyes. The guy didn't flinch.

"You Frankie Deans?" I asked.

"Yeah."

"Can we ask you a couple of questions?"

"What about?"

The smile never wavered.

"Henry Turner."

Flit Construction had the contract for the subway dig too. Small world when hand-outs and pay-offs had been spread around.

"I'm Mo Gold and this is Arthur Birdwell. We're private investigators."

Deans looked from me to Birdie and back again. I didn't see anything come into his eyes or face. I'd know. I'd seen it enough times over the years.

"Ask away," he said.

"You were the area site foreman on the Yonge Street subway job?"

"Yup."

I could see that he wasn't going to offer up information. I'd have to yank it out of him.

"Henry Turner worked for you?"

"That's right. Him and a lot of other guys."

"But you remember him?"

"Sure."

"Was he a good worker?" I asked.

"He was fine," Deans said.

"What does that mean?" Birdie interjected.

Deans cast a glance up at him.

"It means he came to the job on time every day, didn't shirk off like some clowns and carried his weight. Henry was stand-up. I was sorry about what happened to him."

"You mean the accident?"

"That's right. On any construction site, something is bound to happen. Digging tunnels can be tricky sometimes. You have to go slow from time to time but we were under a lot of pressure."

"You saying that this pressure caused Henry's accident?" Birdie asked.

Deans rubbed a dirty, meaty paw around his stubbly jaw line. The limpid eyes told me he liked his beer cold and often.

"No, I'm not saying that but it can be a factor, you know? You have to have eyes in the back of your head in this job and you can't always anticipate every problem. You do your best, that's all."

I prodded him. "So what happened when Henry got hurt?"

Deans sighed and licked his lips. He was thinking about a long tall cold one and I couldn't blame him with all the dust swirling around.

"A couple of days before, there'd been a lot of rain. The ground was soaked and the section of the tunnel we were digging got flooded." He shrugged. "I mean, it happens, we drained it as best we could, then laid down some forms but they hadn't dried completely. This was a cut and cover job which is cheaper and faster than boring through. Henry was with a crew down in the trench helping to pour some cement into an archway. Another crew was positioning beams overhead. Normally, it would have been fine but the rain softened the support and part of it crumbled under the weight. A couple of beams came down and took Henry with them. Lucky he wasn't crushed and luckier that his back wasn't broken or he woulda been in a wheelchair for the rest of his life. He was busted up pretty good and had to spend a few months in hospital."

"Anyone else get hurt?"

Deans shook his head and his jowls wobbled a bit.

"No. Henry was unlucky. The rest of the crew had time to get clear but Henry caught his boot on something."

"He get compensation?" Birdie asked.

Deans face coloured then and he stared down into his gut.

"Not really. He wasn't union yet and the company anted five hundred bucks. I tried to get him more but I was turned down flat."

"Who'd you ask?"

"Mr. Flit. He looked at me like I was crazy even asking."

"Let me understand this," I said. "You're telling me that you went out on a limb for Henry Turner?"

Deans nodded. "That's right."

"Why?"

"Henry was a bright kid. He only had high school but that didn't matter to me. I'd marked him in my mind to train him up as a site engineer." He poked a thick forefinger onto the blueprints. "Then the accident happened."

"What about after? You could have taken him on then, couldn't you?" Birdie asked.

The heavy shoulders went up.

"Yeah, maybe. I told him to call me. Then I heard he got another job and never heard from him. After that, someone told me he disappeared. Is that why you're here?"

"Henry get along with the guys in the crew?" I asked.

"Sure. Why wouldn't he?"

"Because he was a Negro for one thing," I said.

"Take a look, mister." And he pointed at the guys crawling like ants over the site. "We got all kinds–Negroes, Chinks, Spics, Wops, Polacks, Indians, Limeys, Krauts–you name it. These guys have to work together and I don't put up with any crap from any of them. They don't have to love each other and what they do outside of working hours is their business. They could be Nazis or Communists for all I care. On the job they stick to the job or they're out of a job. End of story. That's how I run my site and always have."

"Nice speech," I said. "Save it for the United Nations when you come up for Commissioner. Now, was there anyone in particular that Henry was having a problem with?"

"Not that I remember but it was a long time ago, over 10 years."

"What about buddies?"

Deans smoothed out the blueprints in front of him and looked longingly at the field phone praying it would ring.

"There was a guy he seemed on good terms with, yeah."

"Name?"

"I'm thinking. Ricky, Ricky Garcia."

"He still work for Flit?"

Deans shook his head. "After the tunnel was finished, never saw him again."

I had a thought. "You keep employment records?"

"Of course we do. Everything is legit," Deans replied with some heat.

"You got them that far back, on the tunnel job?"

"Dunno. I'd have to check in the office."

"A list of names, addresses and phone numbers would be very helpful," I said. "I'd appreciate it. And Henry's mother would too."

"That's a lotta names, mister."

I shrugged.

"You working for the old lady? That figures," Deans said.

"Why's that?"

Deans raised a finger like a shaman.

"Mothers always care–no matter what. I call my mother every day without fail."

"Good for you," I said. I took out a pad and pen and wrote on it. "Here's my number. If you could get us that list as soon as you can, it could make a difference."

Deans took the piece of paper, glanced at the number and stuffed it into the side pocket of his vest.

"See what I can do," he said. "Mothers…" And he smiled.

As we drove away, Birdie asked, "Think he'll call?"

I shrugged. "Probably not."

But then Frankie Deans surprised me. A couple of days later, a package of mimeographed sheets came to the office by messenger. There must have been 200 names on it. Deans scrawled a note in handwriting a five-year old would be ashamed of: For Mrs. Turner, it said. The clown really was sentimental. I leafed through the sheets and whistled. "Quite a list."

Birdie took a look at it and scowled. "Hope it's worth it," he said.

Birdie and I spent the rest of the day working our way up and down both sides Spadina Avenue and then along Dundas Street, the heart of Chinatown. We flashed the picture of the young Chinese girl I'd found in Ying's place in markets, laundries, corner stores, dim sum joints even a steam room. But it was a closed trap. No one knew anything. No one saw anything. Most didn't even bother looking at the photo, just turned away when we approached them, waved their hands then ignored us. Even though Birdie is hard to ignore, the merchants weren't cowed by him. They looked up, blinked, then turned away. We didn't exist.

14

I drove us back to the office. We'd stopped off at Fran's for a burger and a slice of apple pie with pomelot sauce. They did pomelot sauce better than anybody at Fran's on College Street. The usual moneyed crowd hung out there. Working stiffs and their families came for the blue plate special and ate their fill for a buck and a quarter. Later on, the winos and rubbies took over the booths in the back slumped in front of murky coffee waiting for nothing to happen. Ashtrays overflowed with butts they'd bummed or picked up from the street.

I admired the smooth operation–well planned and executed. I'd just turned down the alleyway to the office when a large, dark sedan closed off the entrance crossways. The other one hunkered in the lot facing our way when it hit us with its brights. Blinded, I hit the brakes. We were sitting ducks. Couldn't get out of the car because the alley was narrowed toward the back lot. Two guys in front and two guys in back approached. Each guy wore a dark raincoat and hat pulled down over his face. They carried some serious looking weaponry in the form of M60 machine guns and for fun, a couple of sawn-off 10-gauge shotguns. Looked like they expected a war. One of the guys in front pointed an M60 in our general direction while his buddy motioned us forward. What the heck, better to go forward than back, I thought. Apart from putting the Chevy in gear and inching ahead, Birdie and I remained motionless.

"What's with the hardware?" I asked getting out of the car. No reply. They leaned us up against the Chevy, hands behind our heads and frisked us. Both of Birdie's .45's were slipped into the pockets of a raincoat while my .38 snub-nosed followed quickly after. "Deep pockets," I said.

"Shut up," the guy frisking us said casually with only a slight hint of menace. He crouched down and felt Birdie's ankles then yanked his back-up piece out of its holster—a pretty little .25 with a mother-of-pearl grip—and held it up with two fingers like he handled someone's dirty underpants. He tsked under his breath and gave each of us a disapproving look.

I shrugged.

"Sorry Dad, I forgot. No guns on Sunday."

"Shut up, I said," the guy growled. I wanted Birdie to slap him silly but there were three other guys with weapons pointed our way.

Apparently, the others had lost the power of speech.

"Get in the car," the first guy said and jerked his head sharply.

"Say please."

"Huh?"

I figured that only two outfits acted this way, all tough and mysterious and wore long raincoats when it wasn't raining and brandished M60s. Had to be the feds or the military. Since the military didn't have a beef with us, at least not at the moment, it occurred to me these guys must be on the federal payroll. I decided they weren't going to give us each a couple of bursts and leave our bodies to the mercy of the unnatural surroundings. Even the Mounties weren't that crude.

"A little courtesy goes a long way," I said. Birdie guffawed.

One of the other guys started to move in and by the angry expression on his face, I gathered he didn't like being sassed but the first guy put out a dense arm and stopped him before he could get too close and make a bigger mistake. He made a sweeping motion with his hand and grimaced.

"If you wouldn't mind, gentlemen."

I nodded. "That's better. See? That wasn't so bad." I patted his cheek as I passed on by. I looked up at Birdie. "Your tax dollars at work."

Birdie grunted. "Yours maybe."

They bundled us into the back seat of an aging Ford Fairlane. The suspension sagged on Birdie's side. His head pressed into the roof. One of the seams on the seat had split, the door handles had been removed along with the window cranks and the interior smelled like someone had barfed limburger all over the moth-eaten carpet. The guy on Birdie's right looked like a midget. Two others rode in the front while the last guy drove the other car, also a black Ford Fairlane.

"Nice wheels," I said. "Don't suppose you could crack that window open? It smells like last year's lunch in here."

The driver smiled into the rear view. "One of our previous guests," he said nastily. "Had a bit of an accident." Nonetheless, he wound his window down a full inch to show he wasn't such a bad guy after all.

"You never showed us your ID," I said. "All law enforcement officers engaged in their duties are obliged to identify themselves when encountering the public–and that's a quote."

No response. All quiet in the cab.

Birdie turned to the guy beside him. "Show me your shield," he said.

The guy looked at him, flicked his gaze to the driver who shook his head slightly and back at Birdie. "No," he replied.

"I can ask you again politely," Birdie said. "Or I can ask you again–period."

The guy licked his lips, swallowed hard and gripped the M60 a little more tightly. "You gonna shoot that thing off in here–a moving car?" Birdie asked him and his eyes went big and wide like he narrated a ghost story. "Chances are you'll take out your pals first spraying bullets all over the place, and by that time I'll have that itty bitty thing wrapped around your throat. So, what's it gonna be?"

Beads of sweat peppered the guy's brow. The coats hung long and heavy, the hats the same. He swiped at the sweat with his sleeve.

"I'm reaching into my breast pocket," he said. His hand came out with a leather badge holder. Clearly visible, I saw the red crown and the *Maintiens le Droit* motto in the center surrounded by the laurel of golden maple leaves. The big giveaway though–*Royal Mounted Canadian Police* on the scroll at the bottom.

"Always liked that badge," I said. "Classy."

"Now you can shut up and stay that way," the driver said.

"I'll get your names later," I said. "No rush."

Within about ten minutes we'd pulled up in front of the King Edward Hotel on King Street near Jarvis, an inn of former grandeur. It looked like a massive Brownstone that had seen better days. The exterior looked grimy and the ratty blue awnings hadn't been cleaned since Queen Victoria's coronation. Named after King Edward VII, the King Eddy had been a class place once with a spacious marble lobby and one of the swankiest bars in the city. They used to let in only the high-class call girls who worked the lounge after 10 pm when all of the respectable customers had retired to their rooms. Now, you found them working the bar and the lobby from noon onward. Somehow, the management hadn't got the message that the joint had gone down market since the room rates remained among the highest in the city.

Occasionally, they'd find a body in one of the rooms, usually a suicide. People seemed to like the idea of spending their last day on earth in a hotel where they could order anything they wanted from room service knowing they wouldn't be paying the bill.

The M60s and the sawn-offs disappeared behind the folds of the long raincoats as we marched through the lobby in a ragged phalanx to the bank of elevators. The King Eddy led the trend toward self-service elevators in the city. The hotels found it easier and cheaper to let guests punch the buttons. Two couples checking in lined up ahead of us. Our minders let them take the first car that showed up. When the second car came along, the guy bringing up the rear turned around and barred the door preventing a couple of conventioneers from boarding.

"Sorry, private car," he rasped in what he hoped sounded a menacing tone and punched the doors close button. The businessmen stared. One started to protest but his companion wisely tugged him away.

"Smooth," I said. "Bet you can scare little kids too. What're you doing on Halloween? I could stick you in a hole on my front lawn and you could jump out and shout, Boo. How about it?"

The guy clammed up. Birdie shrugged.

"See what I get for trying to be sociable? So much rudeness in the world today." And I shook my head sadly.

The guy behind me said, "You've got a smart mouth. No wonder you didn't make it in the force."

I turned and looked at him, feeling the weight shift as the car ascended. He stood about my size, maybe a little taller with a lot more girth. He looked soft, even under the coat. Like the others, he wore his hair cut short, military style, down to the bristle and he'd shaved carefully that morning. Red patches blotted his cheeks and even though he might have been a couple of years younger, he had the blotchy look of a boozer. Under the brim of the fedora, his eyes had a yellowish tint.

"Better watch it, sonny, or you'll be singing soprano," I said.

The guy snorted and tried to smile but then the elevator doors swished open. We'd made it to the fourteenth floor in one piece, despite my trying to provoke something. We filled up the corridor and somehow, found our way to room 1410. Blotchy Face knocked. A sound like a grunt responded and we went in keeping better formation than the Argos when they took the field. I noticed a tartan sofa and a couple of loungers.

The floor was covered in grey carpet that had probably started out as beige. At the far end of the room, a man sat behind a desk, his back to the windows. The curtains had been drawn. He had a fag going in a mammoth cut glass ashtray, smoke curling to the ceiling. He'd placed his dark jacket carefully over the back of his chair to preserve the creases and his shirt looked crisp and white. He wore a bowtie and slicked back hair parted in the middle. He bent his oily head over a pad where all of his attention seemed to be focused on some dissertation he appeared to be writing. I cleared my throat. That drew a vicious look from Blotchy Face but I didn't care. The guy behind the desk glanced up for a second, then bent over his task again. We watched for a few moments. It was fascinating. Like a countdown to death by boredom.

"I can give you a hand with that," I said. "My penmanship is pretty good."

The guy didn't respond, just kept writing for a few more minutes, taking his time. Finally, he paused, sighed, reread what he'd written and set the pen down. He pushed back from the chair and stood up. He yanked the jacket off the chair back and slung his arms through it neatly, tugging the lapels to make sure it sat just right, and shot his cuffs precisely. He reached into his breast pocket and removed a leather wallet and allowed it to fall open, almost carelessly.

"I'm Inspector Tobin," he said. He waved his hand. "Please, gentlemen, take a seat."

"Mind if I take a closer look?" I asked.

Tobin swallowed hard then thrust his ID in my direction. I took a long look. I saw the insignia and his name, rank and badge number, then handed it back.

"And these goons?"

"Work for me," he said.

"That's very reassuring. So we weren't kidnapped by gangsters."

Tobin laughed but it was a little bit nasty.

"Kidnapped? I wouldn't think so. I believe you accompanied my men voluntarily."

"If that's how you want to describe it. Having an M60 jammed in your gob doesn't leave you much choice."

Tobin showed a few teeth.

"That's exactly what I call it. Please," he said and indicated the chairs. We sat. Tobin sat. Everyone else remained standing. We waited while Tobin scanned the pad again. It was never a good idea to volunteer anything especially with the feds. Learned that in the military. Birdie took the same course. Tobin took a long pull on his fag and appraised us through squinting eyes as he exhaled. Just to make him feel at ease, I smiled.

"You're related to Jake Gold, am I right?"

So, that's where we headed. I shrugged.

"You already know the answer to that. It's common knowledge. Is that all you wanted to know?" And I made to get up.

"That must have been difficult," Tobin said. "Known gangster with a cop for a son."

"Uh-huh." I'd heard it all before.

"Is that why you left the force?"

I'd been asked that one too.

"No. I left the force because I happened to punch the wrong guy."

Tobin nodded and consulted his pad briefly. "That would have been Superintendent Murphy?"

"That's right."

"You decked a superior officer?"

I pointed at him. "Right again. Batting a thousand, Inspector. My god, you feds are good."

"Now you're old man is up on a murder beef in the second degree."

"So I hear."

"You're not close?"

"I spoke to him about ten years ago. We had words."

"Nothing since?" He had an amused look on his face like I'd been kidding or tried to make him look like an idiot.

"My old man and I travel in different circles. We always have. Now, if there isn't anything else…?" I started to rise when Tobin barked.

"Sit down. You'll leave when I say you can." He sounded like my old fusspot geography teacher, Mr. Flook.

I sighed and looked over at Birdie who gave me his amused look. I stayed on my feet.

"It's like this, Inspector. Unless we're under arrest, you can't hold us. So, either charge us with some sort of fake crime, like I know you guys like to do, or unless you've got something meaningful to say, I think we'll be going." I turned toward Blotchy Face.

"And I believe you have some items that belong to us."

Tobin didn't have the look of a guy who liked to be crossed but I could see he'd immersed himself in deep thought. He smiled but it wouldn't have melted an icicle.

"Okay, Gold. I know you're a tough guy, you and your partner both. Take a seat and we'll all try to act a little more civilized, okay?"

"Speak for yourself." But I sat back down.

Tobin cleared his throat. "Why are you looking for Liu Chen?"

"Who?"

Tobin slid a photograph across the desk. I picked it up. It appeared to be the same girl as in the photo I found in Ying's flat. I flashed it to Birdie. "I don't know her name," I said. "I just found her photo."

"Where."

"In Ying Hee Fong's flat."

"What were you doing there?"

"Looking for clues. That's what I normally do when I'm working a case."

"What sort of clues?"

"Don't know until I find'em," I said.

"Who's the client?"

I shook my head. "That's confidential. Of course, you could try and beat it out of us." And I glanced at Blotchy Face who, suddenly, had an eager, almost hungry expression.

"That won't be necessary," Tobin said, as if he'd given it some thought. He stubbed out the fag. "So you don't know the girl in the photo?"

"No."

"She's Ying's sister–and we're looking for her."

Join the club, I thought and remembered the guy I'd winged and the feel of his sap on my head. "Why?"

"She's a material witness," Tobin replied as if that answered the question.

"To what?"

Tobin smiled. "Sorry. My turn. It's confidential."

"Why do you care about her or Ying?"

Tobin picked up his pen and tapped the end of it on the desk. Then he sighed as if he'd made a momentous decision. "Ying was our snitch. He was giving us good stuff on John Fat Gai, who I understand, is a friend of yours?"

Well, well. Ying got around. He was snitching for just about everybody. Who else, the Boy Scouts? "I wouldn't call him a friend. Far from it."

"He's a dangerous man. I'm sure I don't have to tell you that."

"Your concern is very touching." And Birdie guffawed. "Now, what do you want, Inspector?"

Tobin picked up Liu Chen's photo. "You find her, you let us know, simple as that."

"Now why would I want to do that?"

"Because you're a good Samaritan and a pillar of the community, and anything you do to help us put John Fat Gai away will be seen in a favourable light and you never know when that could come in handy."

"You're appealing to our sense of patriotism."

"That's right," Tobin replied. "Got it in one, Sergeant."

This time I stood for good.

"We're reasonable men, Inspector. We'll think about it and if we find Liu Chen before you do then we'll do the right thing, I can assure you."

Tobin's face clouded. I hadn't delivered the answer he wanted. "We can make things unpleasant if we have to."

"Heard that before," Birdie boomed.

"Wouldn't help you find her, though, would it?"

"Maybe not." Tobin stood up. He didn't hold out his hand. "Cut'em loose," he said.

Blotchy Face made a move to lay a hand on my arm but I put a hand on his chest and pushed.

"Keep your distance," I said.

He started to go for me but one of his barren-faced brothers held him back. The third guy placed our hardware carefully on Tobin's desk, where we picked it all up, checked that everything still worked and all parts remained present and accounted for, then stowed them all away in various pockets and holsters. Then we took our leave.

"Been a pleasure," I said but Tobin didn't even look up. He'd got back to his report writing.

We stayed silent in the elevator down to the lobby. An elderly couple along for the ride edged away from Birdie. He ignored it but I noticed. We strode through the lobby. Outside, I said to the doorman. "Whistle us up a cab, would you?"

The guy saluted. "Sure thing." And that's what he did, let out a piercing blast from between pursed lips then waved his arm. A cab turned the corner and slid up to the curb. "There you go." I gave the guy a buck.

"You're wasted in this job," I said.

The doorman laughed. "I've been telling myself that for years. Beats hawking programs at the Argos home games though."

I laughed with him. "Yeah, guess it does at that." We slid into the back and the cab took off. The cabbie meant business. I gave our address. We rode along for a few seconds.

"You thinking what I'm thinking?"

"Uh-huh."

Here's what we figured: if Callaway had been the only guy downtown who ran Ying as a snitch and the feds were doing the same thing without Callaway knowing about it, then the leak, or whoever took Ying out, must work for the cops or the feds. Me, I put my money on Blotchy Face. He looked shifty. Proving it was another thing.

15

I found Callaway at his favourite watering hole—a dump called The Embassy on Dundas Street just a little east of Yonge. He had a tumbler full of Canadian Club and wrestled with a slab of leather billed as a steak. Callaway sawed at it diligently. When he managed to break a piece off, he swirled it around in viscous-looking gravy and popped it into his mouth where he took a short eon to chew it into oblivion before giving up and swallowing it whole. I watched the wrestling match for a few more minutes when he set the knife and fork down symmetrically on the plate, clasped his chubby hands together and stared at me. "What now?"

"Nice to see you too."

I looked around the joint. Calling it dingy came as a compliment. I wanted to clean the grease from the soles of my shoes. "Looks like they've kept the standards up around here."

Callaway grunted. I knew he liked The Embassy because no cop would set foot in the place. It was owned by a guy named Enzo Carlucci who'd spent 15 years in Kingston pen for first-degree murder. The victim had been a cop. Callaway hadn't believed that Carlucci was the guy. Sure, he'd been mixed up with some bad characters and sainthood would never be bestowed on him by the pope but Callaway proved he didn't pull the trigger either, that the evidence had been tainted. Well, more than tainted, reeked to high heaven.

On his release, Carlucci sued the police department for wrongful conviction and Callaway testified for him. That didn't go down too well with the brass. With the cash he'd been given by the court, Carlucci bought The Embassy. The question remained why. It looked like a place where hoodlums hung out all night and smelled even worse. Clearly, Carlucci hadn't plowed any of his gelt into the décor or the kitchen either. Callaway figured he was doing his job, looked hard at the evidence in the case, felt it lacked hugely in credibility and went about the business of being a cop. He found the shooter and got Carlucci sprung. Didn't stop other cops from resenting him, even hating him for it. Made the department look bad and worse, bumbling and incompetent.

The chief at the time, Phil Bevins, lost his job over it. The mayor, Ziggy Callwood, fired Bevins for making the city look stupid. Now, Callaway had become an untouchable. If he got the can, the press would scream payback for Carlucci. So he'd become a pariah on the force and the only guy who'd work with him was a weasel like Roy Mason—even then he hadn't been given any choice. So Callaway ate his dinner in a shithole like The Embassy where no one would bother him, except me, of course.

"Am I going to like this?" Callaway asked. He drained the shot and set the tumbler down on the scarred wooden tabletop.

I shrugged. "Maybe this is just a social call."

Callaway snorted. "Blow another one by me, why don't'cha?"

"Okay. It's not a social call." A busboy scurried over and cleared Callaway's plate.

Callaway pointed to the glass and the kid nodded.

"You?" he asked me.

I shook my head. I couldn't be sure what pissoir the stuff came from even if the labels on the bottles looked glued in place. The kid took off into the kitchen and Callaway ripped out a belch. He grimaced. I felt his pain and smelled it too.

"So, what's eating you?" he asked.

I thought, briefly, about making a crack about the shoe leather that passed for his dinner but held back. I held back a few other things too. "Had a chat with Mrs. Lawson," I said.

The kid bustled over and replenished Callaway's drink. He took a gulp. "Oh yeah? Do tell?"

"You haven't heard from hubby?"

"He was there?"

I nodded. "Stopped in for his pre-lunch martini after slugging it out at the office for an hour or so."

"It's a rough life."

"So?"

Callaway shook his head. "Not a peep–or you woulda heard from me before now."

"That's what I figured. The guy's a lot of show with nothing behind it."

Callaway checked his watch–a pretty nice-looking Bulova. He caught my eye. "Anniversary gift from my wife," he said.

"Nice."

"My reward for 25 years of suffering," he added drily. "So, do I have to ask?" And he tapped a stubby forefinger against his temple.

"Sure," I said. "Not a lot of detail in that police report you sent on Henry Turner."

"Not a lot of detail to put in either. Besides, I didn't write the report."

"Do you remember the officer that pulled Alison Foster and her friends over the night they were joyriding?"

Callaway rubbed his face as if he didn't quite believe what he heard. "No, I don't remember."

"Can you find out?"

"I'll call you. What else you got?"

"One of Alison Foster's pals was a kid named Rance Callaway. That mean anything to you?"

Callaway sighed heavily. "Wondered when you'd get to it. Yeah. My kid sister's son. My nephew."

"You didn't say anything."

"That's right." And his voice took on an edge. "Didn't see the point at the time. Figured you'd understand."

"Understand what?"

"That kids do stupid things sometimes, well, maybe in his case, a lot of the time."

"He wasn't driving the car."

"No, he wasn't, thank god."

"How'd he know Alison Foster? I'm guessing she'd be out of his league."

"You got that right. Rance didn't know her. He knew the boyfriend."

"Harvey Troyer. They knew each other from school?"

Callaway shook his head. "Rance left school when he was 16. He, uh, worked for the Troyer family as an apprentice gardener. Got to know the son and the rest, as they say, is history. The Troyer kid liked to live life on the edge."

"Did he know Henry Turner?"

"I don't know. I don't think so. How would he?"

I knew Callaway didn't like this. Usually he'd peppering a witness with questions. "Not sure. Just thought I'd ask. Where's the kid now?"

"Back living with my sister."

"And her old man?"

"Gone. Took off years ago. Merchant seaman. He kept staying away longer and longer. Then finally, he just never came back. Good riddance. When he was on leave, he sat around the house and drank. And he wasn't a pleasant drunk."

"Sounds tough."

"What if it was? People deal with worse."

"Okay," I said. "I'm not accusing anyone of anything."

"She's my kid sister and I look out for her."

"What's the kid do in his spare time?

"Works in haulage. Drives for some company or other. Spends a lot of time picking stuff up at the docks."

"What sort of stuff?"

"Don't know. You'll have to ask him."

I put my hands out. "Okay, I will. You got an address?"

Callaway nodded, then reached into his jacket pocket and pulled out his pad.

After rummaging around in the side pocket, he found a pencil and jotted down his sister's address, ripped the sheet off the pad and tossed it on the table.

"You'll find him home most days around four. He works the early shift."

"I just need to ask him a few questions."

"Sure."

"Won't take long."

"I said sure." He raised his glass and signaled to the kid for a refill. He caught my look. "I'm off duty–not that I have to explain myself to you."

"Didn't say you did."

"Damn right." The kid brought the bottle over and splashed in a generous measure, then faded to the other side of the bar where he continued wiping out the glasses with a dirty dishtowel.

I thought about what to say next and whether I ought to mention the feds but something held me back. "Guess I'll shove off. Look, uh, don't let them get to you," I said.

Callaway held on to the tumbler like it was a life jacket.

"Not much choice. The girls are about to start college and I'm not ready to work as a hotel dick or run security in Eaton's department store. So I take whatever shit they throw at me. Just have to wait'em out, that's all. I'm good at that–waiting."

"Sure you are. The best."

"I'll get you the cop's name."

"Thanks."

Callaway nodded, then drained the glass. As I left, he held it up for another refill.

16

I drove back to the office and parked the Chevy in the back alleyway. I lived in the third floor flat. More of a shoebox with two rooms, a kitchen and a toilet with stand-up shower. If I hadn't been mulling over my conversation with Callaway, I might have been on guard. Just as I slipped the key into the steel reinforced door, they came for me. Melted out of the shadows and caught me with my back turned. Three of them dressed in black with balaclavas covering their faces.

Two of them pulled my jacket over my shoulders pinning my arms while the third came toward me with his fists balled up. I lashed out with my right foot and caught him square in the groin. He grunted in pain doubling over. I put another one into the soft tissue of his gut using the two goons on either side to support my weight when I kicked up. They didn't expect that. My fun was short-lived though. My buddies didn't let go and I'd only winded the other guy, who after a moment, pushed himself straight and approached me warily. As he came closer, I spat into his eyes goading him into making a mistake. He hissed, wiping away the spittle with one forearm. He landed the first punch—a decent right cross that caught me on the jaw but I could tell his hands were soft and if my luck held, he'd break a few fingers.

"Come on girlie, you can hit harder than that," I said.

"You freakin bastard," he spat.

"Thanks," I replied and managed to form a tight-jawed grin.

He gave me two more good shots to the head then one to the body that had the full English and I doubled over in pain. They let me go as I coughed some blood and that's when the other two decided to get in on the fun. I sagged down to my knees and the three of them worked me over getting their shots in with hands and feet. I'd never been on the receiving end of it like that but I'd seen it plenty of times. Cops working suspects over in the cells picking their spots where the damage hovered on maximum and the bruising minimal. I drowned, lost track of time, sat on the edge of some other place. Finally, I thought I heard one of them say, "Enough". And I imagined that the other two dragged the first guy away but not before he got in one last kick that caught me flush in the temple. That one put me out for the count. I don't remember colliding with the pavement.

17

I dreamt that I rode the Grey Ghost headed for England but the ship had been torpedoed. I swallowed water and woke up sputtering. It took a few years to bring things into focus but a facecloth smothered me and I gagged, then swatted it away thinking the bad guys had come for me again. I heard a high-pitched cry of surprise. The guy really was a girlie, except–the back alley had disappeared and I lay in someone's bed. The room looked vaguely familiar but I couldn't place it.

"How are you feeling, Mr. Gold?" a voice belonging to Aida Turner asked and when I took a look, her face and body seemed attached to it too.

I shifted my back but felt nothing but pain radiating up and down my spine and my legs. The boys had done a good job. They could be proud.

"How do I look?" I asked.

Aida Turner actually chuckled. "Are you that vain?"

"Yes," I breathed.

"Let me get you a mirror then."

I felt her weight lift off the bed and soft shoe taps disappeared into another room. A moment later, the taps returned. She held a mirror out in front of me. I took a look. All things considered, it wasn't too bad, not as bad as I felt. I had a split lip and a nasty bruise that looked like a rotting eggplant embedded in my right temple. Apart from the complexion of week-old fruit, I looked almost human. I put a finger in my mouth and probed around. No loose teeth. Another blessing. My eyes were bloodshot like I'd been on a bender.

"Hhmmph."

"Is that all you have to say?"

"Uh-huh. Oh yeah. How'd I get here?"

I could see her face now and it filled, full of concern.

"Your large friend brought you here. I told him you belonged in a hospital but he wouldn't hear of it. Said God would look after you. I think he wanted me to feel guilty."

I tried to laugh but it came out more like a sick wheeze.

"Sounds like Birdie. We try to avoid hospitals when we can, Mrs. Turner. The rooms cost a bundle and the food is lousy too. But thank you for your kindness."

I made a supreme effort and managed to lift my chest off the bed about an inch. With a forefinger, she pushed me back down again.

"No you don't, Mr. Gold. You need your rest and my Henry's room is available. Besides, whoever your friends were, they won't look for you here. But I must confess, it troubles me that this happened to you because of your search for my son. It troubles me a great deal."

"Mrs. Turner," I wheezed. "I don't know that this–incident–is related to Henry at all. Could be something completely different. I've ticked off a lot of guys over the years."

"Nonsense. This makes me responsible for you. Mr. Birdwell was right about that. You'll stay here until you're feeling better."

"Since you put it that way..." She kept talking but I didn't hear much more of what she had to say since I'd used up just about all the reserves I had left and slipped back into the black hole.

The next time I came to, I wore someone's pajamas. I knew they couldn't be mine because they smelled strongly of mothballs. Expecting to see Aida Turner, I was surprised to see her niece, Adele Rosewell, at the other end of a spoon. In her neatly manicured hands, she held a bowl.

"Hungry?" she asked. I nodded. "Well, open up then." I opened. "This sort of thing happen to you often, Mr. Gold?"

"All the time."

"I see," she replied, clearly not seeing at all.

"How're your ankles," I mumbled.

She snorted and for a second I thought she'd dump what I took to be chicken soup from the aroma, all over me.

"Please," she said. "No jokes. I don't want you to make me spill this on you."

"I don't think I'd look very good wearing chicken soup either."

"How is it?" she said, shoveling more in.

"Salty. That's how I know it came from a tin. Homemade soup isn't salty at all."

"I wouldn't know," she murmured looking at me with a pair of lovely brown eyes. "I've never made soup."

She fed me a few more spoonfuls and then asked, "Does this mean you're getting close to something?" Always business with this woman.

"Not necessarily. All it means is that I've ticked off the wrong people."

"Oh." More soup came my way. "You know, I almost became a nurse."

"What happened?"

She frowned, then actually smiled. "I realized I didn't have the aptitude for it. Not enough empathy and that's why I went into banking instead."

"Good choice."

"Do you think I lack in empathy, Mr. Gold?"

"I just think you've grown a thick skin, probably for good reasons, Miss Rosewell."

She looked down at the bowl. It was empty.

"Now I should pinch your cheek and tell you what a good boy you've been for finishing all your soup."

"But you won't. The empathy thing." She didn't say anything but kept looking at me in a probing way. "Er, these pajamas…"

"Yes?"

"How did I…?"

"Well, it was my aunt and I who changed you, if that's what you're asking."

"I see."

"Yes," she said. "And so did I," she replied with a wry twist of the lips.

I cleared my throat. "See anything interesting?"

She grinned. "I've seen men naked before, Mr. Gold."

"White men?"

She pursed her head and shook her head. "No comment."

"White, Jewish men?"

"My lips are sealed."

"They're nice lips."

"Thank you, Mo. That's sweet of you to say. Now..." She stood up and smoothed her skirt. "I should let you get some rest."

"What time is it?"

"About seven-thirty."

"At night?"

"That's right."

"What day?"

"Tuesday."

It had been two days since the beating. "Where are my clothes?"

"I don't think you're going anywhere, Mo."

"The clothes, Adele?"

"Well, the shirt was ruined–covered with blood–and other things. The jacket was pretty mangy too but Auntie managed to get most of the stains out. One knee was ripped out of your pants."

With a Herculean effort, I managed to get propped on my elbows but the room rotated a bit and the pain crackled and radiated the way nature intended–from the centre. Adele stood in the doorway with her arms crossed holding the bowl and soup spoon, an amused expression on her face. "You really like to be the man, don't you?"

"Last time I looked, that's what I was." I glanced down then back up again and swore she blushed.

"You're staying put. You really don't have a lick of sense. I'll be in the living room and believe me, you won't get by me, not when I'm on watch, okay?"

I knew that I couldn't get to my feet without help and clearly no help would come from her quarter so I decided to give in for now and lay back down.

"I take my work very seriously."

"So do I," she said and closed the door.

After that exchange, I was exhausted. But the soup wasn't half-bad.

Three more days and I could move better than an 80 year-old with two canes. When I had some conscious moments, I began reading *The Invisible Man.* I know how he felt. Birdie brought some clean clothes from my flat. I used Mrs. Turner's shower to clean up and managed to cut myself only a dozen times with a disposable razor. It only hurt when I dropped the soap and had to retrieve it. Birdie waited patiently while I got dressed. Mrs. Turner fretted in the front room.

"Are you sure about this, Mr. Gold? I don't believe you're well enough."

"I've overstayed myself, Mrs. Turner. It's time to get back to doing what I do best."

"I hope that doesn't include any more beatings," she said. Birdie guffawed.

I shot him a dirty look. "I wouldn't worry about that."

Friday night and everybody celebrated the end of the work week.

"We'll be in touch," I said.

On the front step, Birdie said, "Want me to carry you to the car?"

"Wise guy. I'm pretty sure I can make it. Just give me a couple of days."

I took a deep breath. I felt pain but it didn't knock me over. I felt hungry. Hadn't eaten a full meal all week. In the car, I said, "Let's go to Shopsy's. I could murder a corned beef on rye and a cold beer."

"Now you're talking."

He fired up the Chevy and bolted from the curb.

"Hope you been busy," I said.

"Hmm-mm," he replied in a neutral way while keeping his eyes on the road. Dusk trickled in.

Although it hurt to chew, it was the best corned beef I'd ever tasted. Piled as thick as a giant's fist, slathered with French's mustard and the rye freshly baked with seeds, just the way I liked it. The deli hopped but then it always had clientele. The beer had the right amount of bubbles and a frosty temperature. More than that and I didn't care. I managed to down two in short order. I sighed. Nice to feel human again.

After demolishing a plate of smoked meat and three pumpernickel bagels along with half a dozen dill pickles, Birdie heaved a deep sigh. I lit a Sweet Cap and shared his contentment. We ordered coffee and Danish. He poured cream into his cup and added half a dozen sugars. I drank it black. That way I could taste the coffee.

"I found Ricky Garcia," he said.

"Who?" I'd lost a few facts along with brain cells as a result of the conk on the noggin.

"Henry's pal from Flit Construction."

"Where'd you find him?"

"He's a big macher at the union now," Birdie said. "Vice-President of the local."

I liked it when Birdie used Yiddish expressions. Made me believe in the universality of language.

"Is that so? Seems odd that Deans wouldn't know him. The guy must be in his face every time there's a big job and Flit only gets the big ones."

"We're meeting him at the union hall in 30 minutes."

18

Local 183 of the Construction Worker's Association had its HQ on Cecil Street, just down the block from Ying's flat less than five minutes from Shopsy's. The union hall looked like a low-slung bunker where they held bingos and chintzy dances on Saturday nights and meetings of the young socialists early on Sunday mornings.

My mother had been a socialist. My dad had only pretended, just to see what graft he could get out of it. Some of his union buddies had been commies just after the war. When it came out how many Stalin had butchered, a few changed their tune. Didn't stop the rackets though. Politics went hand-in-hand with corruption. Always did and always would. Birdie parked the Chevy on the street. I stepped gingerly out of the car and only groaned once or twice. I took a good look at Local 183.

"Not exactly good advertising for the industry, is it? I wouldn't hold a funeral in that joint," I said.

Birdie merely grunted. He felt the same way. The main doors remained locked so we rang the bell. After a few moments, a light clicked on inside the foyer and a stocky figure came to the glass door–one reinforced with heavy wire mesh. That's when I noticed the windows had been done up in the same motif. The guy unsnapped half a dozen locks and finally, swung the door open. He looked up at Birdie. It took a while.

"You the guy I spoke to?"

"That's me. And this is my partner."

Garcia turned his gaze on me. "You better come in. I was just closing up."

"You expecting trouble?"

"I always expect trouble," Garcia said and ushered us in then reset the bolts and chains. I watched him for a couple of minutes. "My office is this way."

We followed him down a dim corridor, through a meeting room, down a shorter corridor that led to an open work area with offices on the perimeter. Only one office had its lights on.

"Please," Garcia said and gestured to two battered chairs opposite his desk, the surface of which, boasted papers in teetering stacks. "Contracts. It's always contracts."

Judging by his girth, Ricky Garcia hadn't worked a construction site in a while but you could tell by the condition of his hands–swollen fingers like they'd been broken, the palms callused–that he'd done heavy lifting. He wore his graying hair slicked back and sported a Pancho Villa moustache. The skin around his eyes gleamed tight and shiny, testament to a pockmarked youth. He looked older but I figured him to be in his mid-thirties.

"Thanks for seeing us," I said.

"What happened to you?" he asked. "That's a pretty nasty bruise. You're also not walking too good."

I shrugged. "Occupational hazard."

Garcia put out a thin smile. He reached down beside his desk and brought out a baseball bat. "I keep this in case of unexpected company." He hefted it then smacked it into his thick palm before setting it back on the floor. "You wanted to talk about Henry Turner?"

"That's right. What can you tell us about him?"

Garcia leaned back in his chair and the joints creaked. Not sure if it was the chair or him. "We worked together at Flit Construction during the subway contract. We got to be friendly, went out for a beer that sort of thing. Henry was a good guy."

"Was?"

"I heard he disappeared."

"Henry make any enemies while he was at Flit?"

Garcia gave that some thought. "Don't think so. If anyone made enemies, it was me."

"How so?"

"I was the union steward back then. I had run-ins with management at the time."

"Frankie Deans?"

"That's right."

"Deans told us he liked Henry. Wanted to train him as a site engineer, that he had a lot of potential."

Garcia snorted. "Deans said that?" I nodded. "What a two-faced bastard."

"Why you say that?" Birdie asked in a deep rumble.

"Why?" Garcia repeated. "I'll tell you why. Henry got a stinking deal, that's why. How do you think that accident happened in the first place? Deans knew the crew shouldn't have been pouring concrete when it was so wet. That it wouldn't harden and couldn't support the weight of the overhead beams. He sent our crew down into the pit knowing an accident could happen."

"Why?"

"Deans was cutting corners to save money. Wherever and whenever he could cheap out, he did. Flit made sure he was handsomely rewarded, a bonus based on how much money he saved. You know the old man went to jail right?"

I nodded. "He's due out in September. But five years is a long time to be out of circulation."

"He deserved more than that but there's justice for the rich and a different type of justice for the poor."

I didn't want to get into a political debate with the guy. "Deans told us he fought with Flit over compensation money for Henry. That Flit didn't want to give Henry anything."

The thin smile reappeared. "Henry was in hospital for almost four months. Then he was bedridden at home for another three. That's seven months without being able to work not to mention the hospital bills. And when he was, he couldn't do half of what he could before. You call that fair? You think five hundred bucks can make up for that? The medical costs were three times that. It was the union anted up for that, not those pricks Flit or Deans. Don't get me started," he muttered.

"So you don't think Deans was looking out for Henry's interests?"

Garcia shook his head. He didn't have much of a neck I noticed. "Deans is a sonofabitch. Between him and Flit, they figured the five hundred was enough to keep Henry quiet. Henry wasn't a fighter. He just took it, you know?"

"Not like you, you mean?" Birdie said.

"That's right, big man. Not like me. I went after Flit and Deans for breaking the labour code. I filed grievance after grievance but it came to nothing. Flit had his lawyers all over it. I'm surprised the damn tunnel hasn't collapsed by now. You won't find me taking the Yonge Street line."

"Hundreds of thousands do every day," I said.

"Well, one day it's going to cave in on them."

"Then you'll be happy?" Birdie growled.

"Hey, I didn't say that," Garcia said. "I'm no ghoul. I hope it doesn't happen."

"You and Henry stay in touch after?" I asked.

"Yeah. For a while. I visited him in the hospital. Saw him at his mother's once or twice. And then we both moved on."

"When was the last time you heard from him?"

Garcia rubbed his chin. "Maybe 1950 or 1951 sometime? I'm not sure."

"He say anything about getting married?"

"Nope."

"What about working as a chauffeur for a wealthy family."

Garcia's expression brightened. "Yeah. I remember something about that. Can't think of who though."

"He say anything else about this family he was working for?"

"Yeah. He said there was a daughter, a teenager and she was pretty wild. Part of his job was to babysit her. Make sure she didn't do anything stupid. Sounded like a full-time occupation."

"He mention anything?"

Garcia ran a wide palm over his fleshy chin. "Some joyriding, maybe. Nothing too serious. That's all I remember, honest. The next thing I heard, Henry was gone."

"So Henry wasn't active in the union?"

Garcia shook his head. "Not really. I mean, if there'd been a strike I'm sure he woulda walked the line like everybody else. But he wasn't an active member. Paid his dues and that was about it. I don't even remember him coming to any of the meetings."

"You got a city map?" I asked.

Garcia gave me a curious look. "Yeah." And he opened the top drawer of his desk. "Right here."

"Can you show me where the collapse happened?"

"Yeah, sure."

Garcia turned the map around so we could see it. The subway ran north from Union Station. He plunked his stubby forefinger on a spot just above Queen Street near City Hall and diagonal to the law courts. "Right about there."

"Just the one tunnel?" I asked.

Garcia shrugged.

"Just the main one but there's a few spurs that the trains don't really use anymore. They're kept for storage mostly, spare track and occasionally some cars are stowed there but mostly they're dormant. They keep everything up at the marshaling yards now. But when we were building the tunnel, it didn't exist then."

"So there are other tunnels that aren't used for anything?"

"That's right." Garcia rubbed his fleshy chin.

"Thanks."

"Does that help?"

"I don't know," I said. "Maybe."

"I don't get it. You guys looking for Henry?" Garcia asked.

"That's right. Why?"

The shop steward shrugged. "Well, either he don't want to be found or…"

"You think he's dead?" Birdie boomed.

Garcia paled. "I don't know. I just think it's strange that he just disappeared like that. I mean, who does that? My mother would kill me if I did that to her."

I stood up. "Thanks for your time, Mr. Garcia."

"Sure. You find out anything, lemme know, okay? I always liked Henry. He was a good guy. Honest, you know? Not many like that left in the world."

"Amen," Birdie boomed again. Garcia shot him a curious look.

"We'll do our best," I said.

19

Birdie dropped me off at my flat. I let him keep the Chevy and he drove off into the night. Although it wasn't early, I felt restless, edgy and found the walls to be closing in on me. I limped up and down and back and forth for a while but that didn't do it for me. I hadn't invested in a television as yet finding most of the programs idiotic. The radio held no interest for me although there was a big band program I occasionally picked up that broadcast Friday nights out of New York City. It came in on a clear night.

Outside on King Street, I hopped a cab and gave the driver Aida Turner's address. I paid him off then noticed no lights were on and it occurred to me that maybe the old lady was in bed. Throwing caution to the wind, I rang the bell. After a few tries, nothing stirred and I figured she wasn't home, which for a detective, made pretty good deducing. I wasn't looking for her anyway. I headed down the walk and unlatched the gate, then carefully latched it back up.

Bloor Street lay only a few blocks north and even though it felt like a balmy night, I needed to feel some heat, some life. Chasing ghosts chilled the soul. A block up, I found a phone booth and looked up her name but couldn't find a listing. Stymied again. Reaching the brighter lights of Bloor, I hailed a cab and told him to take me to the Colonial Tavern, one of the city's premier jazz spots. I'd never been a rabid jazz fan like Birdie but occasionally they had some big band music. The Colonial spoke of the land of the living and that would do.

The main floor had round tables jammed tight together. Your neighbor could end up sitting on your lap and you wouldn't know it. The stand-up bar stood opposite the stage. I walked into a blast of Dixieland straight from New Orleans. After being in purgatory for a while, I felt warmed by the sound. The heat lay like an extra layer of air along with the fug of cigarette smoke and the buzz of voices talking over the music.

The bar staff had thrown open the windows and doors so the music and talk spilled out into the street. I headed straight for the bar and that's where I found her. Except it wasn't her. Just someone who reminded me of her. She nursed something in a tall glass. She stood taller and willowy with a thrusting bosom in a low-cut red dress with sequins festooned down the front. Her hair was cut long on one side and swept over her forehead and down into a flip. I checked out her ankles; bony as flints on an archeological dig. I turned the other cheek. I caught the bartender's eye and that required Olympian effort. The drinkers piled in three deep and had a yawning thirst.

"I'll have a Canadian Club and whatever the lady's drinking," I shouted.

She fired a gap-toothed smile in my direction. "Why thank you," she said. "Rum and coke for me. That's awfully sweet."

I grinned back at her. "I'm just a sweet guy."

"Are you?"

"Uh-huh."

"Well, somebody didn't think so, honey. Judging from that nasty bruise you got."

I touched my temple and winced. "Oh, that. That was just a simple misunderstanding."

"Really?"

"Really," I affirmed.

The barkeep brought the drinks and I tossed him five bucks and told him to keep the change. He shot me a grin and a thumbs-up.

"You like jazz?" she asked me.

"Mo," I said.

"You like jazz, Mo?"

"That's why I'm here, sugar."

"Evelyn," she said.

"Pleased to meet you, Evelyn."

"Likewise."

"Shall we find a table?"

"Lets."

Along with her ankles, she boasted skinny legs and heels skyscraper high. I found a table in the corner and we settled in. Several drinks later the pain had receded. We talked but I don't remember anything we talked about. The music went into my head and stayed there. Some time later, I found her hand on mine and discovered my hand on her thigh. She let me keep it there. After a few more drinks, I think we got up and left. The music disappeared. Suddenly I found myself in the back of a cab. The cabby was a beefy white guy with an unlit cigar stub jammed in his face. His porcine eyes kept flickering into the rearview. I sensed disapproval. I felt disdain radiating from the front seat.

"You got a problem, buddy," I said. His eyes flicked away. I leaned forward propping my elbows close to him. "I said, you got a problem, buddy?"

"Hey," Evelyn said. "It's okay baby, really."

"What about it," I shouted.

The cabby shook his head once. "No problem."

"Good. Keep it that way."

I don't know why I felt so angry but I think I would have ripped that guy's head off if he'd made a move. Instead, I looked out the window and watched the lights turn into a blur. Sometime later, the cabby pulled up to the curb. I stumbled out, leaning on Evelyn. I threw ten bucks into the cabby's face and told him roughly to keep the change. He didn't bother to pick it up from the floor but gunned the cab down the street.

"You've got a bit of a temper, Mo."

"Huh? Oh yeah. Sorry. That guy–made me angry–I..."

"Thanks," she said.

"What for?"

"Sticking up for me. Most guys wouldna done that."

"AAhhh…" I waved my hand and almost fell over. Evelyn laughed and grabbed me.

"This way," she said and I looked up at what seemed a mountain of stairs. No way I could make it up there.

"Where's the elevator?"

Her laugh spilled out kind of tinkling, like broken glass showering the pavement. "Come on." She wrapped my arm around her shoulders and swaying together we teetered upward. At the top, she rooted around in her purse for her keys. They jangled in her hand. Her fingers were long and slim. "Now when we get inside, you got to be quiet, okay?" She touched my lips. "Okay?"

I nodded. "Okay."

She unlocked the door careful not to jiggle the keys too much. We stepped inside and she pushed the door closed behind us. I leaned back and felt my knees begin to buckle. We were in a living room of some kind. I saw the shapes of furniture. Something had burned earlier and the odor hung heavy. "You need to use the toilet?"

"Uh-huh."

"It's over here." She took my hand and led me to it. "Go on. Do your business."

"Oh, I will," I said.

I should have figured it out from the number of toothbrushes but alcohol makes you thick. I snapped the light on and looked at myself in the mirror. I saw a dark face with a five o'clock shadow and a demented expression stare back at me. No wonder the cabby had been spooked. I looked like a maniac. I ran the cold water and doused my face. I noticed some Ipana toothpaste. I managed to uncap it and squeezed a blob on my finger and ran it around inside my mouth. Then I urinated–mostly in the basin I hoped–profusely. I pressed the lever and washed my hands with a gooey bar of soap. I didn't see a hand towel so I dried my hands on my pants.

"You okay in there," Evelyn whispered through the door.

"Uh-huh."

I opened the door. She smiled at me. "Come on. This way." She led me to the bedroom and clicked on a table lamp. The bed was unmade. "You get undressed and I'll be right with you."

"Okay." I had some thoughts about what I was doing there but the fog had descended earlier and hadn't lifted yet. It must be someone else. A small chair stood beside the bed. I got undressed, tossed my clothes on it then slid under the covers. They felt clammy but it wasn't my skin that felt it. I stared up at the shadowed ceiling.

After a few minutes Evelyn came into the room. She sat on the other side of the bed and kicked off her shoes. Then she stood up and unzipped her dress. It slithered to the floor. She bent down and picked it up and placed it on the dresser. She unhooked her bra and slid her panties off. For a slim woman, her breasts were heavy and full, the nipples dusky. Her buttocks were cream colored. Before clicking off the light, she turned and smiled. That gap-toothed grin. Kind of endearing. Then she disappeared. I heard her move across the floor and felt her weight on the bed and the covers moved.

"C'mere baby." Her heavy breasts pressed against my chest and her full lips lay on mine while her hand worked its way down to my crotch. When I rolled her over I grunted in pain but she didn't seem to notice and I felt her slim thighs part, her pelvis arched and she breathed in my ear. I disappeared into her. Her callused heels slid up and down the back of my thighs and she dug her long, slim elegant fingers and sharp nails into my back. We panted like animals. I drowned in her heat. There was fire and more fire as the flames licked me sweetly up and down. She bucked and heaved and cried out softly sinking her teeth into my shoulder as she whimpered and finally let out a long sigh. She wouldn't let me go after that and I stayed where I was. The night melted in a sequence of motion with caught breath punctuated by yelps and whimpers. I'm not sure whose. We both seemed to need something but it had to be somebody else, I thought. It couldn't be me.

I awoke to find two pair of bug-eyes staring at me with unabashed curiosity from the end of the bed. A young boy of about three and his older sister, maybe five. Her frizzy hair had been pulled into pigtails and tied with pink ribbons.

"Jesus," I exclaimed and shrank back under the covers. My immediate reaction–shame and embarrassment.

"Don't take the Lord's name in vain," the little girl said. Another Birdie in the making I thought. "What's your name?" she demanded.

"Mo."

"What kind of name is that?"

"The only one I got," I said.

"That's a silly name," the little girl retorted while her brother stared at me wide-eyed like I was some kind of monster or demon he'd seen in a puppet show.

"Marcus? Carmen? Where are you?" Evelyn called, then appeared in the doorway dressed in a robe. She crossed her arms and the robe fell open. "What are you two doing in here? You're disturbing Mo. Now out, the pair of you. Go on and have your breakfast. It's waiting for you. Go on now." Carmen gave me a haughty look as she marched out while Marcus merely scampered off. "Sorry about that. How are you feeling?"

"A little hung over." I sat up with the covers pulled up to my chest. I didn't know what to say.

"You hungry?" she asked. I shook my head. "How about some coffee then?"

"That'd work."

"I'll leave you to get dressed." She turned and called out. "You two better be at the table now." She turned back and smiled at me. "My babies."

I nodded and she closed the door after her. Now that the alcohol had worn off, it wasn't only my head that throbbed but every muscle and ligament. Even the cracks between my toes ached. I half-staggered into the kitchen. The two children sat in front of a black and white RCA Victor television watching cartoons. They seemed riveted. Didn't move an inch or utter a peep. Maybe that's what television did? Hypnotized the masses. The kitchen had enough space to hold a small table where three could just squeeze in. I slumped down and Evelyn placed a steaming cup of coffee in front of me. The saucer was badly chipped. "You don't look too good. I got some Bayer in the cabinet."

"Yes," I croaked. "That would be good. Better get me four."

"But the bottle says two tablets."

"Trust me. I need four."

She frowned then shrugged and came back with the bottle and placed it on the table in front of me. She sat down. She watched me tap out four tablets then down them one by one. "You got some bad bruising all over you. I didn't see it in the dark. What happened? You look like you got beat up real bad."

"Something like that."

"Maybe you should go to the hospital. I could go with you. I work down at St. Mike's. I'm a nurse down there and I've seen plenty of beat-up bodies and worse, I can tell you."

"I'm sure you have but I'll be fine, Evelyn." She gave me a skeptical look. "Really, it's okay."

She laid her hand on top of mine. "Baby, you in some kind of trouble?"

I shook my head. "No."

"Then what kind of work you do where you get beat up like that?"

"It doesn't happen often," I said.

She snorted. "Doesn't have to happen much before it gets out of hand. You could have broken ribs or internal injuries."

"I don't."

"How do you know?"

"Because the guys who did this were experts. They knew what they were doing, that's why."

She pulled her hand away. "You're not some kind of gangster are you, Mo?"

I tried to laugh but it hurt so much I just shook my head. "Well it's your business I guess." I hadn't buttoned my shirt and had rolled the cuffs up. She pointed at the tattoo low down on my forearm. "You in the war?"

"Wasn't everybody?"

"Was it bad?"

"Isn't it always?"

She conceded my point. "Fair enough. You don't want to talk about it. No man ever wants to talk about it."

"The kids," I said. "Their father. Where is he?"

She shrugged. "Don't know. He ran off when I was pregnant with Marcus. Haven't seen or heard from him since."

"Sorry."

"Don't be. He was a jackass and more's the fool me."

I shouldn't have said it but I did. My brain lags my tongue, sometimes. It was really none of my business. "Who was here with them last night?"

"What?" Her thin brows came together in a furrow.

"Your kids. Who stayed with them while you were out?"

Her lips went into a line. "They were asleep. They always sleep through the night."

I couldn't keep my gob shut. It slipped out before I could blink.

"Evelyn, but what if something happened? An emergency, a fire, something. They'd be on their own. Alone."

She pushed her chair back. It scraped along the floor and I felt like it scraped my skull. "Don't you be telling me. I got to have a life too. You don't know what it's like raising kids on your own. How hard it is. You men. You just come and go as you please..."

"Sorry. I didn't mean...."

She stood up now angry and defiant. "Oh yes you did. Don't you judge me and what I do." She turned her back. "You better leave now."

"Evelyn."

"I said now and I don't want to ask you again."

I sighed and stood up slowly. I picked my jacket off the back of the chair.

Just as I was fixing to leave she said, "Who's Adele?"

"What?"

She still hadn't turned around but I heard the hardness in her voice and the anger steeling her shoulders. "Last night. You called me Adele."

"I don't know. I must have been dreaming," I stammered.

"You must think I'm a fool." She dipped her head. Her shoulders began to quake.

I didn't have an answer for that.

"Thanks for the coffee," I said.

As I left, the two kids didn't even look up.

At the bottom of her stairs, I took a good look around. She lived not more than two blocks away from Aida Turner. The Junction–the city's dumping ground. I decided to walk back and clear my head. It was early yet, a little past eight o'clock but the day already had heat seeping into it. The pills had kicked in and I felt a little better. The exercise would do me good.

20

Callaway reached me at home. When I walked in, the phone rang. Claimed he'd been calling for a few days.

"I was on a rest cure," I told him.

"Rest from what?" he spat.

"The usual."

"That says a lot."

"I know. So what have you got?"

"The patrol cop you asked about. The one who pulled Alison Foster and her friends over? You remember that much?"

"Sure. What's his name?"

"Don't laugh. It's Paddy Kernahan."

"Let me guess...Irish?"

"Got it in one. I guess that rest cure did you some good."

Kernahan lived in Leaside, a leafy suburb just northeast of the city's core, about twenty minutes drive on a good day. I called Kernahan and he was home working on his garden, he said. He didn't sound too friendly but said I could drop by. To be honest, I didn't think Kernahan could tell me much but it formed part of moving forward. I told myself that Henry had been gone a long time and to find out what happened to him would also take time. We lifted rocks to see what was underneath. I hoped something would slither out.

I stripped off my clothes and dumped them in the laundry hamper. I had a maid come in a couple times of week to tidy up and she took care of the washing for me. I shaved carefully and stepped into a hot shower letting the water pound my skin for a while. When I felt clean on the outside, I dried off and got dressed. Then I called Birdie. I didn't have a direct number for him, just a contact where I left messages. I told him to pick me up in half an hour. While I waited, I made some coffee and burned some toast. I began to feel normal. The swelling had gone down on my temple and the bruise had faded. It glowed a light green and purple now with a yellow tinge. Not bad enough to scare little kids if Evelyn's were anything to go by. Half an hour later, I stood outside on King Street scanning the Toronto Telly dragging on a Sweet Cap when the Chevy appeared. I folded the paper, flicked the butt down a sewer grate and climbed in.

"What happened?" Birdie asked. I never could figure out how he knew things. It was like he could read my soul.

"Tell ya later."

"Yes, Boss."

"Ah, don't be like that. I will tell you later."

He grinned. "Just yanking your chain, master."

"Go on, ya big lug." I gave him Kernahan's address and told him who he was.

"He still on the force?" Birdie asked.

I shrugged. "Yeah, I think so."

Kernahan's house ended up being a neat little bungalow on Millwood Road where it crossed Bessborough Drive. The brick looked clean like it had been washed down every other morning. The lawn neatly trimmed. A figure I took to be Kernahan pushed a hand mower up and down in precise rows. Each window had a freshly painted wooden shutter. A guy with too much time on his hands. We pulled up at the end of the driveway. The property lacked a garage, just a carport where a Rambler rested on its haunches. Kernahan resembled a lean gull short of bread crumbs who stopped his mowing when he spotted us. He mopped his brow with a kerchief he yanked out of the back pocket of his denims. As we approached, he shook a cigarette out of a crumpled pack. I heard the snick of a lighter and saw the tight cloud of smoke. He watched us carefully as we strode up the drive. He flicked his eyes up and down at Birdie but his expression didn't change. I spotted the anchor tattoos and didn't have to speculate that he'd seen active service. He just had the look.

"Officer Kernahan?"

He nodded curtly. Before I could say anything else, the front screen door banged open and a blond tyke of about four came shooting out.

"Tommy. Back in the house," Kernahan barked. The kid stopped on a dime. He stared for a long second, then turned around and went back inside.

"We're…."

"I know who you are," Kernahan said.

Birdie took a step forward but I put my arm out.

"Just want to ask you a few questions, that's all, Officer Kernahan and then we'll leave you in peace on this lovely Saturday morning."

"Go ahead and ask," he spat.

"Man, what's eating you?" Birdie said with a hint of menace.

"Take one more step and I'll have you up for assault," Kernahan said.

I was puzzled by his hostility.

"Something on your mind, Kernahan? We haven't even had time to say a good morning yet."

Kernahan worked his thin lips then took a long pull on the fag.

"You guys in the service?"

"Yeah." I told him where and when. His cheek twitched a bit and it was then I noticed the crease on his forehead, near the hairline. He'd grown his bangs to cover it up.

"I guess that's all right then. Go ahead and ask your questions."

I looked around at the other neat little bungalows and the tidy lawns and the trimmed hedges and the whitewashed shutters. I guess we were talking on the lawn. He hadn't made a move to ask us in.

"About eight years ago, you pulled over a bunch of kids who had been joyriding. Took them down to the station and booked them. They called their parents who got them bailed out. You remember that evening?"

Kernahan snorted, then something that resembled a grin appeared on his face.

"I pulled over lots of joy riders mister. Too many to count. Especially kids out for a good time."

"These were four kids, some from wealthy families. You remember an Alison Foster and her boyfriend, a kid named Harvey Troyer? They would have been about 16 at the time. There was another couple, Gayle Sorenson and Rance Callaway."

At the mention of the names, his face went slack.

"Yeah, I remember them."

"Can you tell us what happened?"

Kernahan took a final drag on the cigarette, then stubbed it out on the bottom of his sneaker. He put the fag end in his pocket.

"Got a call about a stolen vehicle. Brand new Caddy. I just came out of Fran's after picking up a coffee and a piece of pie. Spotted the Caddy going east on Wellesley Street. Hopped in my patrol car and pulled them over between Church and Jarvis."

"They drinking?"

Kernahan allowed himself a small grin.

"Well, the open mickey they were passing back and forth led me to believe so. The driver was an uppity little shit, the kind of kid who was made for slapping around, you know what I mean?" I nodded. "I never touched him, didn't lay a finger on his precious sleeve. Didn't stop him from getting his daddy to file a complaint against me. Got suspended over it too. After a week or so, I was cleared though."

"Any charges filed?"

"All dropped. The Caddy belonged to old man Troyer. He knew his kid had taken it without permission and wanted to teach him a lesson. Waste of time," he muttered.

"You knew this kid?"

Kernahan nodded. "Yeah. Pulled him in once before, same beef."

"Was he on his own?"

"No, the girl was with him that time too."

"Alison Foster?"

"That's the one. A real looker. What she was doing with that kid, Troyer..." He shook his head in disbelief.

"Any charges that time?"

Kernahan actually grimaced. "Well, I brought them both in but the charges were dropped. They were given a warning, that's all. Wasn't my call, believe me. On both occasions."

"Whose call was it?"

Kernahan shrugged but didn't answer. I prompted him again.

"Not sure. I heard the word came down from the Chief Super but it was Inspector Callaway who told me to kick'em loose."

"I guess that must have bit some, especially after the second time."

Kernahan looked at me. His eyes went hard. "Yeah. It did. Rich kids," he spat. You could see what he thought. That he busted his hump for everything he'd got. Nothing handed to him. It was all down to him not like those spoiled rich kids he'd pull in on a Saturday night.

"You remember who came to pick them up?"

"Troyer's old man picked up his son and a chauffeur came for the girl."

"He a coloured man?" Birdie asked.

Kernahan nodded. "Yeah. Didn't envy him that's for sure."

"Why's that?" I asked.

"Both times–the girl tore a strip off him because he'd kept her waiting. She'd no call to talk to him like that. No call to talk to anybody like that. But the guy didn't say anything. If it were me, I'd have put her across my knee and let her have it good."

Birdie grinned. "Me too."

Kernahan looked up at him and his expression softened. He'd found a kindred spirit. "Damn straight. No kid should ever sass an adult. That's what I was taught."

We saw that in action as the little tyke through the door had frozen in fear at his father's words. I wondered what kind of punishment made a little kid so afraid.

Suddenly, the day soured. "Anything else you can tell us?" I asked.

"Don't think so. It burned me a little but out of my hands, like I said."

"Okay, thanks." We turned to go.

"What's this about, anyway?"

"The chauffeur."

"What about him?"

"Right after you ran those kids in, he disappeared. Hasn't been seen since."

I could tell he was confused. "Thanks again for your time." He watched us pick our way down his drive to the Chevy.

21

Birdie pled hunger so we sat at the counter of the Avenue Road Coffee Shop and munched fried egg sandwiches. I drank black coffee while Birdie guzzled a couple of malteds. The counterman watched Birdie with awe as he demolished the food in seconds. I ate slow. I pushed the greasy plate away and lit a Sweet Cap.

"You said you'd been busy," I said.

Birdie nodded. "Dean's list from Flit," he said.

"What about it?"

"Half the guys were casual and disappeared. Eighty-seven of 'em are still on the rolls working different construction jobs. Six died. Seven unaccounted for. That's it."

"What else you been doing?"

Birdie snorted, gave me a look then sucked his second malted dry.

"Not much, 'cept…" And he let it hang like laundry fluttering in the breeze.

"What?"

He broke into a wide grin.

"Tobin's boys. I know where they're at."

I thought about that long and hard.

"You're twitching," Birdie said.

"I know." They were Mounties but then I decided I didn't care. "It's a date." Birdie kept his grin. Revenge was a concept he understood.

"What now?"

"Callaway's nephew. Let's see if he's mowing his lawn."

I put down five bucks and the counterman gave us a wave. I looked at the address Callaway had written out. Callaway's sister lived on Caledonia close to St. Clair.

It turned out to be a white clapboard house that listed so badly I thought it would fall down. I rang the bell, holding the buzzer down for a long time. It echoed into emptiness.

"Should I knock?" Birdie asked.

I stepped back. "Be careful," I said.

Birdie knocked and the frame vibrated from the force of his blows. I expected to hear creaking and wood snapping and the whole shebang tumbling into the neighbor's yard but somehow it held. Birdie shook his head and smiled.

"You're slipping," I said. "Let's try around the back."

We sidestepped down the narrow corridor between the two houses, threaded around a low bush and found him. He lay in a hammock strung up between two spindly maple trees, saplings really, a fisherman's cooler by his left arm. He swigged from a Black Label stubby when we entered the yard, although calling it a yard was a compliment. He didn't hear us at first or pretended not to, but I could see the breadth of Callaway in him and the fair hair and ruddy complexion. He'd tuned a transistor radio to Dave Mickey, the rock and roll jock at CKEY. Buddy Holly sang *Rave On.*

"Rance Callaway," I said.

Without looking up, he drawled. "It's my day off–so beat it."

Birdie moved quickly. I saw the flash of his polished toe. The kid tumbled on to what was left of the lawn.

"Hey," he shouted. "What was that for?"

The stubby rolled away oozing foam. The kid fell on his knees and would have made it to his feet if Birdie hadn't put a paw on top of his head.

"Manners," he boomed. The kid tried to pull Birdie's hand away but he might as well have been flailing at a steel hawser with a toothpick.

"Awright. Awright. Lemme up already…" Birdie looked at me and I nodded. The saucepan of a hand slid away. "Whaddaya want?" Birdie took a step forward and the kid shrank back. I picked up the stubby and handed it to him.

I pointed at the transistor. "Turn that down for a second."

The kid reached down and clicked it off. Buddy cut out mid-wail. "I'm Mo Gold and this is my partner, Arthur Birdwell."

"So?" He plonked himself down in the hammock but stayed upright digging his heels into the dried turf.

"Just want to ask you a few questions."

"What about?" The kid pulled a packet of filterless Export A's from the roll in the sleeve of his T-shirt and fired one up. Made me want to give up smoking.

"You were friends with Harvey Troyer?"

"Yeah?"

"Used to go joyriding in his daddy's Cadillac?"

The kid grinned. Cute. He had dimples. "That was a long time ago. It was just kid stuff, that's all. Nothing serious in it."

"You got pulled over by a cop named Paddy Kernahan?"

"I never knew his name but yeah we got pulled over, what about it?"

"Who else was with you?"

"Couple of girls, that's all."

"Names?"

"Alison Foster—she was Harvey's girl and Gayle Sorenson. I knew her in high school."

"She wasn't your girl?"

The kid shook his head, even grimaced a little. "No, not really. It was just one of those high school things, you know?"

"And Alison Foster?"

The kid's expression hardened. "I told you, she was Harvey's girl."

"But you tried her on, am I right?"

He took a long pull of the cig smoking it down to the nub. "She was a stuck up bitch, if you must know."

"Turned you down, huh?" Birdie said.

"Like I said..." the kid sneered and ground the butt with his sneaker into the dirt.

"What else did you get up to, Rance?"

"Huh?" That threw him and suddenly I wanted to know why.

"You were joyriding, we know that. What else did you do for kicks?" The kid busied himself with peeling the label off the stubby. "Rance?"

"Nothing. I told you. That was it." But he stared at the ground, not looking up.

"Kid," Birdie boomed. "We're not cops so we're not going to turn you in for something if that's what's eating at you but we can still give you a whupping if you don't tell us the truth."

"You guys know my uncle is a cop, right?"

I nodded. "And if you don't talk to us right now, Rance, your uncle is my first call. We used to work together in homicide. I imagine he can make your life unpleasant if he wants to. So do yourself a favour."

The kid made a show of thinking. Expected to see steam coming out of his ears. "This doesn't go any further, right?" I nodded again. "Okay. Sometimes we'd go to this club. Harvey knew a guy at the door and they'd let us in."

"What kind of club?"

"I was told it was private and to get in, you had to have connections."

The kid fired up another Export.

"Why?"

"Because of what went on there."

I was getting exasperated and I thought of having Birdie just squeeze it out of him. "So, what went on in there, Rance?"

"I don't know." He must have seen the expression on my face. "Honest, I don't know. They had these private rooms upstairs. All I saw was the bar and the bandstand."

"So who went upstairs in this club?"

"Alison and Gayle."

"Just them?"

The kid nodded. "Yeah. Just them. Then after an hour or so they'd come back down and they'd be different."

"Different how?"

The kid shrugged. "I dunno, sorta quiet. I figured they were doing some kind of dope up there but I don't know for sure."

"What did you and Harvey do while you were waiting?"

"We'd have a couple of drinks and listen to the music."

"And you never talked about it, what was going on?"

"I tried once but Harvey shut me down. Told me not to say anything and not to think anything because it could be dangerous. So, I didn't. I kept myself to myself. Then we got busted by that cop and that party was over. Haven't seen any of them since."

"What was the name of the club and where was it?"

"I think the club was called Blackwells or Blackstones, something like that. There was no sign, you know? It was all hidden. Down in the docks somewhere. I never drove so I didn't pay much attention to where it was."

"You think you could find it if we took a little drive?"

The kid shrugged. "I don't think so. It was a long time ago. I've never been back since."

"You remember Alison Foster's chauffeur, Henry Turner?"

Rance's face brightened. "Oh, you mean the ni…" and then he stopped himself and glanced fearfully at Birdie. "I mean–the coloured guy? Yeah, he came to bail Alison out those times. Her parents were away somewhere. He seemed decent."

I nodded because I wanted him to think I believed him. The kid was being economical with the truth but how much remained anybody's guess.

"When was the last time you saw Harvey Troyer?"

"I told you, years, since the last time we got busted for joyriding."

"Where you working?" I asked.

"Etobicoke. Haulage. I pick stuff up and deliver it where it needs to go. Warehouses, factories, that sort of thing."

"Company name?"

"Eagle Trucks and Cargo."

I shook out a Sweet Cap and lit it. “Okay, Rance. Thanks for your help. Sorry to disturb your Saturday.”

“Hope it was useful,” he said and the dimples came out again.

“We might have to talk to you again.”

The dimples disappeared. Birdie pointed at him just to let the kid know we had him covered and a frown emerged. We left him sitting in the hammock. A moment later, the transistor radio came back on.

“Well?” I asked as we walked back to the car.

Birdie snorted. “Half truths, maybe.”

“Which half?”

“That’s the big question,” he replied.

I really didn’t know if any of this would get us any closer to Henry Turner. Ying’s sister and her baby were still out there somewhere too.

22

"Are you sure you want to do this?" I asked.

Birdie grinned and nodded. We sat in the Chevy watching the entrance to a bar on Queen Street called the Ratskeller, some fantasist's idea of a German beer garden complete with whitewashed walls and wooden shutters painted black. I thought the name appropriate since Tobin's boys had gone in a couple of hours ago. Saturday night. Yowling time. I knew it wasn't a cop hang-out but then the Feds didn't like to mix–not by choice. Nobody on the municipal forces liked them. I could think of a few good reasons. I shifted in my seat and winced. We drank coffee from paper cups.

A few minutes before midnight, the four of them poured out of the bar. They weren't falling down drunk but they didn't look cold sober either. We followed along. Two blocks east, two of them peeled off and got into a black Ford Fairlane parked at the curb in front of a hydrant. Pure arrogance. We heard some loud goodbyes and slaps on the back and the Fairlane pulled out and screeched its tires. The other two guys kept on walking.

I pulled the Chevy over and we got out. The street had settled for the night. Only the rumble of a passing streetcar and the singing of its steel rails split the quiet air. It seemed a good night for sitting on the back porch and hoisting a few, if you had a back porch. Most of the places in this part of town had a stoop or a steel-ribboned staircase. We followed them across Yonge Street, then Church and finally at Jarvis, they slowed. Birdie gave me a big grin. We both knew what that meant. They ventured into hooker alley to pick up some cheap tail. Real cheap. Some cops would pick up a girl, go back to her place and let her do him. After it was done, he'd flash his badge and threaten to run her in and what could a working girl do? Of course, she'd go along with it. Not much choice. Some guys had that princely quality and it didn't surprise me that these two, especially Blotchy Face, would pull that scam. Cops had all kinds of ways of making extra money and receiving any number of services. Certain kinds of cops, that is.

Two ladies of the night melted out of the shadows and approached the two Mounties. I heard them murmuring, negotiating the deal in the oblique way that they spoke so nothing incriminating was said. All stated with nuance and suggestion. Blotchy Face and his pal laughed. They enjoyed themselves in anticipation of more joy to come. Birdie and I came up. I lit a Sweet Cap and the click of the lighter caught their attention. One of the girls stared at Birdie and not without admiration.

"Maybe you'd like to dance with us, instead?" I blew some smoke.

Botchy Face turned toward me. "Well, well, well," he said, the articulate type. "Didn't expect to see you standing so soon."

I smiled. "You're not as good as you think you are and I'm a lot tougher."

"So you say."

I nodded at him, still smiling.

The other slob put a hand on his arm. "Phil, this isn't a good idea." Botchy Face shook him off.

"Girls–you better beat it–take off," I said.

They didn't need much prompting. They could smell the danger. Their high heels clacked in the night as they hurried away, their shoulders touching in a tight phalanx.

"Hey," Blotchy Face said. "Don't run away. This will be over in a minute and then we can have our own little party." The girls didn't even glance back.

"They got off lucky," I said. "Saved them from your little scam, not to mention the general nastiness of seeing you naked."

The other guy appeared genuinely puzzled. "What the hell are you talking about?"

"Oh, you mean, your buddy didn't tell you? About screwing the hookers in more ways than one? Then pulling rank so you wouldn't have to pay them?"

I dropped the butt end and ground it out under my heel.

"Like I said before, you got a big mouth, fella," Blotchy Face said.

Since training and fighting as a middle-weight in the army, I'd lost a few steps and gained a few pounds. Booze and fags didn't help but I'd kept up the training at Sully's Gym, a few blocks down from the office. Sully, a trim guy in his 50s, usually beat me into the canvas but he instilled what I call, motivation. I didn't have to look far for any tonight. I think Botchy Face and his pals had gone a little rogue on this one. Not that Tobin would have blinked about beating me up if it served his purpose. In this case, I figured Blotchy Face wanted back at me for needling him at the King Eddy.

"Guess what, fatso? We're not hiding behind dark clothes and balaclavas. We're doing this above the line so if you want to run and cry to your boss, Tobin, you go right ahead."

Blotchy Face went blotchier. "Not necessary–after I clean the pavement with you…"

"Phil, this is really not a good idea…" His pal practically whined now, thinking about his career going up in flames.

"Shut up," Blotchy Face snarled. "And whatever happens, you say nothing, understand?" The other guy went red up to his crew cut hairline. "Understand?"

"Yeah, sure."

Birdie reached over and tapped the guy on the shoulder. "It's okay, man. You and me are just bystanders." The guy's face flooded with relief just as Birdie flicked his hand out and the guy crumpled to the ground. "Guess I lied," Birdie said.

An alleyway opened up just behind us. I jerked my head and Blotchy Face, glancing nervously at his pal, nodded. Birdie blocked the view of any haphazard onlookers. We moved toward the alley, Blotchy Face, a few paces ahead. I watched the back of his shoulders and got ready. His meaty shoulders hunched. I stopped. As he whirled I had my hands up. He came around with a thick fist and a soaring overhand. I blocked it with my left forearm and hit him with a sharp jab to the gut sinking up to my wrist in flab. His eyes widened and his mouth opened like a hooked lake trout gasping for air.

I let him flounder for a second. "It's different when it's one-on-one, isn't it? Don't worry, I'll make this quick."

Blotchy Face straightened up.

"Come on," he gasped and motioned. "You suckered me."

"Yeah, sure I did. Keep telling yourself that, fatso."

I knew he'd get the boots in. That's what they were for. He didn't sit around and polish them all day long for nothing. The color came back into his face, a natural shade of puce. He came forward flat-footed keeping his hands busy. I kept my arms up parrying his blows then gave him two shots to the ribs with my left. He dropped his right and I gave him two more to the ribs on his right and felt the satisfaction of feeling something crack. His right foot shot forward and I took it off my hip. It hurt like hell since I already had a dozen bruises there but it was worth it as I caught him with a toe to the groin and I didn't spare the horses. Puce turned to chartreuse as he doubled over but I hadn't finished yet. I held him up. He tried to bring his arms around me but I stepped away putting together a one-two to the jaw then hammered the bridge of his nose. The cartilage exploded. Blood splattered his face.

The other guy had just shaken off Birdie's tap and stood up somewhat unsteadily. He choked out a hoarse yell. "Hey."

Birdie put a paw on his chest. "It ain't over yet."

Sure wasn't. Blotchy Face shook his head. He wheezed now and listed badly. Time to finish it. A straight left to the jaw, then a hard right hook that connected with his chin. I felt the concussion down my arm, through my elbow and up into the shoulder. Blotchy Face spun on his axis and like a slaughtered mastodon his knees went and he crumpled to the pavement. I shook my right hand. It hurt like hell.

"Now it's over," Birdie said and stepped away. The other guy moved slowly to Blotchy Face and rolled him on to his back. Birdie and I each took an arm and dragged him over to the side of the building and propped him up. He looked like a beached whale. For a moment, I almost felt sorry for him. Maybe two moments.

"Can't have him choke on his own blood even if he is a Fed," Birdie said.

The other guy straightened up putting his hands on his hips. He looked down at Botchy Face then looked over at us. "He had it coming," he said. "For the record, I didn't partake of your beating, Gold. I was against it. I don't go along with that kind of crap and I didn't know about his little hooker scam either."

"Just a choir boy, is that it?" I sneered.

The guy colored slightly. He nodded.

"I look the other way. You know how it is. You don't and you can kiss the job goodbye."

"I'm crying," I said.

"Don't be such a hard case, Gold. We can help each other. The name's Jack Dunn. I know how to get in touch. In the meantime, I'll look after Philly boy here. Looks like he'll need a few days off."

"Tell your friends to keep looking over their shoulders," I said.

Jack Dunn grinned. "I'll pass the message on. Watch out for Tobin. That's all kinds of misery."

Birdie and I walked back to the Chevy. He glanced at my knuckles. "Better soak that in cold water before it swells too much."

23

I knocked softly at her door. In one hand, a bunch of cut flowers and the other a mickey of Canadian Club. After a while, I heard some movement and then some fumbling with the chain. The door opened a crack and a blurry-eyed Evelyn peered out at me.

"Mo? What you doing here so late–waking me up–I was fast asleep."

I stepped back and showed her the flowers and the mickey. I was too wired to sleep but not too tired to get into bed–if it was the right one. "Couldn't keep away, Evelyn. And I wanted to apologize for what I said before."

"You could have done that in the daytime not the middle of the night, Mo."

"Sorry. I was a little busy tonight."

Her eyes flicked to my swollen hand.

"I can see you been busy. Up to no good more like it. That hand needs attending to." She sighed and stepped back. I heard the chain lock slide through and the door opened. I handed her the flowers and she smiled almost shyly.

"These are nice. I've got a vase, somewhere."

I stepped in and she closed the door behind me. Suddenly we were close together. I leaned in and kissed her and she kissed me back. The robe she wore was frilly and flimsy. She took my right hand, tsked and shook her head.

"Let me get these in water. Both of them."

We sat in her tiny kitchen. I had my hand in a bowl of ice water. Some of the ice went into tumblers topped off with rye whiskey. I was nursing my second and felt the heat spread its joy.

"Want to tell me about it?" she asked.

I shrugged. "I returned the favour to one of the guys who beat me up."

"Then what happens?"

"What do you mean?"

"Mo, you know it ain't gonna stop there. What's round three?"

"Maybe there won't be one," I said.

"Oh sure," she said. "Didn't you get enough of that in the War?"

"Apparently not."

Something in my tone made her snort and I was happy to see her mood lighten. For all kinds of reasons. She shook her head but she smiled. "You men," she said and pointed to my swollen knuckles. "That's all you get out of it."

"There could be other compensations," I said.

She gave me an amused look. "Like what?"

"Sympathy from a beautiful woman maybe."

"Oh yeah?" She leaned forward and the front of her robe billowed. She didn't move to close it.

I shrugged. "A guy can hope, can't he?"

"So you think some flowers and booze will be enough to get me into bed?" She reached out and took my good hand. She kissed the fingertips cold from holding the tumbler, then slid the hand inside her robe. "It should warm up in a second."

"Getting hot already," I murmured.

"I know," she replied.

I dried my hand on a dishtowel and she led me into the bedroom closing the door behind us. I untied her robe and slid my hands around her waist pulling her close. We kissed for a couple of years and there were all kinds of fires burning. I nibbled on her neck moving down to her nipples. They'd gone rigid. She moaned.

"Let me help you, baby." She undressed me like she knew what was doing. I'd never let a woman undress me before. I felt like a king with his courtier except that I doubt that courtiers did to their kings what Evelyn did to me that night. She swiveled lifting the back of her robe, backed in and began moving her high, firm buttocks against me. I felt every pulse and quiver in her strong limbs. She took my hands and placed them on her. As she writhed, I hung on for dear life cupping her swollen breasts, pinching her erect nipples. Every whimper and moan cracked like a whip. She ground into me in a frenzy rotating faster and harder until I felt like I was part of her, connected into her. Evelyn growled and moaned deep in her throat then dropped from her waist bracing herself on the bedpost urging, cajoling me to thrust deeper and deeper. Her limbs pulsed and shook and trembled and she clung to that bedpost like she was drowning. She slumped over. A long minute later, she straightened up and laid her cheek against mine. Her breath slowed from frantic gasps to mere panting and we stood there like that caressing each other. After, we got into her bed, she pulled the covers over.

"Now it's just the two of us," she breathed. I forgot my pain. Just disappeared into her dusky skin. This time she did what she wanted–and I let her.

The next morning I awoke and when I could focus I saw that Evelyn was fully dressed and perched on the side of the bed. She wore a prim blouse and skirt, a double-breasted jacket and some sort of pointy hat on her head.

"Good morning," she said and smiled.

"Good morning," I croaked. "What's going on?"

"It's Sunday, silly"

"Yeah, so?"

"I'm going to church. I go every Sunday."

"I see."

"Want to come?"

I sighed. "Evelyn, I'm Jewish."

"I know," she said.

"How do you know?"

She pulled back the covers and grabbed my crotch. "By this," she said and kissed me there.

"Hey," I exclaimed going instantly stiff.

"I know when a man's circumsized, Mo. I'm a nurse, remember?" She worked her hand a little bit. "How's that? Feel good?"

"Uh-huh."

"Thought so."

"You better let go now or you can forget about singing in the choir."

She released me and covered me back up. "You gonna come with us?"

"I don't think so. It would feel a bit strange–a man like me."

"Because you're Jewish or you're white?"

"Take your pick."

"That's okay. I didn't think you were the religious type."

"Well, you know what they say...."

"What?"

"Even an atheist can find God in a foxhole."

She frowned for a second.

"Mama, come on," her little hellion screeched.

"Okay, baby. I'm coming. Got to go," she said and stood up.

"You look nice, Evelyn."

"Why thank you, Mo."

"Listen, I got some things to do today so..."

She waggled her finger. "I understand."

"No, really. Something I'm working on."

She sighed. "I'm not going to tie you up to me, Mo. You got to come on your own. I can't make you. I won't make you. I made that mistake before–too many times. But my door is only open for a short while, so you better make up your mind sooner than later."

"Have a good time at church."

"Mama..."

"Got to go before little Missy explodes."

She wore clunky heels and moved awkwardly. She was tall, almost gangly. I had a hard time putting together the image of the church-goer with the woman who ravaged me repeatedly the night before.

24

"Where's Mrs. Turner?" I asked.

Adele Rosewell smiled at me coolly. "Well, hello to you too, Mr. Gold."

"Sorry. Bad manners."

After leaving Evelyn's, I'd returned to my flat, tossed my clothes into the hamper and stood under boiling hot water for a short eon, scrubbed myself top and bottom and tried not to think too much about what I got up to the night before. I dried off, shaved twice and changed into a fresh suit. Now I was looking at Adele and felt a lurch in my gut.

"Hello Miss Rosewell, nice to see you again."

"That's better, Mr. Gold. Please come in. My aunt is at church."

It was then I realized, in a sudden flash of insight that Aida Turner and Evelyn probably attended the same church. Maybe even knew each other. Gave myself a mental kick for not thinking of it sooner.

"Of course. You don't partake?" I asked as I stepped into the narrow entrance.

"Just Christmas Day and Easter, I'm afraid. Would you like some coffee?"

"That'd be swell, thanks."

"Just put your hat anywhere and please have a seat."

"Sure."

"You're looking well after your–little adventure."

"Thank you."

She spotted the swollen knuckles on my right hand. "Although it appears as if you've been up to something new recently."

I grinned and dropped my hat on to a low side table and parked in a hard-backed chair. Adele pivoted to head into the kitchen. I dropped my eyes toward the floor and her pant cuffs. She stopped and caught my eye. She appraised me in an unhurried way. I almost felt like blushing. Today, she wore tailored grey trousers, a short-sleeved yellow cotton blouse and an onyx necklace with matching earrings.

She folded her arms tapping her forefinger on her chin. "There's something different about you, Mr. Gold."

"And what might that be?"

She shook her head and her glossy hair cascaded across her cheek. "I'm not quite sure. You look a bit like the cat who got the cream. Speaking of which?"

"Just black, please."

"Coming right up." I watched her go and she knew it.

While she fixed the coffee, I wondered just who in the room was the feline. I knew it wasn't me. A moment later, she returned with a small carafe of coffee, two cups, a miniature jug of cream and a plate of chocolate biscuits. She set the tray down, settled herself and poured the coffee. "What did you want to see my aunt about?"

"I wanted to brief her on our progress."

"Has there been any? Progress, I mean," she asked handing over the steaming cup.

"Not a lot," I admitted.

"Why don't you fill me in?" And took a demure sip. "Biscuit?"

I shook my head while she helped herself. A smear of chocolate found its way to the corner of her mouth. She licked it with a flick of her tongue and I nearly tumbled off the chair.

"Mr. Gold?" she prompted.

"Mo."

"All right, Mo."

I brought her up-to-date which didn't take long. She listened carefully sipping the coffee intermittently. She wiped her lips then patted the corners of her mouth with a patterned napkin. "Where do you go from here?" she asked.

I drained the cup. "We need to speak to the other joy riders and find out about this club and what went on there."

"Blackstones?"

"If that is the name, yes."

"And why is that important?"

I shrugged. "It may not be but it's a loose end and loose ends need to be tied up. Perhaps Henry had been there. Maybe someone at the club is connected to his disappearance or the owners of the club might have a connection. We won't know until we take a look. We'll continue to run down any of Henry's work associates too."

"Sounds a bit, vague, Mr. Gold."

"Mo. And yes it does. A lot of our work involves chasing shadows, Adele. It's a little different from banking I imagine."

She laughed this time, full and throaty. "Oh, you'd be surprised at some of the phantoms we see at the bank, Mo. And I don't mean in a good way."

"Right."

"More coffee?"

"No, thank you."

"Is there anything else you want to tell me, Mo?" I felt like she was toying with me. She tilted her head slightly and again the subtle smile formed on her shapely lips. Mutely, I shook my head. "I'm so glad to see you have recovered."

"Thanks Adele."

"I'll share your information with my aunt."

"That'd be swell."

"You're sure there isn't anything else?"

"There is one thing," I said.

"What's that?"

"The box your aunt showed me. The one with the stuff she said Henry left for her."

"What about it?"

"I'd like to look at it again, if you don't mind."

She seemed puzzled and amused. "Not at all. I'll fetch it." And went off. I heard her rummage around in a closet. A moment later she was back. "Here it is." She set it on the coffee table.

"Thanks." I pried off the lid. I hadn't really noticed before but the box was gold, battered and dirty now but once it contained something rather expensive. "This box," I began.

"What about it?"

"What do you think it was used for?"

Adele shrugged and assumed an expression that you see on orderlies in a mental institution when talking to the inmates. "Why do you want to know?"

"Humor me."

"All right." She took a closer look at the box, ran her slim fingers along the edge, peered into the corners, lifted it up and looked at the bottom. I held the lid face down on my lap. Adele shrugged. "Could be anything really."

"You sure about that?"

"Uh-huh." Her eyes narrowed. "Now you really do look like the cat that ate the cream."

"Do I?"

"You do." And she gave me a chilly kind of smile, so cool in fact, that I shivered involuntarily. "What do you see?"

I turned over the lid.

"This was an expensive box holding pricey things. See? Look here." And I pointed in the corner. "There's a piece of fabric here that had been stitched in. Not just any fabric, silk. And if you look carefully in the centre, you can see through the dirt and grime the lettering there. Lettering that had been printed originally in what looks like gold leaf. Some sort of trademark or monogram. Too bad it's small, faded and covered in dirt. I'd wager that the original fabric had the same, only larger and screened in."

She was listening to me now. I'd become suddenly more interesting than the Ed Sullivan Show. "Fascinating Mr. Holmes."

"Just trying to impress you, Adele."

"Well, I'm impressed."

"I think this was a dress box, maybe even for a wedding dress. Something fancy and special anyway."

Adele took another look. "Yes, I suppose that makes sense. How does this help you?"

I shrugged. "Not sure, yet. Every fragment of information adds something, brings things into focus." I took a look at the contents.

"See anything?" Adele asked.

"Toys," I murmured.

"What?"

"They're all pieces of broken toys, tokens of childhood."

Adele bit her lip. "That's a little too deep, don't you think?"

"You said Henry was a good guy, right? Everybody liked Henry. Everybody has good things to say about him." I'd annoyed her.

"So?"

"So, maybe a guy like that needs something to hang on to, something to connect back to the time he was happy, something like his childhood. You said he had a happy childhood, didn't you?"

Adele nodded slowly. "Well, apart from my uncle, Henry's dad, dying so young. We were well taken care of. I don't remember worrying too much when I was a kid. Henry and I spent a lot of time playing together."

"What about other kids?"

"Sure, we played with the kids in the neighborhood."

"This neighborhood? Your aunt and Henry lived here?"

"Uh-huh."

"Anywhere special?"

"Gee, this is a trip down memory lane. We played in the lane out back but mainly Henley Park two blocks over. They had swings, a slide, a sandbox and a jungle gym. The usual stuff."

"Still there?"

"I believe so."

"Okay." I placed the lid back on the box. "You can put it back now." She didn't like taking orders either but with a jaundiced look, she flounced out with the box and put it back in the cupboard.

She re-appeared looking thoughtful. "Is there anything else you need, Mo?"

"No, nothing else Adele. Not at this time anyway."

"Thank you for stopping by. It's been enlightening."

"Sure." I rose to go. "Thanks for the coffee."

"My pleasure, Mo." I asked myself if she was conning me. I couldn't figure why or for what.

Henley Park lay like a bedraggled square plot of dirt with some withered grass thrown in at the last minute. The swings hung there still but the chains were blotched with rust. I noticed the cracked, splintered seats of the teeter-totter while the jungle gym leaned at a sharp angle. But none of that stopped kids from fighting over the swings or crawling over the jungle gym like energetic ants. Somehow, it didn't seem to matter. This perfect May day opened up before me with a clear, blue sky, light breeze and the temperature right around 70 degrees. Hopped up kids on some natural high while their parents chatted in groups or basked in the warmth on the few rickety benches scattered at each of the corners of the square. Kids in this neighbourhood didn't have a lot. Maybe this was it and that was all it took to make them happy. Just like it made Henry Turner and his cousin Adele happy some years back when I'm sure the state of Henley Park looked cleaner and brighter. I glanced around. Along with the kids, I saw toys scattered in the sand and the dirt, some in need of serious repair. I'd found buried treasure in Henley Park. Is this where Henry had been digging?

I entered the flat to the sound of the phone ringing.

"Yeah?"

"Mo, it's your aunt Zelda. Your uncle Lou is dead."

No holding back with Zelda, she hit you between the eyes without hesitation. Don't get me wrong, my uncle's death caused me sincere regret, but his death led to something else altogether that caused me considerable grief.

"What happened?"

"Stroke. Dropped like a fly while playing bridge. Too bad. He had a slam going."

"When?"

"Last night about eleven."

"I'm sorry, Aunt Zelda."

"Yeah, me too. Fifty-two years we were married and in all that time that man didn't listen to me once. How many times did I tell him to stop with the cigars? Fell on deaf ears and this is the result."

"When you're right, you're right."

She sighed heavily. "Don't I know it," she said sadly. "This is one time that being right doesn't feel so good."

"When's the funeral?"

"Tomorrow morning at ten-thirty. Dawes Road, you know it?"

"Yeah, I know it." I hesitated, then cleared my throat. "Is he..?"

"They're giving him a day pass so he can see his brother buried and spend a few minutes at the shiva."

"Right. I'll see you tomorrow Aunt Zelda."

"Of course, darling. Wear a nice suit."

"The nicest."

She hung up. As if funerals didn't give me heartburn, having to see the sorry excuse for a human being that, according to rumour, was my father, would make it worse. Jake Gold was about to put in an appearance.

25

Dawes Road cemetery lay situated in the east part of the city, so far east it seemed like another country. Why sane-minded people would buy burial plots in the middle of nowhere defied belief. It took at least 45-minutes to drive from civilization–a schlep of the highest order. Brick bungalows dispersed in large plots distanced from each other and the road. An actual landscape existed out of the city, one of gentle hills and swaying trees. And headstones of different hues–onyx, rose-coloured marble and sandstone–all resembling jagged teeth set against the recently shorn grass. Each headstone carried a family of pebbles on its shoulders—blessings for the departed.

For an inmate, however, the trip made for a nice day out especially as the dry, warm weather continued. Far too nice a day for a funeral, I thought. Too cheery and life-affirming. Funerals should take place in dark, gloomy conditions where wind and rain whipped up the leaves around the gravesite, inverted umbrellas, and blew hats off bowed heads. Serious weather befitting a solemn occasion. Not a day when you'd rather be at the beach.

I parked the Chevy on Dawes Road opposite the chain link fence bordering the cemetery. Plenty of parking. My uncle Lou hadn't been mister popular. I removed my hat and put it in the back seat and fitted a yarmulke on my head. Birdie already wore his and I have to admit, it suited him. He resembled an African prince. Made of burgundy velvet with gold brocade, its seams sharp and crisp. Mine shouted cheap, wrinkled, black nylon. I'd pilfered it from Aaron Finkleman's bar mitzvah in 1948. I'd worn it twice since then, both times for funerals. But it matched my suit. Birdie wore an electric blue, double-breasted number that radiated in the warming sun. It was his preaching suit, he said and always drew favorable comments in church from the congregants, especially the ladies.

Nevertheless, he drew more than a few bewildered looks from a huddle of mourners. I heard the mutterings. "Schwarze," they intoned. He ignored them with grace and elegance. But I grabbed the elbow of a distant cousin at the centre of it, a guy about my age but portly in stature and arrogant of expression.

"Button up, yid," I hissed. "Or I'll do it for you."

The fat cousin yanked his elbow away, scowled like a flatulent bulldog and moved off. I'd confirmed that my branch of the family consisted of gangsters, men of violent nature. I would have felt an enormous feeling of satisfaction slapping him out but then I remembered it was a funeral, after all.

It blew over when Zelda, looking like a small child, reached up to Birdie and gave him a kiss. He bent down to her and she smacked him on each cheek and spoke to him in a loud voice.

"Thanks darling, for coming to see my Lou off. He would have appreciated it."

"You are most welcome," Birdie boomed and Zelda beamed up at him, reflecting the sunshine back toward his smiling face. Birdie had that effect on older women. They just loved him. As for me, that was a different story. They could take me or leave me. Zelda turned to me and gave me a hug. I smelled the Estee Lauder–White Musk perfume–she always wore and the hint of powder. She looked brittle. I could feel it through her mourning suit.

"Nice to see you, Mo, my darling. Your uncle Lou always liked you."

"He was a prince," I said.

"Well, I wouldn't go that far," she replied. "But he wasn't a frog either. A few warts here and there, maybe," and she sniffed into the handkerchief she held in her gloved hand.

The group comprised perhaps twenty mourners in all, some relatives, mainly cousins. I shook hands with Zelda and Lou's son, Brian, who earned an honest buck as an accountant. The others consisted of old cronies of my uncle's, bridge partners, guys he knew from the 'Y', guys from the old neighborhood at Spadina and College. My uncle worked in the garment industry on Spadina his entire life. He made a decent living and more than that, the living he made had been honestly earned. No graft. No corruption. No double deals. Sometimes, I found it hard to believe that he and my father came from the same family. That they grew up in the same house and came from the same parents. They went to the same schools and haunted the same streets. At the all-important corner, though, Lou went one way and Jake went the other. The rabbi stood expectantly at the open gravesite but nobody moved. There was an anticipation of something happening.

The answer came in the form of a patrol car that turned languidly on to Dawes Road and pulled up opposite the crowd in a no parking zone. That was the cops for you. Didn't care about the rules. The chauffeur got out. An officer in uniform. He opened the driver's side back door first and a burly guy in a rumpled suit stepped out holding his creased fedora in a pair of mitts the size of a first baseman's glove. The uniform went to the other side and the burly guy followed him. Another cop in a rumpled suit exited the patrol car.

The three cops stood around the door peering in. Finally, a head appeared but the rest of him remained obscured. He still wore his hair in a ducktail but now it looked like moldy plastic trowelled on to his scalp. The cops stepped back and I got a better look. Still the same swagger but his chest had sunk to his gut and he had that green-white prison pallor. Dark blotches under his eyes made him look owlish. He wore an old suit from the Forties that hung on his shrunken frame. No tie. His hands had been cuffed in front and the two burly cops moved him forward between them. He looked like a midget. The ever-present smirk creased his thin lips. The one I couldn't wipe off no matter how hard I tried.

Birdie put his paw on my shoulder and I nodded. Couldn't say that Jake didn't make an entrance. All eyes focused on him as he walked stiffly toward the motley crowd of the bereaved. As he approached, the other mourners turned and began to file slowly toward the hole where the rabbi stood waiting. The rabbi's assistant had placed a plastic tub filled with water and a roll of paper toweling on a rickety stand. Each of us dipped fingers in the tub and dried them on a sheet of paper provided. Now we were cleansed. Didn't think that would work for Jake. I knew he looked at me. I could feel him bore a hole in the back of my head.

The rabbi, who showed a hefty paunch–looked beyond middle-aged and had the yellow skin and dark teeth of a heavy smoker–beckoned us over. The crowed shuffled forward. Punctuated between coughs and rasps, his voice rumbled out of a flabby chest. It sounded deep and sonorous. The brim of his hat looked frayed as did the cuffs of his midnight blue suit jacket. His bearing remained dignified, his demeanour sober. He held a small prayer book but didn't refer to it.

I recalled the words, striding out of the mist of childhood: *Yitgaddal veyitqaddash shmeh rabba*....May His great name be exalted and sanctified is God's great name... *Be'alma di vra khir'uteh*...in the world in which He created according to His will... *veyamlikh malkhuteh*...May He establish his kingdom... *veyatzmakh purqaneh viqarev (ketz) meshiheh*...and may His salvation blossom and His anointed be near... *behayekhon uvyomekhon*...during your lifetime and during your days... *uvkhaye dekhol bet yisrael*...and during the lifetimes of all the House of Israel... *be'agala uvizman qariv ve'imru amen*...speedily and very soon. Say, Amen.

I remembered from Hebrew school that the prayer had been inspired by Ezekiel in the Old Testament. Its purpose was to acknowledge the sanctity of God, not to mourn necessarily. Seemed like a bit of a paradox but I had to admit with everyone mumbling the words, swaying in the gentle breeze, standing before the open pit where my uncle Lou would soon reside, it did have a powerful effect even on the lapsed and the ignorant like me. I glanced at Birdie. He swayed to the rhythm of the words keeping his eyes closed. The cops had shed their hats and held them down at their sides. No one corrected this behavior because they were goyim and probably figured it didn't matter, either to God or to Uncle Lou. They marked respect in their own manner, heathen or not. The old man bowed his greasy head and kept his gaze on the ruptured turf striving for some shred of piety.

The service didn't take long. They never did. No point wasting time when the corpse needed to be put in the ground. The hearse had pulled up as far as it could go. Birdie and I and four other men under the age of 80, carried it forward, trying not to trip on the narrow path. The diggers laid a harness over the hole and we set the coffin down readied to be lowered. As it descended, the rabbi continued to intone. The diggers removed the straps and Lou was all set to embark on his eternal rest. My cousin, Brian, picked up the shovel. The diggers stood back respectfully. Each of the men, in turn, took the shovel and spread dirt over the coffin. There was a thrum on the lid as knotted clods rained down. Birdie wielded the shovel one-handed. I dipped the blade in once, twice, three times watching as my uncle disappeared for the last time, then I turned and handed the shovel to the next in line.

"You'll come back to the house," my aunt said.

"What about him?"

"Him too," Zelda said. "And his escorts."

26

Birdie and I stopped at the threshold of my aunt's bungalow.

"You go ahead," I said.

He nodded, pulled open the squeaky screen door, its hinges screaming and disappeared inside. Better than a guard dog, my uncle had said. The cops beat us there. The patrol car rested out front. Uncle Lou's folding chair stood in the same place it had always been where he'd sit on the porch, smoke a cigar and drink some tea watching the world go by, taking in the life of the street. We'd lived in a similar house half a block down but only for a short while. The bailiffs chased us out. They always chased us.

I used to like hanging out on the porch. Kids from the neighbourhood gathered and we'd sit around and jaw until it was time to go in for supper and all the Moms started calling out into the street. I sat down and fired up a Sweet Cap enjoying the light and warmth of the day. People came to the house to pay their respects and I nodded to them as they went inside. I took a final drag, ground out the butt, flicked it into the mangy hedge and went in. Zelda had put out a spread. People balanced plates and cups and yakked like it was a party. I guess in a way it was. Birdie delicately held Zelda's arm and ran interference on anyone too pushy.

"Uncle Lou doesn't know what he's missing," I said.

"He knows," Zelda replied. "He was always sharp that away. Go on, help yourself to something. I don't suppose it would do any good to say you're too skinny and you look like you've been fighting." Birdie snorted and I gave him a sharp look.

"She's got your number," he boomed.

"No, it wouldn't," I said to her. "But a decent bagel, some lox and cream cheese and a strong cup of coffee wouldn't hurt."

"I made some mandel brot too. I know it's your favourite."

I almost blushed. "Thanks."

Any second and she'd grab a hunk of my cheek. I spotted the old man in the living room seated at the end of the sofa bed. Zelda had finally removed the plastic cover. It had been a while since I'd been there. The cops stood around him and I noticed their plates piled high with potato and egg salad and rye bread while Jake nibbled on a cheese blintz. He'd always had a weakness for them and I doubted that the cafeteria in the Don Jail had them on the menu. He caught my eye and winked. He leaned over to the nearest cop and spoke to him. The cop laughed and nodded. My old man put his paper plate down on the coffee table. I noticed he hadn't been given any cutlery–as a precaution I supposed. He got to his feet awkwardly. The cuffs had been removed, as a gesture of goodwill. Hitching his pants up, he moved toward me. He knew he took centre stage in that small house. No one said anything or even looked obviously in his direction but he could feel it and so could everyone else. People eased out of his way.

"Boychick," he said.

"Don't call me that," I replied.

"Sure, Mo, whatever you say."

He put his hands up to show his sincerity. I glanced over his shoulder at the cops, who had paused in their conversation and lunch to watch. The older one, the senior man of the trio held my look then nodded in my direction and turned his attention back to his plate. I don't think they figured me as an accomplice aiding in my old man's escape. Not with my years on the force.

"I'd say you were looking good but I'd be a liar," Jake said.

"You don't look so hot yourself. Your chest is down around your testicles," I replied.

"You always had a sharp tongue, even as a kid." His face crinkled into what might have been a smile or a grimace. "I'm not here to apologize…."

"Why change now?"

"Look…" Jake paused. "I could do with a smoke. Let's step out on to the porch. I know your aunt doesn't like smoking in the house." I didn't say anything. He craned around. "Sid–going for a smoke–all right?" The older cop looked at him, then at me and waved his hand. "Guy thinks I'm going to make a run for it," Jake muttered. "That's a laugh."

We stepped out on to the porch. I shook out a Sweet Cap and lit it for him. He took a long pull.

"Neighborhood hasn't changed that much," he said, taking in the neat lawns, the kid across the street washing his daddy's Biscayne–white with red leather interior–the guy opposite pushing a hand mower. I think I saw Jake shudder in fear and loathing at the domestic scene in front of him. Never enough action for Jake Gold and certainly not in this boring neighborhood where the strip mall two blocks down had a Laundromat, a cinema, a hairdresser's and a bowling alley. Nowhere to buy a beer or place a bet.

"How would you know? We only lived here five minutes."

He gave me a sour look like I caused all his problems.

"Can't we just talk without gouging each other's eyes out?" he asked.

"Probably not," I replied.

He wheezed out some smoke. "You haven't changed."

"Either have you and I don't mean that in a good way."

"You still think and talk like a copper."

"Better than acting like a goniff," I said.

Jake shrugged. "It's a living."

I almost laughed. "No, it's not. What kind of living you going to make when they send you up to Kingston Pen for 10 years? Oh right. You can save the pennies you earn in the prison laundry or bank your take home pay from weaving baskets."

"Who says I'm going up to the Pen?" he asked.

"Well, that's where convicted felons go, especially those who commit murder."

Jake took another long drag but couldn't keep the smirk off his creased face. "Maybe some guys end up there but not me."

"Oh, really?"

"Yeah—bigshot–really."

"How do you figure?" Jake didn't answer but gave a shrug in response. The sort of gesture that if he hadn't been so decrepit as well as my old man, I would have slapped him around. Hard. Family. The buttons they push.

"You'll see," he said.

"I don't give a shit."

"You're not as sharp as you used to be," Jake said. "I can see that someone laid into you real good. In fact, I heard about it inside. I hear about a lot of things. I've still got connections in this town."

"As you can see I'm still standing."

"I heard something else too."

"Yeah? What's that?"

This time he didn't hide the sneer. Jake always wanted to win. It was a compulsion. It explained why he was a lousy gambler and a rotten crook. Couldn't walk away when ahead of the game.

"You're looking for a little Chink girl and her kid." He took a final drag then flicked the butt on to the front walk. "Am I right?"

"Where'd you hear that?"

"Like I said, Boychick. I still got connections."

He began to turn away to head back inside. I grabbed the meaty part of his shoulder and squeezed. "I asked you a question, Jake."

He snorted. "Tough guy. Doesn't even call me dad…."

"So?"

Jake peeled my fingers off him. "You come see me and maybe I'll let you in on something. Something that could see you through."

"Tell me now."

Jake shook his head. "Sorry, Boychick. Doesn't work that way." With the old man, there'd always been a price to pay. He yanked on the screen door and stepped inside.

"Son of a bitch," I muttered. "Son of a bitch."

27

I said, "If Henry Turner was still alive, where would he be hiding?"

"What are you thinking?" Birdie asked.

I explained it to him.

"I can't get those damned broken toys out of my mind and Mrs. Turner's unshaken faith that her son isn't dead. Let's start with Aida Turner's place. It makes sense that if he was alive he'd want to stay somewhere close but out of sight. So, why don't we start there and work our way out and see what we find?"

"You mean, like concentric circles?"

I looked at him. He never ceased to surprise me. "Exactly."

We took our time driving around the streets with Aida Turner's apartment at the centre, gradually working our way outward. Eventually, the circle grew wider and wider until we ended up at the knacker's yards. Canada Packers slaughterhouse.

"He wouldn't be here," Birdie said. "The smell alone would kill him."

I shrugged. It wasn't just the odour of animal parts or tanned hides that assaulted the senses. It was the smell of fear. "Maybe that's why no one would look for him here," I said. "But I agree, it's a long shot. I wouldn't last five minutes."

We pulled up to the gatehouse, minus the gate.

A guy who put his belly first, ambled out of the guard hut. I could hear the radio–tuned to a Bison's ballgame from Buffalo.

"What happened to the gate?" I asked.

"Drunk trucker drove through it a while back. Been waiting for it to be fixed," the guard said.

"How long ago was that?" I asked.

"Five years, give or take," the guard replied.

"No worries about security, I guess?"

"Not too many cows break out of here," the guy drawled. "Not since I've been working here. And I don't think any would try to sneak in, neither."

"How you doing, Muldoon? Been a while."

"Not bad, Sarge. How about you?"

"I'm not on the force anymore. Working private now."

Muldoon, lifted his frayed cap and scratched his graying head. "No kidding. That's too bad."

I introduced Birdie, who reached across to shake Muldoon's hand. The ex-cop hesitated then extended his arm tentatively.

"You like working here, Muldoon?"

"Can't stand the smell, to be honest. Gets under your fingernails, seeps into everything. The wife hates it. Even bleach won't get it out. Apart from that, it's fine. I got no complaints."

"We're looking for a guy," I said.

Muldoon chuckled. "Well, you can take your pick of 855 of 'em and 47 women too."

"Don't think he's working here. I'm wondering if he could be shacking up somewhere."

Muldoon looked surprised. "Here? He'd have to be crazy. No one in their right mind would want to spend an extra second in this place."

"Well, for a guy who doesn't want to be found, it could make sense," I said.

Muldoon gave it some thought. "A fella would have to be pretty desperate," he said.

"Yup. Mind if we take a look?"

"I gotta call the production supervisor. Let him know you're coming."

We drove along the gritty road toward the complex of buildings that looked like a giant cow shed made out of industrial-sized many bricks. An ominous looking smokestack stood to one side. I didn't like to think about what was stoking the ovens or whether it would end up on my plate beside the potatoes and peas at supper. The road followed along a dry riverbed that had leached all its water. The banks appeared crumbly. Good place to toss a carcass or two if you were in mind of it.

"Not a happy place," Birdie intoned.

"No sermons," I said.

The road opened up into a marshalling yard where hundreds of trucks stood parked in neat rows. Waiting their turn to ferry the dead. As we drew closer, I saw half a dozen guys scurrying between the trucks left off to the side. They climbed into the cabs, started up the engines and maneuvered each rig into alignment. All of the slots were numbered. Then they'd hop down and move on to the next one, all in a coordinated dance.

"Truck jockeys," Birdie said.

"How'd you like to do that for a living?" I asked. He answered by giving me a pitiable look. "Thought so." We'd had enough of regimentation in the army. To the right of the marshalling area stood a vast parking lot filled with jalopies. Here too, each spot was numbered.

"Guess they don't get many visitors."

Just in front of the main entrance, four spots had been earmarked for guests. Three of them were taken. I pulled into the fourth spot and cut the engine. We stepped out of the car and the animal smell felt like a frontal assault. I shook my head.

"Smells like Normandy," Birdie said.

Not to me. It smelled like Bergen-Belsen. A heavy-set man wearing a weathered hard hat, a badly stained smock, holding a clipboard, stood outside the entrance. He hugged the clipboard to his grimy chest and spread his feet to keep his balance.

"You the production supervisor?" I asked. He didn't answer. "It wasn't a trick question."

The beak of the hard hat dipped. "Yeah, that's right. Dick Olsen. I help you gentlemen?" His face was pale and doughy as if he didn't get outdoors much. "Mr. Muldoon said you were looking for someone?"

"That's right. Someone who may be hiding out."

"You think he's employed by Canada Packers?" Olsen asked.

I shook my head. "No, hiding out here somewhere. This is a big place."

Olsen's jaw dropped and his doughy face creased. I realized he'd put a smile on his wide kisser. "Impossible. This place is locked up tighter than a drum. We operate seven days a week, 24 hours a day. You've got a bum steer, no pun intended."

"Even so," I said. "Mind if we take a look?"

"You been inside a slaughterhouse before?" Olsen asked.

"No, but I've seen plenty of slaughter in the War. Is it as bad as that?"

This time Olsen laughed outright. "Not even close," he said. "This here's the most modern facility in the country."

"Impressive."

"You'll need coats and hard hats," Olsen said. "Come with me."

We went through the main entrance into the reception area consisting of a long wooden counter and a desk behind it where a secretary sat typing forms with staccato precision. He pointed to a logbook where we signed our names, the time in and the date. Olsen watched us carefully, checking if we knew how to read and write.

"This way," he said.

He pushed his way through a low swing door and took us into an enlarged cloakroom. White coats hung on pegs and each peg had a number. He walked down the line of coats staring at the numbers. He took one off and tossed it to me. "Your friend might be a challenge." Olsen walked right to the end of the row. "This is the largest size we have," he said.

Birdie took it and shrugged it on. It was tight in the shoulders and the sleeves came partway down his forearms. He looked ridiculous. "It'll have to do." At the far end of the cloakroom, hardhats were laid out on wooden shelves. Each of these was numbered too. Olsen tossed me a hard hat. It fit perfectly.

Again, he went to the end of the row, shook his head and held out the hardhat in his hand to Birdie. It added three inches to his height. "Better duck through that doorway."

We went through a door marked, Slaughterhouse One. Olsen led us down a long, industrial corridor bare of any markings to a door with a push bar marked, Holding. He pushed the bar and we stepped out onto a concrete platform. The sound of the cattle was deafening, louder than any cattle drive I'd seen in the nickel westerns I'd enjoyed as a kid at the Odeon.

"These here are the holding pens," he said. "Cattle are shipped by truck or rail." He pointed to his left. "Over there is the marshalling yard for the incoming transports." Then he pointed to his right. "The rail line is on that side, just over that long berm. The rail cars unload at the front of the pens down yonder."

I looked but couldn't see that far. The vast pen seemed to disappear into the horizon.

"Why is it curved?" I asked, indicating the line of fence leading up to the plant.

Olsen flashed a macabre grin. "Animal welfare and a bit of psychology," he said.

I must have looked surprised because the besplattered production man actually laughed.

"Yeah, that's right. Came out of the anti-cruelty legislation of the Fifties, if you can believe it. Cattle, like all animals, have a survival instinct and they get spooked. If they were lined up straight, they could see and sense what was coming and cause a ruckus. If the animals are spooked, it also affects the quality of the meat. With the fencing set up in a curve, all they can see ahead of them is the butt end of the cow in front. Keeps them calmer and easier to handle."

"And this works?" Birdie boomed.

Olsen nodded, his helmet bouncing on this round head. "Seems to. That's what the knackers say, anyway. Those that have been around for a while and came up using the old methods."

"The psychology of death," I said.

With a twinkle in his eye, Olsen replied.

"That's one way of looking at it. I like to think of it as the way of commerce. This is a big business in a bigger industry. You enjoy a steak or a roast for your Sunday dinner, don't you? We're past the days when people went out and slaughtered their own. Now it comes in a nice, neat packet on the supermarket shelf ready to go into the fry pan."

I swallowed trying not to breathe in the stink of too many bodies pressed into a tight space.

There was no way down from the platform so he took us back inside.

"Here's the good part," he said, pausing before a door that he had to unlock with a set of keys. When he opened it, we heard the sound of industrial machinery hammering and whining away in addition to the pitiable lowing of the cattle.

An assembly line of death. The cattle were fed into a kind of chute that kept them immobilized from the neck down. I could see the panic in their eyes. A worker clad in soiled apron, pants and rubber boots picked up what looked like a pneumatic drill and placed it against the cow's forehead. He pulled the trigger and gave it a jolt. The cow's body went slack, the eyes rolled up.

"That's a captive bolt pistol," Olsen intoned. "We use it to stun the animal. This way, they can't resist. If they thrash around, our guys could get hurt plus, of course, it slows down production and that costs money."

"Of course," I said. "Maybe they should use them in prisons." I must have been thinking about Jake and our recent conversation.

Olsen laughed uncomfortably. "I think the death sentence has been repealed if I'm not mistaken."

"Sure it has," I replied. Nothing but gruesomeness followed.

The knacker shoved a huge hook into the animal's underbelly, yanked on a pulley and hoisted it in the air, forelegs and head down.

Using a razor sharp knife, the worker jabbed the cow at a point just above the neck and behind the jaw line. He brought the blade forward and around, efficiently slitting the cow's neck. The animal jerked on the hoist. I watched the blood spill out. It splashed over the guy's thick rubber boots. Gradually, the cow's eyes lost their luminescence. The floor became slick with globules of fat, littered with bits of gristle and sinew.

"The carotid artery and jugular are severed," Olsen lectured. "This leads to exsanguination which means…"

"I know what it means. I was a cop for 10 years, Olsen."

Olsen stopped for a moment, perplexed. I threw him off his rhythm. "Right. Sorry." He continued. "Once the animal is dead, we remove the head and front and rear feet."

The knacker sliced down the corpse vertically, two lines in front and two lines in back. Using what looked like a large pair of pliers, he grabbed the edge of the hide and peeled it off in strips.

"Those are called 'pullers' for obvious reasons," Olsen said.

"I wouldn't mind using those on a guy I know," I said.

"Just one?" Birdie asked.

"You've got a point," I replied.

Olsen chuckled. He seemed to enjoy our banter. I'm sure he liked doing the tour just to see what sort of reactions he got.

The knacker cut into the belly of the cow and ripped out its viscera. I noticed he separated the heart and the lungs then the liver and dumped them into separate bins.

"That's called the 'pluck' ", Olsen said. "for…."

"Yeah, I know," I said. "Obvious reasons. Why did he separate the liver?"

"New regs," Olsen replied. "Gotta check it for disease."

The knacker deftly lopped off the tongue and stuck it on a hook then went to work sawing off the head. It looked tricky and required some muscle. After he was finished, he stuck the head on a smaller hook. With a bloody finger, the knacker pressed a button and the head and the carcass lurched off down the line.

"The carcass goes through a steamer to kill any bacteria," Olsen continued. "Then it's sent into the cold room before distribution. The beef is always split in half then quartered before heading out to market. Local butchers then make up the cuts you see on the shelf."

"What do you do with the leftovers?" I asked indicating the various organs left in the bins.

"Some of it is used for human or animal consumption. A lot of people like organ meat and the rest is ground and mixed with feed," Olsen explained. "The waste like the bones, lard and tallow are sent to a rendering plant."

He paused. "There's not much else to see."

The knacker already worked on his third cow since we'd entered the area. Fast work, slaughtering.

"You have any storage units in the main building or off-site?"

"Yep. But we keep them locked at all times. And there are only three sets of keys. A master is kept in the office. I have another set and the plant foreman has the third."

"Can you show me, anyway?" I asked.

Olsen sighed, then glanced at his watch. He figured he'd had his fun but we didn't bite. "Okay, but it's got to be quick. It'll be faster on these." He pointed to a brace of bicycles propped against the wall.

Olsen grabbed one and just like a 10 year-old riding home from school, hopped on and took off. I took one and followed suit. It had been over 20 years since I'd actually ridden one of the things and took it a bit wobbly at first. That was nothing compared to Birdie, whose knees tucked under his chin as he pumped the pedals. He kept it moving though.

Olsen was right. It took some five minutes or more of hard riding, ducking around concrete pillars and skirting metal rails to get to the far end of the plant. As he stated, the storage areas were locked up tight and I couldn't see how somebody like Henry Turner could be able or even interested in breaching their security.

"I just don't think your man is here, gentlemen. Be a crazy way to live, wouldn't it?" Olsen asked.

"There's probably worse but I'm having a hard time thinking of it," I admitted. "Thanks for your time, Olsen. Sorry to have dragged you away from your regular duties."

"That's okay," Olsen said. "Is there anything else I can do for you?" He glanced pointedly at his watch.

"There is actually."

Olsen sighed. "What's that?"

"When's the next break?"

"About five and a half minutes."

"Do you mind if I ask a few questions of the men?" Olsen rolled his eyes but didn't say no. We walked the bicycles over to the canteen, a large room lit by interior fluorescent light. Along the back stretched a counter. Under glass sat a row of tin trays belching steam. A guy in a white smock and cap stood sweating behind the counter. A bell clanged and almost immediately, the din of conversation filled the outside corridor.

The door sprang open and groups of knackers pushed their way in ready for some refreshment despite the horror they'd left behind them in the plant. An easy camaraderie came with the men who filed into the canteen punctuated with barks of laughter and shouts. When the room had filled, Olsen grabbed a spare chair and stood on it. I watched the seat bend dangerously. He blew a shrill whistle through his lips. That caught their attention.

"Men, we have a couple of guys here who are looking for someone–" He didn't even have to finish before a groan went up. This was their free time and we'd spoiled it. "–just hear them out, will ya?"

I didn't stand on the chair. I just spoke up. "Gentlemen, we just want you to look at a picture and let us know if you've seen this guy. Won't take but a second of your time. Please carry on with what you were doing." The men didn't hesitate and lurched back into action.

Birdie and I circulated the room showing Henry Turner's picture as wc went. One guy laughed.

"What's so funny?"

"Take a long look around the room, Mac."

I did.

"No offence," the guy said "but you won't find too many coloured working here." As he spoke, the crowds of men drifted apart. I noticed one black man sitting at a table by himself, ignored by the men around him. He sipped at a cup of coffee keeping his head bowed. Alone. Across the room, I spotted Birdie as men moved nervously out of his way. They gave him a darting glance before sliding off to grab a drink or a doughnut before going back on shift. My one true friend and these men avoided him like he had a disease.

We didn't get any other reactions. Most of the men took a quick glance then shook their heads. They weren't curious. They didn't ask any questions. Their minds were focused on the few minutes of pleasure they had before them, cherished time ticking off until they returned to the mechanized slaughter they undertook day in and day out. It had been worth a shot but we didn't get a hit.

I thanked Muldoon on our way out.

"Find your man?" he asked.

"Nope. Just a lot of dead cows."

Muldoon chuckled. "That's money on the hoof, Sarge. Big money."

"Guess you're right. So long, Muldoon."

He waved as we set off down the drive. Two minutes later, we found ourselves back in the heart of the city. I wondered who in their right mind would choose to live near a slaughterhouse. We weren't any closer to finding Henry Turner. Or Liu Chen and her baby.

"Wanna go for a burger?" Birdie asked. He looked serious.

I considered it for a moment, then shrugged.

"Yeah. Sure."

We made our way to the Brazier King on St. Clair and demolished four burgers between us, one for me and three for Birdie plus two malteds each. For some reason, it just felt right.

28

I slung my jacket over the back of the scarred, wooden bench and sat down to read on the periphery of that sad patch of moth-eaten grassland known as Henley Park. Birdie had dropped me off and gone to the office. I thumbed through the well-annotated copy of *The Invisible Man* I'd lifted from Henry Turner's bedroom.

I glanced to my left as a city worker idly speared bits of flowing paper with a stick and flicked them into a canvas sack he carried on a strap across his shoulders. He wore government-issue coveralls and a straw hat and didn't seem to be in a hurry. Two mothers sat on the other side of the park, hunkered down by the sandbox watching a pair of toddlers chop away with tiny plastic shovels, filling tiny plastic buckets. The mothers chatted and smoked enjoying a few minutes of freedom away from the drudgery of domesticity. The sun continued to shine and a light breeze rustled the leaves in the trees. It came easy to think the world operated in peace and didn't have a care, that no one suffered or felt pain and happiness reigned supreme.

Turning my attention back to the book, I leafed through some pages finding myself caught up in the machinations of the Brotherhood, Ras the Destroyer and the funky rhythms of Harlem before the War. I'd read the passage where the narrator's friend and colleague, Clifton, had been arrested then shot in the street after struggling with a beat cop. Clifton had left the Brotherhood and become a street vendor selling little black Sambo puppets making them dance obscenely before crowds of grinning whites. Puppets that horrified and offended the narrator's sense of morality.

During that dangerous time, the narrator discovered an alter ego called Rhinehart who assumed the personas of a gangster, a pimp and the pastor of a Holy Roller church. Merely by donning a hat and dark glasses, the narrator transformed into Rhinehart even fooling the criminal's closest associates. *The Invisible Man* had become less of himself and more invisible as the story progressed, merging into what he thought others, his associates in the Brotherhood and neighbors in Harlem, wanted him to be.

"*...I was invisible, and hanging would not bring me to visibility, even to their eyes, since they wanted my death not for myself alone but for the chase I'd been on all my life; because of the way I'd run, been run, chased, operated, purged—although to a great extent I could have done nothing else, given their blindness and my invisibility. And that I, a little black man with an assumed name should die because a big black man in his hatred and confusion over the nature of a reality that seemed controlled solely by white men whom I knew to be as blind as he, was just too much, too outrageously absurd. And I knew that it was better to live out one's own absurdity than to die for that of others...*"

Until there was nothing left of himself. In the end, the narrator tumbled down a dirty coal chute into a filthy cellar and couldn't find his way out. Thinking about all of this made me shiver and I wondered if that's what Henry decided to do, make himself invisible. His life appeared self-effacing. Well-liked at school but no stand-out. Kindly thought of at Flint but after the accident, he faded away. Then he became a non-entity for the Fosters, merely a servant, someone for Alison Foster to harangue and abuse. Henry's life was all about being invisible and I found that sad. My thoughts again turned to Birdie, who was anything but invisible. How did he control his anger? I knew I couldn't.

A shadow fell across the pages.

"I never took you for a man who lounges around parks, Mr. Gold."

I looked up. Her hair was framed in a halo of light blurring out her features. She wore the saucer-sized sunglasses.

"It's not something I do often, Miss Rosewell." I shifted over. "Take a pew."

Today, she wore a short-sleeved maize-coloured blouse, tan slacks and low heels without hose. I glanced down to be sure. "May I?" she asked, reaching out for the book. I nodded and she took it from me. Our hands touched for a moment. Her skin was warm and moist, the palms plump. Adele riffled the pages stopping to look and skim the notations.

"Henry sure loved this book," she said.

"Looks like it."

"He wrote all over the margins."

"Yes, he did."

"Doesn't get you any closer though, does it, Mo?"

There was a gentle teasing in her tone, a bit of a smirk at the corners of her full lips.

"Probably not," I admitted.

I glanced around. The city worker had left, ambling on to the next park most likely. The mothers hauled their toddlers out of the sand swatting off their bottoms to howls of protest. I reached into my jacket and pulled out a packet of Sweet Caps.

"Smoke?"

Adele shook her head. I shook one out of the pack, popped the head of the lighter and flicked it into life.

"Those things will kill you," she said.

I smiled at her. "I don't think so. Plenty of others out to get me first."

"Ooohhh," she trilled. "Such a dangerous man with a dangerous life."

"Now, you're mocking me".

Behind the glasses, I saw her eyebrow lift. "Me? Little old me? Don't be silly."

"Now I know you're mocking me. How's your aunt?"

Adele Rosewell sighed.

"Bereft if you must know. This thing is eating at her and it's affecting her health."

I blew out a plume of smoke. "Are you, bereft?"

"Now, who's mocking who?"

I sighed. The heat of the sun felt good on my skin. "I never mock," I said.

"Women must find you rather infuriating," she replied.

"Not just women."

"Still, I guess you'd be a challenge."

"Is that how you look at relationships? As a challenge?"

"You don't understand."

"Understand what, Miss Rosewell?"

"What it's like for someone like me."

I took another hit on the cigarette. "You mean, an intelligent and attractive black woman making her way in a white man's world?"

The line around her lips tightened. "Something like that."

"Listen, sister. What makes you think you're the only one who's got it tough?"

"I never said I was, the only one, I mean. Just that a white boy like you doesn't get it."

"And what is it I'm not getting, Miss Rosewell?"

"That men, all kinds of men find me, attractive. But what they really want is for me to lay down and spread my legs." That idea of her, that image, ran through me like an electric current. "And you're no different, Mr. Gold."

"What makes you think so?"

She tipped the sunglasses up toward her forehead and looked at me directly. "I can see it in your eyes and your attitude. Feel it radiating off your skin."

"You think I'm just interested in getting you in the sack?"

"Aren't you?"

"There's nothing wrong with physical relationships between men and women," I replied.

"You didn't answer my question," she said.

I laughed and it came out as a nervous snort. "Miss Rosewell, I won't deny that I find you attractive in all kinds of ways."

"Now you're thinking I'm a prude."

I shook my head. "Well, you're pretty direct."

"...the way I like it..."

"What if I offered to take you to dinner?"

"Are you? Offering I mean."

"Yes."

Adele set the glasses back on her nose, straightened her posture and leaned forward. "Find Henry first. Then we'll talk."

"It's all business with you, is that it?"

"I think you're getting the picture, Mr. Gold. It's how a girl survives in this cruel world. My body is my own. I decide who gets to see it and when. Understand?"

I ground the stub of the cigarette under my heel. "Beginning to."

A tall shadow blocked out the sun. Birdie loomed over us.

Adele glanced up, then shook her head. "Ah, the sleeping giant awakes."

She got up from the bench and flicked at imaginary dust mites.

"Thank you for the chat. It was most interesting."

She nodded at Birdie then strode off down Dundas Street. I watched her hips and buttocks churn and those ankles slashing through the atmosphere.

"Did I spoil the moment?" Birdie asked, then grinned.

"Did you ever. Brother, did you ever. What have you got?"

"Found joyrider Number two."

29

The Royal Plaza Hotel at the corner of Bloor and Avenue Road had a rooftop pool and lounge area. That's where we found Harvey Troyer, Alison Lawson's ex- boyfriend. He lay face down on a lounger while a young woman in a bikini that barely covered her assets massaged baby oil into his shoulder blades. In fact, a number of young women in bikinis did the same to young men fanned out around the pool's edge. On the far side, stood a cabana bar. To the right the hotel had set up a number of tables with umbrellas. Those bright young things that tired of soaking up the sun sat and sipped their drinks behind dark glasses pretending to be movie stars. A light breeze kept the sun from being oppressive.

"That's it, baby," Troyer oozed. "Lower it down a little."

The only ones out of place were Birdie and I. Definitely overdressed. I felt like stripping down to my skivvies and cannon balling into the minty blue water. Troyer looked a lanky lad with skin the colour of putty. His hair looked like tar and he had it combed like Elvis. A fag dangled from his right hand. A fruity-looking cocktail sweated on the small table to his left. As the girl, a honey-coloured blonde, worked her fingers into the muscles in his back, her bra strap slid down her tanned shoulders revealing just about all that nature had given her.

Wearing a dark suit and a fedora on a warm day at poolside makes you stick out. Birdie's natural consumption of space and the colour of his skin drew looks from the club clientele. A fussy waiter hurried over and I knew he was going to try and tell us the place was off-limits. I cut him off before he could open his mouth.

"Two beers, Pedro," I said. I nodded toward Troyer. "Put them on his tab and make sure they're frosty." The waiter gulped, looked at Birdie who stared back at him impassively. When he raised his Ray Bans to tighten that look, the waiter nodded and took off.

"Think we'll get the drinks?" he asked.

"We better," I replied.

We sauntered over to Troyer while the blond exercised her fingers.

"You do good work," I said. She peered up at me and then took in Birdie and smiled guilelessly.

"Thanks," she said. "I work at the club here."

Troyer lifted his head. He had smarmy good looks, cleft chin, hollowed cheekbones, blue eyes and an irritating smirk.

"That's enough, Alice," he said as he pushed himself up, then reached for his sunglasses. Alice backed off as Troyer swung his legs around. Men, instinctively, don't like to feel they're in a vulnerable position when in the company of other men.

"You Harvey Troyer?" I asked.

"Who're you?" he replied.

"Asked you first, Harvey," I said in a tone with just enough edge in it to make him wonder.

"Yeah, I'm Harvey Troyer, so what?"

He reached for a packet of silver-tipped Benson and Hedges on the small pool table, shook one out of the pack and lit it with a gold-plated lighter.

"You didn't offer one to Alice," I said.

"Huh?" A look of juvenile confusion flooded into his face.

"Rude Harvey," Birdie boomed. "Just plain rude."

Alice grinned. "I don't smoke," she said.

"I help you with something?" Troyer said.

"Sure, Harvey, that'd be swell."

"Okay, shoot."

"You know a lady by the name of Alison Lawson? Used to be Foster?"

Now Troyer looked genuinely quizzical. "You guys cops?"

We didn't answer just gave him our stone faces.

"Alison? Yeah, sure. We dated in high school. That was a long time ago. Now she's married to some nob her daddy picked out for her. Is that what this is about? What's she done, anyway?"

I sighed. "Too many questions, Harvey. You remember being pulled over by a cop one night when you were out with Alison and a kid called Rance Callaway and his girl, Gayle Sorenson?"

Troyer gave a nasty little laugh. "She wasn't his girl. Gayle didn't even like Rance. She only came along because I asked her to."

"You had something going with her?" Birdie asked.

Troyer glanced back at Alice. "I didn't say that, okay? We were friends, that's all. I was dating Alison."

"Things got a little wild, did they Harvey?" I asked.

Troyer smirked. "Maybe a little. Alison was a thrill seeker. She liked to do crazy things."

"Like what?"

Troyer took a long drag on the fag. "I don't recall if you guys said you were cops?"

"Used to be. Private."

"You got a badge or something?"

"Uh-huh. What sort of things did Alison like to do, Harvey?"

Troyer laughed but it was a bit queasy. "Alice, honey. Why don't you go powder your nose or something while I talk to these guys, okay?"

"Sure, Harvey. If that's what you want?" she replied in a brittle tone.

Instead of heading to the ladies toilet, Alice stood up. She had a set of long, graceful limbs. She replaced the bra straps, strode athletically over to the pool and dove in elegantly barely making a ripple. Every male in the area couldn't help but watch as she stroked along the bottom and surfaced at the other end barely puffing for air. Her hair looked like spun gold laid sleek and wet against her tanned skin.

"She's something, isn't she?"

"I'll give you that," I said. "We were talking about Alison."

"Yeah, right. She was just kind of wild, you know?"

"In what way, Harvey?" I felt like smacking him around a little to hurry things up. The waiter still hadn't brought our beers.

"Drinking, going out to bars. It was her idea to boost my old man's Caddy that night we got stopped. She dared me to."

"And you fell for that?" Birdie asked him quietly.

Troyer grinned sheepishly. "Yeah. I guess I did. I mean, you've seen her right? She knew how to get her way. She was good at that. Always got what she wanted."

"Anything else happen that night?"

"Like what?"

"You tell me. You were hauled into the station. Alison called her old man in Palm Springs. Do you remember who came to pick her up?"

"Yeah. It was the chauffeur. Henry, I think his name was. Geez, I felt sorry for the guy."

"Why was that?"

Harvey glanced nervously at Birdie. He confirmed the story about Alison and Henry told to us by the cop, Kernahan and Rance Callaway.

"Alison says she broke it off with you after that night," I said.

"Oh yeah? Well, she would, wouldn't she?" Troyer said. "Pride and all that. No. I definitely told her we were quits."

"How'd she handle it?"

"Not good. Threw an ashtray at me. Lucky for me, it missed."

"What can you tell us about a club down by the docks?"

Troyer reared back. "You know about that?"

I nodded. "Blackstone's wasn't it?"

"Who told you? That little fink Callaway?" I didn't answer but it didn't stop him. "I should have known. It was a mistake hanging out with him. The guy's a deadbeat. Drives a truck for a living."

"And what do you do for a living, Harvey? When you're not lounging around the pool getting a nice massage, that is."

"It's my day off. I'm a stockbroker at Chisholm's. I handle some big league clients too."

"That's swell. Now about Blackstone's. Exactly what went on there?"

"What do you mean?"

"You know what I mean. The girls, Gayle and Alison used to head upstairs while you boys stayed at the bar. What were they doing up there?"

Troyer mashed his cigarette out in the onyx ashtray. He slurped the melted ice in his drink crunching the cubes between his molars.

"Don't know a thing."

"You mean, you aren't going to say."

"Take it anyway you want, okay? I don't have to answer your questions. I don't have to talk to you. In fact, I should have you thrown out of here. Maybe that's what I will do."

"Just try it," Birdie said.

Troyer gulped. "Hey, just kidding, okay?"

"Right," I said. "Now that we know you've got the spine of a garden snake, just answer the question." Troyer clammed up. He shook his head. "What was it? Pills? Reefers? What was it Troyer?"

He resembled a little kid now getting a tongue-lashing. He bowed his head and rocked in his lounger. It made creaking noises as he shifted in the canvas seat.

"We could beat it out of him," Birdie suggested.

"We could."

I stood up and saw Alice giving us a look. Three guys were huddled around her as she sat by the edge of the pool.

"Looks like Alice has got some company, Harvey. You might lose another one." He went to say something but stopped himself. We never got the beers.

30

I had parked the Chevy on Prince Arthur just around the corner from the back of the Plaza. It was a one-way. When we got back to the car, we were blocked in–a two-toned Buick Roadmaster front and back–touching the bumpers. Four of them waited for us in their baggy suits and floppy hats, flashing their .45's. One of them sat on the Chevy's hood. Birdie and I strolled up making sure to keep our hands in the open.

"I'd appreciate it if you didn't do that," I said.

The gunsel grinned then slid down the hood dropping on to the pavement like a gymnast, light on his feet, good balance.

"John want his money," he said. "John say you not looking hard enough."

"Is that right?" I replied.

"That's what he say," the gunsel repeated keeping the grin going.

I turned to Birdie. "What do you think of that? We're not trying hard enough."

"Others have made that mistake," Birdie said.

"What else did John say?"

The gunsel removed his hat, then shrugged off his jacket and handed it to one of his associates. The leather straps of his harness rode high on his chest. He slipped that off too.

"John say that I give you a reason to try harder."

I watched him as he rolled up one sleeve then the other. I glanced at Birdie, who shrugged. The other three gunsels grinned now too, sharing the same joke. This was a quiet street in one of the posh areas of town, not the time or place for gunplay. But not many people about either. The block remained practically deserted. I sighed. I handed my hat to Birdie and then my jacket. I unstrapped my harness with my left hand and held it up while John's men watched me warily. Just as Birdie hooked it in his big paw, I pulled the handle of the .45 and aimed it at the gunsel's chest. The others flinched but didn't move.

"I could just plug you here and now," I said. "Maybe John would get that message loud and clear."

"You wouldn't do such a thing," the gunsel sneered.

"Try me, sport. It's nice and quiet. We'd be gone in no time and so would you." I cocked the trigger and he flinched. From under my coat, the barrel of Birdie's cannon poked out. "Up to you but if you're smart, you'll go back and tell John we got the message and understand. We are trying our best to find his money for him."

"You won't find it here," the gunsel said, pointing at the hotel. Then he spat.

"Don't be so sure," I said, and motioned with the .45. "Tell him we've got lucky number eight horseshoes up our backsides. Him, he's a number four. Get it?"

The gunsel grimaced and gestured for his hat and jacket.

"Okay, we leave it for now but we are watching. You will hear from us again."

He barked in Mandarin. The four gunsels got into their two-tone Buicks, fired up their engines then screeched away from the curb. We gazed after them as the cars peeled down Prince Arthur tires squealing.

"No need for that," I said sadly.

"John's nervous," Birdie said.

I nodded. "That's the way I like it. Let's keep pushing his buttons, keep him off-balance." Then I had a thought about hotels and who they employ. We'd been to the penthouse to jaw with Troyer but a small army labored behind the scenes, sometimes in the basement. Ying's sister might have found a refuge in one of them.

I snapped my fingers to wake myself up. "Come on. We might have missed something back there." Birdie looked at me in surprise, just for a moment.

We walked back to the Plaza, pushed through the revolving doors and made our way up to the main reception. A nattily attired young man with enough Brylcreem in his hair to grease a watermelon, pretended to be busy.

Finally, he decided to look up and acknowledge us. "Yes, gentlemen. Can I help?" he asked in a nancy-like drawl.

I drew the girl's picture from inside my breast pocket and laid it flat on the counter in front of him.

"Just wanted to know if you've seen this girl in here."

He glanced at it. "I don't think so."

"Are you sure?"

His dark eyes flickered up at me. "Yes, quite sure."

"Do you have any Chinese on staff?" Birdie asked.

The young man smirked. "Only in the laundry area but no one under the age of 50."

"What about guests?" I asked.

"I should think not." And he actually wrinkled his nose.

"You're sure?"

"Yes. Quite sure. Now, if there isn't anything else?"

"Stringer around?"

Stringer was the house dick. He'd been turfed off the force for drinking on the job. Seemed like he just forgot when his shifts were and hedged his bets by drinking during the day and the night.

"Of course. I believe he's in his office." He picked up the house phone. "Whom shall I say…?"

"Don't sweat it," I replied. "I know where he hangs his hat."

Ray Stringer's office, if it could be described as such, lay at the far end of a corridor through a doorway opposite the incinerator. You could smell the burning garbage. Showed how much management thought of Ray. I didn't knock but went straight in. As usual, Ray drank his lunch.

"Hey, hey, Mo," he said and nearly tipped his chair over. His size 12 brogues were propped on the scarred surface of his desk and he hung by his scuffed heels. "You startled me. Don't get many visitors down here."

I looked around. No windows. Single overhead light. Wobbly desk and rickety chair. No kidding. "I can't imagine why. This place is swell."

Stringer waved a meaty paw at the air. "It's a dump but it's my dump. Hello Mr. Bird." For some reason that's what he called Birdie. A sign of respect, I imagined.

"Ray," Birdie replied.

"Drink?" He held up the bottle. Bell's Whiskey. Not my tipple.

"No thanks, Ray. A little early for me and you know that, uh, Mr. Bird, rarely imbibes."

Ray nodded. "Okay." And poured himself a generous measure. "To what do I owe the pleasure," he said, tilting his snap brim further back on his head.

"Looking for someone, Ray. Thought you might have seen her around."

I took out the girl's photo and placed it on the desk in front of him. Ray shifted his weight bringing the chair forward. He lifted his feet off the desk and placed them on the floor to get a better look.

"Chinese, huh?"

"Yeah."

"You're looking in the wrong part of town, boys."

I sighed. "Thought she might have worked here at one time or another, Ray."

"Couldn't tell ya."

I scooped up the photo. "Thanks anyway."

"Hey," Ray said affably. "I'm not finished, but I know who might." He picked up the phone on his desk and dialed an extension. "Hey, Barry. Can you do me a quick favour? Come on down to my office for a minute, will ya? Thanks." He hung up. "Barry might know," he said.

A minute later, discreet knuckles rapped on the door. A middle-aged Chinese man with Buddy Holly glasses, poked his head in. He was pudgy with iron-grey hair buzzed close to his scalp. He wore whites, like an orderly in a hospital. Even his slip-ons were white.

"Barry, c'mon in," Ray said as he gargled more booze.

Barry nodded at me and Birdie. "Barry Wong," he said and put out his hand.

"Nice to meet you, Barry. Mo Gold and this is my associate, Arthur Birdwell," I replied and shook. Then Birdie did the same.

He blinked at Birdie, then at me. "How can I help you gentlemen?"

I held out the photo. "We're looking for her." Barry adjusted his glasses and took a good look. "You know her?"

Barry handed the photo back to me. "I'm not sure. Maybe."

"Either you know her or you don't."

Barry swallowed and looked uncomfortable. "I could say they all look alike to me."

I gave him a sour look. "Come on, Barry. Don't be cute."

"Why are you looking for her?" Barry asked.

Birdie leaned toward him. "I think you know why, Barry. You do, don't you?"

Barry's round face took on a baleful look. "I might," he admitted.

"Look, Barry, we don't mean her any harm. We think she might know the whereabouts of something quite valuable that's gone missing. We just want to talk to her, nothing else. Ray will vouch for us. We used to work together on the force."

Obligingly, Ray chimed in. "He's telling it straight, Barry. Mo's a stand up guy and that's saying a lot coming from me. Most of the cops I knew were as crooked as a bent stick. Why Mo even punched the deputy chief. I should know. I was there and it was a doozer," said Ray. Whatever Ray was and that included being a drunk, he never took a backhander. And he could handle himself in a scuffle. Those size 12's had a pair of meaty fists to go with them.

"Listen Barry," I said. "Better we find her first. Otherwise, who knows what could happen? We can help her out of a jam. We just aim to return whatever's gone missing, that's all."

"I'm a man of God," Birdie intoned. "And I don't tell lies."

"Aww, Birdie, not now, okay?" He gave me a look. I sighed. "Okay, Barry, Birdie is a man of God, like he says. We're playing square. Do you know her?"

Barry chewed his lip. "She worked here about three months ago. Chambermaid. Said her name was Wendy Ling."

"You got a file on her?"

"Nope."

"Address?"

"Nope."

"Guess it's too much to ask about a phone number?"

"You gotta understand," Barry said. "She was a temp. I had a couple of girls off, one had a baby and the other was in the hospital. We hire girls by the day, pay them cash. All the hotels do it. We keep it off the books."

"So, they're illegals?" I asked him.

He nodded. "Probably. We don't ask them any questions as long as they do the work and don't steal anything. This girl. Wendy, she was here maybe three weeks, then she disappeared. Never came back. That happens a lot too. They go on to other jobs. Some get arrested. They leave the city, all kinds of things go on. Not our business."

I reached into my jacket pocket where I kept a random poker chip. "You play, Barry?"

He shrugged. "Sometimes."

"Where do you play?"

"Here and there."

Birdie placed a huge paw on his white shoulder. "Where's your regular table?"

"A joint on Cecil, a few blocks in from Spadina. There's usually a game going there."

"Really?" Ying had lived on Beatrice not far from Cecil and his sister with him. "You know any of the dealers by name?"

Barry shrugged again. "Maybe."

"What about Ying Hee Fong? You know him?"

Barry shook his head. "Don't think so." His expression went tight.

I held the photo up. "This could be his sister."

"I wouldn't know. Look, I've told you everything I know." He glanced pointedly at his watch. "I really should get back."

"Sure, Barry, we understand. Thanks for your help." I slipped the poker chip back into my pocket and came up with a card. "If you hear of anything, you let me know, okay? This girl could be in serious trouble. A lot of people are looking for her. Most of them are not as nice as we are."

Barry looked from me to Birdie and back again. He took the card and stuffed it into his pants pocket.

"Sure," he said. He backed away and slipped out the door.

"Geez," Ray said. "You sure scared the crap out of him."

"I hope so," I said.

31

When I still worked on the force, I had a tout in Chinatown. He was an opium dealer and small time crook named Danny Chow. I'd busted him a few times and then put him on the payroll. We'd kept in touch over the years. I knew where to find Danny but there was no point in looking until after midnight. I dropped Birdie at St. Paul's Cathedral. He liked to sit there and reflect. I went home. I had a date.

I took Evelyn out to dinner at Hy's, one of the classiest steak joints in the city. The waiters wore tuxedos and they actually fit. The carpets grew deep and the silverware was the real deal. Even the chandeliers sparkled.

"My, this is nice," she gushed. She wore a shimmery, sleeveless dress that had tassels hanging from it that accentuated her height and colour.

"Glad you like it," I said and ordered a vodka martini from the waiter. Evelyn opted for a gin and tonic.

She reached across the table and covered her hand with mine. "Thank you," she said.

"For what?"

"For this. I don't get to go out to nice places like this very often, Mo. I just want you to know I appreciate it, that's all."

"My pleasure. You deserve it. You work hard and you take care of your kids." The first thing she told me when I picked her up was that her sister agreed to sit for her. I met the sister, briefly, an older, stouter version of Evelyn and got a short "hmmpphh" by way of greeting. Clearly, she didn't approve. Probably thought I shilled used cars or chased ambulances. "Well, I didn't impress your sister much."

"Don't worry about her. She's always been protective of me. Her husband left her too and she's bitter. Thinks all men are rotten. You know the type."

"I've met a few," I said. More than a few, I thought.

Hy's really did serve up a good steak and we each ordered a sirloin the size of a small city-state served on a platter. Evelyn's eyes lit up when she saw the food. "Oh my. Haven't seen that much food on one plate since my last Italian wedding. One of the girls at the hospital. Must have been ten courses at least. Felt like that anyway."

I'd ordered a nice Cabernet to wash it down. We dipped into it liberally.

"How's your case going?" Evelyn asked between chews and swallows.

"Case?"

"Isn't that what you call it?"

"Yes."

"Well, all the fighting you've been doing, I just figured you had to be on a case, that's all. Was I right?"

"Kind of, Evelyn. To be honest, I don't know what I'm on or doing for that matter."

"Want to talk about it?"

"And spoil the evening?"

"What is it about some men and their work? It's like the war. Nothing to say. And then they expect their women just to go along with it like everything is normal when it isn't. Does that make sense to you?"

I looked at her. Her skin looked smooth and her eyes bright. She'd put her hair up and it suited her. Even still, we got some looks from other diners. I knew she noticed but ignored it. I wasn't that forgiving.

"Maybe it's a form of protection, Evelyn."

She crossed her arms and sat back in her chair.

"Okay. Men don't talk feelings. It's just not a manly thing and I do think we want to protect the people we care about. There are certain jobs that you just don't want to talk about because it means reliving something you want to forget."

"And is that how it is for you, Mo? You just want to forget?"

"Yeah. A lot of the time. Why do you think I'm not married?"

Evelyn picked up her wine glass. "Well, maybe you haven't met the right girl."

I grinned at her. "Maybe you're right."

We clinked and drank a little more.

We just finished the main course when she came in. She didn't see me. The maitre'd seated her across the large dining room at a table in the corner shielded by a pillar. But I saw her and her ankles flash by and the smooth looking white man she came with. I ought to have recognized him. Alison Lawson's husband, Reginald. I have to admit, my first reaction came steeped in jealousy. Then boiling rage. I must have stared for too long. I willed myself to believe there must be some simple explanation.

"You know that woman, Mo?" Evelyn asked sharply.

I jerked my head back to her. "No," I lied. "Him, actually. He's married and that's not his wife." It sounded unconvincing, even to me. What were they doing together?

Evelyn took another look. "Why is that a surprise?" And then I saw the look of contempt on her face. "I think I know her."

"Oh?"

"Seen her in church," she murmured. "Only once or twice. She was with an older lady. The older one's a regular. I see her every Sunday."

Neither of us ordered dessert and Evelyn stayed silent in the car all the way back to her place. When I pulled up to the curb, I'd made a decision.

"You were right," I said.

Evelyn looked at me expectantly. "About what, exactly?"

"I do know her. The old lady you've seen her with in church is my client. The old lady's name is Aida Turner and we're looking for her son, Henry. He disappeared about eight years ago. The looker is named Adele, Adele Rosewell. She's the niece, Henry's cousin."

"Adele?"

"Yeah, Adele."

"That Adele?"

I pondered this turn of phrase. "She's the only one I know, Evelyn. And you're the only Evelyn I know too."

"What about the man she was with. That slick looking white guy?"

"The husband of Aida Turner's employer, a woman by the name of Alison Lawson." I shook my head.

"What?" she asked.

"Well, this Alison Lawson is a real looker, so....?"

"You're wondering why her husband is playing the field?"

"Something like that, yeah."

Evelyn gave me a direct look. "Well, don't you know, honey? We're forbidden fruit..."

"Evelyn..."

"Some white men get their kicks having sex with a black woman...they like that black pussy...then they're ashamed and want to be punished by their mamas just like little boys."

"You think that's me? I mean, I like having sex with you, of course, but it's more than that..." I floundered and she let me hang myself. "Maybe that didn't come out right...."

"I don't want you to mention her name to me again."

I was going to point out to her that I had been at pains to avoid mentioning anything about her but I gave in.

"Sure. I won't mention her again."

"Especially not in your sleep."

"Not even in my sleep."

"'Cause if you do, I'm gonna sock you one and I don't care if you're awake or not, you hear?"

"Yeah, I hear."

"Okay," she said sweetly and leaned across and gave me a lingering kiss. "You coming up, baby?"

"I've got til midnight."

"That's all right, I'm a working girl. Need my beauty rest."

I waited by the door as the sister, Hortense, gathered her things. I wished her a goodnight as polite as could be and only got a prolonged "harrumph" for my consideration. I could see that Evelyn's daughter took after her auntie. After she left, Evelyn and I got undressed and thrashed around in her bed praising the lord for our good fortune.

32

I picked Birdie up in front of the office. I kept the windows of the Chevy rolled down. If we intended to search the gin joints and opium dens of Chinatown, and we did, then any fresh air would be welcome. I parked right on Spadina opposite John Fat Gai's place. Although late, the joint hopped. You'd almost think John had a legit business going. With the kind of trade he did, it made me wonder how much more he socked away illegally. Must have been a bonanza.

Our first stop–the alleyway where we'd found Ying's body. You could always find a lively game of craps taking place in back of Mr. Ling's Grocery. We edged around John's restaurant sticking to the shadows at the opposite side of the street. I could hear them before we saw them as we turned into the alleyway. About 50 feet in, half a dozen guys sat on upturned box crates, smoking, drinking and rolling dice. They were parked just about on the spot where Ying died. I could hear the clink of the glass as the die hit its sides and the clackety-clack as they rolled on the pavement. That and the yells and groans of the players marking the winners and the losers.

A pair of look-outs took the watch–as custom dictated. We didn't hide ourselves as we strolled into the alleyway and the watchers melted out of the shadows. They knew we hadn't come to play craps.

"What you want, fella?" one of them said, a wizened fellow in a pair of blood-stained overalls. A rusty machete lay against his thigh. Some chickens had died tonight.

I kept my hands clear. "Nothing. Just looking for someone."

"Who?"

"Doesn't matter," I said. "He's not here."

"Big man," the other one said. "Dark face, like the devil..." The Chinese were nothing if not superstitious. I hoped Birdie didn't take offence. A burst of Mandarin followed this acute observation along with a surfeit of spitting. The players stopped the game and watched us suspiciously. We backed out of the alleyway. I'd seen what I needed and there was no one of interest. We kept walking along Dundas Street, Birdie's size 17 brogues clopping on the cracked pavement. After a moment, we heard quick steps behind us. One of the players. Once we'd turned, he pulled up keeping his distance.

"Who you looking for?" he said in unaccented English.

"Danny Chow. You know him?"

He was hatless and wore a dark jacket over a dirty white shirt and a pair of trousers that didn't match. He wore different shoes too. They were odd but looked about the right size for each foot.

"I can take you to where he is."

"Okay."

"Five dollars," he said.

"Sure."

I handed over the half sawbuck and it disappeared into the folds of his jacket. I slipped my hand into my jacket pocket and the guy tensed.

"Relax," I said. "Just want to show you a photo."

I pulled out the picture of the girl and handed it to him. He held it up to the streetlamp to get a look. "Know her?"

The guy shook his head once and handed back the photo.

"This way," he said and jerked his head in the opposite direction.

"You better be on the level," I said. "Or you'll be wearing a hole where your head used to be."

"Don't worry," said our new guide.

Looking for a Chinaman among other Chinamen made the rest of us stand out like a sore thumb. Tough way to work the shadows if you wanted to be discreet. We crossed Spadina heading west. Near the corner of Portland, our guide pulled up before a storefront. Chen's Hardware.

"Wait here," he said and disappeared down the walk and around the back.

I glanced at Birdie who shrugged. It was gone one in the morning now and I felt it a little. The night air remained balmy and the smell of garbage didn't make you gag at this end once you moved away from the small markets, the restaurants and the alleys where they dumped the trash fresh every night for the morning pick-up.

I heard some light footsteps and spotted Danny Chow's slight figure round the back of the building. He paused to light fire to a cigarette drawing on it like it was a long lost friend before plodding down the walk to greet us.

"Looking for me?" he asked.

"Nice to see you, Danny. Been a while."

"What you want, Mo?" His dead eyes flicked at Birdie then back at me.

"You look a little rough, Danny. Things been tough for you?"

Danny barked a short laugh. "You might say that but then they've never really been good, have they?"

"I guess not." I reached into my pocket and took out the girl's photo. I handed it over. "We're looking for her."

Danny didn't reach for it or look at it. "I know you are and I can't help you."

"You didn't even take a look."

"I don't have to. Looking for her can get you killed. I don't want to have nothing to do with it."

"What have you heard, Danny?"

"That she don't want to be found, okay? Is that good enough for you?"

"Not really. Not when we need to find her. I'm looking for fresh ideas."

"Then you're out of luck," Danny snorted. "For once, it's you and not me."

"What's that supposed to mean?"

"I think you know, Mo. I'm not your stoolie anymore. If I had something I could give you I would. But I don't. I'm not touching this one with a barge pole. And if you were smart, you'd do the same," Danny said, then spat a thick wad of phlegm at his feet. "I gotta go. Don't come looking for me again, Mo, or things could get, difficult."

"How much you want?"

I could see he was hurting. He kept licking his lips, had a case of dry mouth and even though it cooled off now he sweated like a pig and his hands shook. Something told me he'd jump into the bottom of the barrel along with a needle if he could get his hands on some gear.

He shook his head, trying to control the shaking in his hands.

"I ain't got much of a life but at least what I got, is mine." Danny started to back away. "Don't come looking for me again, Mo. I mean it…"

I heard the quick scuffling of shoes. Danny had stepped out of the pool of light thrown by the streetlamp. They came out of the shadows, half a dozen of them, guns drawn. Birdie and I stood back to back in a defensive posture while the gunmen surrounded us like Indians circling the wagons on the old two-reelers I used to watch. They found their spot and went still. The wise guy from before, the one who wanted to teach me a lesson, pushed through the pack, still grinning. He seemed abundantly happy at the moment. Really pleased to see me.

"Good evening," he said. "Pleasant evening."

"Sure it is," I replied. Birdie snorted his answer.

"Now, maybe, we have a little fun," the wise guy said.

"What kind of fun?"

"You find out." I thought his face would crack open he smiled so much.

I glanced at my watch. "It's a little late and it's been a long day. Maybe some other time."

The smile disappeared. "He want to see you, now. You come with us."

"What if we don't want to?"

"Then you make a big mistake."

I shrugged. "Your party."

The gunmen closed ranks around us and we quick-stepped back the way we came and crossed Spadina against the traffic, to John's restaurant. Now it stood empty. The fearless leader of our little expedition rapped sharply on the front door rattling the glass. One of John's flunkies opened it and stepped aside. We shuffled through.

John gave us a cold welcome beckoning from his usual table at the back. More of his men occupied two tables and stared silently and hostilely at us through the thick cigarette smoke that hung in the air. This time no food came on offer. Not even a complimentary cup of green tea. The guy with the happy face poked me in the back. For a second, I thought about putting an elbow in his jaw but Birdie gave me a cautionary look. I suppose the two dozen or more henchmen giving us hard looks could be interpreted as some sort of deterrent. If so, it seemed to work.

"John," I said. "Nice to see you. We should get together like this more often, us and your friends."

John Fat Gai sighed. His thin face looked strained and I noticed a nervous tic in his right cheek. As usual, the eight cards lay spread out before him. He played with the ring of jade coins. "Always the joker, Mo. I'm not amused, as you can see."

"Okay."

"What progress have you made in finding my missing money?"

"Not a lot," I admitted.

"You're looking for the sister?"

"That's right."

"Why haven't you found her? It can't be that difficult to find one woman with a young baby, now can it?"

I shrugged. "Someone has hidden her well."

"I don't have a lot of patience. You should know that by now."

"Well it is a virtue, so they say."

"So is forgiveness," Birdie boomed and took stock of the room ensuring he made eye contact with each and every gunsel standing. Most wouldn't have understood him anyway. I doubted if they spoke much, if any, English.

John smiled thinly. "Spare me the platitudes. I hear your attention has been, diverted."

"Oh?"

John went on. "Yes, apparently, you are looking for some fellow who went missing eight years ago. His mother has hired you to find him. Is this true?"

"I never talk about one client to another John. We keep things confidential. It's our stock in trade."

That remark caused a guttural response from John's good friend who took the opportunity to whack me in the back of the head with the heel of his palm, a blow that brought me to my knees. It felt like being hit with a cement bag with the cement still in it. Birdie caught the Chinaman's hand and twisted viciously. Suddenly, everyone in the room went for their guns and the tension notched up a few degrees. I stood up shakily rubbing the back of my head. My knees felt a little loose and the room took on a different perspective, like that of Alice after she swallowed the pill.

I picked my hat up off the floor. Everyone hung there suspended for a few moments while a slow clock ticked off in my head. Then John spat out a command and reluctantly, the guns went back into their holsters. It had been a bit unnerving looking down the muzzles of a dozen .45 caliber pistols.

"We're not your flunkies, John," I said quietly trying to control my anger.

"I'm sure this incident has been distressing for all of us," John said. He spoke again in Mandarin and turned to Birdie. "You may release him now. I have something for you."

I could see that Birdie had twisted the guy's hand to the point of breaking his wrist. One small turn and it would shatter. I looked at him and nodded. He released John's henchman. The guy rubbed his wrist with his good hand and kept on smiling but now everything except malice drained his expression.

"Like what?" I asked.

John reached into the side pocket of his suit jacket and tossed a snapshot on the table. "Take a look," he said and smirked. All of his gunsels smirked too.

I picked up the snap—a Polaroid. I saw my brother, Eli, tied to a chair, his face bruised and bloodied, staring up at the camera. I flipped the snap over and read the date. Taken yesterday. Rage washed over me but I bit it back.

"Where is he?"

"In a safe place," John replied. "Perhaps this will act as an incentive for you to look harder for the girl."

"She's not hiding anywhere in Chinatown. If she were we would know about it and would have found her by now," I said.

"I urge you to find her and find her quickly and recover what is mine," John replied. "For your brother's sake."

"Then he can go free?"

John cleared his throat and took a sip of tea, then adjusted his tie. "I don't care what happens to him assuming my property is returned." His answer offered no reassurance.

"We'll keep looking," I said.

"Make sure you do that. I'll give you three days." John waved his hand in dismissal and the small army of gunmen parted to make way for us. He rolled the jade coins in his left hand and fingered the jade dragon pendant with his right nervously.

I pocketed the Polaroid but didn't move. I stared John in the eye. I spoke calmly but forcefully.

"If anything happens to him, John, we will come and burn your house down. I will rain fire and destruction on your head. You will burn in hell. Your soul will wander forever. You have my personal guarantee." I flicked over the eight of spades and it fluttered to the floor. I held up four fingers. He stared at me through yellowed eyes and the tic worsened. Slowly, we took our leave careful not to make any sudden moves.

Outside, I took a deep breath. "That could have got ugly."

"I can do ugly," Birdie replied.

"Stupid idiot," I cursed. "I told him to get lost. I gave him 300 bucks."

"Your brother never did have much sense."

"You're being too kind. After all is said and done, I'll kill him myself," I said. "This is the last time I bail him out of a jam."

"Helluva jam," Birdie said. 'I'm ready. Are you?"

Ever since we'd spoken to Rochelle Dodson and he'd seen how O'Rourke treated her, Birdie had been itching to lash out at someone. He'd become a powder keg waiting for a lit fuse.

We walked back to the car. "You know what this means?" Birdie said.

I looked up at him and nodded. It meant paying a visit to Jake at the Don Jail. He dropped a loud hint at my uncle's funeral that he had some information about Liu Chen. It meant I had to go to him. Just what he wanted, the putz.

33

The Italianate face of the Don Jail made you think of an opera house but the fake front hid its horrors within ominous stone walls. Over 30 men had been hanged at the Don. The building dated back to 1862– designed by one of the city's most prominent architects. Inside, he built a magnificent rotunda where hefty sopranos could have belted out an aria or two.

At one time, the Don existed as the largest jail in North America. The corridors bleeding off the rotunda led to the cell wings. The women's block got stuck up on the fourth level. It's ironic that the building of the jail pre-dated the creation of Canada as a country by at least two years. Made you wonder what the founding fathers thought when one of the first stepping stones to democracy comprised a penal institution used to house men, women and children. They'd hung a 10 year-old kid for stealing a loaf of bread.

In those days, the hangings took place outdoors so the community could have some entertainment while eating their picnic lunch. Prisoners were supposed to stay in the Don until arraigned for trial or sentencing before being shipped off to one of the permanent correctional centres like the Kingston Pen. Yet some guys languished there for years.

The cells measured three feet by seven feet with three prisoners crammed in each. They slept in hammocks one over the other and had a slop bucket for a john. The Don was a swell place and it did me good to revisit it. Of course, I could think of nothing better than seeing my old man locked up. Unlike the more modern prisons, no visitor's area had been provided and no cafeteria to get a cup of coffee. Visitors weren't welcome. The Don cut the prisoner off from the outside world. No family. No friends. And especially, no lawyers. It became a concrete tomb. Blocked windows kept the atmosphere dark, dank and gloomy. No talking allowed or you'd get punished–taken to the 'recreation' room and flayed by one of the gunbulls. It certainly wasn't a happy place nor did it engender fond memories among the denizens who lived there.

Every other year some politician wanted to close the place down calling it a disgrace. But after nearly 100 years, the Don kept going strong. Nowhere else to stick the bad guys. It served its purpose. Those on the outside didn't care. Most of the inmates got what they deserved, didn't they? Especially that ten year-old kid.

I took off my jacket and hat and handed them to one of the guards. I unbuckled my belt and put it on the counter, emptied my pockets of cigarettes, lighter, pack of Juicy Fruit and thirty-seven cents in change, three dimes, a nickel and two pennies. The guard searched through the pockets of my jacket, found my wallet and went through every compartment.

"I'm not gonna slip the old bastard a key if that's what you were thinking," I said. The guard glared at me but didn't respond. Finished with the jacket, he patted me down, not lightly, starting with my arms and working his way down to my ankles.

"Take off your shoes," he said.

I slipped off my brogues and he felt around inside the soles then tested the heels with his fingers. You never know. They could have been hollow. I wasn't packing because that would have delayed things even more and I didn't think I'd need a weapon inside. My mistake.

"Okay," the guard said with a great deal of reluctance. I guess he hoped I had a penknife or a blasting cap on me. I slipped the brogues back on and threaded the belt through the loops on my trousers. I grabbed the rest of my stuff and put it away. I held the hat in my hand.

Birdie went through the same rigamarole. The guard nodded to his buddy on the other side of the heavily barred gate. The bull then riffled through a set of keys he kept on a large ring secured by a chain to his leather side belt, inserted one into the lock, twisted it around half a dozen times, leaned forward and pushed the gate open.

"Come on in," he said. "Welcome to paradise." Even the gunbulls had a sardonic sense of humour.

"I've been before," I replied. "And it's overrated."

Birdie elected to stay down in the main common area while I went up. He liked to observe the families visiting the inmates. "Wouldn't want to ruin your reunion," he said. I snorted.

The gate clanged shut behind us. Always gave me a shiver when I heard that cold sound as the guard reset the lock. Without waiting, I started down the corridor to the visitor's enclosure when a hand clamped my shoulder.

"This way," the guard said.

"Where we going?"

"Warden's office," he muttered and buttoned up. I shrugged and gave Birdie a look.

The guard led me down a series of corridors then up some metal steps toward the newer wing. The other staircases had shifted or crumbled accentuating the Don's medieval atmosphere. This particular block could have been situated in any office building in the city. We climbed the stairs and the guard huffed and puffed as we made our way up. When we got to the top, his face glowed red and shiny.

"That's almost work," he said.

I smiled at him but didn't answer because I felt the same way. Before long, we found ourselves before a wooden door with a small glass window and the appropriate gold leaf lettering that read, Warden's Office. The guard opened the door without knocking and we found ourselves in an anteroom with a desk, a telephone, a typewriter and a stack of neatly placed files still in their folders. A secretary's station without the secretary. On the far side, stood another door without a window.

The guard crossed over and knocked. There came a guttural response and the door opened. The guard stood aside and nodded me through. He didn't follow. The door closed behind me. It was a large office and spacious with a bank of windows that overlooked the meager exercise yard below. A large desk made of shellacked pine that shone pale yellow in the light had been set on the opposite side of the room facing the door.

In the high-backed leather swivel chair sat Jake Gold, my old man, looking smug and pleased. I glanced around. Instead of the warden, there sat Tobin and his boys. I gave Blotchy Face a hard look and a grin and felt pretty happy to see that his nose stayed swollen and his eyes black. One of his front teeth had chipped. He wouldn't catch my eye. That made me even happier.

"Here we are again, Mr. Gold," Tobin said in a sharp tone and I shifted my gaze. He wanted me to know he saw himself in charge.

"So it would seem, Inspector."

"Surprised to see us here?"

"Maybe a little."

I glanced at Jake. No cuffs or shackles that I could see. In fact, he looked relaxed and at home. He reinforced that impression when he dug into the warden's cigarette box, put one to his lips and lit up with the warden's silver desk lighter.

"Your father is helping us with an investigation," Tobin said. "We're moving him out of the Don but he wanted to see you first."

"What investigation?"

Tobin shook his sleek head. I could see the braces tight against the pressed white shirt underneath his suit coat. Today, he wore sober-looking charcoal, almost funereal.

"Not at liberty to say," he replied. He glanced at his watch. "We haven't got much time."

"I want to speak to my son," rasped Jake. And before Tobin could open up, Jake added, "Alone."

Tobin pursed his lips and brooded for a second. I could tell because he knit his brows together like a spinster at a quilting bee.

"Five minutes," he said. "We'll be right outside."

"Don't worry," Jake laughed, breathing smoke. "I ain't gonna throw myself through the window."

"Mind you don't," Tobin said and yanked open the door then jerked his head. Obediently, the three officers followed. Just as he cleared the doorway, Blotchy Face gave me a hooded glance. I held it without blinking until the door slammed shut.

"You give him that nose and shiner?" Jake asked.

"What's it to you?"

Jake shrugged. "Nothing. But I've seen hatred plenty and that guy's got it in for you. I'd watch my step."

"You're giving me advice now? A little fatherly guidance?"

Jake leaned back in the chair and took another pull. "Yeah, yeah. Sing from another song sheet, will ya?"

I yanked out the chair opposite the desk and sat down. I shook out a Sweet Cap and fired it up. "Okay," I said. "You wanted me here and I'm here."

"I told you I wasn't gonna do hard time," he said.

"Yeah, you told me. You're cooperating with the feds. What are you giving them that makes it worth their while?"

Jake smiled shaking his head. "Sorry boychick. That's between me and Tobin."

"How do you know he won't kick you loose when you give him what he wants?"

"You just leave that to me. Stupid, I'm not. I know how to play the game."

"Right. The one that got you here in the first place. That went well."

Jake shrugged. "Everyone makes mistakes. We're all human, even you."

"Sure." Suddenly, I was tired of playing games and Tobin had given us a short leash. "You said something about the girl."

"Yeah, that's right. Before I tell you, I need you to do something for me first."

I should have known. There was always a debt to be paid with Jake.

"What," I spat.

He enjoyed my discomfort. So he told me what I needed to do. I didn't like it but I agreed. Under the circumstances.

"Give," I said.

"Okay, boychick. I'll have to trust that you'll hold up your end of the deal."

"I said I'd do it," I replied through gritted teeth.

Jake nodded. "I know you will. That was something I could always count on. Good as his word. Mister reliable, that's you."

"You were saying?"

"John Fat Gai has these rolling card games all over Chinatown..."

"Uh-huh."

"You think that nobody knows about them?"

"And so?"

"How do you think they keep going without getting busted every night?"

"John's got juice, everybody knows that."

Jake looked up at the ceiling. "Now he thinks he knows everything. What kind of juice?"

"Whatever it takes," I said. "Politicians, ward bosses, commissioners..."

"And cops," Jake added.

"Hardly a surprise, so?"

"One of the cops has her."

"What?" He surprised me. "That doesn't make any sense. If a cop had her and he was working for John, then John would know."

"I know," Jake said. "That's what's strange, boychick. You don't hold out on a guy like John Fat Gai and live."

"What cop?" I asked.

Jake shrugged, doing his three stooges impression. "That I don't know."

"Could be anybody."

"He was in the service."

"So were a lot of guys," I replied.

"You wanted something, now you've got it," Jake said.

"There's one more thing," I said.

"What's that?" Jake thought he had it all covered.

"It's Eli," I said.

"What about him?"

"He's in hock to John. That's why we're looking for the girl, to square it with him. I gave Eli some dough and told him to skip town. Either he didn't make it or he came back. John's got him now and he's given me and Birdie three days to find the girl or else."

"Or else what?" Jake asked.

"Use your imagination," I said. "John doesn't make idle threats."

I have to admit, I almost never saw Jake rattled but his face looked puffier and the dark circles under his eyes deepened. His sun-deprived complexion went waxy. He could have had his own consignment at Madame Tussaud's. Eli had been made in his image and Jake cared about him. "Then what are you wasting your time for?" Jake demanded. "Get out there and look for her."

"You're a sorry sack of shit," I said as Tobin opened the door.

"Time," he barked. Jake walked around the desk. "We have to put the cuffs on," Tobin said.

Jake held out his hands. Tobin took a set off his belt and snapped them around Jake's wrists. I watched all of this like I witnessed some stranger being collared.

Jake nodded. "I'll see you when I see you," he said. "So long, boychick. Don't forget what I said."

I thought about asking where they were taking him but decided I didn't really care. He'd made his pact. But I did think about what he'd told me. If some cop had the girl and her baby, that could be the reason John hadn't found her yet. That made sense at least. But why? Then I began to wonder again about the baby and who'd sired it.

The gunbull stuck his head in the doorway.

"Come on," he said. "I've got to take you out." I mashed the cigarette into the warden's ample cut glass ashtray.

"Sure," I said. "You know the way."

I followed the guard into the corridor. He turned and locked the outer door to the Warden's inner sanctum. The guard rattled the knob behind him. He turned and started down the corridor.

Just at the stairwell, I heard a commotion and heavy feet on the stairs. The alarm sounded. I recognized it—a riot had broken out on the cell block. I couldn't see past the guard. Inside the Don jail, guards weren't armed. They carried nightsticks and restraints. The outside guys watching the yard carried rifles and pistols and always patrolled in groups.

The guard fell backwards into me. I crashed into the wall. When I looked up, I saw three inmates standing over us. One had scars all over his face including a thin line that ran from the corner of his right eye down to his cheek. It made that side of his face look droopy. He had short grey hair shaved at the sides and blue eyes so pale they looked almost white. He had a powerful build with broad shoulders and large hands. He looked agitated. His companions looked hopped up and crazed. One was tall and skinny with a dark complexion and wiry hair. His skin tone said mulatto. The other one stood short and thick with red hair, a blunt nose and freckles on his hands. I could see a tattoo etched into his wrist under the prison issue denim shirt. From the corridor, I heard yells and banging.

"Where's the warden?" Pale Eyes snarled and grabbed the guard by his collar bunching up the material until his throat bulged. In his other hand, I saw a shiv, a shaved down fork probably smuggled from the canteen. He pressed it hard under the guard's chin. A trickle of blood ran down his neck.

"Not here," the guard rasped. "Out of the building."

"Bullshit," Pale Eyes spat. "Where's he at?"

I got to my feet slowly. "He's telling the truth. The warden's not at home. You're wasting your time."

Pale Eyes turned to me. "Who the hell are you?"

"Just a visitor."

"You were in the warden's office."

"You're barking up the wrong tree here, pal. Better end it before it goes all wrong. You'll never get out of here. The building will be locked down by now," I said. Just trying to be helpful.

The skinny one moved in my direction. "Shut up," he yelled. "You just shut up."

"Easy there Amos, I'm just telling it like it is," I said.

"Well, I don't want to hear it," the skinny inmate yelled. "Red. Tell him I don't have to listen to him. And I ain't no Amos neither."

"That's right, mister," Red said quietly. "He don't have to listen to you if he don't want to."

I nodded. "Swell. So don't listen. I'm just talking to myself anyway."

"Grab the keys," Pale Eyes said. Quickly, Red stripped the keys from the guard's belt. He tossed them to Pale Eyes who caught them in his other hand. He hauled the guard upright and pushed him ahead. "We'll just take a quick look," he said. "Unlock it." And gave him a shove for good measure.

"All right, all right," the guard muttered. He fumbled with the keys, found the one he was looking for and opened the door. We were shoved through first. Red slammed the door behind us and locked it.

'Amos' went ape shit. He ran over to the secretary's desk and swiped it clean. He swept all the files, trays, lamp, family photographs, on to the floor in a heap. Then he jumped up on the desk and did this crazy sort of spastic jig, kicking out his heels, pumping his knees up high. A skinny barn dancer fueled by some kind of speedball. We were then treated to Amos unzipping his trousers and pissing in all directions.

"Jesus," yelled the guard.

'Amos' giggled. "That feels a lot better," he smirked.

"What's 'Amos' in for?" I asked.

Red snorted. "Public indecency."

"What a surprise," I replied. "Well done, Amos."

'Amos' stopped and stared at me malevolently, still flying low. "My name ain't Amos. It's Earl. Earl. You got that?" He jumped down off the desk, awkwardly, one hand holding his pants up, spittle flying from his lips. "Earl…Earl…Earl…," he cried, like a whiny kid. He raised a shiv as he came. I kicked him in the nuts and he crumpled to the floor. When he started to struggle up, I punched him in the temple and he went down for the count.

Red had an amused expression on his face. Pale Eyes just nodded.

"That shut him up," was all he said. Then motioned to the warden's office. "Let's take a look."

Me and the guard went first with Red and Pale Eyes right behind us.

"Siddown," Red said and pushed us each into a chair. Pale Eyes went around behind the desk yanking out drawers. There came a satisfied chuckle as he lifted a half full bottle of single Malt above his head.

"Now, that's more like it," he said.

Eagerly, he spun the top off the bottle and put it to his lips taking gigantic gulps. Then he breathed a deep sigh and handed the bottle to Red. He took a long pull. They'd emptied half of the contents.

Red wiped his lips and smiled lazily. He looked over at the guard. Slowly, he put the bottle down. "Now for some fun," he said and approached.

"I ain't got nothing against you," the guard said. His knees practically knocked together.

"Well, I got something against you," Red replied.

"What? I don't even know you."

"Doesn't matter. You're a bull, aren't you? That's good enough for me. You're all scum."

In a measured way, he hit the guard a good shot in the jaw and gave him another one. The guard didn't resist.

"Come on, stand up," Red demanded and hauled him to his feet and as he did, hit him low in the abdomen. The guard crumpled over. Red held him up and hit him again and again pounding his clenched fist like a sledgehammer. The guard's nose oozed blood and his right eye swelled shut. Red stepped back and snapped a hook into his jaw putting his weight into it. The guard staggered back and fell into the chair unconscious. Red massaged the knuckles of his right hand. He had a satisfied look on his face like he'd done a good day's work.

"Mind if I smoke?" I asked.

Pale Eyes wiped his mouth in surprise and looked at me. He snapped his fingers. I handed him the pack of cigarettes and my lighter. He shook one out and lit it holding the smoke in his lungs for a long time. He pulled out the warden's swivel chair and sat in it contentedly. He tossed the fags and lighter back to me. I eyed the heavy glass ashtray. It was the only weapon within reach.

"You know that there must be 30 armed guards out in the corridor by now."

Pale Eyes nodded like it was a foregone conclusion.

"We know," Red said.

He came across, dug his hand into the warden's cigarette box and helped himself to a dozen smokes. I held the lighter up but he slapped my hand away grabbing the warden's silver lighter instead. He bent his head over the flame.

"So why the riot?" I asked.

Pale Eyes looked at me. "The guys needed to let off steam. You don't know what it's like being cooped up down there. Guys blow up all the time. This time it's a little better organized."

"But you'll just get put back in the can and they'll add to your time, so what's the point?"

"It's worth it," said Red, taking another pull from the bottle. "Even for a few minutes of freedom, it's worth it."

I shrugged. "If you say so."

"We do say so," Pale Eyes snarled.

"What're you boys in for?" I asked.

"Armed robbery," Red replied and smirked.

"Yeah? Who'd you rob?"

"They say we robbed a few banks and some trust companies but personally, I think the case against us is weak." Obviously, he thought his legal skills and experience outpointed the real deal.

"Oh yeah? Why's that?" I asked always interested in the habitual con's point of view.

"No witnesses," Red replied

"No witnesses left," Pale Eyes added and laughed. They both laughed at that one. I think they and their pals must have shot some dope down there, something that got them so hopped up they couldn't think straight.

The telephone on the desk jangled.

"Answer it," I said.

Pale Eyes and Red stared at the phone. Pale Eyes licked his lips then snatched it up.

"Yeah?"

He listened for a long moment and held the receiver away from his ear staring at it.

"It's for you," he said holding it out to me.

I took the receiver from him. "Uh-huh?" I said.

"Having fun yet?" Birdie asked.

"Not really." The others watched me intently. Pale Eyes seemed suspicious.

"I'll be up in a minute," Birdie said and hung up.

I handed the receiver back to Pale Eyes who stared at me. "Wrong number," I said.

I thought he'd snarl and spit smoke the way his face contorted. He stepped back from the warden's desk. The guard lolled in the chair moaning. He looked like he might roll off onto the floor. Pale Eyes and Red watched me like I was the most fascinating thing they'd seen in years. I was flattered.

We heard heavy footsteps in the outer office then a fierce knock on the warden's door. Red and Pale Eyes froze. The knocking resumed, fiercer this time. Pale Eyes jerked his head and Red took a few hesitant steps toward the door. Then took a few more. When he was about four feet from the knob, the hinges exploded. The door flew inward slapping Red in the chest. He staggered backward. I grabbed at the thick cut glass ashtray and swatted Pale Eyes in the jaw with it. He went down under the desk, out cold. I looked up as Birdie, with fire and brimstone in his eyes, trod over the smashed door, picked Red up and hurled him against the wall. Red bounced off the wood paneling, crumpled into a heap and lay still. The guard moaned again.

"Took you long enough," I said.

"Ten flights of stairs," Birdie said. "And a few bodies in between."

"What's happening out there?"

"It's a hoo-ha," he replied.

"Hoo-ha?"

Birdie nodded. "They've got it under control now."

I looked over, saw that Red was still out. I stood up and peered down at Pale Eyes. He'd have a nice bruise down his jawline, maybe even lose a few teeth.

"Looks like our work is done here," I said. Birdie grinned.

We both looked up as Tobin blew in. His face shiny with sweat, his tie askew and the charcoal suit jacket torn at the elbow. "Where is he?" he demanded.

"Where is who?" I asked.

Tobin ignored the scene in the office. Instead, he looked like his face might blow apart. He marched over to me and snatched at my lapels. I stepped back grabbing both his hands and twisting.

"What are you playing at?" he hissed.

"I don't know what the hell you're talking about, Tobin. Why don't you fill me in?"

"Your old man," he said.

"What about him?"

"He's gone."

"But he left with you in cuffs and he's not exactly Speedy Gonzalez."

I let go of his hands. He massaged his wrists. "Tell me what happened."

Tobin stared at me and there wasn't a lot of warmth in his look.

"Just as we were about to go through the control gate, a bunch of cons came out of nowhere. They overpowered the guards. We were unarmed. We'd left our weapons on the other side. I was hit over the head and went down. When I came to, Jake had disappeared. I found the cuffs lying on the floor. One of the guards saw him get into a jalopy and speed off."

I gave a low whistle. "Impressive. Even for Jake."

"If you know something…" he said in a low tone.

"Don't threaten me, Tobin. This is as much of a surprise to me as it is to you. I had no idea what Jake was planning or if he was planning anything. Before my uncle's funeral, I hadn't spoken to him in almost 10 years. We're not close. Never were, not even when I was a kid."

"He's practically a dead man now."

"Maybe you should tell me about this case he's helping you with."

Tobin smiled thinly. "No can do."

I smiled back. "Well, good luck with it. Time for us to ride. See you around, Tobin."

"Count on it, Gold. I'll be watching you like a hawk."

"The dirty piece of chewing gum stuck to the sole of my shoe."

"That's right."

"Tootles," I said. "This guy needs a doctor." Right on cue, the guard moaned. Birdie and I waded through the debris out to the corridor and the exit.

34

The sun still shone out in the parking lot even if the atmosphere remained dark inside my soul. We'd gone down the stairs and out the doors. At the control gate, the guards stared at me with contempt and suspicion but didn't say anything. I supposed Birdie's presence kept things civil.

When we reached the Chevy, I shrugged off my suit jacket and lay it across the back seat. I pulled at my tie working it away from the collar, then rolled up each sleeve. I got in the passenger side. Birdie drove us out carefully, turning on to River Street heading toward Queen just as a dozen patrol cars, sirens blaring, screeched toward the entrance. I looked at the rubbies and the pawnshops and the greasy spoons as we drove away from the mayhem. A group of guys stood on the corner, shucking and jiving, passing a bottle in a brown paper bag between them. Just another productive day.

"What the hell is Jake up to?" I asked. Birdie smiled and shrugged. It was the best answer under the circumstances.

"Where to?" he asked.

"The girl," I replied. "What's her name, the other one who was in the car that night. Let's talk to her."

"Gayle Sorenson."

"That's the one. Maybe she's knows something about Henry. Maybe he's hiding in her bedroom closet."

I'd run out of ideas about where to look for the Chinese girl. If Jake's information turned out to be legit, then it meant talking to some of my old pals on the force, not a happy prospect. Not when I'd be looking at them as suspects.

Gayle Sorenson's parents lived in Forest Hill, on the swanky side, north of St. Clair Avenue, west of Spadina Road adjacent to the park. Vesta Drive, number four. The street was leafy and tranquil, a short block up from the Village, an enclave for the wealthy where the prices for everyday items doubled up anywhere else in the city.

Number four backed on to the park. If you didn't know any better, you'd think you'd stepped into the countryside even though the hurly burly of the city boiled over less than a mile away. That's what money bought–the hushed sense of calm and quiet. That and a three-storey, Gothic-inspired monster with mullioned windows and a faux spire in dark stone topped by a grey-slated roof. I expected Bela Lugosi to slide down the drainpipe.

We left the Chevy at the curb and strode up to the heavy oak door. It had a knocker the size of Arizona. I leaned heavily on the bell and heard chimes ringing distantly inside. They should have a butler named Igor. Instead, the door was opened revealing a querulous, gnome-like servant who must have come with the house when it was built. It surprised me that she managed the heft of the door given her age and size. She wore a black maid's uniform and a white cap that had slipped low on her forehead. Her pale, damp skin glistened. She levitated a pointy nose and aimed it first at me then at Birdie where it lingered, longer than politeness allowed. I flinched but Birdie didn't. He let it roll over him. Somewhere in the recess of her brain, she decided to give us the benefit of the doubt. We wore decent suits and didn't look like hobos or encyclopedia salesmen. We might have been proselytizers of one ilk or another but she seemed willing to find out.

"Yes?" she asked in a sharp tone.

"Is Mrs. Sorenson in?" I asked politely.

"What is the nature of your business?"

"It's personal." I reached into my side pocket and removed a card. I held it out to her. "We just need to speak to her daughter, Gayle, for a few moments."

The elderly maid's eyebrows went up and stayed there. She examined the card with disdain, sniffed loudly and pursed her lips.

"Step inside," she commanded. She shut the door heavily after us. "Wait here," she said.

She scurried off toward the inner sanctum. She had five directions from which to choose. She lurched to the right. We stood in a large marble foyer having stepped through a small anteroom. That's why the chimes sounded far away. The second door muffled the sound. To our left, an expansive oak stairway swept upward to a second floor. I glanced at the mahogany wainscoting and wall panels. The house felt solid, immovable. Light filtered weakly through the stained glass of the second door we'd stepped through. Harder to see the dust on the tabletops, I reasoned. The maid came back wearing a disapproving look.

'This way," she warbled.

Mrs. Sorenson looked to be a well-preserved woman in her late forties with peroxide white-blond hair done up in a beehive that could have shattered granite. She perched on a leather settee that might have comfortably seated a dozen obese guests at a health farm, stroking a white Angora cat with fur so long it made my nose itch. The feline stared unblinkingly out of luminous green eyes.

She wore a pearl-grey blouse and matching skirt and pumps. Around her neck I spotted a fashionably small diamond necklace on loan from the Tower of London. The rock she wore on her wedding finger must have been four or five carats. It surprised me she could lift her hand. The maid walked us into the sitting room then turned on her heel and marched out without saying a word. Mrs. Sorenson had an unruffled expression and stared at us unabashedly as if we were two specimens in a lab dish she scrutinized under her microscope. The eyes were blue and sharp.

"Mrs. Sorenson?"

"What do you want with my daughter?" she asked. Her voice purred low and throaty with an edge to it.

"We're investigating a disappearance," I replied. "We think your daughter may have some information that is relevant to the case."

Mrs. Sorenson turned her gaze on Birdie, following the length of him up and down without any embarrassment or thought that it might be rude, as if it was her right. He reflected it back at her and after a long moment, she glanced away.

"Whose disappearance?" she asked.

"A man called Henry Turner," I said. "He was the Foster's former chauffeur."

At the mention of his name, Mrs. Sorenson flinched. Once. "Did you know him, Mrs. Sorenson?"

"On whose authority are you here?" she said quietly but she'd injected some steel in it.

"We're acting on behalf of Henry Turner's mother."

Her hand halted over the cat's fluffy mane.

"His mother?" she repeated as if it had just occurred to her for the first time he might have had one.

"That's right. Mrs. Turner asked us to find her son. Did you know Henry Turner, Mrs. Sorenson?"

Suddenly, there came a screech and the cat sprang off her lap and scooted away. Mrs. Sorenson held the meaty part of her hand where the cat had bitten her. Blood dripped on to the white carpet. I glanced at Birdie who gave an almost invisible shrug. I strode forward, removed my handkerchief from my suit jacket, took her hand and bound it up.

"You're bleeding, Mrs. Sorenson."

She had a dazed, unfocused expression on her face. "What?"

"Your hand." Maybe she took happy pills for luncheon.

She looked down distractedly.

"Oh yes. It's nothing. Thank you." And there appeared the briefest of smiles, as if it was something she rarely did, if ever.

I stepped back. "May we speak with your daughter, please, Mrs. Sorenson."

She held her hand wrapped in my handkerchief in her lap. "I'm afraid that is impossible, Mr., Mr...."

"Gold. Mo Gold and my associate, Arthur Birdwell."

"Yes, well. Gayle is ill. She can't see anyone. You'd get nothing out of her, in any case. She hasn't talked to us in years."

"Do you mean, you are estranged?"

Mrs. Sorenson looked at me with a hysterical expression.

"If only," she cried. "If only...no...I mean, she hasn't said a word to anyone in almost eight years. She's had a nervous breakdown, locked away in her own mind all this time. We don't know what goes on in her head, Mr. Gold. We can't make sense of it. Not at all."

"I'm sorry." I might not have said it at all for the lack of reaction. "But you knew Henry Turner?"

She nodded slowly. "Oh, he drove me once or twice when I went out with Mildred–Mrs. Foster–but that's all. I never really spoke to him, you see. He was just the driver, nothing more. I never took much notice really. I know how that sounds...." She glanced at Birdie then looked quickly away. I thought to myself, invisible.

"You said that it's been eight years since your daughter's breakdown?" Birdie boomed. His words caused her to flinch like she was being slapped with every syllable.

"Yes, that's right."

"About the time Henry Turner disappeared," he said.

"I guess...yes..."

"Don't you think it's strange that Henry disappeared around the same time as your daughter's illness occurred?"

"Not really," she replied. "I can't see how the two are connected. They never had anything to do with each other. It's unthinkable. No," she said. "Impossible."

"Do you know what caused the breakdown, Mrs. Sorenson?" I asked.

She stared at me wide-eyed then shook her head.

"But you have some suspicion, surely? We know that Gayle used to go out with friends, one of whom was Allison Foster and two boys, Rance Callaway and Harvey Troyer. Do you remember that?"

"I remember Harvey Troyer. He was well-bred with lovely manners. I don't know this Callaway person, I never met him. I haven't heard of the family."

Suddenly, I wanted to slap her. To smack the snobbery out of her.

"Well, you wouldn't. Not quite the same class as Harvey, Gayle and Allison. They used to go to a club, Mrs. Sorenson, a place down by the docks called Blackstone's, I believe. Have you heard of it?"

"Club?" she murmured, as if it was all a little too much to bear.

"Yes, some kind of nightclub. Did Gayle ever mention it to you?"

She laughed then, a kind of frenzied giggle.

"Mention it? A teenaged girl telling her mother anything? Are you serious?"

"Still, you must have known or suspected. We believe it is all connected, Mrs. Sorenson. Something happened. Don't you want to know?" I raised my voice without realizing and she shrank back into the cushions of the settee.

At that moment, Gayle made her appearance. Or rather, she danced into the room in ballet slippers, a leotard, a tutu and a silk pajama top. She pirouetted across the room. Her mother couldn't look at her. We heard the indiscriminate humming and the girl whirled around so quickly and wildly, she crashed into the far wall and fell to the floor.

Her mother jumped up and went to her. The girl sobbed and laughed all at once then moaned like a ghost. As her mother approached, she jumped up and skittered away. She stopped in front of Birdie and stared up at him then began to scream hysterically. Blood-curdling screams that gave me the heebie-jeebies, enough to make your hair stand up and flesh crawl.

Mrs. Sorenson wrapped her arms around her daughter from behind in a straitjacket effect and dragged her backward, still screaming, to the couch. Just as she did the cat, Mrs. Sorenson took the girl's head in her lap and stroked her hair, murmuring to her, shushing her, wiping away the girl's hysteria. After a long moment, Gayle quieted down to gulps of air and whimpers. Mrs. Sorenson looked at us with an expression of resignation and deep, undiluted pain.

"I'll have your handkerchief laundered and sent on to you, Mr. Gold. Good day to you. Good day to both of you." She turned her attention back to her broken daughter and forgot we were there.

"Creepy," Birdie said as we strode down the walk.

"Brother, you can say that again." I lit a Sweet Cap and inhaled it like it was the first fresh air I'd sucked into my lungs in a long, long time. "Don't say it," I said.

Birdie shook his head but he smiled.

Back in the Chevy, I turned to him and said, "What have we got?"

"Not much, man, not much."

And it was true. Henry was still missing. I could still see the red blood on the sparkling white carpet.

35

That night, I sat on my sofa with a bottle of Johnny Walker, a glass and the radio for company. I let Birdie be, doing whatever he did when he went on his own. So the Sorenson girl scrambled her marbles. Something had to fracture her personality. I'd seen guys in the war who'd broken down like that. Nerves shattered into little pieces. What or who had happened to her? I felt restless and edgy, couldn't get settled. Ying's sister hid out there somewhere. I thought about taking another slug but set the bottle aside. Where to go from here? And then I had a thought. Occasionally, it happened.

He wouldn't be happy but sometimes it's safer and more discreet to talk to a cop at home than out in the street. I grabbed my coat, my piece and my keys and headed down to the back lot. I fired up the Chevy and nosed her down the alley. King Street kept fairly quiet that time of night, getting on toward eleven-thirty.

As I edged out into the street and swung east, I noticed a car with its lights dimmed, pull away from the curb. Looked like a Buick Roadmaster but it hung back far enough to make it difficult for me to see in the rearview. That would be John's boys keeping tabs on me. Another pair of headlights came on facing the opposite direction just as I approached Bathurst Street. The car, a large, dark sedan, possibly a Ford Fairlane, pulled a U-turn and dropped comfortably in behind the Buick. No one seemed to be in a rush. Everyone relaxed and took their time.

I figured the dark sedan belonged to Tobin. Everybody present and accounted for. I let them tail me as far as Yonge Street. I turned south on Yonge and just as the light changed to red at Wellington, I jack-rabbited through the light leaping west. I turned sharply into an alley-way, pulled over in front of a dumpster and killed the lights keeping my eyes on the side view mirror. The Buick and the dark sedan sped past. I gave them a moment figuring they'd double back. I spotted the Buick go by retracing its route on King. The dark sedan sniffed at its heels. I eased the Chevy up the alley and took a good look in both directions up and down King Street. Then turned west on King moving quickly away from the centre of town.

I rapped on the screen door. A moment later the porch light came on.

Callaway glared at me through the screen.

"I'm in a bit of a jam," I said.

"What else is new?" he replied.

"Can I come in?"

A voice I knew belonged to Florence, his wife, sounded behind him. He turned and barked something then beckoned me in. He took a quick look up and down the street as he held the screen door open.

"Hurry up," he said. "We got mosquitoes in this part of town."

"Don't worry," I replied. "I didn't bring any company."

Callaway closed the door and switched off the porch light.

"Better be good, Mo. Drink?"

"No thanks."

We stood on the threshold of a small living room stuffed with rumpled sofas and chairs. A crumpled newspaper had fallen on the graying carpet. I smelled fried fish. I followed his burly back past the living room, through the compact dining room to the rear of the house and the den. Callaway's private sanctuary, I surmised by the state of it. Hadn't been dusted in months and carried the fuggy smell of cigars and sweaty socks.

"When's the last time you opened a window in here?" I asked.

"Remember, I didn't invite you over," he said and gestured to a cracked leather chair. He plunked his bulk down on to the love seat.

I pulled out the pack of Sweet Caps and held them out with a quizzical look. Callaway nodded. He reached down to the floor and tossed me an ashtray. Fortunately, it had been cleaned.

"What gives?" he asked.

I took a good hit on the fag and quickly summed up what we'd found in terms of the Chinese girl–nothing basically. I told him Jake's tidbit and Callaway flinched. Then I mentioned Eli and his particular circumstances. "You sure you want to stay part of that family," Callaway said when I'd finished.

I shrugged. "Hard to divorce your family. Jake, I got no time for but my kid brother, well, he's a schmuck but for some reason he thinks he's the old man. He's not a bad guy, just reckless and stupid. Anyway, if what Jake says has any truth in it, then the only way to find the girl is to find the cop who has her."

"So you came to me thinking I would finger the guy for you?"

"Ying was your snitch. That means, you have a connection, almost a responsibility to the guy. I know what that means."

Callaway sighed and ran thick fingers through his hair digging the nails into his scalp. "Yeah. Some guys might feel that way." He paused, chewing something over in his own mind. "I been looking at some old case files," he said. "Trying to cross reference the ones connected to John and the cops who worked them. See which names kept cropping up. Maybe then I can find the guy who ratted out Ying."

"Any luck?" Jake mentioned that John Fat Gai had his hooks into the force and given the pay scale, it wasn't a surprise some guys would be interested in a little extra dough for dropping a hint or making a phone call. You don't get rich if you're an honest cop.

"That's the problem," Callaway said. "Too many names. If I'm right then half the precinct is on the pad, one way or the other."

"So what have you got?" I asked.

"Could be any one of about eight guys or maybe all of them. I don't know," Callaway said. "There's no evidence, at least, not yet. I can't do this on my own. If the Super found out, he'd have my badge."

"His name's not there, is it?"

Callaway shook his head. "Not yet," he smirked.

"Let me and Birdie take a look. We'll keep you out of it so there's no blow back."

"I don't know," Callaway said.

"Listen, I've got three days until we find Eli's body parts or the girl. I'd rather it was the girl."

"John won't let her live, you know that," Callaway said.

"We'll cross that bridge when we come to it. First things first. Gotta find her or..."

"Or what?"

I looked at him carefully. "You don't want to know," I said. "I can't let John hurt him. You know what that could mean."

"The War's over," Callaway said quietly.

"Maybe it is and maybe it isn't," I replied. "Let's see what you've got."

Callaway sighed again but finally nodded. His knees cracked when he stood up. He went over to the sideboard, took out a small key ring, found the one he wanted and unlocked it. A stack of files lay where there should have been bottles. He shifted the files, dropped them on to the coffee table in front of me and shut the sideboard back up.

"I hear your old man disappeared again. Took Tobin by surprise." He smiled thinly.

"Yeah, Jake is nimbler than I thought. Say, what's the case Tobin's working on? What's Jake go to do with it?"

Callaway's face sprung open in surprise. "You mean you don't know?" I shook my head. "Jake is Tobin's star witness. He's supposed to be testifying for the Crown against John Fat Gai in a racketeering case. Gambling and loan sharking plus some prostitution. Your old man fronted one of the joints for John, one that catered to a white clientele and rumour has it they split the profits between them. Then Jake got pinched on the manslaughter beef and the Crown wants to put him away forever but your old man cut a deal."

"Well, Jake kept his business to himself. I didn't want to know about it." I thought for a moment. "Swell. With Jake and the girl missing, Eli is as good as dead. He probably thinks he can save the day, the schmuck."

"That's only if you look at the bright side," Callaway said and smiled grimly.

I started leafing through the first file. "One of those joints John ran. There wasn't one down by the docks called Blackstones by any chance, was there?"

Callaway grunted in surprise. "Was and is. The place is still open for business."

"Where is it?"

Callaway shrugged. "Not sure. Down by the waterfront, off Cherry Street somewhere."

I wanted to find this place–Blackstones and I wanted to find it pronto. We spent a couple of hours going through the case files. As I went through them, I made notes to take away and mull over. Then it hit me. I snapped my fingers. I knew who could take me to Blackstones.

I fired up the Chevy and found my way to Caledonia and the Callaway kid's house. He pulled away from the curb as I drove up, manhandling a clapped out Edsel that belched black smoke every time he changed gears. I turned around and followed him. He drove west on St. Clair then hooked a left on Old Weston Road heading south toward the industrial section of the west end. As he continued, the houses became smaller and meaner and run down–they turned into slums, each decaying building had a sad, sick air. Gradually, the houses cleared out taken over by factories.

The traffic had faded now. I kept a block back and dimmed the headlights. Rance turned down a laneway and I rolled to a stop. I slid out of the Chevy and clicked the door shut and locked it. I headed down the laneway keeping to the shadows. I unholstered the snub .38 I'd brought along for company. I didn't like laneways particularly because bad things often happened in them, especially late at night. I crept as close as I could.

A truck sat hunched in the laneway. The back doors had been lifted off and set along the side of the warehouse while the canvas tarp had been rolled back a bit. It was a warm night and I could imagine the inside of the back of the truck must have been sweltering. Nothing like canvas to keep the air close and dank.

Birdie and I lived in a canvas tent for almost three years and nothing about it was enjoyable. In the winter, you froze your nuts, in the wet, you slept in sop and in the summer you couldn't breath and the canvas stank. Only in the cool, clear weather of autumn were the damn things tolerable. And that didn't last long before conditions turned miserable again. Army life. Couldn't beat it, man.

I heard the murmur of voices and some smothered laughter. Rance and another guy hauled cases and loaded them on to the truck. The loading door had been lifted and the cases stood over six feet high and plenty deep. I didn't see the Edsel so the Callaway kid must have stashed it somewhere. As the kid hefted a wooden case onto the truck's tail, I heard the pinging of glass and I knew what they were loading.

While Rance could only manage one case at a time, his buddy carried two. And that's because he was a big sonofabitch and he looked damned familiar. I wracked my brain staring at them through the gloom. I recalled the low whistling as he came up his walk carrying a lunch pail jammed under his arm, and remembered the lupine features and the wary eyes. I remembered the fear in her voice when she spotted him and how quickly she fled inside the house. I saw the grey yard and the sagging line of laundry. A big guy with a hairy chest and a cruel expression. I pegged him now–Steve O'Rourke–Rochelle Dodson's man.

I zipped across the lane to the other side so I could get a better angle and saw a lot of cases had yet to be loaded. In fact, Rance climbed into the back of the truck and began shifting them further to the front to make more room. That told me they'd be a while.

I remembered a phone box about half a block away and slipped into the darkness to make a call. Walnut 4-2134. Birdie's contact number. I dropped a dime into the slot. I told the guy on the other end where Birdie should have the cab drop him off and how far he had to walk in. I checked my watch and suggested he tell Birdie to make it snappy. The guy on the line said, okay, he'd pass the message along and the line went dead. I hung up and went back to my listening post. Well, well. Steve O'Rourke. This got better and better.

Just about 30 minutes later, I felt his presence before I saw him. Birdie moved like a cat, sure-footed and silent. By the time I looked over my shoulder, he had crouched down beside me.

"Quick enough for you," he whispered.

"Sure," I said. "Didn't think you'd want to miss out on this. Take a look." Birdie peered into the gloom for a long moment.

"Who's that with the kid," he muttered. He could only see O'Rourke from the back as he handed up wooden cases to Callaway's nephew. The kid grunted each time he hefted one, bending at the waist as he disappeared toward the front of the truck. Finally, the penny dropped.

"Sweet Jesus," he intoned. "God is merciful, merciful indeed."

I almost expected him to break out in a round of hand clapping and hymns but he didn't. "You see," I said. "Good things happen to those who wait."

"Yes, indeed."

We watched them hefting cases for another hour. Rance huffed and sweated but O'Rourke merely mopped his Neanderthal brow with a kerchief he'd tied loosely around his neck. He'd stripped down to a singlet and I could see the muscles bunch tightly under his hairy shoulders as he lifted the cases upward. He stopped and lit a fag but otherwise kept moving like a machine with a full tank of oil. As stevedores go, he made a good one. I wondered about the destination of the cargo.

Finally, O'Rourke nodded and Rance jumped down from the tailgate. His face and neck ringed with grime and sweat. O'Rourke lifted the doors and slotted them into the back of the truck ramming the pins home. From his pants pocket, he drew out a padlock and clipped it through the pins to hold them in place. Those old GM trucks bounced a lot. I remembered from the War, the doors could shoot right out of the slots and hit the ground behind. Then the cargo was fair game. Clearly, O'Rourke didn't take any chances.

The kid lit up and went around to the passenger side of the tarp truck. I tugged at Birdie's sleeve and we faded back out of the alley to the Chevy. We got in and I turned the engine over leaving the lights off. I backed out the way I came and parked around the corner with the engine idling. We didn't have to wait long. The truck chugged slowly through the laneway poking its nose out into the street. Its springs had seen better days and with the load it carried, the undercarriage rode halfway down the wheel wells. Not only that but it listed badly to the passenger side. I knew that the maximum speed on a truck like that was maybe 60 miles per hour but with the cargo in the back, O'Rourke would be lucky to get it up to 50 and that would be pushing it. The truck made a right turn and trundled off down the street. I let it go for almost a block before I pulled away from the curb.

"Heading for the lakeshore," Birdie murmured.

"Looks like it."

The truck meandered through city streets before turning down Dufferin Street near the entrance to the Exhibition grounds and gunned it. At least, I heard the engine strain as O'Rourke pushed the pedal but it didn't seem to make much difference. At this rate, he might blow a gasket. We passed the occasional cabby or patrol car. I dropped back as far as I could while still keeping him within eye contact.

I rolled down the window and sniffed.

The water in the harbour resembled a dank, murky oil slick from all the ships and boats that passed through. Yet, every summer, residents flocked to the beaches in the east and west ends and on the islands, parking white bodies on grit, putting their toes in the frigid lake. I smelled the distinct odour of wet rot from driftwood washed up on the shore, dead fish, weeds and surface scum mashed into a sickly sweet perfume. Throw in the barley and hops from the Molson's brewery and the air stoked into an unmistakably potent mix.

We headed east on the Lakeshore passing under the steel and concrete overpass of the Gardiner Expressway. At Parliament, the truck turned right heading closer to the lake. Gulls shrieked over the water. I pulled over and let it go for a moment, watching its taillights fade into the dusk then followed. The air grew thicker here and I rolled the window back up. The truck took a left on a dusty dirt track. I stopped at the corner and shut off the engine. “We’d better go on foot from here,” I said.

We stepped out of the car and closed the doors quietly. Sound carried at night and carried even better over water. Along the dirt track we spotted two rows of low concrete buildings. We kept close to the walls and traversed going from one to the other. I looked for the truck. After the fourth building, I spotted a sign, Warehouse 14. I peeked around a corner and saw the truck backed up to a loading dock. We stood still in the shadows.

“Let’s get a mite closer,” I said. Birdie nodded and we shimmied along until we positioned ourselves opposite the loading area. In front of us sat a wide metal bin for dumping trash. We crouched behind it. It didn’t sound like they wasted any time. I heard low voices and the clinking of glass. More than two voices this time, quite a few more. Then he came around the front of the truck walking slowly, keeping a look out. He cradled a machine gun in his arms casually. As he lit a fag, the flame caught his face. I had pretty good night vision and unless I was sorely mistaken, it appeared to be my good friend from John’s little gang. Birdie nudged me.

“It’s your second best friend,” he hissed. I nodded and grinned. The fact that John seemed mixed up in this didn’t surprise. The surprise came in the form of Callaway’s nephew and O’Rourke being part of it. I didn’t like the thought of having to spill the news to Callaway. He wouldn’t take it well. As for O’Rourke, it just gave Birdie another reason to hate him and he’d plenty of incentive already.

“Let’s go,” I said.

“What?” Birdie was surprised.

“Nothing more we can do here.”

“But…”

“In case you hadn’t noticed,” I said. “They have machine guns.”

“So?”

I sighed. “Our beef isn’t with John on this one. We’ll wait for them back at the other place, okay?”

Birdie thought for a moment. It must have seemed reasonable to him because he nodded. "Cleaner that way," he said.

We drove back the way we came. I parked the car and we waited. After about an hour, I heard the rumble of the truck.

I had parked adjacent to a concrete abutment. The building next to it threw a deep shadow. The truck, noticeably lighter on its springs now, bounced on by. As it did, we got out and strode over just as O'Rourke backed it up to the loading bay. Neither of them noticed us at first. It had been a long night for them, especially after spending the day shifting boxes down at the docks, something I assumed O'Rourke had been doing. I hoped it had tired him out too. O'Rourke stepped out of the truck. The Callaway kid slid out the other side and slammed the door. They had their backs to us as they headed toward the loading bay.

"Hey," I called. Birdie and I walked toward them. O'Rourke turned. Rance poked his head around the front end of the truck.

We moved in a little closer but not too close. O'Rourke and the Callaway kid watched us. Then Rance reached into the rolled sleeve of his T-shirt and pulled out a pack of Export A's. He fired one up.

"Whaddaya want?" he asked.

"Hey, bad grammar, kid. Still no manners, I see," I replied. I could see O'Rourke staring our way and then he focused on Birdie and some light came into his eyes.

"So, you're not salesmen," he said. "I knew it."

"Doesn't give you the right to smack her around," Birdie said.

"Huh?" O'Rourke couldn't believe what he was hearing. "Come again, big man."

Birdie walked up and tapped him hard on the chest with his forefinger. "A man," he began, "who beats a woman isn't a man. He's a coward."

O'Rourke's eyes lit up. "You challenging me, big man?" Like he couldn't believe his luck. O'Rourke loomed large but Birdie stood at least three inches taller. The stevedore was broader, made for the rugby pitch, arms and legs hewn from oak.

I pulled out my snub nose .38 and motioned to the kid.

"Hey, jerk. Over here."

The kid moved forward carefully circling around O'Rourke and Birdie who stared at each other. I grabbed him as he came near.

"Your uncle's not going be happy when he finds out what you've been up to."

"Whaddaya talking about?" the kid cried.

"Boosting booze is still illegal in this country, kid, haven't you heard?"

"Who says I was doing that? I was just driving a truck, that's all."

"Yeah. Filled to the brim with bottles that you loaded yourself. The two of you."

"Shut up," O'Rourke snarled at the kid. "Before you say something stupid."

"You really gonna tell my uncle?"

I looked him over. Sweat and dirt had congealed on his face and neck but he perspired hard now. "You got a better idea?"

The kid shook his head." I. . . ."

"I said, shut up," O'Rourke roared.

At that instant, Birdie turned his back on O'Rourke and walking away, began to shrug off his pea jacket. Hobnailed boots pounded the pavement. As O'Rourke went for him, Birdie sidestepped, ducking in one smooth motion. O'Rourke missed completely and ate some dirt. Birdie looked down on him, shrugged off the pea jacket and tossed it to me with a wide grin on his face.

I looked at the kid who didn't seem to be taking it all in. "Front row seats," I said.

Wary now, O'Rourke got to his feet slowly. He went into a wrestler's crouch with his arms out. Birdie held his fists high, under his chin, elbows in tight and peered over his knuckles. He bounced on the balls of his feet. A gleam of light came into his eyes, a saintly radiance in his face. O'Rourke lunged at Birdie but only grabbed air. Stumbling, he swung around snarling like an animal.

"Stand still, boy, so I can get my paws on you. I'll rip your throat out."

"Don't think so," Birdie replied calmly.

O'Rourke swung back around. He lashed out with his fist with such force the momentum yanked him forward. Birdie pivoted and stung him in the side of the head with a solid right jab then a left to the jaw. The brawny stevedore went down on one knee. He put his hands down to brace himself and came up with an iron bar he'd found nestled in the dirt. He held it up like a baseball bat, ready to swing.

"Let's see who's so damn clever now," he sneered.

Birdie widened his stance and parted his elbows. O'Rourke moved in cocking the iron bar. Birdie kept moving, watching O'Rourke carefully. O'Rourke swung out. Once. Twice. The bar swooshed perilously close.

"C'mon O'Rourke, you can't hit me? I'm a big enough target. Come on, man. "C'mon wife beater," he hissed. "Let's see you do something. . . ." And he slapped him in the face, then again.

O'Rourke bellowed, raised the bar above his head and charged. As O'Rourke brought the bar down aiming at Birdie's forehead, Birdie caught it in the palm of his hands. The smack of metal against his flesh made me flinch. The two of them, stood toe-to-toe and grappled, locked in a contest of strength and will. Birdie pushed back on his right leg for leverage and slowly, like a rusty wheel turning, he began to twist the bar out of O'Rourke's grip.

For a time they deadlocked, neither moving, grimacing, face-to-face, muscles rigid with strain, sweat and saliva streaming down. O'Rourke looked maniacal, like a rabid lion baring its yellowed teeth. Birdie seemed evangelical, forcing his will on the sinned and sinning. Breathing became hoarse grunts, the sounds of animals in bloodlust. Then. You saw it in his face. O'Rourke appeared a little desperate as the bar twisted, bit by bit, out of his grip. With a final surge, Birdie stood straight, using his height and weight to pry the bar out of O'Rourke's hands.

"C'mon Steve," Rance called weakly. "Get him. Get him." I clapped my hand over the kid's mouth and hissed at him, like a cobra.

The iron bar hit the dirt with a thud. O'Rourke put his head down and charged, wrapping his arms around Birdie's chest driving him to the ground. The air choked with dust as they grappled and rolled.

Birdie's torso bucked and his long legs snaked up, wrapping them around O'Rourke's neck. O'Rourke pawed, trying to break the hold. He pounded his fists into Birdie's thighs. Birdie tightened his grip. O'Rourke's face turned red, then blue, then puce. Birdie squeezed. Blood leaked out of his nose. He bore a serene, determined expression. O'Rourke's grappling weakened. His eyes bulged and his jaw slackened. Finally, O'Rourke went limp. His eyes rolled back in his head. Birdie released him. O'Rourke slumped back in the dirt. Carefully, Birdie got himself into a crouch position then slowly stood up. He glanced casually at O'Rourke sprawled in the dust.

"Is he dead?" said the kid.

"Just unconscious," I replied.

Birdie blew out a funnel of air and kicked some dirt over O'Rourke's face.

"I should have finished it," he said.

"Why didn't you?" I asked.

He shrugged, then glanced briefly upward. "Maybe I'm going soft," he replied with a hint of regret.

"Feel better now?"

He grinned at me. "It was better than confession."

I gestured. "Come on."

We turned to go. The kid protested. "What about him?" he asked.

"What about him?"

"But…but…we can't just leave him here…"

"Why not?" I replied. "He'll come around in a while."

"It don't seem right, somehow."

I laughed. "O'Rourke's a big boy. He can look after himself. You, on the other hand, have other things to worry about."

The kid swallowed hard but didn't say another word. We marched him back to the Chevy and I shoved him in the back seat. Birdie, flexing his knuckles in a menacing way, got in beside him, just in case the kid decided to try some funny stuff.

"We're going to take a little ride," I said. "Down to the lake."

"Why should I care?" the kid replied.

I started the engine. "It's always a good idea to take an interest in the things around you, kid."

"Yeah?"

"Yeah. Now, you're going to be a good boy and show us where this club, Blackstones, happens to be."

"What if I don't know where it is?"

I laughed but it came out more like a dust-choked wheeze.

"You saw what my friend just did to your buddy back there, didn't you? Just think what he could do to you and not even work up a mild thirst. Just point us in the right direction. It'll go better for you, believe me."

"Why should I?" The kid put on a brave face but the façade melted fast. Birdie grabbed his dirty bicep and squeezed. The kid winced.

I turned around to face him square on. "Well, there's a couple of things that could happen here, kid. We could just hand you off to your uncle, that's one option. The second option is to let John Fat Gai know that you ratted out his little operation back there. How about that? Now I know which option I'd pick. What about you?"

The kid paled. He looked like he was going to be sick. But he didn't have to think about it very long. "Drive," he said.

It turned into a pretty drive. The sun came up on the horizon and the water lay calm and flat. The kid took us through a rabbit warren of old storehouses then told us to pull up outside a low building with a slanted wooden roof made up to look like an elongated sea shanty. No sign or number that I could see.

"This is it," the kids said dully. "This is Blackstones."

"You sure?"

"Course I'm sure," he snapped. "You got my cookies in the squisher. I ain't gonna lie to you now."

"You better not, kid. Or it'll be more than your cookies that get squished, believe me. What time does this joint kick off?"

The kid shrugged glumly. "Dunno. Eleven, twelve, something like that. You had to be a member. Now it's just a bar. Anyone can get in."

"And your buddy, Harvey Troyer, he was a member?"

The kid made a sour face. "That dip ain't my buddy, never was. No, it was her, she was a member."

"Who?" I asked, thinking I already knew the answer to that one.

"Alison," he said. "Alison Foster. She got us in." The kid lunged for the door grabbing the handle. He kicked the door open and scooted out. We watched him tear up the street and disappear around a corner.

"Guess we're letting him go?" Birdie said, after a moment.

I shrugged. "He won't get far. Where's he going to hide? He's got nowhere now."

"He won't be talking to John."

"Nope."

"What about Callaway?"

I thought about the stocky, volatile cop. "Yeah. There is that. Guess we'll have to say something."

Birdie looked at me skeptically. "We?"

I sighed. "Okay. Me."

Birdie smiled. "My prayers have been answered."

36

That evening I decided to take Evelyn out to a club. I heard that Blackstone's might be good–a hopping joint down by the waterfront. The scary sister agreed to babysit. She gave me the evil eye when I rolled up dressed in my best blue suit. Evelyn ignored the undercurrents and kissed her children goodnight, gave her sister a hug and told her she'd made up a bed for her in the spare room. I kept my smile low and tight. Evelyn looked nice in a black cocktail dress with spaghetti straps. She wore a Bolero jacket to cover her bare arms.

"You look swell," I said as we descended the stone stairs of her stoop to the car.

She gave me a look of quiet surprise. "Well, thank you. Compliments now. Ain't that something?"

"I meant it."

"I know. I'm just teasing you, Mo."

I opened the door for her and helped her in. I caught a flash of thigh as her short dress rode up while she maneuvered her way on to the seat. "No peeking now," she admonished.

I grinned at her. "That's like asking a dog not to grab at a bone."

"I know." Still, my gaze lingered for a moment longer. "Shut the door," she said.

"Sure."

I followed orders then got in beside her and fiddled with the ignition. "They have music at this place?" she asked.

"I honestly don't know."

Not much seemed to faze her. "Well, let's find out."

"At your service, Ma'am."

"I like the sound of that."

I'd arranged for Birdie to meet us there. Evelyn stared out the window as we drove through the docklands. "Kind of out of the way, huh?"

"It's off the beaten path," I replied. "If you don't like it, we can leave. Just say the word."

"Don't worry. I will, baby. I will."

I parked the Chevy in an industrial lot around the corner beside a row of silent trucks, a backhoe and a road grader. Evelyn gave me a look but held her tongue. I helped her out of the car.

"This had better be worth it," she muttered under her breath while she plumped her hair. She took a last look in the side view topping up her lipstick under the glare of a streetlight. I gave her my arm. She held it tight.

"Don't be nervous," I said. "You look great."

"Hhmmphh," she snorted. Her heels clacked on the pavement.

The entrance to the club was stacked with cars and people. The cars looked shiny and the people even shinier. A lot of glitter and gold, the flash of diamonds. The muscle hunkered menacingly out front. As we joined the queue, I felt a nudge in my back. I turned to find Birdie grinning down at me.

"Saw you pull up," he said and he looked expectantly at Evelyn who gave him an icy stare.

"Evelyn, this is my partner, Arthur Birdwell. Just call him, Birdie."

"My pleasure," Birdie boomed and stuck out his paw.

Evelyn gave him a quirky smile. "Likewise," she said and reluctantly, gave him hers to shake. It disappeared into his mitt. After he gave it back to her, he motioned to the front.

"See who's on the door?"

I took a better look. My good friend, John's right hand. Just a few hours earlier I'd seen him cradling a Tommy gun. "He gets around," I replied.

"No kidding," Birdie said.

"That delivery we observed earlier was probably for this joint."

"Seems like a good bet," Birdie replied.

The line moved slowly but steadily forward. I could buff my car with all of the Brylcreem the guys in line used to glue their hair to their scalps.

"Trouble," I said. The men were being patted down before being let in the front door. "You carrying?" I asked Birdie. He nodded. "Me too." I glanced at Evelyn's small pocket purse.

"Something wrong?" Evelyn asked.

I cleared my throat. It wasn't the sort of thing you normally asked a date.

"Er, you got anywhere you can stash a couple of heaters?"

And I flipped open my jacket to show her my snub .38. Birdie did the same. She gave us a wide-eyed look, then shook her head, tut-tutting to herself. I was hoping she didn't think that maybe her sister had been dead right about me.

"Give me some cover," she said and held out her hand. I slipped her the .38 discreetly as I could. "Move in closer," she said. "You too, big boy." In a flash, her skirt had flipped up and the gun disappeared. "Now yours," she said to Birdie. He handed it to her and she quickly repeated the same tricky maneuver, then tugged her dress down "You're gonna owe me a new pair of nylons," she said.

"Okay."

"And garters too."

"Only if I can watch you try them on."

She slapped my shoulder but it was a kind of playful slap.

"That your only piece?" I asked Birdie. He shook his head. "Good," I replied. Better to let them take something than nothing. Otherwise, they'd look a little more thoroughly.

We came to the front of the line and my friend with the crumpled hat and screwy smile looked at me with amusement.

"You," he said. "You want to get in?"

"That's right. I hear the beer and sauerkraut are good in this joint."

"Them too?"

"Yes."

"I'm glad you could make it," he said. "I will enjoy the pleasure of your company. Please." And he indicated that I should hold out my arms. The goon beside him patted me down. He flipped open my jacket and saw the empty shoulder harness. He gave me a quizzical look.

"Left it in the car. No need to carry here. I'm sure it's safe."

"Good thinking," the gunsel replied. He turned to Birdie, who flipped open his jacket and showed him the piece he was carrying, a .32 that looked like a toy. The guy smiled finding the size of the piece amusing. He hefted it in his hand, then slipped it into his coat pocket. "I hold for you. You get when you leave."

Birdie shrugged. "Fine by me," he said.

The gunsel looked from me to Birdie then settled on Evelyn. He looked her up and down slowly then went for another round. It seemed to take a long time and a group behind us became a little restless.

"Seen enough?" she asked him.

"For now," he replied. He stepped back and beckoned us in. "Welcome. Enjoy your evening." His lopsided grin held no mirth showing nothing but menace.

Inside the lighting burned low, practically non-existent. The main room opened up into a long bar sheathed in leather and zinc. Wooden pillars chopped up the sight lines in between round tables. A small stage rose to the left of the bar. Shiny instruments lay inert on their stands.

"Looks like there's music, after all," Evelyn said with a smile.

We found a table toward the back, in the shadows. A cocktail waitress came up and using a battered Zippo, fired up a candle.

"There now," she said sweetly. "What can I get you?" I ordered a CC on the rocks, Birdie asked for a tomato juice and Evelyn went rogue opting for a Singapore Sling.

I looked at her. She cocked an eye back at me. "What?" she asked.

I reached my hand under the table and laid it on her thigh.

"You can hand back the hardware now," I said. "Must be getting a little itchy."

I felt the cold steel meet my fingers and I slid it discreetly back into its holster. Birdie did the same.

Evelyn sat back and sighed. "That's better," she said. "Now I can relax. You aren't planning on using those things, are you?"

"Haven't planned anything," I replied. "We're just here to enjoy the music."

"You didn't know they had music," she said.

"Then it's our lucky day."

Evelyn shook her head. "Honestly, you are a strange one sometimes, don't you think, Mr. Birdwell?"

"I do, I honestly do," he intoned. "Call me, Birdie."

The waitress brought the drinks and set them on the table. Birdie put a ten on her tray and told her to keep the change. Although the lighting had been set low, I thought I saw her blush a little. She smiled at him, and he smiled back and that's when the trouble started. I looked around. Just a bar, I thought. What's special about it? Directly opposite, on the far side of the room stood a staircase. I wanted to climb those stairs. Eight years ago, Alison Foster and Gayle Sorenson had climbed those stairs and something had happened. Something that caused the disappearance of Henry Turner.

Two tables over sat four beefy Americans in ill-fitting suits. They looked like hunters who wandered off the trail. I wondered how they found their way here, to this place of all places. They didn't have to be Americans, they could have been anyone of a small mind and ugly demeanour. Two of them had moustaches that drooped over their upper lips and I bet they sported tattoos under the wrinkled sleeves of the cheap suit jackets they wore. At least two of them glared, in a squinty way, in our direction. Fair-haired boys, all of them. It could prove to be the distraction I needed.

I nudged Birdie's foot under the table and he followed my line of sight. Now the four of them glared at us. "More trouble," I murmured.

"That ain't trouble," Birdie said. "That's amusement."

"The band's about to start," Evelyn said, as if that would make it all go away.

The musicians filed on to the small stage; a trumpet, sax, stand-up bass and guitar player. They wore turtlenecks and sunglasses. The bass player had on a fedora and the guitar player opted for a wool cap. None of them looked white. They swung into the first number and the music poured out fluid and icy cool.

"Coon music," I thought I heard from the hunters' table plus a round of sniggering. A lot of empty glasses sat before them. The table seemed set to spark an explosion.

"Excuse me," I said and stood up. I leaned over and whispered into Birdie's ear. He listened without looking, turning his gaze on the musicians but his attention on the hunters.

"Where you going, baby?" Evelyn asked.

I smiled at her reassuringly. "Be right back."

I made my way across the room threading through the tables passing directly by the hunters. They watched me in scowling silence but I kept on going to the far side of the room. I was noticed. She had a momentary look of panic on her face before her expression settled back into one of composure with a hint of wry amusement. He remained neutral.

"Good evening," I said. I had to admit my heart pumped more over this encounter than what I knew was to come.

Her smile dazzled in its coldness. "Why, Mr. Gold. What a surprise," said Adele Rosewell.

He had stood up and buttoned his jacket. "Hello Gold. What are you doing here?"

"I might ask you the same thing, Lawson." I could hear the ice cubes swirling in his voice but I didn't mind.

"Why don't you join us for a minute," Adele Rosewell said. "I can see you're with friends."

"Thank you." I sat.

"I suppose you'd like a drink too," Lawson chided.

"No thanks, I'm fine." I let silence hang over us.

"They're really good," Lawson said, indicating the combo. "It's not often you get to hear really exceptional jazz played live."

"You're a jazz fan?" I asked.

Lawson glanced quickly at Adele before answering. "Well, I've been introduced to it rather recently."

"Mr. Lawson is a valued client of the bank," Adele Rosewell said.

"Of course he is," I replied. "And what is Mrs. Lawson doing this evening? She's not a jazz fan, I take it?"

Lawson frowned. "No, not really."

"But then, she's been to this club before–on numerous occasions."

Lawson perked up, his expression tightened. "What are you implying, Gold?"

"I'm not implying anything Lawson. Of course, it's part of the normal course of business to be seen out in a jazz club after hours with a very attractive single woman who happens not to be your wife. What I am saying is that your wife, before she assumed that title, used to come to this club on a regular basis. Something interesting happened here eight years ago. Something that caused a man to disappear and a young girl to lose her mind."

Lawson's face had become pinched. "You're out of order, Gold. Now you'd better get out of here or...."

"Or what? You'll have me thrown out? I don't think so, Lawson. You're not man enough to try." I thought he would go for me then but I stopped him with my next remark. "You do know who owns this club, don't you?"

"I couldn't care less."

Adele Rosewell had turned away from us, pretending not to care about what took place. "Do you know who owns this club, Miss Rosewell?"

"I haven't the faintest idea," she muttered icily.

"All right, Gold. You've had your fun…"

"Does Mrs. Lawson know you're here this evening? Does she know you're out on a date?"

"That's it," Lawson roared and began to push back his chair and reach for my jacket at the same time. I grabbed his wrist and twisted it downward forcing his shoulder forward. With my left hand, I smacked him in the face and he sat down heavily. I released his wrist and he grabbed at it. It had unfolded in about three seconds. A trickle of blood ran from the corner of his mouth. His neat blonde hair had become tousled. Adele moved toward him but he pushed her away. She glared at me–fire and ice.

I stood up.

"Enjoy the rest of your evening."

The jazz combo continued to play through. I glanced at the guitar player and he winked at me. I guess they'd seen it all before.

On the way back to the table, I bumped into one of the hunters knocking a glass of beer from his hand. It spilled down the front of his trousers. He looked down in disbelief.

"Excuse me, fat boy," I said.

"Jesus. H. Christ," he exclaimed. I kept moving back to my table but I heard a commotion behind me. I'd only gone a few steps when I felt a meaty hand clamp down on my left shoulder. I pivoted around. Using the momentum of the turn, I caught him in the jaw with an upper cut and he went stumbling back into the arms of his buddy who'd jumped up to help him. I gave him a cool look, pulled down on my jacket and went back to our table. Birdie stood up. He grinned. Two fights in two days. Heaven.

"Think you can handle it?"

"There's only four of them," he replied.

I shrugged. "We could always look for a few more."

Birdie shook his head. "They'll have to do."

"Holler if you need a hand."

I grabbed Evelyn by the elbow and lifted her out of her seat. "I need you to step away for a few minutes," I said.

"What are you doing?" she asked.

"Creating a distraction," I replied.

"What? What for?"

"Something I need to do." She tottered in her high heels beside me. I steered her to a chair against the far wall. "I need you to sit here out of the way. I can't have you get hurt."

"What about your friend? There's four of them and only one of him."

I nodded. "I know. It hardly seems fair but then Birdie would be insulted if anyone came to his aid. Four against one hardly seems like much of a challenge for him."

Evelyn stared at me. "You sure you know what you're doing?"

"I hope so."

"Where are you going?"

I indicated the staircase. "Upstairs for a minute. I'll be back directly. Now sit. We're wasting time."

I took a quick glance. Two of the hunters had gone out for the count and the other two circled warily. One had a bottle in his hand. Birdie stood his ground coolly, waiting for them to make a move. The jazz combo kept playing. Nothing distracted them from making music. I kissed Evelyn on the cheek and pushed her into the chair.

"Wait for me here. Won't be long."

I legged it up the staircase. Birdie had commanded everyone's attention. John's main man stood watching, arms folded on his chest, an amused look on his broad face.

Two flights of stairs brought me to a landing and a set of doors with chiseled French glass. I went through and continued on down a corridor. On the way, I passed doors on either side. I turned each knob as I went but they were all locked. I may have to do something about that. At the end of the corridor stood one last door and this time, the knob turned.

I found myself in a deserted outer office. A secretary's desk with a typewriter neatly covered, a coat rack, some file cabinets and a water cooler. Dull as dishwater. I focused on the inner office. The knob on this door turned too, so I twisted it and went in. I looked around–a large room with a thick carpet and two leather wingback chairs. Facing the chairs stood a mahogany desk large enough to launch a jet fighter. The executive chair on the far end of the desk faced away. Someone sat in it. I could see the top of a greasy, dark crown. The chair swiveled my way.

"Hello boychick. Fancy seeing you here. Of all places."

He'd caught me out. I stumbled around, taking some time to get my voice to work. "What the hell are you doing here?"

He smiled. "Always asking questions. Nothing ever changes."

"How about an answer for a change and throw some truth into it."

Jake's paunchy face lit up. "Truth, he says? What is that? I'm not sure what you mean." He flipped open a box in front of him. "Cigarette?" I shook my head. Jake shrugged. "Suit yourself."

He dug his fingers in and fished out a fag and lit it with a desk lighter in the shape of a dragon. He held it up as he puffed away contentedly. "Neat, huh? These Chinks love their symbols. Their cultural artifacts."

I grew conscious of time draining away. "You working for John Fat Gai? I know he owns this club."

"Relax, boychick. Why don't you take a seat? We'll talk reasonably, like men."

I reached across the desk and grabbed his tie wrapping it around my knuckles until they crimped his chin.

"I want some answers. Something happened here eight years ago and I need to know what that was."

Jake gurgled a little and his eyes popped. Smoke leaked out of his twisted mouth. He slapped desperately at the tie and finally yanked it out of my grasp. I watched him wheeze into his shirt.

"Jesus. I'm your father, remember? You got no cause to treat me this way."

"Just answer the questions."

"I don't know nothin' about eight years ago, boychick," he spat. "Before my tenure. And I told you I wasn't going to serve any hard time and I'm not. There," and he spread out his knobby hands. "Simple enough?"

"What about Tobin? The feds aren't going to let that go. You made him look like a sucker. He'll turn the city upside down looking for you."

Jake shrugged. "Like I care. Let me worry about Tobin. Believe me he's not going to be a problem."

"What's John got on you? Why have you thrown in with him? What are you doing for him? Answer me."

"Who the hell do you think you are, boychick?" Jake said and his face clouded with anger. "You think you can tell me what to do? You got another think coming."

What should I do? Beat answers out of my own flesh and blood? Believe me, I considered it. Jake chuckled and all I could think about were the umpteen times he left my mother crying, the slaps and punches I got for sticking up for her. I must have shown something on my face. My hand snaked in under my jacket. Jake eased his chair back but the smile hardened. He glanced up looking past my shoulder. Something hard came down behind my left ear. A fireball exploded in my head. I crashed forward across the desk.

I thought I heard Jake say, "Served him right, the prick."

37

Waking up from a conk on the head never came easily and harder still if your head felt like it had been split open like a ripe cantaloupe. An ever-expanding, elasticized balloon of throbbing pain worked its way from the back of my ears forward.

Gingerly, I worked my fingers around the side of my head and gently probed a swollen lump of stinging flesh sending shock waves down my neck into my shoulder. I'd been coshed hard. I recognized that fact and it seemed a good sign that my brain hadn't been scrambled, that most of the wires, although pulsating, remained intact and connected. I didn't groan or moan out loud. I wouldn't give them the satisfaction. I also realized that I was lying down.

"Here, take this," and someone shoved a cold compress into my hand. I slid it under the lump and winced but it felt better.

"That was pretty stupid, boychick. I thought you was smarter than that. It's clear that you didn't get your brains from me."

I risked opening an eyelid. Jake swam into view looking much the same disheveled person as before. He wore an amused expression on his face. I opened eye number two and waited for the image to stabilize. Next to Jake stood someone resembling John Fat Gai but not quite enough to actually be him. Someone older with grey hair and a drooping moustache. Profound insights in my present condition. This man's expression carried benign concern.

"Hello Mr. Gold," he said. "Feeling better?"

"No," I replied. "Who the hell are you?"

The Chinaman chuckled. He turned to Jake. "He's a tough one, all right."

"He's got a hard head, I'll give you that," Jake muttered.

"Someone want to fill me in? What's going on? And I asked you a question, mister."

Jake sighed. "Tough guy. Always has to play it hard."

"An answer will do me fine," I said and winced.

The Chinaman stood over me then reached a hand down. I took it and he hauled me to my feet. I felt woozy and the room spun a few times. He steadied me. Jake wheeled over a chair and I dropped into it. "I'm afraid Quan was, shall we say, enthusiastic?"

"Quan?"

"Yes, you met him outside. He was guarding the door."

"But he works for John," I said.

"He works for me. I just want it to appear that he works for John Fat Gai."

"And again, you are who, exactly?"

"You can call me, Mr. Li."

I looked around. Still the same room. In the same building. "Isn't this John's club we're in?"

Mr. Li stepped back. Jake moved behind the desk and sat in the same chair where I'd found him. He smoked moodily staring at the ceiling.

"Technically, yes. But actually, no. It is my club. John Fat Gai is supposed to be looking after my interests."

"Your interests?"

"Yes, that is correct," Li said. I glanced at Jake, who shrugged.

"It's complicated," he said.

No kidding. If my head hadn't been spinning already, it'd be in orbit by now. Li continued. "John Fat Gai has disobeyed my instructions and I have come here to find out what he has been doing. Instead of sticking to business, I find he is involved in matters that complicate things unnecessarily."

"What things?" I asked.

Li's eyes narrowed. "That is none of your concern. His behaviour recently has been strange and out of character. I find these things troublesome and bad for business. It is messy and will only cause trouble."

"What are you going to do about it?" I asked.

"Me?" asked Mr. Li and pointed to his chest, then laughed harshly. "Not me, Mr. Gold but you."

"What?"

"Yes, your father has been telling me how good you are at your job. That you can find anyone. That you fix problems for people. I am just a stranger here, on my own, without any influence to speak of. This girl that John Fat Gai seeks, she didn't steal just money, but something infinitely more valuable. Something that money cannot buy."

"What's that?" I asked.

"A ledger," Jake said. "It's got everything in it. Every financial deal, who's on the pad, you name it. That ledger, in the wrong hands is dynamite. It's got cops, judges, politicians, the whole shemozzle."

"Yes, if it fell into the wrong hands, it could be very dangerous for everyone," Mr. Li said. "Do you want to see your brother again?"

I hesitated. Jake stared at me. He'd always liked Eli better. Two peas in a pod, the two of them. "Yeah, sure," I muttered.

"Then get the ledger back, Mr. Gold."

"Why can't you just order John to let Eli go and shape up?" I asked.

Mr. Li shrugged. "I tried but he was not responsive. How do you say it here–I believe that John Fat Gai has gone off the line."

"So you want me to do your dirty work for you."

"Yes, precisely," Mr. Li replied. "I am pleased that you recognize this. Get me the ledger and I will deal with John Fat Gai and you will get your brother back safe and sound."

"What if I get the ledger and I give it to the cops?"

Mr. Li nodded as if it seemed a reasonable choice. "I wouldn't recommend it. Most of them or their superiors will be in the ledger, in any case. Who would you be able to trust with it? No one. It is better that the ledger should come back into the hands of the owner–its rightful owner. And that would be me, Mr. Gold. I will also authorize a payment of $10,000. A finder's fee. How does that sound?"

"How do I know you're on the up and up? How do I know you're who you say you are?"

Jake cleared his throat. "You've got my word on it, boychick."

I didn't know whether to laugh or cry. "That's reassuring. A thief guaranteeing the word of another." I looked at Li who stiffened. "No offense, Mr. Li." Li nodded but didn't reply. My head pounded. "What's your role in this, Jake? How the hell are you going to stay out of prison? Your face is plastered all over the papers. There are constant reports on television about the breakout. Every cop in the country is looking for you."

"A few of the boys owed me a favour or two. Wasn't hard to get a riot going in that place. You've seen it. Not exactly the Ritz."

"And the car you jumped into?"

"Courtesy of Mr. Li," Jake said. Li took a short bow. "When I heard about Eli, I knew I had to get out, that John was out of control."

"You heard about Eli before I did?"

"Naturally."

I thought about the layout of the Don. All of the armed guards faced into the inner courtyard where the prisoners congregated. None of them would be positioned by the main entrance. Jake had a police escort that far, so he wouldn't have been stopped. It meant something strange happened in the hand over area, between the locked gate to the prison and the foyer leading out. It'd be unusual to find prisoners hanging around there. Only visitors and guards normally moved through that area. "Tobin did you a favour and didn't know. He walked you through the locked doors and the armed guards."

Jake laughed. "Yeah, it was pretty sweet."

"Doesn't explain how you overpowered Tobin and made it out the front entrance."

Jake just smirked. "I'll leave that to your imagination, boychick." I really did want to slap him. "Besides, don't worry about me. I'll lie low for a while. It'll be fine."

"I don't really care what happens to you, Jake."

Jake winced. "Ooohh. That hurt."

I started toward him when I heard a commotion at the door. It swung open and Birdie filled it. He marched in but didn't look happy. Behind him came Evelyn. Behind her, holding a shotgun, strode the smiling goon I'd come to know as Quan. I felt the back of my head.

"Baby," Evelyn cried. "You all right?" She threw her arms around me. "What happened to your head?"

"Him," I replied, indicating Quan who just grinned at me but didn't loosen his grip on the shotgun any.

"It's all calm downstairs," Birdie said. "We cleared the place."

"Great. I see our little plan worked well," I said ruefully.

Birdie cracked his knuckles. "It wasn't all bad. I had fun."

"Who are these men?" Evelyn asked.

"Time to go," I said. I turned to Mr. Li and Jake. "We'll be in touch—speaking of which?"

Mr. Li handed me a slip of paper. "You may call at any time day or night," he said. "I wish you the best of luck, Mr. Gold."

"Sure." I turned to Birdie and Evelyn. "Come on, let's get outta here." I noticed Jake look at Evelyn in an admiring way.

"You going to introduce me?" he asked.

"No." I took Evelyn's hand and began to pull her toward the door.

"But..?" she protested.

"It's late, kid." I had two heads, one that pounded and one that just ached like the blazes. I looked at Mr. Li and nodded. I didn't say goodbye to Jake. Screw him.

38

We dropped Evelyn at home. She gave me a lingering kiss and told me to be careful. I staggered down the steps to the car. I told her I might not be able to see her for a while. Not until things blew over. She didn't look very happy. I pulled myself away reluctantly. Birdie had kept the engine running. Back at my place, I grabbed some ice from the freezer, wrapped it in a towel and held it to my throbbing head.

After thirty minutes or so, I dumped the ice in the bathtub and washed up in the sink splashing cold water over my face. I took a fresh shirt from the drawer and put it on. I strapped on the .45, took the snub .38 and stuck it in my belt. I made sure I had enough ammunition to weigh down both jacket pockets. Birdie had twin .45's in a cross-hatch holster under both armpits. He carried a chopped down 12-gauge in his right hand. He had two boxes of shells in his pants pockets. I gulped down four Bufferin then took a shot of Scotch to chase them down.

"Let's go," I said.

"We're going to war with John?" he asked.

"Looks like it." I knew the feeling and I liked it. "I think I know where Henry is," I said.

Birdie hesitated. "You do?"

"Well, I think I know how we can find him, let's put it that way."

"Good."

I hoped the dope kicked in soon. The pain in my head screamed.

First stop. Alison Lawson. She'd cough even if I had to beat it out of her. I'd lost track of time. Being unconscious warped your inner timepiece. Darkness hung over the sky like a warm blanket. No sign of the sun coming up. We moved in that dead of night zone, the one where terrors happen.

Birdie drove us out to the Lawson residence. I could hear the tires humming. The streets hushed quiet. Sane people tucked up in bed. Two identical Cadillac convertibles parked in the driveway. His and hers. Cute. Except one Cadillac had crashed through the hedges, its engine running and the driver door ajar. Like somebody had stumbled out of it drunk and giddy. We stepped out of the Chevy. I reached in and switched off the Cadillac's ignition and pocketed the keys.

"This don't look good," Birdie said. No kidding. It got worse.

"Front door's open."

"Hmmppphh."

Birdie cracked open the 12-gauge making sure the shells were in place, then snapped it shut.

I slid the .45 out of its holster. "Let's go."

We each took a side and moving quickly, approached the doorway. I toed the door open and went in first, nice and low. Birdie came in high. The lights blazed. So bright my eyes stung.

"Mrs. Lawson?" I called. "Mrs. Lawson? It's Mo Gold and Arthur Birdwell. Are you here?" Nothing in the foyer. Too many rooms, too many corridors in the damn place. We heard a rustling sound and a muffled cry.

"Upstairs," I whispered. Birdie nodded.

Then a sob sounded. "Up here," an anguished voice called. "Quickly. Please."

We knew enough not to come just because we were called. We took the stairs quickly but carefully covering as many angles as we could.

"Down here," the voice called.

At the top of the landing the corridor split into a T-shape. It went left and right and straight. The voice came from straight ahead. I heard serious sobbing. The walls had been done up in crimson brocade and gold trim, enough to make me puke again. Some maniac had installed gargantuan chandeliers that had enough candlepower to smoke the Brazilian rainforest. It felt like gamma rays burned through my skull. After wading through plush pile carpet we came to the entrance of the master bedroom. We heard some commotion going on inside. Birdie eased the door open with the barrel of the 12-gauge. It swung noiselessly.

Reginald Lawson sat on the carpet, his legs splayed out before him with the bloodied corpse of his dead wife draped across his lap. Gussied up in a satin dressing gown infused with blood. In his right hand, he held a bloodied knife. The blade looked long and broad enough to gut a moose. Lawson sat propped against the mattress of a king-size, canopied bed. The kind I imagined in the palace of Versailles. Lawson remained dressed much as he had been when I'd seen him at the club, except that he wore no tie and the buttons of his shirt had been ripped open as if he'd been in a fight. He wept, sobbing helplessly.

"Hello Lawson," I said.

"Please, please…" He looked up at me and I saw what appeared to be genuine tears. "It's Alison, I think…."

"She look dead to me," Birdie said. I glanced at him and he shrugged.

"Yes, yes," Lawson mumbled. "He's right, she, she…is…"

"I think it would be a good idea for you to put the knife down, Mr. Lawson," I said.

For a moment, he looked puzzled. "What?"

"The knife…" And I indicated with my head. "Please."

Lawson lifted his hand up and stared at the bloodied blade, then collapsed into wracking sobs. The knife dropped on to the carpet.

I thought about slapping him for a moment. Even in this pitiable state, he irked me. "What happened here, Lawson? Was there an argument? An altercation of some kind?"

"What?" Lawson wasn't focusing. His eyes were clouded. "What? You think…?"

"Go on."

Then he began to shake his head. “No. No. No.” He pushed his dead wife off his lap and struggled up. The blood in her chest cavity gurgled, bubbling up as he shifted her off him. His hands were bloody. I could see several stab wounds in her chest. The blood must have spurted everywhere and as she lay dying her weakening heart kept pumping it out.

“It wasn’t me. I found her like this. You’ve got to believe me. I would never do this to her. Never, ever. You’ve got to help me, Gold. I beg of you.”

“Call Callaway,” I said to Birdie. “Use the downstairs phone.” Birdie stepped out.

Lawson looked around him as if seeing the scene for the very first time. “I’ve got to get out of here. I can’t stay here.”

“I’m afraid you can’t leave now, Lawson. At the very least you’re a material witness in a very nasty homicide. The police will need to speak with you.”

“But don’t you see? They’ll think I did it. They’ll think I killed Alison. I’ve got to get out of here before they arrive.” His expression screamed bewilderment. He was right about one thing though, the police would think he did it.

“Think about it, Lawson. You take off now and the cops will think you’re guilty without a doubt. They won’t even bother looking for anyone else. You’re a wealthy guy. Get yourself a top-dog lawyer and see it through.”

Lawson raised a bloody hand and pointed a stained finger at me. Then he started to giggle and I knew he’d really gone over the edge. “Rich? Rich? Me? That’s a laugh and a half, Gold. If only you knew…” He looked around the room wistfully. “You think I would have condoned any of, of, this?”

“What do you mean?”

“I gave Alison my name, that’s all. I thought I loved her. I really did but they just wanted my name, my family history. He controls everything, Gold. Not me. I’m just the lackey, that’s all.”

"We haven't got much time, Lawson. The cops will be here soon. If you've got something to say that might help you then you'd better spit it out–here and now."

He rambled. "That's why I was with her—Adele. Adele..." I winced. "She's so beautiful and smart, incredibly smart..."

"So you spent the evening with Miss Rosewell?"

Lawson nodded. He seemed to have forgotten momentarily that he was covered in his wife's drying blood. "That's right. The entire evening. After your friend there, after he caused that disturbance in the club, we went back to her apartment. I stayed there until late and then I came home and I found Alison, like that, lying there–covered in blood..." His face cracked as he broke down again.

"What about her parents?"

Lawson looked up. "Her parents?"

"That's right. Your in-laws. Have they been told?"

"Oh my God," he breathed. "No, I didn't think..." He stared at me in desperation. "I can't. I couldn't. They hate me anyway and now they'll think..." Lawson drifted off and swept his arm around the horrific scene. "You know what they'll think."

Birdie stepped back into the room. The carpet grew deep. I hadn't heard a sound.

"Cops are on the way. Should only be a couple of minutes."

I holstered the .45. "Better make that thing scarce," I said, nodding at the 12-gauge. I turned my attention back to Lawson. He wavered. A good puff of air and he'd topple. "You'd better tell the cops about Miss Rosewell too."

He shook his head. "No, I can't do that. I couldn't possibly involve her."

"Look Lawson, use your head. It will be better coming from you. If the cops find out about her then it will go even harder for you. There are plenty of witnesses that will put you with her at the club. Having an affair with Miss Rosewell is a good motive for murder and the cops will jump all over that. But if you tell them it will make it look like you have less to hide and that your conscience is clear on the killing of your wife. Miss Rosewell is involved whether she likes it or not and she could end up being your alibi. As it is, things aren't looking too good for you but even if you can't afford it, get yourself a good lawyer anyway. Understand?" I almost added, 'dummy' but bit my tongue.

"I'll put it in the car," Birdie replied indicating the 12-gauge. We'd had a special rack fitted into the trunk.

Lawson stared at me as if he hadn't seen me before. "Why are you doing this? You don't like me, Gold. The feeling is mutual."

"You got that right, Lawson. I couldn't give two figs if you went down for this or not. I'm doing it for her, not for you."

"Adele?"

"That's right, and her aunt. She's a decent, hard-working woman who's just trying to find out what happened to her son."

"I don't know anything about that, I swear to you."

They came in a brace of squad cars with the sirens screaming. Nothing too subtle. We'd taken Lawson downstairs to the den and allowed him to pour himself a stiff Scotch. Birdie met the first couple of cops at the door but wouldn't let them in until Callaway showed up. I could hear sharp words exchanged but Birdie remained an impenetrable wall.

A few minutes later, Callway's guttural voice chimed in. I kept my eye on Lawson. He sat slumped in a chair holding a heavy, cut glass tumbler but didn't even take a sip. A pair of patrolmen appeared in the doorway. I knew I wasn't going anywhere and Lawson showed no signs of anything at all except a slight intake of breath to prove he was still alive.

I heard a heavy thumping coming down the stairs and a moment later, Callaway and his shadow, Sergeant Roy Mason, shouldered their way through. Mason worked a wad of gum in his narrow jaw and had a smirk on his weasel face. I could see he limped. Callaway had thunderstorm etched into his expression.

"Do I need to ask why you're here?" he asked me.

"Didn't Birdie tell you?"

"Wouldn't tell us anything," Mason said with disgust.

"You mean, he wouldn't tell you anything, Mason."

"All right," Callaway snapped. "Let's not forget we have a particularly nasty murder on our hands here." He nodded at the comatose Lawson. "What's he been saying?"

"That he didn't do it. Came home and found her like that."

"How'd he get the blood all over his shirt?" Mason sneered. "Dancing with the corpse."

"You'll have to ask him," I said. "There was a lot of blood. Looked like she took a direct hit in the heart. There would have been a lot of spurt." Mason limped his way a bit closer.

"Save the analysis," Callaway said. He went over to Lawson, who didn't even bother looking up at him. "Show me your hands, please, Mr. Lawson."

"What?" Lawson barely acknowledged him.

"I'd like to see your hands please. Hold them up for me, will you?"

Lawson set down the drink on the carpet and tentatively held up his hands, palms out. Callaway didn't touch them but took a close look.

"Turn them around please, palm side in." Lawson did what he was told like a good little boy. Callaway gave them the eyeball. "Roy," he said. "See if you can find a couple of those small plastic trash bags in the kitchen, will you? And a couple of rubber bands."

"Huh?" Mason looked startled.

"You heard me. Just get them." Mason winced but he disappeared. He returned a moment later. No one had said anything.

"Nasty limp you got there, Mason," I said.

He glanced at me. "Just slipped on the stairs, that's all."

"Sure."

Callaway took the bags and rubber bands from him, slipped a bag each over Lawson's hands and snapped the elastics around his wrists. He grunted with satisfaction.

"Mr. Lawson, you're going to have to come with us down to the station for questioning, okay?"

Lawson nodded then stared down at his drink on the carpet hungrily. "Check and see if the coroner is here," Callaway said. Mason snapped his gum. "Roy?"

Mason glanced up. "Right."

"And nobody gets in the bedroom until the lab boys have finished."

"I know the drill, Inspector."

"Then act like it."

Mason winced then slunk out.

"We didn't get much past the doorway," I said. "We didn't go right into the room. I just talked to Lawson while Birdie called you from the downstairs phone." I paused.

"Boys," Callaway called. The two patrolmen stiffened. "Come and take Mr. Lawson down to the station. Make sure he's comfortable and put him in one of the guest suites. Stay with him. You might want to get him a jacket to wear. It can get cold in there."

"Yes sir." The two patrolmen approached Lawson from either side, each pinching an arm. "Right this way, Mr. Lawson." They escorted him out, his sleek head slumped to his chest. He didn't look up.

After they left, Callaway noticed Lawson's drink on the carpet. He picked it up and downed it. "Shame to let it go to waste," he said. "Now what the hell were you doing here?"

I cleared my throat. "Well, we were just passing by as it happens and I spotted the Caddy up on the grass. The driver's door was open with the engine running. I thought that was a little strange. Then Birdie noticed the front door. We decided to see if the homeowners were in distress so we entered the premises. I called out and identified myself. A voice called and asked for help. We went upstairs and found Lawson cradling the body of his wife. She looked dead and he was covered in her blood. That's about as much as either of us knows."

Callaway gritted his teeth and rocked back on his heels. There were dark pouches under his eyes and his skin looked puffy. "Oh really? You just happened to be passing by?"

"That's right."

"And you expect me to believe that?"

"Sure. Why not?"

"And the door just happened to be open?"

"That's the way it was," I said.

Callaway glared at me. I didn't want to add to his troubles but couldn't see any other way. I wasn't going to endanger my stupid brother by telling him the truth. That I wanted to beat information out of the now deceased Alison Lawson.

"By the way," I said. "Her parents haven't been told yet."

Callaway rolled his eyes upward. "Ah shit," he said.

"Thought we'd leave that to you, make it official and all."

"Nice of you."

"Sure. No need to thank me."

He was about to open his mouth and let me have it when the coroner appeared in the doorway, a fat old bird named Doc Nelson. He looked like an obese owl with white hair parted in the middle that came up in points on either side of a pink, rotund skull. His thick, black-rimmed glasses made him appear myopic. "Okay, Inspector, we're removing the body now."

Callaway looked at me then sighed. "Thanks Doc. What's the preliminary?"

"Well, definitely deceased," he chuckled. "Murder weapon matches that of the knife found on the floor. She was stabbed about a dozen times, twice straight through the heart, took it from the front while she was standing. Must have caught her by surprise. We're not looking for anyone too tall though, the angle was slightly downward but not too much. Could be a shorter man maybe but we'll need to let the pathologist take a closer look, okay?"

"What about a straight thrust then, Doc?"

The fat coroner considered this for a second. "Unlikely," he replied. "The wounds would have been lower down, in the abdomen area. These were higher up and angled downward."

Callway nodded. "Sure, okay. Thanks Doc."

"Hi Mo, haven't seen you in quite a while."

"How are you, Doc?"

Doc Nelson grinned and patted his stomach. “Losing weight, can’t you tell?”

“Withering away before my eyes, Doc.”

Doc chuckled again, then turned and lumbered away.

“Rules Lawson out,” I said.

Callaway gave me a withering look. “We’ll see.”

I stepped in closer and lowered my voice. “Listen. About Ying.”

“What about him?” he asked warily. He glanced over my shoulder to make sure we were alone.

“Seems like you weren’t his only handler.”

“What?”

“He was singing to the feds too.”

Callaway grabbed my lapels and I thought he was going to yank them off. “How do you know this?”

I disengaged his hands from my jacket. “Easy on the material. I’m not a public servant like you. I cover my own expenses.”

Callaway swallowed. “Sorry.”

“I had a visit from that pompous ass Tobin. He told me that Ying was his guy on the inside with John Fat Gai.”

“Why did he tell you that? Why was he talking to you in the first place?”

It had to come out some time. “Tobin thought I knew something. He got wind that we were looking for Ying’s sister. He was trying to play me like I’d feel guilty for having Jake in the family.”

“And do you know anything?”

“No, I don’t.” I hesitated. I hated to do this but I figured it was time to get it all out on the table. I heard a slight rustle of fabric and turned to see Birdie fill the doorway. “There’s more,” I said.

“Jesus,” spat Callaway. “Maybe I should just hang it up.”

“That’s your call. It’s about Rance.”

“Rance? What about Rance?”

I put my hands up. “Hey look, I know he’s family and you want to protect your sister that’s why I’m giving you a heads up on this, okay?”

“Spit it out,” he said.

"Earlier this evening, we happened to catch Rance and a buddy of his, a big Irish bastard named Steve O'Rourke. He's a stevedore down on the docks. The two of them were engaged in a little moonlighting."

"What kind of moonlighting?"

"Unloading a truck with illegal booze and delivered it to a warehouse near the port area. John's men were there to receive it."

Callaway rubbed his jaw. "Jesus Christ, Mo. Is there anything else you'd like to impale me with?"

I grinned. "No, that's it, I guess. John probably doesn't even know who Rance is, he's the lowest of the low in the chain."

"What if he does know? What if Rance is working for him full-time? How would I break it to my sister? I'm obligated to turn him in, you know that."

I shook my head. "I don't think he's working for John full-time. I think he's looking to pick up some quick cash and is being stupid about how he does it, that's all. You need to step in before he gets in too deep or else you won't be able to help him."

"Yeah, yeah. Sure. I'll rip his heart out, the little idiot."

"That's it. Some guidance in his young life."

"He'll get it from the toe of my boot," Callaway growled.

"That could work," Birdie boomed.

"Yeah, sure." Then he looked at me. "Where's Jake now?"

I shrugged. "Don't know and don't care. If I never see that shifty bastard again, it'll be too soon."

Callaway rubbed his meaty paw over his face. He looked tired and worn. "You boys better beat it. It's going to be a long enough night as it is."

I looked at Birdie. "Works for me." Birdie nodded. "We'll see you around."

Callaway shouted at our backs. "You stay away from John Fat Gai, you hear me? I don't want you going near him."

"Sure, we will," I said. "We've got no business with him anyway." I didn't look back but kept on going. Callaway was good at reading faces and I wasn't sure what mine would show him.

39

The next morning, Birdie watched me as I sat hunched over the desk reading through the notes of the case files Callaway had shown me, pausing to take sips from coffee in a paper cup he'd brought from the Italian bakery down the street. The coffee tasted strong and sweet. My head and body ached. I'd spent half the night going over those files cross-checking names, dates and events. Wrote them out on a chart. Cops tied to John Fat Gai, allegedly. The picture showed me some fuzzy edges but it came closer into focus. "You figure it out yet?"

I looked at him sourly. "If only it was that simple. But I'm getting somewhere, yeah. I've narrowed it down to five names. Take a look."

Birdie scrutinized the pad. "Very interesting," he said.

"I know who my money's on."

Birdie sighed and shook his head. "Maybe we're making it too complicated."

"How do you figure?" I asked.

"I don't. I put my faith in higher powers."

I sighed. "Don't think that's going to help us this time." But I spoke too soon.

The phone rang. I snatched it up expecting Callaway or Tobin to growl in my ear. "Yeah?"

I heard hesitation on the line mainly because no one spoke for a minute. Then, "Er, Mr. Gold?"

"Yeah. Who's this?"

"Barry Wong…we met at…"

"I remember, Barry. What can I do for you?"

"Well, I've been thinking about what we discussed that time."

"Okay, what about it?"

"I may have some information for you. I'm wondering if we can meet someplace?" I glanced up at Birdie who caught my eye.

"Where and when?"

"I get half an hour for lunch." He named a greasy spoon on Bloor Street, not far from the hotel. "Twelve-thirty, okay?"

"See you there," I replied and hung up.

We got there early. Barry sat at a table nursing a bowl of tomato soup. Cracker crumbs layered the Formica tabletop. He'd taken a table at the back facing the door so he could watch who came and went. When we entered, he stood up and beckoned. Still dressed in his whites with the shoes as good as new, like they just came out of the box. Birdie and I sat down.

"How you doing, Barry," I said by way of greeting.

"Okay, I guess," he replied. "You guys want anything, soup, sandwich, cup of coffee maybe?"

"Coffee will be fine," I said. Barry went to the counter and ordered two coffees.

"Seems edgy," Birdie said.

"Uh-huh."

Barry brought the two coffees with him and set down a small metal jug with cream. The sugar shaker stayed with the table.

"You guys weren't followed, were you?" he asked.

"No," I replied.

"Are you sure?"

"I'm sure," I said. "Now why don't you clue us in here so we can help you?"

Barry swallowed and nodded, then pushed his glasses up with the tip of his finger. "It's my wife…" he began. "The girl you're looking for–she's my wife's cousin. Close family. You guys know what families are like."

"Why don't you tell us?" I said.

Barry shook his head again. "Her brother was a fool. Greedy and stupid. He stole from a powerful man. These men make their own laws, follow their own rules."

"You're talking about John Fat Gai?" I asked.

Barry nodded. "You must understand, my family knew nothing of what Ying was doing. But he stole from this man. He took money and worse."

"Meaning?"

"He took something of great value."

"What?"

Barry choked the words out. "A ledger. Financial transactions. Important people are incriminated. Something that can get you killed."

"I get it."

"My wife's cousin is scared. We all are. She needs protection. She's frightened for the baby."

"This baby," I asked. "Who's the daddy?"

Barry shrugged. "I don't know. Honestly. Liu Chen wouldn't tell us. I think she was ashamed. She's not married."

Birdie leaned in. "If she's got the ledger then that's all she needs, man."

Barry shook his head. "She gives John Fat Gai the ledger and there's nothing to stop him from killing her and us. That's the only thing that's keeping her alive. He hasn't found out about our connection yet. But he might."

"What do you want from us, Barry?" I asked him.

"You give him the ledger."

"In return for what?"

"A guarantee of our safety. And we'll need money to get my wife's cousin out of the country where she'll be safe."

"What about the money that Ying skimmed? Doesn't she have it?"

Barry shook his head woefully. "Don't know anything about any money."

It raised an interesting question. Who did take the dough? "You know who killed Ying?"

Barry shrugged. "My great-grandparents came here to work on the Pacific railway in the 1880's. They came as coolies—slave labour. Conditions were hard. The white men they worked for were cruel. Many died and a lot were injured. No compensation. You just lost your job if you couldn't work. They laid track in all kinds of conditions–blistering heat and freezing cold. They blasted through mountains and crossed the Prairies. Paid pennies a day by the rail company and whipped by the overseers. With those coolies came bad men who preyed on them bringing vice to these shores. Men like John Fat Gai. My family didn't slave for pennies sacrificing everything so men like him could take it away. I hope you understand. This is why my wife's cousin wishes for a chance at a new life for her child. That's all she wants. That's all we want."

"Where is she now?" I asked.

Barry's expression went tight. "Better you don't know–for now. When you've worked things out, you call me at this number and I will bring you the ledger." He slid a business card across the table to me. I slipped it into my jacket pocket. Barry checked his watch. "I need to get back to work. Can't be late. The boss is very fussy."

I glanced at the front door. "Is there a back way out of here?"

"Yes."

"Then I suggest you use it. Birdie and I will wait a few minutes before leaving."

Barry put out his hand. I took it. He did the same with Birdie. "Thank you gentlemen. I hope we can all rest easier soon."

"Amen to that," Birdie intoned.

I watched Barry go while Birdie kept an eye on the front door. We walked back to the car.

"What now?" Birdie asked.

"We let John know we've got the ledger and set up a meet for him to hand over Eli."

My mind spun with the possibilities. Tobin and Callaway wanted the ledger and John but if we gave them the ledger, then there'd be little hope for Eli or the girl and her baby. Then there was Jake and Mr. Li—they wanted the ledger too. Finally, we had Henry. He was mixed up in all of this yet I didn't know how. Our best chance at finding out had died last night. The odds on finding Henry hadn't improved much.

"How we going to make John leave the girl and Barry's family alone."

"Only a couple of possibilities come to mind," I replied.

"Like?"

I had the key out to open the Chevy's passenger door. I stopped and faced Birdie square on craning up, squinting into the early afternoon sun. "Well, we could take John out."

Birdie nodded but didn't seem convinced. "Risky. If it didn't work, everyone suffers and a lot get hurt. Or?"

"We spook him. Make him roll up and get out."

"That sounds better. How do we do that?"

I gave Birdie a soulful look. "Working on it."

Birdie grinned. "Time for some praying then."

40

I took out Mr. Li's card and studied it. We'd returned to the office, hanging around for a couple of hours. I called the number. He picked up after the third ring.

"Yes?"

"Mr. Li?"

"Hello Mr. Gold. Have you found the ledger yet?"

Nothing like getting down to business. "Why don't we discuss it in person?" I glanced at Birdie who quietly thumbed through his bible.

"Excellent idea, Mr. Gold."

"Where and when?"

"Midnight sounds like a good time." Then he gave me the address of a warehouse at the bottom of a back alley in Chinatown.

"Be there or be square," I said and then rang off. Hopefully, he knew what I meant. We'd see.

I didn't like back alleys. Too quiet. Too hidden. Too spooky. We'd found too many dead bodies in similar surroundings. Birdie parked the car a block away and we walked in. Just to emphasize our seriousness of purpose, I carried the .45 in its holster and the snub.38 down my sock. Birdie had twin .45's, one in each armpit and held the sawn-off, double barrel, pump action 12-gauge down at his side. A lone, sputtering streetlamp emphasized the dark inkiness away from the main drag. I looked for a green door. Li said it would be open and we should walk on in. Something else I didn't like.

"There it is," I muttered.

"Well, he got the colour right," Birdie said.

"Hmm," I replied.

We fanned out and took it from either side. I touched the knob then twisted. Like Li had said–open. I nudged it with my toe and it swung back revealing darkness. From my cop days, I always carried a flashlight. I flicked it on, sweeping the beam back and forth. Dusty emptiness. I sighed.

"Shall we?" Birdie asked.

I went first, Birdie after. I didn't even hear him. He took up a position behind me and to the right. I flicked the light around. Looked like an abandoned warehouse all right. Cement floor. Cinder block walls. That feeling of damp and the smell of humidity, of fungus and mold. A few wooden crates sat impassively on the cold floor. Apart from that–nothing. We moved ahead carefully, stepping cautiously and slowly.

Despite the damp and the chill, I sweated through my white shirt, feeling the beads of perspiration pool up in the waistband of my trousers. My eyes hurt from the strain of peering through the gloom, burning under the contrast of the white beam against the shadows. I stopped. Something moved. I flicked off the light. We stood and breathed for a long moment. I shook it off, snapped the light on again and we continued. Rats, most likely. The large, damp room seemed to be empty.

When it came, it was almost a relief. But the pistol shot made me jump. I snapped the light off quick and waited.

"Came from the far end," Birdie said. "Think I got a glimpse of a staircase too."

I flicked the light back on and we moved ahead. Birdie had been right. A cement staircase grew out of the back wall. Nowhere to go but up. I had the .45 in my right hand now and I knew that Birdie had cocked both barrels on the 12-gauge. We stepped upward lightly. After two flights, the stairs opened up into an alcove. A metal railing fenced it off like a corral. It connected to a corridor. At the end of the corridor, I saw a dim light glinting under the frame of a door.

"Looks like the place," Birdie murmured. It was a death trap. We both knew it but we headed toward the light anyway. Just as I reached for the knob, a voice I knew called out.

"Come on in, boychick, it's open." The voice belonged to him but the tone came out different. An old man's voice, cracked and fearful.

I flicked the light off and stowed it in my jacket pocket. I nodded to Birdie, who lifted his right, size 17 foot and applied it to the door in a thunderous kick. It flew off its hinges and we stepped inside. Another cavernous room, brightly lit. A wooden table had been pushed aside.

"A very dramatic entrance," John Fat Gai said and cackled. Beside him stood Quan, casually cradling an M-60 while a dozen of John's henchmen had their weapons out, trained on us. Sprawled on the floor lay Mr. Li, not quite dead. I smelled the burnt cordite and focused on the gaping, oozing hole in his abdomen. An expanding pool of blood threatened to lap at John's polished toe. Li's chest heaved, the breath coming in and out, raspy and whistling. He gasped out some words in Mandarin. His deadening eyes looked over. John stared at me. He didn't notice the blood reach his shoe.

"Hear this, Mr. Gold," Li wheezed like a creaky bellows, then craned around to stare at John. John looked away. "My spirit shall haunt you through the ages. You will find no peace and your soul will burn for eternity. The ghosts of my ancestors will steal into your soul and poison your mind, John Fat Gai. Hear me and be cursed from this moment forward. I curse you. My ancestors curse you. My descendants curse you forever. Look," he gasped and slumped back. Li's eyes rolled up into his head. Blood bubbled out of his lips.

John didn't look so hot. Sweat rolled down his gaunt cheeks. He looked down at his shoe then jumped back letting out a piercing squeal. He hopped around on one foot flicking the other in front of him. Finally, the shoe shot away hitting the far wall. As he flicked it off, a spray of blood came from the toe. The gunsels shrank back. They ducked as John hopped around like a maniac. You could eat the uncertainty and fear in the room. John stood panting, off-balance on one foot. He turned. A rivulet of Li's blood ran down his cheek. It could have been acid burning through paper. John's hand lunged into his trouser pocket. He dragged out a handkerchief and swiped at his cheek trying to rid himself of the cursed blood eating into his face. He swiped once, twice, three times. Finally, he threw the handkerchief on to the floor in disgust. He pressed his palm against his cheek and hissed. He turned and glowered at me with maniacal hatred.

John held a small caliber pistol in his right hand. He turned its snub barrel, pressing it into Jake's right ear. Jake didn't look so hot either. Pale at the best of times, his skin had turned practically translucent. I took another look at Mr. Li.

"Now is that any way to treat a fellow countryman?" I asked.

John mopped his face with his sleeve. The dragon pendant dangled outside his shirt. "A slight misunderstanding. But we settled our differences amicably," he panted, his lips trembling.

"For you, you mean."

"Li didn't understand his position here," John answered.

"I guess he does now."

"Exactly," John replied. "And now, to business. Do you have the ledger?"

"Not yet." John's finger tightened on the trigger. "Go ahead," I said.

"Boychick," Jake pleaded. That was the wrong thing to say.

"I don't care if you blow his head off."

Birdie raised the 12-gauge, pumped in two shells and pointed it at John's head.

"Your brains'll look mighty fine splattered on the ceiling," Birdie said.

"You will die too," John replied but didn't move.

"You'll be the first and then maybe Quan over there," I said and pointed the .45 at Quan's heart. His smirk froze.

"Fair point," John conceded. He grimaced. "I want the ledger, the girl and the chauffeur and I want them now. I will not tolerate any more delays."

"I've still got 24 hours," I said. "Your terms."

We stared each other down. It felt like looking into a cataclysm of darkness. After an eon, John broke away. "Twenty-four hours, no longer. If not for your father, then your brother. It would be a shame to have all of the Golds eliminated at the same time."

I thumbed the hammer on the .45. "I think you're speaking out of turn, John." I took a step back and motioned Birdie to do the same. "I'm not the one who's been cursed. Twenty-four hours."

I took another look. Li's eternal expression looked like one of contentment. Slowly, we backed out of the room. Jake didn't take his eyes off me once. I could see he tried to figure it out. Would I have let him die? I didn't give him the satisfaction of leaving any doubt.

We walked briskly back to the Chevy. No one followed us.

41

My head pounded but it had subsided to a vigorous tapping inside my skull rather than the relentless drilling of a jackhammer. Some progress. "Where we headed?" Birdie asked.

"To see if we can find Henry."

Birdie thought for a minute. "It's two o'clock in the morning."

"I know, but we don't have a lot of time."

"I need to stoke my fire," he said and pointed at his belly.

"Right."

On College Street, there was an all-night diner called Mars. Its slogan was "Food Out of this World." I didn't know about that but the countermen whipped up hot food on the spot. Quick and cheap. Particularly famous for their bran muffins. It called out to the denizens of the night.

We took a seat at the counter. One other guy who'd seen better times, nursed a coffee. One of the night men sat at a booth in the back smoking and reading the paper.

"What'll it be, gents?" the counterman asked.

He looked to be about 50. He wore a dirty white apron smeared with grease and a paper hat. He had a sallow face and the heavy-lidded eyes of a boozer. A fag smoldered in an ashtray by his left hand.

"Four fried egg sandwiches and two large orders of French fries," Birdie said. "And a large chocolate malted."

"And you?" the guy asked. He didn't even blink. Not once.

"Just gimme an order of French toast, coffee and one of your famous bran muffins."

The counterman nodded. "You got it." He took a last drag of the cigarette then crushed it out. "Coming right up."

He slapped down a saucer and a cup and poured out of a fresh pot. He rolled a couple of creamers my way. "To get you started," he said.

He turned his back to us and began cracking eggs for the French toast. "You want those sandwiches toasted?"

"You have to ask?" Birdie boomed.

"I figured."

I liked watching these guys work. They were models of efficiency. Took my mind off things. He sliced four slabs of egg bread, dipped them in the egg mixture then tossed them on to the grill. I almost felt the sizzle. The fries burbled in oil. He cracked six eggs beside the bread. In his right hand, he held a metal spatula. He shifted the spatula over to his left and filled four toasters with white bread and banged them down. With deft strokes, he slid the spatula under the French toast and turned the slices over and flipped the eggs in succession, lining everything up in a neat, sputtering row. He grabbed a plate, covered it with the French toast, sprinkled some icing sugar over top and slid it over to me.

A second later he set down a metal pot of syrup. "There you go," he said. "French toast, hot off the griddle."

The toast popped and he buttered each slice in turn, scooped up the eggs, ground on some pepper, sprinkled a little salt and put it all together in a stack. He lifted the fries out of the oil, drained them and dumped them into some grease paper. The sandwiches were neatly arrayed as he set the plate carefully in front of Birdie. The grease paper had done its work, and another plate, a platter really, appeared beside the sandwiches, along with a bottle of malt vinegar and the same of ketchup.

"Malted coming right up," he said but before I could ask he refilled my coffee cup. He began to mix the malted ingredients up in a long, metal container. The French toast was the best I'd ever had–hot, crisp on the outside, soft on the inside–steam wafted up as I cut into it. I slathered on some syrup and dug in. The milkshake machine whirred away and a moment later, he poured out the thick, creamy liquid into a tall glass, stuck a straw in it and set it down in front of Birdie just as he was taking a bite of the second egg sandwich.

"Lemme know if you want anything else," he said. I think the whole thing must have taken all of two minutes.

Birdie nodded.

"Sure thing," I said, as he placed an enormous bran muffin, the size of a flying saucer, on the counter in front of me.

"Enjoy."

He sidled down the counter, leaned back and lit another fag, then poured himself a coffee. He held up the pot and I nodded. My cup was refilled efficiently. He moved back down the counter, replaced the coffee pot, picked up his fag and took a long pull.

I looked over at Birdie. He had just demolished most of the third sandwich. Half the malted disappeared. "You let John shoot Jake?" he asked.

I pondered that for a second or two. "Yeah, I would have." Birdie took a last bite of number three and picked up number four.

"That's what I figured."

"You think that's cold?"

Birdie shrugged. "That's between you two. You know I got someone always looking over my shoulder."

I began to peel the wax paper off the bottom of the muffin. I broke off a piece, it was nice and moist, and took a bite. I'd inhaled the French toast.

"I know. I just want to get Eli back. Jake's on his own," I said.

Birdie chewed thoughtfully, took another slurp of the malted that just about emptied it and nodded. "Like I said…"

"You and your god will forgive me. I know that too."

Birdie polished off the last sandwich. "Can I get a coffee, please?"

The counterman looked up. "Yessir, you can." He grabbed a cup and saucer and a couple of creamers and poured out the cup, then set it down carefully in front of Birdie's plate. "Guess you were hungry, huh?"

Birdie grinned. "Famished but I'm feeling good now. Real good."

"What do I owe ya?" I asked the guy.

The counterman did a quick calculation in his. "Six-fifty," he said.

I laid down a ten. "Keep it," I said. "You earned it."

"Thanks. Anything else I can get you?"

I looked over at Birdie. He shook his head. The coffee in his cup had evaporated.

"That's it," I replied. I emptied the cup, took a last bite of the muffin and stood up. "See you again."

The counterman nodded. "Right. See you."

I could feel his eyes on us as we left. Birdie usually made people nervous. Even so, the guy had been a pro and I appreciated it. No complaints about the grub.

A guy in desperate straits could count on his friends. I figured that Henry Turner was no different. Otherwise, my options had expired.

Reaching Cecil Street took five minutes, even less early in the morning. I'd heard Garcia kept a flat in the Local 183 building and I hoped he bunked there tonight. Cars lined the street but I found a spot half a block down. None of the houses had lights on. The dead zone–a time when few ventured out and those that did often regretted it. I rang the night bell, leaned on it heavily and heard its muffled ring from inside. After about five minutes of putting my weight into it, a light came on in the hallway. A rumpled Garcia appeared. A short lifetime later he'd unlocked the deadbolts and the door swung open. He held the baseball bat in his right hand and looked like he'd use it without a moment's hesitation. He blinked at us and finally, recognition flooded into his face.

"What the hell do you want?" he rasped. "Especially at this time in the morning."

"Need your help, Garcia," I said staring at him, willing him to understand what we needed.

He returned my stare for what seemed a long time. But then he nodded grimly. "You better come in." And he stood aside to let us pass. When we'd entered, he took a quick look in both directions up and down the street, then bolted the door clicking into place a complex array of locks and bolts.

A moment later, we were seated in his office. "When I'm working late, it's more convenient for me to sleep here than go home."

"Safer you mean."

"Yeah. That too."

I glanced at the family photo on his desk. "Divorced?"

"Separated."

"You know why we're here?"

Garcia smiled and shook his head. "Enlighten me."

The office felt small and cramped. Stale odours lingered. I stood up. "We need to find Henry Turner and we need to find him fast."

"So?" Garcia knitted his brow.

"You know where he is."

"Look, I've told you, I haven't seen Henry since he disappeared."

"Tell us another one, Garcia. You're his pal. Maybe his best pal. Henry disappears but has the ability to reappear when he wants. He can leave his mother small gifts on her birthday for example and then he disappears again."

"Yeah, so maybe he's really Harry Houdini."

"I know you think you're protecting him but things are coming to a head. A young guy's life is at stake. An innocent party who did no harm to anyone." My voice broke a bit and Garcia gave me a quizzical look. "I have to speak to Henry. I have to know what was going on and why he felt he needed to disappear. And why he couldn't say anything about it all these years. I know it's dangerous but it's going to be worse if we don't find him. Henry may have disappeared but his mother hasn't and there are parties out there who know that and won't hesitate to use her to reel him in. Do I make myself clear? Innocent people may die here. His mother is in danger. He doesn't have any options left." Garcia's eyes narrowed. He chewed on his upper lip under the moustache.

"I made a promise," he said but his brain was ticking over.

"Look Garcia, I understand. A man gives his word. Often it's all he's got. But if Aida Turner ends up dead, how you gonna feel about your promise? How will Henry feel?"

"How do I know you're not just trying to sucker me?" Garcia asked. "Henry told me that under no circumstances was he to be found. That no one, including Mrs. Turner should know where he is."

"I know that but the circumstances have changed. Everything is cracking open. The family he used to drive for, The Fosters, the daughter, Alison–she's dead—murdered—a beautiful, 24 year-old woman and young wife, and there could be more to come. If Henry can help us prevent anything else from happening, don't you think he'd want to? Henry strikes me as a decent guy trying to do the right thing. He'd make the choice. He's sacrificed a lot. It's time to put an end to all that so he can come back and live in the real world."

Garcia drummed the desktop with his stubby fingertips. "I don't know," he said. "I just don't know."

"Look," I said. "You know we've been looking for him, covered a lot of ground. And then I got to thinking about him and you and where you worked before. Somewhere you can't be seen and a place that's difficult to find or even think of. You and Henry worked on those tunnels. I think you know exactly where Henry is and can lead us to him. I need you to do that now for all kinds of good reasons, least of all, Henry's own welfare."

"Whaddaya mean?"

"If we've figured it out then others probably have too. Those others include a Chinese gangster with a vicious posse. Come on, Garcia, don't you see? It won't be long before they go gunning for him–and he's on his own without any help. At least we…" and I spread the flaps of my jacket to reveal the mini-arsenal I carried and Birdie did the same. "…can even the odds a little bit."

"You'd do that for him? You don't even know him."

"Like I said, there's more at stake here. We need Henry's help to figure it out."

Garcia slumped in his chair staring at his lap. "Goddammit," he said. After a long moment, he raised his head, then nodded wearily.

42

Garcia rode in the back of the Chevy. I checked my watch: 3:17 a.m. Fatigue seeped into my bones but I knew I had to stay sharp and focused. Garcia directed us to the Rosedale subway station. Rosedale. A swanky address even if it was underground. We parked opposite the station. It was shut up tight for the night. The last train ran at midnight except on special occasions and certain holidays.

Garcia led us to a utility door. A key that looked more like an Allen wrench appeared in his hand. He fitted it into the lock and the door swung open. Garcia took a quick look around. He ushered us in closing the door behind us and locked it from the inside. He switched on a feeble light that revealed a metal staircase pointing downward.

"Come on," he said.

As we descended, I shivered. It felt dank and distinctly colder. Birdie gave me a look, one of those that said 'what have we got ourselves into?' I counted 75 steps before we hit bottom and another door. This one was open. Garcia waited for us.

"This way," he said.

He led us down a long, narrow corridor–concrete floor, walls and ceiling. The corridor veered sharply right and we followed that trajectory. After roughly 100 feet, Garcia stopped at another door. Out came the curious little key and it swung open. We stepped inside. A storage area. I spotted a rack of slickers, one below for boots and up above for hard hats.

"Grab a slicker and some boots," Garcia said. He looked at Birdie. "You'll have to make do. You don't want to ruin your coat or your shoes. It's pretty damp down here. Water flushes down from the open grates and vents on the sidewalks." He picked up a hardhat that had a light built into it. "You'll need one of these too. Not much light where we're going."

I managed to find a slicker and a pair of boots that corresponded roughly to my size. Birdie squeezed himself into the largest he could find but still ridiculously small. Same with the hard hat. Garcia expanded the headband as best he could and handed it over after firing up the torch. We looked like odd-shaped glowworms.

"C'mon," Garcia beckoned. "It's a bit of a hike." I wondered when he'd done it last. He didn't look like he'd been very active lately but surprisingly, ambled forward comfortably.

The slickers helped with the dampness and chill permeating the air, but they sat awkwardly and the boots dragged. I began to sweat as we slogged through the next corridor. Disoriented, I couldn't tell our direction, how deep underground we were or how far we'd walked. Probably not too far. Less than a mile.

Garcia banged through another door with a push bar and we found ourselves on the edge of the subway platform. The entrance to the platform consisted of a metal gate. Garcia prodded it open with the toe of his boot and we went through to the platform proper. The conductor's booth and the newspaper kiosk sat shut up tight like the ticket taker and candy-floss maker of an abandoned fair ground. We strode to the end of the platform where we encountered another gate. The railing hung low and awkwardly, Garcia, stepped over it. We followed, descending a narrow set of steps to the floor of the tunnel.

"Walk in the centre, away from the rail," Garcia said. "You can get fried pretty quick. It stays hot all the time."

We moved gingerly into the centre of the floor. Slimy debris littered its bottom.

"Stuff blows in," Garcia said, stopping for a moment focusing his headlamp by my feet. "People toss stuff on to the track and when the wind comes up from the trains or the grates, it blows on through and turns to mush after a while."

He lifted his head up shining the beam on a grate I hadn't noticed and I could see the dripping of water from the surface. "When it rains heavily or we get melting snow, you can get a lot of water down here. The tunnel is built on a slant from the centre so most of it drains away from the rails. The water never gets high enough to short out the system."

"Nice," I said. "Remind me to put in a job application with the transit authority."

Garcia chuckled and made it sound like a gurgling tap. "Come on," he said. "Better make tracks." When we looked at him, he said sheepishly, "Transportation joke."

We walked for a while and I tried to get a rhythm going in the heavy boots but it became a slog. The beams from the headlamps darted around like artificial moonbeams doing a crazy sort of a dance.

"How far we going?" I asked.

"To Bloor," Garcia said then chuckled again. I figured it was another joke. Bloor was the next station south. Garcia stopped. We stopped behind him. "See anything?" he asked.

I peered around. "Nope. Just a dark, nasty tunnel."

"You?" he asked Birdie.

"Same."

"That's what makes it such a good hiding place," Garcia said. "You blink and you're by it. Only if a bright light shone right over the entrance would you even know it was there and if a train is going fast enough, it probably wouldn't register anyway."

He resumed walking but stopped after about 50 feet. He turned to his right. When I drew abreast, I followed the line of his headlamp and saw an opening in the tunnel wall.

"It's an old spur line," Garcia explained. "But after the tunnels were finished, they filled most of it back in but left a small opening. No one uses it now."

"What was it used for before?" I asked.

"Storage mainly and they could put some of the rolling stock in here while they went ahead with the blasting and they knew it would be protected. You've got 20 feet or more of solid Canadian Shield there plus they built a metal frame and covered it over in concrete. Pretty solid. Take a major earthquake to bring it all down. I'm not saying it couldn't happen but it's unlikely."

"Great," Birdie muttered. "Earthquakes now…"

"I said it was unlikely…"

"I heard you…Jesus…deliver me from evil…"

"Amen to that," I said. Garcia looked at us both strangely. "Just a little thing we do," I told him. "Picked it up during the War."

Garcia nodded, then turned into the opening. "You said that before."

We had to go single file as it ran like a vertical slit trench just barely wide enough for a man to walk through normally and that was why Birdie struggled and appreciated the slicker at the same time. It became hard going though as we scrabbled over the uneven ground. Two hundred yards or more along, the slit veered left. We continued on. As the space narrowed, it pressed closer in, made the dank air moist and clotted. Garcia had begun to wheeze and I wasn't far behind. Birdie grunted with effort. I hadn't noticed but the ceiling had swung low and he had to bend his head to get under it, walking hunched forward with his neck stuck out like a flibbertigibbet. If I wasn't so uncomfortable myself, I would have laughed.

"I know what you're thinking," he said. "Don't say it."

"I don't have to."

There wasn't enough room for Garcia to turn around comfortably, not with his bulk so he kept moving forward. "You can see why Henry hasn't been found," he said. "Who'd want to come down here and put up with this crap?"

"How'd he find it in the first place?" I asked, hearing my voice echo back like a ghost.

"We'd worked this section a few months before Henry got hurt. He'd seen the plans. Remember, he was Deans' guy and he showed Henry the blueprints–practically every day they were going over them, so Henry remembered it."

"How'd he get through the doors and gates?" I asked. "He would have needed one of those screwy keys, wouldn't he?"

Garcia couldn't look at me but he shrugged. "Keys go missing all the time. You think they keep an accurate count? Serves them right anyway, the union hating bastards."

"So, this is a form of revenge?" I asked.

Garcia kept trudging along. "Let's say I enjoyed the fact that he was taking advantage of the Transit Authority's hospitality without their knowing it."

"It'd be living like a bat," Birdie said. "Wouldn't take long before I was sleeping upside down, hanging from the ceiling."

"That I'd like to see," I said.

"Almost there," Garcia said.

I shone the headlamp on my watch. We'd been walking for over half an hour, maybe closer to 40 minutes. I had to admit, it was a good hidey-hole. The narrow corridor we'd been following opened up into an antechamber. The area lay bare and the ceiling skyrocketed. I peered up and in the gloom could barely make out where it ended. The air felt warmer too and fresh.

"Because the guys were working down here, they put a couple of vents up into the surface to keep the air circulating. It's funny how the air warms up as it's drawn down, like a natural heater. Even in winter, the temperature stays fairly constant, almost pleasant. If we weren't 100 feet or so underground, it would almost be ideal."

"Except there's no natural light," I said.

"Yeah, that's a problem for most people," Garcia replied.

"And Henry?"

"You'll see." He gestured. "This way."

We crossed the antechamber and found another door recessed into the wall. If you didn't know it was there, it would have been difficult to find. Even the door handle, a semi-cylindrical piece of brushed metal, was hard to see. Garcia used his screwy key and the door opened inward. He beckoned.

We stepped into a strange, other-worldly landscape. It could have been a movie set. This second antechamber appeared double the size of the first, perhaps larger. Lines of lights hung from a series of wires cross-hatched above ceiling height. Lit up like Christmas. Amazingly, we stood before a front yard with a green lawn, a picket fence freshly painted white and a cozy looking cabin nestled behind it. The cabin had a wooden porch and a rocking chair, two picture windows and a slanted, wood shingle roof. Both Birdie and I must have looked as if we'd been stunned.

"Sweet Jesus," Birdie exclaimed.

Garcia chuckled. "Gets me every time too."

"How did he...?" The question remained incomplete.

Garcia looked at me. "People throw stuff out–you'd be amazed. Not just residences; building sites, industrial parks, whatever you need can be acquired for free–and that's what he's done. Took him a while to put all this together."

"Running water? Electricity?" I asked.

Garcia nodded. "Yeah, we'd put in the water pipes when we were doing the construction, so that was easy. Henry figured out how to tap into the grid so he's got more juice down here than City Hall."

We made our way to the front yard. I stepped on the lawn and heard it crinkle.

"Fake grass," Garcia said. "This lawn came from a golf shop that had its own artificial putting green, you know, like when you play mini-putt? Looks pretty good, almost like the real thing."

It was extraordinary and weird, like looking at some kind of exhibit in a museum for the strange and unnatural. I looked at Birdie and he shrugged as if he was saying, who were we to judge? Henry had to do anything necessary to survive.

We stepped on to the porch and it felt solid; weathered oak timber that could last centuries. To one side, stood a grocery cart and I figured that's how he moved stuff in and out. It looked like it had been polished and oiled recently. Garcia tapped gently on the front door. It was painted an ocher colour. I saw a box at my feet, filled with discarded objects, broken toys and beheaded dolls.

"Henry?" Tap. Tap. "Henry?" We listened. Nothing. No movement within. Garcia peered through the closest window shifting his headlamp in an arc. "Don't see anything inside." He tried the door handle. "Locked. Looks like he isn't home."

"Where could he be?" Birdie asked.

"Anywhere," Garcia replied. "He travels the entire city. Knows it like the back of his hand. He's always out doing things, finding things, collecting stuff and he keeps an eye on things too."

"Now what?" I asked.

"Nothing," Garcia said. "We go. No point waiting for him. He could be out for hours or days even. He knows places to stay in just about every part of town. Places where he isn't seen."

"Where are they?"

Garcia shook his head slowly. "Honestly, I don't know. This is only the third or fourth time I've even come down here. I haven't actually set eyes on Henry in almost six months."

"Leave him a note. Say you've got to talk to him."

"What good will that do?"

"It will save us chasing him around the whole damn city for one thing," Birdie snorted.

"Birdie's right, Garcia. We're short on time. It's important we get to him as soon as we can."

Garcia blew out a long sigh. "I don't know about this."

I reached down and picked up one of the broken dolls. "Tell him you need to meet him at Henley Park at two o'clock. Tell him you'll be there until six o'clock and he can pick his time."

"Where's that?"

"Henry will know where it is."

Garcia reached into a side pocket and pulled out a piece of crumpled paper. He rummaged around in the slicker until he came up with a pen.

He lay the paper flat on the porch rail and wrote out the note, re-read it then stuck it into the door frame.

"Hope you guys know what you're doing," he said.

"Yeah, me too." I took another look around. Henry had found his refuge, his hidey-hole, just like in the book.

43

We dropped Garcia back at his union infused fortress just as the sun peeked up over the horizon. While it was still early and the world shook off the night tremors, I figured a return to the docklands might be fruitful. Fortunately, I knew a bakery on Lansdowne that opened early. We grabbed half a dozen danish, some hard rolls, butter and cheese and four coffees to go. I kept the window rolled down and we ate as we drove which was easier for Birdie since I sat behind the wheel. He ate five of the Danish, most of the rolls and drank three of the coffees.

A fruit vendor hosed down the sidewalk in front of his shop and the cobbler next store winched out his awning. Mostly, it seemed calm and hushed. By the time we got down to Blackstones, the sun rose several fingers above the horizon. I drove around back thinking that might be the way in. No cars parked anywhere near by or in the perimeter around the building. They should have blown off by four or five in the morning at the latest, even with the additional kerfuffle Birdie initiated. I had forgotten to ask him how all that went.

"What happened with the Yanks?" I asked.

"Very disappointing."

"How so?"

"Didn't last more than two minutes, maybe two and a half. I was hoping for a little more fight in them."

"Well, they'd had a skinful so blame it on that."

"You saying I took advantage because they were drunk?"

"Did I say that?"

"It's what you meant," he retorted hotly.

"You gonna eat that last Danish? If not, I wouldn't mind one."

He grinned at me. "That's what I like about you, Mo. You stick to the important things."

"Took a lot of practice." I launched into a big bite. "Thinking about Eli."

"I know."

"Whatever it takes."

"I hear you."

We took a look around. At the back we found a metal security door.

"Wanna grab my picks from the glove?"

Birdie tsked at me but went back to the car. He came back with a set of lock picks I liberated from a second story man I'd busted years back. The guy had been more upset about losing his picks than getting arrested, kept telling me he owned only quality tools. He was right. They'd come in handy many times since then.

It took me about two minutes before I cracked the door open. No alarm. Why would there be? Anybody stupid enough to rob John Fat Gai wouldn't be around for long.

"Hmm, didn't know this place had a kitchen," I said as we made our way forward. "Doesn't look like they've used it for cooking recently either." The thick layer of dust on the countertops and the grease-stained walls seemed a clue. Metal pans stacked in the industrial sink looked as if they'd been sitting there for weeks.

"Guess the music is the attraction," Birdie said.

"Must be."

We entered the bar area. The cleaning crew hadn't been on the scene. Half a dozen tables lay overturned and toward the centre, where the Americans had been sitting, three chairs broken, bottles and smashed glasses littered the floor. I stopped and took a good look. "What a mess. Aren't you ashamed?"

"I'm trying," Birdie said. "I'm sure I will be remorseful."

"Hah."

A quick tour verified that the main floor of the joint remained unoccupied. We headed up the stairs, pushed through the door at the top and found ourselves in the same corridor I'd trod the day before. I set about unlocking the doors along the side. The first one sprung open and I took a good look. Birdie frowned.

"Looks like a pillow room," I said.

We left that one and I cracked open the next.

"Well, well. Looks like John has a nice little sideline going."

The second room had a movie camera and a reel-to-reel tape recorder. The camera sat on a tripod pointed at the wall that connected the two rooms.

"Alice through the looking glass," I said.

The wall we faced acted as a one-way mirror. From the camera's point of view, the camera guy had a clear shot of the bed. Rumpled sheets. There'd been some action recently. We checked the other rooms and all together found four identical set-ups. That meant John could blackmail four guys at once. Or he'd established his credentials as a maker and peddler of smut. I had more faith in John's commercial instincts. Blackmail seemed far more lucrative with a longer revenue cycle. I slapped my thigh hard.

"What?" Birdie asked.

I shook my head. "John."

"What about him?"

"Think of it this way, okay? John uses underage girls. So, he gets the guy and squeezes him. The girls he uses come from wealthy families. He puts the bite on them too. He gets a cut both ways. I've got to admit, it's smart. He's got double the money in his pocket and nobody dares admit to anything. What a set-up."

"He's the devil."

"Or a close second."

"The girls," Birdie said.

I looked at him. "Yeah–wild girls–like to party and he gets them to cooperate by hooking them on opium." I sniffed the air. The cloying odour of cloves hung heavily, saturating the carpets and the drapes. Opium could be mixed with tobacco and cloves and smoked like a cigarette. Another tradition John Fat Gai had brought with him.

"Girls like Alison Foster," Birdie said.

"Girls like Alison Foster and Gayle Sorenson," I added. "Party girls looking for a kick and not knowing what they were getting into."

"You think Lawson knows?"

I paused. "I don't know. Maybe."

"Her folks?"

"That's an even better question."

The door to the office where I'd found Jake remained locked but not for long. We went through the desk pulling out drawers and folders finding requisition sheets and manifests for liquor orders. Some of the booze had to be legit, they couldn't provide all the liquor by boosting it. The file cabinets yielded much of the same, utility bills, phone statements, nothing of much use. The bottom drawer remained locked. Out came the handy tools and thirty seconds later, I had it open. A bunch of manila envelopes stuffed with reels. I grabbed them and re-locked the drawer.

"This could be important."

Birdie looked at me. "Where there's smoke," he said. I caught his drift.

I locked up all the rooms and we headed back down the stairs.

We crossed over to the car.

I fired up the Chevy and switched on the radio making sure it was tuned to CKOC. Del Shannon's '*Runaway*' came on. Picking up on the rhythm, I tore out of the parking lot burning rubber.

44

Two o'clock found me comfortably seated on a bench on the perimeter of Henley Park. I crumpled a paper cup that had contained bitter coffee and tossed it into a wire-framed trash bin. I fired up a Sweet Cap and surveyed the surroundings. It looked like the same mothers were watching their kids climb and jump and indulge in shrill-voiced mayhem while they gossiped, ignoring but the most strident of entreaties.

A little girl and boy dug around in the sand with plastic shovels filling up tiny buckets then dumped them out again and started over. I wondered when life had become so simple. Their mother sat near by reading a magazine, she stretched her limbs, yawned and turned her face up to the sun in unbridled pleasure. For some reason, I found that painful and turned away. I glanced at the newspaper on my lap but nothing came into focus. Birdie lurked somewhere. He was good at that despite his size. He had patience, something that came to me in short supply.

Three o'clock passed and the first group of mothers left. At three-thirty, another group took their place. These kids were older, having, I guessed, just been let out of school and didn't want to go home just yet. By four-thirty, some teenagers showed up and huddled in the far corner talking loudly, laughing caustically, sharing a few fags among them. The mothers moved their kids away as the teens got louder and rougher.

Two of the boys began to chase each other around the small square, rough housing and generally cutting up. They weren't watching where they were going and knocked over a little girl who began to cry. The mother picked the little girl up and began to harangue them. Being teenagers, they sassed her back. Before I could step in, one of the loudmouths was yanked backward. I could see he wore the same uniform as before, the white coveralls and carried a canvas satchel where he put the garbage he picked up.

The city cleaner held a pole with a long, sharp nail at the end of it. When the teens started to cuss him out, he brandished the pole and told them to clear off or he'd use it. One of the teenagers dared him. The garbage picker's hand darted out in a flash and suddenly, the boy grabbed the fleshy part of his thigh yowling in pain. When I looked at the nail on the end of the pole, a fleck of blood glinted in the light. The teens grabbed their pal and dragged him off hurling insults.

"You're crazy man–you should be arrested–go get locked up…"

The garbage picker ignored them and had words with the young mother who still clutched her little girl. The girl had calmed and the mother thanked him, saying those boys terrorized the park just about every day and no one stood up to them. The man nodded and smiled, then went about his business picking garbage from the ground. I felt the bulky shape in my pocket. I got up and waited for a minute while the garbage picker moved off a ways then went over to him.

"I found something," I said.

The man kept sticking papers in the ground and flicked them into the satchel. He didn't look up. "Oh?"

"Yeah," I replied. "I think it belongs to you."

"What makes you think that, mister?"

I reached into my pocket and removed the copy of *The Invisible Man* and held it out to him. "Here, take a look."

The garbage picker looked at it sideways but kept moving. "Don't think so."

"Take a closer look, Henry. Your name is written on the inside cover. It's definitely yours, all right."

Henry Turner froze. He swiveled to his left away from me and was about to run for it when he banged into a wall of human flesh that turned out to be Arthur Birdwell.

"Howdy Henry," Birdie said.

"We're not here to hurt you, Henry."

"Where's Ricky? He left me a note."

"We're here to help," I said. "Can we talk for a minute? I've got a few questions to ask you. Your mother hired us to look for you."

Henry sagged. "Guess I knew this day would come," he said quietly. We escorted him to the bench. He kept his head down the whole time. Trying to stay invisible.

"Hiding in plain sight, Henry. That was smart. Clever."

"Uh-huh. Who'd you say you were again?"

"I didn't, but my name is Mo Gold and this is my partner, Arthur Birdwell. Call him, Birdie."

"My momma's okay?"

"Fine, Henry, she's just fine. She can't wait to see you."

Henry looked up with fear in his eyes. "No sir. I can't do that. It's too dangerous."

"Why Henry? Why is it dangerous?"

Henry looked away again like a little kid distracted by a bright colour. "She got the things I left for her, I know she did."

"That's right. She always believed in you, Henry. She never stopped believing, not after all these years."

"She'll understand one day. One day…" and he stopped. "Why you talking to me, man? What have I done to you?"

I glanced at Birdie who rolled his eyes just a tad. "You haven't done anything, Henry. We're fine. We're here to help you and your mother but you have to talk to us."

"Uh-huh." But he didn't sound convinced.

"You remember Alison, don't you? Alison Foster? Her name is Lawson now."

Henry started to laugh. "You think I've lost my marbles, haven't you? You think that old Henry's been away so long, he can't function in society any more. Don't you? Isn't that what you thinking, Mr. Gold?"

"I think what you've done is very, very smart. Amazing really."

"Why did you ask me about Miss Foster?"

"She was murdered, Henry. Last night. Stabbed through the heart."

Henry's face went slack. "They know who did it?"

"Her husband's been arrested but I don't think he's guilty. He's in a helluva mess though."

"If it wasn't her husband, then who was it?"

I shrugged and shifted my position on the bench. "I don't know, Henry. I was hoping you could help me find out. I was hoping you could fill in a lot of the blanks we've been looking at."

"Meaning?" His tone was almost accusatory.

"What happened on that night eight years ago? What happened that you had to run away and hide yourself? That's the key to everything, Henry. And if we don't know what happened that night, then we can't help you, your mother, your cousin, Adele…"

"Adele? What's she got to do with anything?"

"Well, she's become very close to your mother and everyone wants to find you…"

"Me and Adele weren't that close. She was always trying to make herself look good, make me look bad, you know what I mean?"

"Yeah. I think so but that doesn't mean she isn't worried about you. I get the impression you were tight."

"Uh-huh. That's right. Just the three of us, against the world. After my daddy died."

"What happened back then, Henry?"

Henry shook his head. Jaw clenched.

"C'mon man," Birdie boomed. "Get it off your chest. You'll feel better for it."

Henry stared at Birdie then swallowed hard. He took a big gulp of air. "You a preacher?"

"Sometimes," Birdie replied.

"I finished with all of that. What good did it do? Didn't help me none."

"Your mother goes to church every Sunday, Henry," I said.

"Yeah. I know that," he replied in a sullen tone. "She think God's gonna help her out and look what's happened. Slaving for that family all those years and what has she got? Nothin, that's what."

"She's still got you, Henry and that's all she cares about." Birdie laid his big paw on Henry's shoulder. "Now, come on, man. If you don't do this for yourself, then do it for her. Talk to us for Miz Turner. For her precious sake."

Henry stared at Birdie for a long moment, then he laughed. "Man, you good. I think you are a preacher."

"Henry?" I prompted.

He sighed. "Yeah. Well. I was driving for Miss Alison. She and her friends were getting into all kinds of trouble. All kinds…"

"You would drive them to Blackstones?"

"That's right. I don't know how she found out about that place but she did and they were going two, three nights a week. Her folks were away a lot. They didn't know what she was up to."

"But you did?"

"Kind of. I knew they weren't going to church, if that's what you mean but I didn't know exactly what went on there."

"When you say they went two, three times a week, was it all four of them, the boys and the girls?"

"Nu-unh, just the girls. Those boys only went a couple of times that I know of."

"And the other girl was Gayle Sorenson?"

"Yeah. That's right. Gayle."

"You never went into the club?"

Henry hesitated. He licked his lips, folded his hands in his lap and stared at the ground. "Only the once," he said. "Only that one time and I wished I hadn't. I wished I'd never set foot in that place."

Birdie reached out and took his arm gently. "Man, you gotta tell us what happened that night."

Henry nodded, tight-lipped. "My life changed forever that night was what happened," he said. He drifted back eight years.

"I'd been concerned for a while. Things were getting crazy with those two. They'd go in that place and when they came out, man, I knew they was trippin' on something. And whatever it was, it wasn't good. Some Chinese guy would bring them out the back. That's where I picked them up. I wanted to tell Mr. Foster about it but Miss Alison made me promise not to say anything. She told me she'd tell him it was all my doing. That she'd tell Mr. Foster I forced her to go and then the police would be called and I'd be arrested for all kinds of things. She'd just gone crazy. Whatever they were doing in there must have made her insane. They'd come out and be all drowsy, barely able to walk and the two of them would just giggle their heads off in the back seat but it was spooky what they sounded like–it certainly wasn't natural."

"Go on."

"That night…they….uh…"

"They got pulled over by a traffic cop, isn't that right?" I prompted.

"Yeah, that's right. I got down to the station a little after midnight. I had to wait. The kids were still being talked to by the police. When they come out, Miss Alison laid into me, really tore a strip off my hide, like it was all my fault they got picked up and held by the cops. She was screaming and yelling but then, I could see she was in a real bad way."

"What do you mean? A bad way?"

"Doubled over and moaning with pain. That's what it looked like."

I was confused. "Miss Foster was in pain?"

Henry shook his head. "No. The other one."

"Gayle Sorenson?"

"Yeah, that's right. She could barely walk. Miss Alison, she was in a bad way too but not like the other one. Miss Alison was jumpy and scratching at herself. I figured it was the dope doing its work, you know?"

"Go on."

"We got outside and the boys split. Miss Alison held the other girl up who was moaning and crying. I brought the car around. Miss Alison say to take them back there... "

"To Blackstones?"

"Yeah, that's right. Back there. We had a disagreement about it. I was worried about the other girl. She looked like she needed a doctor real bad but Miss Alison screamed at me. I never heard a body spew such filth, it just poured out of her. Finally, I said, fine, I had enough. Her call. So I drove down to the club. As I drove, the other girl had her head in Miss Alison's lap. She tried to soothe her, keep her calm and it worked for a while then she'd get a kind of spasm and start screaming again. It was hard to listen to and I felt real sorry for her."

"Finish it off, man," Birdie said. "Go on."

"So we get there and I stopped the car outside the front door. Miss Alison gives me a look like, ain't I gonna help them out of the car but I stayed put. I wasn't gonna do anything else. Fed up with it but the other girl was in such a bad way that I couldn't stop myself. I opened the back door and between the two of us, we kinda half-carried the poor girl to the entrance of that place. But that was as far as I went, you know? We was met by this Chinese guy, the same one who was always there, had a kind of cocky attitude. He stopped me and said he'd take it from here and I said, fine, I'll just go wait in the car. And that's what I did. I put the radio on low and sat there. Must have been an hour or two later. I'd fallen asleep. No sign of the girls. I got worried. I had a bad feeling about this. I had a bad feeling about everything that night. I just didn't know what–I didn't know how–I had no idea... you know?"

"Take your time, Henry," I said.

Henry nodded and swiped at his forehead with his shirtsleeve. "The place was closed so it was real late, maybe between three and four in the morning. I checked the door and it was open. I went in. Climbed up some stairs and tip-toed down a hall to an office in the back. I cracked the door and that's when I saw it... saw it... "

He'd gone into a trance, staring into space. "What'd you see, Henry? Were the girls there?"

"Uh-huh," he replied.

"Did you see anybody else?"

"Yeah," he said. "There was another Chinese guy. This guy was short and kind of skinny with his hair parted in the middle. He spoke funny, like those folks in England. But he was no gentleman, that's for sure."

"What were the girls doing?"

"Just sitting there. Miss Alison, she just stare out into space at something. The other one was crying softly, whimpering like a little...like a little...a..."

"Baby, man?" Birdie asked.

Henry darted a fearful look at him. "Yeah. That's right." Tears welled up in his eyes and his mouth went tight. "I couldn't take my eyes off it...I just couldn't..."

"Off what, Henry?" I asked.

"The child, man. Her child. It was just lying there on a blanket–right on the desk. Its skin all blue. Dead. Poor child never had a chance. When I came into the room, the Chinese guy, the other one, was untying something from around its little neck. Whatever happened, that child didn't die naturally, that was for sure."

Birdie reared back on the bench. "The child was murdered? Is that what you're saying?"

"Yeah. God didn't save a child that night..."

"Jesus," I breathed. All kinds of thoughts spun around in my head.

Henry sighed and rubbed his palms up and down his face like he was trying to scrub the memory of it away.

"The Chinese man, the smaller one–he wrote something on a piece of paper and he handed it to me. I read it and my heart fell through the floor. My blood ran cold. The paper had my momma's address on it. The Chinese man say that I should take the girls home and say nothing about what happened and that as long as I keep quiet everything be okay and nobody get hurt but in case I didn't–he pointed to the piece of paper–he didn't say anything after that. He didn't have to. I got the message loud and clear. So I did what he say.

I got the girls into the car and drove Miss Gayle first and then Miss Alison home. I parked the car in the garage and I walk away. I couldn't stay on, after that. Didn't know where to go or what to do. Just felt I had to disappear, make myself invisible somehow but in a way that I could watch, that I could see what was going on. I called Ricky. Woke him up. Explained what happened and together, we came up with this idea of me going underground–like in the book–and eight years later, here we are. Look but don't touch–that's my life–maybe forever..."

I sighed. Henry looked very alone and I caught a glimpse of what it must have been like for him since he disappeared. A life but not a life. A life of watching everyone else live theirs but not having one of your own. I thought about Gayle and her ordeal. I remember when I was a beat cop, I took a call concerning an abandoned baby. We found the mother—a 14 year-old girl who'd delivered in the school washroom. Her mother didn't know. Her friends didn't know. Kept her condition hidden wearing loose clothing and making excuses to get out of gym class. Said she'd been putting on weight eating too many sweets and cakes. What she went through on her own. I couldn't fathom what Gayle had gone through. It didn't bear thinking about.

"What now?" Henry asked. "I tell you what happened and then what? What's gonna change things."

I looked at him. "We are."

Henry gave a snort, then a harsh laugh. "That's it? You all we got?"

"Afraid so."

Henry sighed and stood up. "Where you going, man?" Birdie asked him.

"Where you think, big man? I'm going back to my life, the only one I know."

"Things are going to change," I said.

"You can't win. This man have the city in his pocket, you understand? He do what he want and nobody stop him. Not the police. Not the Mayor. Not anybody. I can't risk having anything happen to my momma. She hire you to find me? Now you found me. I'll see you around."

We watched him walk away from the playground. He picked up his satchel and stick and moved off, head down, still staying invisible.

45

Birdie and I parked in front of the police precinct. We had about 18 hours until John's deadline. We watched the front entrance. While we waited, he demolished three fried egg sandwiches and half a dozen doughnuts. I ate a tuna salad on rye and sipped coffee.

"There he goes now," I said.

Birdie nodded, swallowed the last of the doughnuts, flicked crumbs off his lap, and slipped out the door. He glided across the street after the lean figure of Roy Mason, Callaway's taciturn sidekick, as he strode down the sidewalk, hands shoved in his pockets, a fag jutting from his thin lips, favouring his left leg. I waited for a minute, locked up the Chevy and headed inside.

I found Callaway in his disheveled office. He looked up from a stack of folders with a miserable expression on his face as I walked in and closed the door.

"Need your help," I said.

"Just my luck," he said. "I was hoping some helpless citizen was going to walk in here and ask for my assistance. And then you show up."

"You're probably not going to like it," I said.

"Tell me something I don't know," Callaway replied and motioned to the chair opposite. I shoved some more files out of the way and sat down.

"Looks like you can use a distraction, in any case."

Callaway sighed. "Already I know I'm not going to like what you're gonna say. So say it fast before I change my mind."

I grinned. "Maybe, you'll like some parts of it."

"Give," he said.

"Sure."

So I told him everything I knew or rather, just about everything. There were a few things I wasn't sure of. I told him about Henry Turner and what happened to him and where he'd been hiding out for eight years. I told him about Alison Lawson nee Foster and what she and Gayle and those boys did all those years ago. I told him about the night Henry disappeared and why he disappeared. Then I told him about Eli and I even mentioned Jake to him. He seemed very interested in that. He got more interested when I told him he could nail John Fat Gai once and for all. Then I told him what I wanted to do and why I needed his help. He sat there listening intently and didn't say anything until I finished.

"That's some story," he said. "My granny used to read me fairy tales when I was a kid before she put me to bed at night."

"Yeah. Well. This is more like a nightmare."

"No kidding." He cleared his throat. "Er, your plan…"

"Uh-huh?"

"There's a few holes in it."

I nodded. "Yeah I know. That's why I need your help."

"I don't think I have the manpower for an operation like you're suggesting."

"I figured. That's why you need to call Tobin and get him to help you out."

Callaway's face creased. It made him look like a sick bulldog. "Tobin? Are you suggesting I bring the feds into this?"

"That's exactly what I'm suggesting."

"Why?"

"Well, he's got some guys and I know they carry a lot of weapons with them and he wants John just as much as you do, maybe more.

And he wants Jake real bad. Besides, not a lot of guys you can trust around here, is there?"

"You don't care what happens to your old man?" And gave me one of his truth or dare looks.

It was a good question. "Jake made his own mess. He belongs in the slam and it doesn't matter to me who puts him there. It could be you or Tobin. Same difference. He's a felon and needs to serve his time just like any other con whether he's related to me or not."

"Very noble."

"I thought so."

"You got Tobin's number?"

"As a matter of fact, I do," I said. I slipped a folded piece of paper across the desk to him. Callaway picked it up and scrutinized it. "There's seven numbers. I counted."

Callaway grunted. "Smart guy. That's why you got busted outta here." He looked up at me. "Anything else?"

"Yeah. Is Dewey still working robbery?"

"Uh-huh. Why?"

"You need to call him too."

Callaway sighed. "Better let me get to work. Don't go too far."

I stood up. "We don't have much time."

"How you gonna get John Fat Gai to show up?"

I smiled. "Just leave that to me."

I lounged in Interview room number two–one of the classier rooms in the building. Over the years, handprints, face prints, puke, dried blood and grime built up from sweaty prisoners and cops had turned the décor a fashionable greenish-gray. A room of no hope for losers. Didn't matter about guilt or innocence. A place where everybody who came to that room suffered. Today wasn't going to be any different.

Birdie poked his head in. "He's on his way up."

"Good."

Birdie stepped inside and found a spot further down the wall without touching it. Didn't want to ruin his suit. I leaned up against the bare, metal frame table. I didn't think too much about what I leaned against. There was always the Chinese laundry next door to the office.

Bare knuckles rapped on the door and it opened. Roy Mason stood there tentatively.

"Come on in, Roy. Shut the door."

He took a breath, squared his shoulders and stepped inside closing the door behind him.

"The desk Sarge said Callaway wanted to see me." He took a long look around the room. It wasn't a big room. No Callaway. "What's this about?"

I stood up and took a leisurely stroll over to him. "Drop your pants."

Mason looked confused. "Huh?"

"I said, drop your pants. That's easy enough to understand, isn't it? Even for you."

Mason looked at me like I was crazy and the beginnings of a smile creased his thin lips. "This is some kind of joke, right? There a bet going round the bullpen?"

I smiled back at him. "No joke, Roy. Either you do it voluntarily…or…" and I shrugged.

The smile hardened. The eyes narrowed. "Now wait a minute. I'm not going to put…"

Birdie grabbed him from behind clamping one big mitt over his mouth while wrapping him up with the other keeping him immobilized. I undid his belt, flicked open the button, unzipped his fly and yanked his trousers down to his ankles. He wore braces on his socks. Flashy. Inside each one he'd stashed a .22 caliber throw away. I removed them. I reached inside his jacket and took the police issue .38 and from his waistband, Birdie removed a pearl-handled .45. He handed it to me.

I piled all the gear on the rickety table.

"Jesus Roy, you got enough weaponry to start a small war. You worried about something?" Mason struggled in Birdie's grip but we both knew it was futile. "Well, you should be."

I lifted his shirttail and took a look at the puckering wound I found on his left thigh. Pronounced bruising turning deep purple with tinges of green.

"Looks like it missed the bone. That was too bad. I really hoped I'd plugged you good when you coshed me in Ying's flat. You wanna tell me what you were doing there, Roy? What was it you were looking for?"

I think he uttered some choice obscenities but they came out muffled. His breathing labored.

"Okay. Maybe you wanna tell John where the girl is and the baby? How about that? Not to mention the money Ying skimmed from him? You see, Roy. I have it on good authority that the girl had been looked after by a cop. That's why we couldn't find her. She wasn't anywhere in the Chinese community. Now I know that cop was you. How do you think John would react knowing that bit of business? Don't think he'd be too pleased, do you?"

Mason's eyes went wide and he began to shake his head. Birdie uncovered his mouth but kept his arms pinned behind his back.

"You'd give me over to John Fat Gai?" he asked.

"What were you doing at Ying's flat?" I asked. "Make it snappy."

Mason stared at me. I'd characterize the look as one of extreme hatred. "I was making sure nothing tied her anywhere, that nobody could trace her."

"Ying's sister?"

He nodded, reluctantly. "Yeah, that's right."

"Where is she now?"

"I don't know."

"Come on, Roy, don't play dumb. One call to John and it's over."

He held his hands up. "Honest, I don't know. A couple of nights ago she ran off with the kid–that's all I know, I swear."

"You helped her get away from John in the first place?"

"Yeah."

"Why?"

Mason visibly slumped now. He hated having to tell and in particular, he hated even more saying it to me. "Because of the kid."

"What about it?"

Mason looked away. His voice went small and quavery. "It's mine, that's why."

Birdie and I exchanged looks. Mason was married with three kids of his own. "Who killed Ying Hee Fong?"

Mason turned and looked at me. This time I saw fear. "Does Callaway know?"

"Not yet."

"Do you have to tell him?" I shrugged but didn't answer. "Yeah, okay. I get it. Fine. It doesn't matter anyway. She's missing and so's the kid. She ran away after she found out what I'd done. I don't know where she's gone. Guess my career is down the toilet. My life too." He sighed. "I set Ying up. I admit that but I didn't kill him. I swear. I'm not a cold-blooded murderer."

"Who killed Ying?" I asked.

Mason shook his head. "I can't tell you that."

"Come on, Mason. Don't hold out on us now."

"He'll kill me too. He's crazy. You can't make me talk," he spat.

"Oh yeah?"

I put my hand over his mouth and leaned in real close. I took the barrel of the .45 and rammed it into the gaping wound in his thigh. Mason arched his back and screamed into my hand. "Now tell me who killed Ying."

Mason, eyes wide, shook his head. I rammed the barrel in again, harder this time, using my knee to up the pressure. His body felt like a piece of steel and his silent scream deafened me. "Feel like talking now?" I pulled the barrel away.

Mason slumped down. Birdie held him up. His breath came labored, a ragged whistling through his nose. "I can't," he gasped. "Jesus, that hurts."

Once more the barrel went in. I pressed my forearm across his face. Mason convulsed like a guy dancing in the electric chair. When I finally released him, he crumpled to the ground, panting.

"What's it to be, Mason?"

He lifted his head, face drained of colour and spat. "You're a bastard, Gold. A fucking bastard." I made a move toward him and he shrank back. "Okay. Okay. I'll talk. But I want protection, you understand? The guy's a maniac. He'll kill me and probably kill you too."

"That's not up to me. It'll be up to your boss, Callaway. Now give."

So, Mason told me what I wanted to know. I looked down at him. "You can pull your pants back on now," I said.

"It's not what you think," Mason said.

I scratched my chin and smiled mirthlessly. "You mean, you're not just some cheap shyster on the pad?"

"You know I'm not the only one," Mason retorted. "How'd you figure it out anyway?"

"I had a look at a bunch of old case files Callaway kept at his house. Five times you had John dead to rights and each time it all went away. That was no coincidence."

"Once you're in, you can't get out even if you want to. I made a mistake, that's all."

"So that makes it right? Other guys jump on the gravy train and suddenly, it's okay?"

"John threatened my family. My old man was a cop. He's retired now. I couldn't have him find what I'd been doing. It'd kill him."

"Who's got the money?" I asked.

"He does," Mason replied.

"Okay."

"So what now?" Mason asked.

"You're going to help us out."

"And?"

"And if you're lucky, you'll end up only with jail time. Stay with him. Make sure he doesn't go wandering," I said to Birdie.

I hurried down to the main desk. "You got the duty roster?"

"You don't work here anymore, Mo," the duty Sergeant replied.

"Come on, Wayne. It'll just take a second."

Wayne sighed then slid over the clipboard. I went down the names, found the one I wanted and headed out the back.

"Hey," Wayne yelled.

"Thanks." I waved as I tore out.

I scanned the parking lot. Shift change. Guys getting into patrol cars. Doors slammed. Engines started. I spotted him on the other side of the lot. He jawed with another cop then removed his hat, opened the driver's door and tossed the hat inside. Had to be careful, how I played this one. But I had to work fast. As I crossed the lot, I eased the .45 out of its holster and held it down by my thigh, out of view. I slipped around cars and cops.

"Officer? Officer?"

He turned, leaning against the open door. With the angle of the sun, the crease at his hairline stood out like a throbbing red line. Less than 10 feet now. I smiled.

"Hey. Remember me? We spoke earlier?"

"Yeah, I remember," Kernahan said. "The chauffeur."

"Right. Good memory." I stuck the .45 in his abdomen and pressed him against the car but he collapsed into the interior and I fell in with him. He head-butted me and I saw stars. Although my weight forced him back, he went for the gun and began to twist it out of my hands. A wiry guy and stronger than he looked. He wriggled around and I fell off the seat onto the floor, my hips trapped by the steering wheel. He had both hands on the .45 now wrenching it out of my grasp. That was fine. I reached around with my right hand and grabbed his service pistol. I stuck it under his chin.

"Let go or I'll blast you," I said.

"You'd shoot a cop in a parking lot full of cops?" he hissed.

"Try me," I replied. "Now ease back"

Kernahan grinned. He pushed his weight off me. "Take it slow or I might just slip on the trigger here."

"Sure. No sudden moves," he said. He backed out of the car and I followed him.

"Turn around." As he turned, I shoved his .38 into my belt and spun him around against the car. I pushed my knees into the back of his and he buckled. I unlatched his handcuffs from his belt and snapped them on him. I stepped back.

"Now, let's go. Inside."

He turned around with an amused look on his face. We'd drawn some attention from the other cops. "I'm not saying nothing," he said.

"Fine by me," I replied. "March." I pushed him forward keeping the .45 trained on his back and did my best to ignore the hostile looks around me. I figured John would find out what happened in about a minute or less. Someone here would put in a call.

Callaway seethed. We put Kernahan in a holding cell. Birdie continued to keep Mason company.

"What the hell do we do now?" Callaway asked.

"Nothing," I said. "We proceed with the plan but we take Mason with us."

"Why?"

"By now, John will know that we've got Kernahan, even if he isn't talking. But he might not know about Mason spilling his guts yet. Even still, John will be spooked. He'll figure his operation could be rolled up anytime. It means we've got him on the run."

"I admire your confidence," Callaway spat. He shook his head. "Never figured on Kernahan. If that don't beat all."

"He fooled me too," I replied. Callaway had let me take a peak at his employee file. "You know the guy turned down promotion three times? That was smart. Wanted to keep his head down low. Nobody would suspect he ran the show inside the precinct. That he was John's main contact. It's only natural to think it's someone higher up, like Mason. Someone who's got some authority."

"At least we've got Mason's statement," Callaway said. "That will help us get the ball rolling against Kernahan and John eventually." Mason had ratted out the other guys on the pad; six others taking backhanders from John, all of them patrolmen. Faces in the background.

"Well, we can live and hope," I said. I glanced at my watch. "Now, we've got an appointment to keep."

46

Dusk approached. The day slipped into the nether world between light and dark.

For the past week, I'd been worrying John. I sensed his edginess and thought I could help send him over with a little bit of help. As a gangster, John was protected. His men surrounded him and guarded him at all times.

Sometimes, it's the simple things. One method rarely failed. The postal service. Each day I'd mailed John a different card; a black one to symbolize death, one adorned with ghosts and eerie figures from the grave, a number four card, a red card representing blood. The last one had come from Mr. Li or at least, someone I had pretend to write a note as if it came from Mr. Li, in Mandarin. The note ragged on about ghosts and spirits and haunting him forever. I hope it cracked his seething brain wide open.

Quan and a couple of goons came out of John's mansion. Quan pulled a Zippo from his pants pocket and lit a kerosene-soaked torch set into a holder by the front door. He took it down and lit the other one opposite. Quan kept the torch with him and walked the perimeter of the grounds lighting torches on his way. A private drive led to the entrance of John's house—a dead end in a cul-de-sac. An iron gate sealed it. The gate featured some nasty spikes at the top.

Adjacent to the gate spanned a solid brick wall. The bottoms of broken bottles had been set into the mortar at the top.

Birdie and I sat in the Chevy opposite watching Quan do his rounds through a set of military binoculars I found at the local Army surplus store.

I counted 20 torches ablaze. The same thing every night. You could almost hear the flames flapping in the wind. The effect looked eerie, like a brace of witches and goblins would swoop down and gambol and cavort on the carefully manicured lawn. The house had been built up a slope some 30 yards from the front gate. I hoped Eli and Jake were in there somewhere. I checked my watch. Just gone 9:30 p.m. The meet to exchange the ledger, along with Henry Turner and Ying's sister had been set for midnight at Christie Pits. We'd get Jake and Eli in return.

I thought we'd hit John's house a bit earlier and see what we could find. Callaway, Tobin and some of his boys had parked two blocks up, waiting for John to emerge. About fifteen minutes later, John showed. Alone.

Earlier that night, Birdie and I had seeded the yards of the neighbours with doctored steak, hoping their dogs would feed on it. We'd laced the steak with hot chilis–guaranteed to get a reaction. And it did. The dogs in the surrounding houses yowled like a runaway storm. Howling dogs. A portent of evil and bad luck to come.

Surrounded by his henchmen, they moved in tight formation to a dark sedan. John flinched and covered his ears. He looked around in bewilderment. Bent his knees to the ground. Quan opened the back door and pushed John in. Quan went around the front. He pulled the passenger door closed, stuck his hand out the window and banged on the roof. The car started up followed by another filled with his goons. They trundled down the drive and waited for the electric gates to open. The lead car pulled out followed by number two. Quickly, Birdie and I sprinted across the street and squeezed through before they closed completely. Birdie just made it. Tobin and Callaway would follow John to see where he headed.

I had a buddy in the planning department at City Hall who owed me a favour. Through him, I got a copy of the plans for John's house. Didn't matter if you were a crook or not, if you built a house, you had to file plans with the city. No ifs, ands or buts. Or the city would halt the construction, charge a hefty fine or both. After studying them, I had a good sense of the layout.

A brace of Dobermans streaked towards us. Didn't know about the dogs. They moved swiftly and silently. Birdie and I stood dead still and let them sniff us. When I moved a muscle, I heard deep growling in anxious throats and saw the baring of sharp teeth.

"Now what?" Birdie murmured. In effect, the dogs held us prisoner.

"We could run for it." He gave me an incredulous look. "Okay, maybe not."

"What if we shot them?" he asked. Now I gave him an incredulous look. He reached into his pocket and pulled out a silencer. "See? I came prepared."

I had a thought. "Hey, you remember, Gomer?" A guy we knew in the service, grew up on a farm where they kept a lot of dogs.

"Yeah, so?" Birdie replied.

"He told me this thing once."

"What thing?"

"Well, it goes like this. Just do as I say. Take off your jacket and carefully drop it at your feet."

"Say what?"

"You heard me. We've got to do something. We can't stay here all night."

Birdie shook his head and muttered something incomprehensible but shrugged out of his suit jacket and carefully lay it down at his feet. I did the same. We straightened up and waited. The dogs had assumed a sitting position and watched us. One by one, each of the dogs stood up, ventured over to each jacket and snuffled around, poking its long nose in the pocket and sleeves. Then each dog lifted its leg and peed.

"Sweet Jesus," Birdie exclaimed. "That dog just peed on my jacket."

"I know. That's good."

"Good? I paid a hundred dollars for it."

When the dogs had finished lifting their legs and doing their business, they went back to their sitting formation.

"Now what?" Birdie demanded.

"Reach down slowly, pick your jacket up and put it on," I said.

"Huh? You want me to put it on after each of those mongrels has soiled it?"

"According to Gomer, they were marking their territory. We'll have their smell on us and they'll let us pass through. Trust me on this."

"Well, you and Gomer better be right. If not, then I'm going to have to look him up."

"He was killed in '43," I said.

"Well, I'll go and dig him up," Birdie replied. But he reached down carefully and shrugged himself back into his jacket. He made a face. I did the same.

"Now what?"

"We walk toward the house. We can get in through the side entrance."

Birdie looked at me. "You first."

"Okay." I took a step.

The dogs watched me curiously but didn't move. I took another step. Same reaction. Birdie followed along. Moving slowly and cautiously, we'd traveled about 10 steps when I heard the low, menacing growl. I turned around. The dogs were up on their feet now. "Keep moving but make it smooth. Nothing sudden."

We marched in step across the field and around to the side of the house. The dogs were out of sight. I got out my lock picks and went to work. Suddenly, there came a yelp and the dogs went on the move.

"Better hurry," Birdie said. I heard the pad of their paws on the thick grass. They moved fast. "Come on, Mo. Anytime would be good."

"I'm working as best as I can. There's not much light," I hissed.

"You got about three seconds," Birdie said. He pulled his .45.

I glanced over my shoulder. The dogs had flattened their stance, ears back, fangs bared. They flew across the lawn. The tumblers clicked. We went through and closed it just as the pack threw itself at us slamming into the door. I heard the yelps and squeaks on the other side.

"Close one," I said.

"My jacket stinks," Birdie replied.

"Well, it kinda worked."

"I think we should just shoot them on the way out. That's my plan, okay?"

We moved quickly through the first floor of the house checking all of the rooms and there were plenty of rooms. Nothing.

"Let's split up," I said. "I'll take the upstairs, you do the basement."

"Why do I get the basement?" Birdie groused. Still pissed about the jacket.

"Okay, I'll take the basement. That way you won't have to bend your head, okay?"

"Better," he said.

Birdie trudged carefully up the expansive staircase. According to the plans, the basement entrance lay off the kitchen. I shone my torch around the kitchen. The remnants of a meal lay scattered about. Plates piled in the sink, scraps on the table. I knew John as fastidious. This seemed out of character.

I opened the basement door and found the light switch. I flicked it on and descended into the bowels of the house. I'd been right. The ceiling height allowed me to stand straight but I removed my hat to duck under the ceiling beams. It consisted of four, large connected rooms. One for laundry with all of the latest washing gizmos. Impressive. John could run his own commercial operation out of there. Another looked to be storage–tables and chairs stacked up in there.

The third room had been servants' quarters once upon a time but no one had lived there recently. I found the fourth room padlocked. With the butt end of the .45, I hammered it off and swung the door open. Wine cellar. Some decent vintages looked like. Clearly, John didn't trust the staff to keep their hands off a few bottles. I closed the door and trudged back up the basement. I met up with Birdie in the living room.

"Anything?" I asked.

"Nothing. Just empty bedrooms."

"Odd. Don't you find it odd?"

Birdie shrugged. "Yeah. Maybe."

"Why wouldn't he leave someone behind to watch the place? You don't leave without having someone watch your back, do you?"

"Not someone like John," Birdie replied.

I sat down on the settee to ponder for a moment. Then I heard something.

"What was that?"

Birdie looked up. He'd heard it too. A tinkle, then a crackling sound. We exchanged looks. I got up and went to the far door. As I approached, I sniffed. I smelled something. Gasoline.

I stepped carefully, put my hand on the knob and twisted slowly. I glanced at Birdie and he nodded curtly, just the once. Slowly, I eased the door open. A fireball blew me off my feet in a vicious whoosh, flinging me backwards. I felt heat and pain. I rolled like a manic tumbleweed. I think I screamed. A hand seized the scruff of my neck and hauled me up.

"The front door," I croaked.

Birdie half-dragged, half-carried me as the flames shot out in evil tendrils engulfing everything up in its path. The living room shimmered like an angry torch. I'd gained my feet now. I held on to Birdie's coattails as he bulled his way from room to room, the fireball billowing after us. My skin blistered.

"Come on," he yelled. "Stay with me." My feet skittered.

My lungs felt like they had burst. Throat raw. Eyes stinging. Couldn't breathe. Oxygen sucked out of the air. Smoke billowed. Acrid fumes ate my throat. Birdie flung the front door open. We charged through it, hit the grass and rolled just as the house behind us erupted. A massive explosion. The war all over again. The sight mesmerized me. Almost beautiful. Like a 500 pound bomb had been dropped from the sky. We scrambled up and lit out as fast as we could until we'd managed to put 30 or 40 yards between us and the inferno. In seconds, the entire house flamed up. We dropped down to the grass panting. I coughed smoke out of my lungs.

"Well at least we didn't have to worry about the dogs," Birdie wheezed.

I looked around. No dogs. The flames lit up the skyline. I heard a deep rumble, felt the vibration of it through the ground. The core of the house erupted shooting fire, ash and debris up into the air.

"That was no accident," I said.

"Booby trapped," Birdie replied.

"No wonder the place was empty. John never intended to come back. Son of a bitch," I said. "That crazy son of a bitch."

"Amen to that, brother. You burned anywhere?"

I shook my head. "Don't think so."

"Your eyebrows look a little bit singed."

I grinned, blew some more smoke out of my lungs. "The latest look this summer."

"Jacket's really ruined now," he said, looking at the remnants of his lapels in disgust.

At least the jackets fulfilled one more useful purpose. We tossed them up onto the wall and climbed up and over gingerly without being slashed by the embedded glass. I fired up the Chevy and drove away as another fireball erupted, lighting up the sky. We drove back to the office to get cleaned up.

"Let's hope Tobin and Callaway find Eli and Jake," I said.

47

Christie Pits at midnight. It had a certain ring to it. We stood in the northeast quadrant near second base. The home park for the Maple Leafs of the Intercontinental Baseball League. A fabled place, the Pits.

Back in 1933, when I was just growing my first set of pimples, a riot erupted between the Jews and the Swastika Club–a homegrown fascist group of bullyboys who admired Hitler. The Jews played baseball regularly in the Pits on Sundays. Fights broke out when thugs from the Swastika Club showed up to disrupt the games. One of those times it blew up into a full-blown riot that lasted the better part of a day. I remember because it was one of the first times that the Jews stood up for themselves in public and also, because my old man had been an ecstatic participant in the proceedings.

I remember how he came home, flushed, sweaty and bleeding but happy as a clam enthusing about what they did to the Swastika Club members–the most excited and exuberant I'd ever seen him. He broke heads and busted legs with a crowbar. That said a lot about Jake. Later that night, we went down to College Street and he took me out for a gelato. Hasn't happened before or since. Within a couple of months he'd left for good. That was something all right.

The elevation of the park sloped downward hence the name, Christie Pits. The top of the sides all around stood at street level. At each corner huddled a family of streetlamps throwing a dim glow that didn't reach the interior of the field where we stood. John Fat Gai had chosen the Pits carefully. At field level, the ground lay flat. Nowhere to hide except near the batting cages and some of the outbuildings by the public washrooms where the players changed into their uniforms. In the western section, lay a playground. The only way to approach the field meant coming down one of the slopes. You'd be backlit by the streetlamps and an easy target. Apart from that, there were many routes in and out but it was difficult to hide, even in the dark.

Me, Birdie, Roy Mason, Ying's sister and Henry Turner stood in a small group. On John's instructions, I'd planted wooden torches soaked in kerosene in a circle. We stood in the centre. Mason pulled nervously on a fag. I'd put manacles on Henry and the girl. I'd taped their mouths shut in case they tried yelling out. We didn't need any distractions or unwanted attention. Henry still wore his city coveralls and a Toronto Maple Leafs ball cap pulled down over his face. Birdie held on to him and the girl so they wouldn't bolt. I held the ledger in my hand. At the stroke of midnight, I lit the torches. They fired up in a blaze of glory. We stood out like a human beacon.

"I don't like it," Mason muttered. "I feel naked out here." Mason had been in the service and knew a good ambush spot when he saw one.

"Now there's a thought," I said. "I'll need to flush that one from my mind."

"Always the joker," Mason sneered.

"That's me."

Birdie scanned the perimeter but it was a cloudy night and tough to see. He didn't comment but harrumphed quietly.

I figured they'd come from the southern quadrant and that's what they did, a pack of them, moving slowly, fanning out to cover the angles, picking their way down the slope carefully. I couldn't make out how many there were but I didn't think John would take any chances. They'd come in numbers and they'd be heavily armed.

For this scheme to have any chance of working, I had to make sure John came with them. The only way to do that was to promise him the missing ledger and the girl. Along with Henry, of course. He knew Mason wouldn't talk and he figured Birdie and me wouldn't spill because of Eli and maybe, Jake. He hadn't been wrong. John sniffed out the weakness in people and exploited it, even in his agitated state, he kept that instinct alive.

We waited for them. They came in two lines, the first protecting the second. Moving in a phalanx, they halted about ten yards in front of us. John had at least eight guys, plus Quan and himself, but no Jake or Eli. We were heavily outnumbered and outgunned. I smelled the acrid smoke from the torches. The flames crackled and snapped.

"That's far enough," I said. The group opposite held up.

"Gentlemen," John said. A nervous tic ate at his cheek. "Lovely evening."

"Isn't it?" I replied. "I was just thinking that myself."

"You have the ledger?" John asked, his voice, high-pitched.

I held it up. "Right here. Now, tell your goons to back off or I'll set it alight." I leaned toward one of the torches.

John barked in Mandarin and the gunsels moved back out of range.

"Now you and Quan can join us here in the inner circle," I said.

John shrugged. Quan smiled.

"All right," John replied and fingered the dragon pendant obsessively.

The two of them moved forward until they'd positioned themselves within the circle. John looked tightly conciliatory and Quan seemed oddly relaxed.

"Where's my brother? I don't see him with you." I pushed the ledger into the flame and singed the pages.

John cracked open.

"Let's not be hasty, Mo. Your brother is perfectly safe as is your father. I give you my word as a gentleman. Now, the ledger please and our two guests." He held out his hands in a placating gesture.

"I'd sooner trust you as drop kick you off a cliff. The ledger becomes ashes unless you produce them." I felt the heat lick up my fingers as John gave me a worried look.

"Give me the ledger now. I will take you to them."

I held up four fingers. "Tell me where they are."

John shrank back. "It seems we are at a stalemate. If you burn the ledger, you will never find them and when you do, it might be too late."

"What are you talking about?" I demanded.

Nothing happened for a long moment but I could sense a lot of hands resting on the butts of weapons itching to use them. The scent of burnt paper filled my nostrils.

"The ledger. Quickly," John hissed.

Then it all unraveled like a film reel unspooling. From opposite directions, powerful searchlights snapped on, blinding us. A scratchy, metallic voice echoed out from the dark. Callaway squawking through a bullhorn. Anger and disappointment welled up in me.

"This is the police," Callaway squawked. "Put your hands up." I spotted dark figures holding flashlights streaming down over the hill. They charged forward yelling like banshees. Both 'Henry' and 'Ying's sister' pulled off their cuffs, tore the tape from their mouths and like Houdini, .38 Police Specials miraculously appeared in their hands from inside their clothes. John and Quan and their men remained motionless. John smiled evilly.

"I'm so disappointed in you, Mo. Now you will never see your brother or father again." He clapped his hands. Once. Twice. He and Quan placed slate dark glasses over their eyes. I heard a hissing sound and felt the ground begin to vibrate. Instinctively, I bent low to maintain my balance. John and Quan remained still, curious smiles on their faces.

The cops continued to pore down the slope but it was too late. I knew that now. The others, Mason, Henry and Ying's sister's doubles looked around, confused and uncertain. The ground erupted in a blaze of pops, bangs and cracks. I reeled back.

Quan shot forward. He snatched the ledger from my hand as a hundred Roman candles exploded around us in a dazzling display. From fissures in the ground surrounding us, rockets, cannon balls, firewheels ignited. The kids in the neighbourhood must have loved it. Electric lights flashed in our eyes. I groped blindly. Quan whirled about and fired a shot then he and John vanished in the dazzle. I dropped to the ground and tried peering through the showers of sparks and erupting explosives. Birdie did the same. We could barely see and couldn't hear. Something soft and heavy fell across my back. I lurched up and rolled it over. Mason. A neat hole carved into his forehead.

Fuzzily, I heard distant yells and screams. Then, as suddenly as it had begun, the display fizzled out. Snaps. Pops. Birdie and I stood up. I looked over at the two cops who'd doubled for Henry and Ying's sister. They seemed confused but okay. I found myself face to face with a resigned looking Callaway and a furious Tobin.

I got it now.

The kerosene torches had been a marker. John's men had stood outside the perimeter of fireworks John had set up at some point earlier in the evening while Birdie and I tried to avoid becoming smoked meat in his burnt out house. Inside the circle of torches, it had been safe ground. The fireworks had been buried just below the surface all around us.

Maybe John had cracked, after all. He'd abandoned his house, and maybe he'd clear out his warehouses now that he had his precious ledger. The only satisfaction came from knowing a technician from Tobin's office had photographed each of the ledger's pages before we handed it over. At least we had the goods on the bent cops, judges and politicians John kept in his pocket. Barry Wong had been as good as his word. He'd retrieved the ledger from Liu Chen, his wife's cousin and given it to me when I called.

I grabbed Callaway's lapels. "He's got Eli and Jake. Tell me you followed him to where they are."

Callaway looked ashamed but cast daggers at Tobin. "We lost him," he said sheepishly. "Sorry, Mo."

I pushed him away and sat on the grass, head in hands. Callaway crouched down over Mason's body. He too seemed dejected. Whatever his faults, the guy had been his partner and a cop. Jake and Eli could be anywhere.

"We'll find them," Birdie said. I looked up at him and wearily stood up. We smelled like burnt out gunpowder.

John had established a theme.

"Callaway," I said. He looked over at me. "Better alert the fire department. Warehouses will be smoking all over the city."

Callaway looked stricken.

"Shit," he said.

"What are you talking about?" Tobin demanded.

"He torched his house, he torched us so he's going to torch everything he touched, leave no trace and then disappear. Fire is a thing with him, kind of sacred. He had it all planned," I said. "He's three steps ahead."

Tobin pointed his finger. "This is your fault. You. You set this plan in motion. I am holding you responsible for this and I will make sure that you…"

I hit him. I socked him hard and he went down in a heap. My hand stung, the knuckles sore. I hadn't felt that good since I'd rocked the deputy chief with a solid right cross.

"Feel better?" Birdie asked. Callaway smirked.

"Yeah, I do."

"Let's get to work," he said. "We probably don't have much time."

"We'll cover whatever we can," Callaway said. "Just give me the word. But first I gotta tell Doreen Mason she's a widow.

48

I consoled myself that John hadn't harmed Henry Turner who still wandered the city as the Invisible Man, hiding in plain sight, popping in and out when he wanted. Ying's sister hadn't been touched either. When I met him to retrieve the ledger, Barry Wong told me he had been moving her between empty rooms in the hotel, a different one each night. He'd kept her and the baby below the radar. No records and completely anonymous.

Even though he'd been spooked by Li's curse and everything else we'd done, I figured John knew when to cut his losses and run taking with him his ill-gotten gains. He had enough influence, contacts and money to buy his way across any border. Birdie drove to the docklands. I took a pull from a mickey of Scotch I kept in the glove compartment. Just to settle things a little. John had gotten into my head and I wanted him out. More than that, I wanted to find my brother and maybe Jake too, alive and well. At least, that way, I could hand Jake back to Tobin with a clear conscience.

We pulled into the Blackstone's parking lot but we'd arrived too late. Half a dozen fire engines had their hoses turned on an inferno where the club last stood.

"Let's hit the warehouse where we saw him the last time," I said. "It's not far from here. Hang on a second," I said. I hopped out and approached the fire captain.

"Excuse me," I said.

"Kinda busy here," the fire captain replied. His gear looked pristine, like he'd never been to a fire in his life. His helmet gleamed.

"I just need to know one thing."

"What's that?"

"Any bodies in there?"

The fire captain took a good look at me. In contrast, I looked like I'd been engulfed in flames. Singed eyebrows, burn marks on my face, bloodshot eyes.

"No, we didn't find anyone in there yet. But we won't know until it dies down completely," he said.

"Thanks," I replied. I could see the guy had become curious. "Carry on," I called and hurried back to the car. "No bodies yet," I said as I jumped into the passenger side.

"That's a mercy," Birdie intoned, as he sped out of the parking lot. I began to think about fires and rockets and superstitions.

"Hey, you know what day it is today?"

Birdie looked at me curiously. "It's the fourth of June," he said. "Why?"

For the first time in a long while, I clapped my hands. "We may be in luck."

"In luck? How?"

"The fourth. The number four. Again." Birdie gave me a blank stare. "We've been playing on his superstitions, making him feel the sting of Li's curse. He can't get away today. Four is the worst kind of bad luck. He wouldn't chance it, I'm telling you."

"Okay, then where is he?"

"I don't know. But it gives us a little more time to look for him," I said. "Let's hit the warehouse and see if we can find anything, if it's not burnt to a crisp by now."

"Okay, let's think about this," I said, as we cruised west along the Lakeshore. "John's warehouses are near the waterfront. If he's moving stuff out, where would he move it to? Somewhere close by. Somewhere that gives him easy access to the border." Birdie pulled over. We sat opposite the harbor. He gave me a dirty look and pointed.

"Okay, so it makes sense for him to move everything by ship. That's how he came into the country 15 years ago. Seems reasonable that's how he'd leave too."

I peered ahead. "There's a phone booth up ahead. Pull up to it." I searched my pockets. "Got a nickel?" Birdie sighed. "I know, I know. You do everything around here. Come on."

I held my hand out and he dropped the nickel into my palm. I climbed out and squeezed into the phone booth. I managed to get Callaway just as he was leaving.

"You got something?" he asked wearily.

"How'd it go with Maureen?"

"Not good. She took it hard. Three kids on a Sergeant's pension? Won't go far."

"John's still in town. We've got a bit of extra time but need to move fast."

"How do you know that?" I told him. "Superstitious mumbo jumbo," he groused.

"Takes it seriously, believe me. You saw the fireworks. How many warehouses went up?"

"Six so far. Might be more for all we know."

"We think he's moving his stuff out by ship, probably after midnight, once the date turns over."

"Great. How do we find him? Must be hundreds of ships along the harbor front."

"Check with the harbor master," I said. "Send your guys to look for a ship that's sailing after midnight and has an eight in it, either number or name. Lucky Eight. Lady Eight, something like that. And you can have Tobin's plain clothes boys check for his car. We know it's a black Cadillac Coupe de Ville. License plate 888UVM. It's gotta be parked along the docks somewhere. Maybe we'll get lucky and someone will spot it."

"Any sign of Eli or Jake?" he asked.

"Not yet," I replied grimly. "I'm hoping he's been a bit too busy to get rid of them but that won't last long. We're still looking."

"Call me back in a couple of hours. We'll work it from our end here."

I hung up. Got back into the Chevy. Birdie pulled on to the Lakeshore driving west. "John's cleaning out his warehouses—booze, cigarettes, opium and any other contraband he's into. But he's got to move his stuff down to the ship by truck, right?"

"Uh-huh?" Birdie asked.

"You don't think that...?"

"The kid could be that stupid?"

It seemed clear from Birdie's expression that he thought it eminently possible. "Worth a try. John would be calling in all of those who owe him a favour or two."

"Just what I was thinking."

We made it to the warehouse, the one where we'd spotted Rance and O'Rourke earlier in the week, in less than ten minutes. I parked the Chevy away from the back alley like I'd done before and we walked in. We crouched behind the dumpster and prepared to wait a while. The bouncy GM truck with the canvas top stood quietly at the loading dock. One lone bulb lit the area dimly. Birdie held the 12-gauge loosely in his left hand. Twin .45's packed the holster at each armpit. I carried my .45 in a holster and the .38 special tucked into my waistband. We came loaded with ammo, just in case. After ten minutes, I got antsy.

"Let's take a look," I whispered.

We stayed in the shadows. I took the left and Birdie went round on the right. He moved fast and disappeared without making a sound. Not a footstep was heard or a pebble disturbed. I crossed the alley quickly hovering by the front of the truck. I felt the hood. Still warm.

The loading dock door sat to the left. The main door locked down. I climbed the cement steps staying low. Birdie came up on the other side. I niggled the door to see if it might be open. If not, I had my set of picks with me. Birdie nodded and moved smoothly toward me. We heard voices and shrank back. A metal latch clicked over with a thunk and the main door scrolled noisily up. We faded to the wall. A large figure stepped forward. O'Rourke. Just behind him stood Rance Callaway. They hadn't seen us yet but remained focused on the back of the truck. O'Rourke bent down to unlock it. I moved in quickly behind them.

"Well, well," I said. "We'd better stop meeting like this."

O'Rourke straightened up quickly and whirled. Rance went to make a run for it.

"Better not," Birdie said lifting the double barrel of the 12-gauge.

Rance froze. O'Rourke smiled grimly but raised his hands in the air and placed them behind his head, like he'd had a lot of practice. His face still bore the brunt of his encounter with Birdie.

"Come back for round two?" he asked.

"Round one worked for me," Birdie replied.

"Working tonight, boys?" I asked.

Rance shook his head. "We're knocking off. Just heading home."

"Really? Then maybe we should have a look in the truck, just to make sure."

O'Rourke said nothing, just kept a wolfish grin splashed on his face.

"Down on your knees first," Birdie said. "Don't want you to try anything foolish." He positioned them by motioning with the shotgun. They stepped back and sank to their knees. Birdie covered them while I went to unlock the back of the truck.

"Key," I said. O'Rourke just smiled. I cocked the .45. "I'll ask one more time."

"Right pocket," he replied.

"Get it out and toss it to me." He reached his hand in. "Make that slow."

He removed his hand holding a key ring. I shifted my weight to the left, glanced at Birdie who nodded in the slightest way. O'Rourke tossed the keys high. I reached up to grab them when he made his move. For a big man, he moved fast. From his knees, he dove bringing me down in a tackle while twisting the .45 from my hand. Rance looked on slack-jawed. O'Rourke spun around behind me holding the gun to my head. He figured Birdie couldn't take a chance of shooting me by accident with the 12-gauge. He was right. The spread from the shotgun would have taken out everybody.

"Rance," O'Rourke barked. "Get the keys and get in the truck. Start it up. Now."

The kid jerked out of his paralysis and jumped to it. He scooped up the keys, looked at Birdie then me. Gave us his best smirk. He vaulted off the loading dock, got in the driver's side of the truck and kicked it over. O'Rourke pulled me up with him, moving me to the edge of the dock. Kept me in front. Rance pushed open the passenger door.

"So long, sucker." O'Rourke shoved me forward roughly, landed on his feet and hauled himself into the truck as the kid pulled away. Just as they peeled out of the loading area, the .45 sailed out the window. It landed in the dirt sending up a small plume of dust. I went to retrieve it. Birdie close behind me. We sprinted to the Chevy.

"How was that?" I asked. "Convincing enough?"

"Looked good to me," Birdie said. "Let's hope they lead us where we want them to go."

"Good thing the .45 was unloaded. I almost expected O'Rourke to use it." I'd forgotten to slam home the clip.

"Nah," Birdie said. "He may hit women but that don't mean he's a killer."

Birdie rode shotgun as we pulled out of the alley. The kid had maybe 20 seconds on us but the truck was slow and unbalanced. Only so many routes back to the harbor. The light traffic made it easy to spot him heading down Dufferin to the Lakeshore. He cut through the Canadian Exhibition grounds. I made sure to hang back in the curves of the road and drove with the headlights off. The kid headed back in the direction where we had come.

"Shit," I said. The truck pulled into a loading area for the commercial ferry, joining a short queue. The ferry took commercial traffic to the Toronto Islands and back. Passenger vehicles weren't permitted. Still too early for the passenger ferry to begin its schedule. I checked my watch. Less than five minutes until departure. Rance and Steve O'Rourke stepped out of the truck and walked forward to the lounge on the second level. You could grab a coffee and a doughnut there.

"Let's go."

I pulled the Chevy into the parking lot opposite the ferry terminal. We ran across the street. Trucks and buses formed a small queue to get on to the ferry. The islands ran a bus service back and forth. I pointed. Birdie nodded. We walked up to the bus and rapped on the door. The driver looked at us, shrugged, then opened up.

We each put a dime in the slot and moved toward the back of the bus. Although early, half a dozen passengers had boarded to go to the island. Once there, the bus went round a dozen or so stops. It wasn't a large bus and held perhaps 25 fares. A moment later, the bus pulled on to the ferry and the driver shut the engine off. The front and middle doors opened. The other passengers stood up and exited the bus. The driver looked around, saw us still seated and called out.

"Everyone has to leave the bus during the ride over," the driver said.

I lifted my hand and smiled reassuringly. We stood up and stepped out of the bus.

The driver gave us an odd look, eased down the steps and closed the door behind him. A narrow walkway led forward, up a cement staircase to the upper levels. We followed the driver along. I touched Birdie's arm and we held back. I glanced behind me. The bus had been the last vehicle let on the ferry. The others in the queue would have to wait until the next departure in about 20 minutes' time.

"Can't take the chance they'll spot us," I said to Birdie. "Especially you."

I had ridden this ferry before and the lounge was miniscule. To get to the outer observation deck, you had to cross through it.

"Thanks for the vote of confidence," Birdie said.

"You know what I mean. Anyway, we should be taking off any minute now."

Just as I finished speaking, we felt the vibrating thrum of the engine and a couple of deck hands winched the back gate into place. I looked back toward the dock as the ferry began to chug away. I lit a Sweet Cap.

"Shouldn't be long," I said.

We walked forward and took a look at O'Rourke's truck. The springs sat low against the wheel wells with the back end shifting to the left. I gave Birdie a poke.

"Ever do any tail riding?" I asked.

He gave me a dirty look. "I've been burnt up and peed on and now you're asking me to play kid stuff off the back of a truck?"

"Uh-huh."

"Sweet Jesus, the sacrifices I make."

"All in a good cause," I replied.

When the bus driver came by after swigging his coffee and gulping his doughnut, I pulled him aside. "Here's ten bucks," I said.

"What's this for?" he snarled.

"For not asking any questions or making any noise when you see me and my friend here hanging off the back end of this truck. Get it?"

The driver frowned but snatched the bill out of my hand.

"Your funeral," he said.

The rest of the passengers made their way back to the bus and the driver opened the door to let them board. I counted on Rance and O'Rourke making their way to the cab without checking the back. Had to make certain they didn't catch sight of us in the side mirrors as we hung off the back doors.

The ferry made its docking and the engines up and down the queue began to fire up. I felt the truck's motor kick over. Almost gagged on the exhaust spewing out in the enclosed space of the ferry's parking bay.

"Here we go," I muttered.

Hadn't done this since I was a kid. The truck drove forward following the vehicle in front of it while the bus came up behind us. I think the driver accelerated and kept the front bumper a little too close just to try and spook us. I smiled at him, then eased my jacket back to show him my shoulder holster. The driver's jaw went slack but he dropped back pretty quickly. I hoped he'd do the right thing and stop at a phone booth and call the cops. After leaving the loading area, the bus turned left toward Ward Island while O'Rourke kept us on the main track. A track that had seen better days when, once upon a time, it had actually been paved and the potholes were only a few feet deep. The terrain on the island consisted of gentle rolling hills but with the potholes, it felt like riding a runaway bull steer. Then the brakes jammed hard. I heard one of the doors open up and O'Rourke's voice.

"Just wanna make sure the doors are secure," he said.

"Shit," I hissed. I looked around. No time to drop off and hide. I looked up, nudged Birdie and pointed. We made it to the roof of the truck just before Rance and O'Rourke came around.

"See?" Rance said. "It's fine."

I heard him tug at the doors. I prayed they didn't look up at the roof. They couldn't help but see us laying there, spread eagle, trying to make ourselves invisible. Fortunately, it remained a good 40 minutes until sun-up.

O'Rourke gave an extra tug. "Okay, let's hit it," he said.

They climbed back in the cab and the truck took off with a lurch. Birdie grabbed my arm. Not too many handholds up there. The truck sped along the rutted track, twisting and turning for a good five minutes or more. The harbor faded in the background but I could see the lights of some steamers on Lake Ontario. We passed a lonely playground empty of the rambunctious kids needed to bring it to life.

The vibration made us slip and slide. I tapped Birdie on the back and pointed. He looked up. Just ahead lay a private docking area large enough to hold a small tanker. And that's what it did. Rance wrenched the truck into a lower gear. Birdie and I slid down the back.

We grabbed hold of the door handles and as the truck slowed further, dropped off the end making sure to keep our feet. A nearby hedgerow provided some immediate cover. We kept low and made for it. The truck stuttered forward and pulled up near the dock. Rance swung it forward, then backed it up to a lading area.

A winch had been set up and a large net attached to a steel cable lay slack, ready to receive its next load. A spotlight from the deck had been trained on the loading area. O'Rourke unlocked the back and lifted the doors out, setting them against the side of the truck.

I gave Birdie a nudge. Quan, cradling an M60, strutted down the gangplank. He engaged O'Rourke in a brief, muffled conversation then slapped him on the back and headed back up the gangplank where his head appeared bobbing along the railing as he walked the deck of the ship. O'Rourke and Rance began shifting wooden crates from the back of the truck to the net. After they'd transferred about 20 crates, O'Rourke held up his hand and the winch kicked in with a whine and the net jerked upward closing around its cargo. Slowly, the bulging bundle rose shakily into the air until it was winched over the side of the ship.

We heard some chatter coming from the deck and I supposed it came from the hands shifting the boxes so they could bring aboard the next load. A moment later, the winch re-engaged and returned, lowered near the truck where Rance and O'Rourke waited. They shifted another 20 or so crates. The air had lightened. I got a look at the side of the ship—Eight Candles—John hadn't taken any chances with the name.

The cable went taut and the third load went up and over the side. O'Rourke nudged Rance. They replaced the doors, rammed home the lock, got into the truck. The engine sputtered into life. O'Rourke raised his arm as the truck lurched off, heading back to the ferry docks. The spotlight snapped off.

"Only one way in," Birdie said and pointed to the gangplank with the barrel of the 12-gauge.

"We don't even know if Eli and Jake are aboard," I said.

"Either they're up there," Birdie said. "Or they're charcoal in one of the warehouse fires."

"That's a comforting thought," I replied. "I can't see why John would have brought them aboard in the first place."

"Insurance," Birdie said.

I nodded. That made sense. That's how John might think. If things went wrong, he could use them as bargaining chips to keep the authorities at bay. And then, once safely on his way, he could simply dump them over the side.

"It'll be daylight soon."

"I don't feel like waiting here until sundown," Birdie said.

I sighed. "I thought the Lord taught you patience."

Birdie grinned. "He's on the side of the righteous."

"Okay. Well, maybe most of the crew are asleep since it's still early. John had about eight guys with him at Christie Pits. We'll have to reckon on that many, maybe more. And if they're like Quan, they'll be heavily armed with M60s."

Birdie snorted. "Pea shooters. No good in close quarters anyway." He snapped open the breech of the 12-gauge, then patted his pockets feeling the comfort of the extra shells.

"Well, they shouldn't be expecting us," I said.

I took a deep breath and shivered. Maybe twenty yards to the loading area. "Let's give it a whirl."

I unholstered the .45 and checked to make sure I'd rammed the clip home this time. Birdie went to the far side of the hedgerow and I stayed to the left. On a silent three count, we took off, heading toward the ship, staying in the shadows, keeping low.

My breath felt loud in my ears. My pulse jumped. We crept along the jetty reaching the bottom of the gangplank from opposite directions. We played Rock, Paper, Scissors to see who'd go up first. I lost. I always lost. I gave Birdie a dirty look and he encouraged me with a grin.

It wasn't easy going up an incline in a crouch position. At the top, I paused to listen and peer around through the gloom. I heard voices in the distance but no one close by. I stepped off carefully and crouched down behind the last load of crates. Birdie joined me.

"Someone will be by soon to haul these away," he said.

I nodded and we moved around the back to wait. I noticed coils of rope stacked up on the deck. Handy. A few minutes later, we heard a couple of the crew talking, making their way along the deck toward the crates. Two guys. As they bent down to pick up a crate each, Birdie and I went around behind them.

Birdie slugged one of them and caught him as he crumpled to the ground. I put the .45 against the temple of the other as I placed my hand over his mouth.

"Any sound and your brains will be splattered all over the deck, do you understand?"

The guy had gone stiff as a board but he nodded. I pulled him around behind the crates. Birdie had finished trussing the first guy up, stuffed a rag into his mouth and knotted some of the coiled rope to hold it in place. Then he dragged the limp body over to a lifeboat, lifted it up and shoved him under. I brought the second guy to his knees. Birdie set the 12-gauge up under his jaw and hooked his thumb over the trigger.

"I'm going to take my hand away and you're going to answer some questions very quietly. If you do something stupid, my friend will blow you to kingdom come. Got it?" The guy nodded. Unlike the other guy, he was Caucasian. About forty with a ragged beard and greasy hair. "Okay." Slowly, I took my hand away from his mouth. I felt his sweat trickle on to my palm. "How many men on board this ship?"

"Ten crew including the captain."

"And?"

"Seven other guys, all armed."

"You all work for John Fat Gai?"

"No."

"Who do you work for then?" I asked.

"Mr. Li. This is his ship."

"Mr. Li?" I glanced at Birdie. "It may interest you to know, pal, that Mr. Li was murdered yesterday by John Fat Gai. Shot through the gut. It wasn't pretty."

The guy jerked his head toward me. "What?"

"That's right."

"Jesus," the sailor hissed. "Look, I'm just a deck hand, okay? I don't get involved in stuff. I just work the ship and go wherever we sail to, load and unload, take orders from the captain and that's it, I swear."

"Where's this tub bound for?"

"Macau."

"Are the crew armed?"

"No. Arms are kept in the gunroom below deck. It's locked and only the captain has the key."

"The other guys?"

"Armed to the teeth."

"Okay. You're doing good so far. Keep it up and you'll also keep your head on your shoulders."

"Sure. I got no reason to lie."

"Anyone else on board? We're looking for someone."

"Yeah. Two guys in the brig."

"Describe them to me."

"An older guy and a young guy. The older guy wears a ducktail and has bags the size of craters under his eyes. The other one, probably his son."

"Sounds like them," Birdie intoned.

"Where's the brig?" I asked.

"It's aft, two levels down."

"Who's got the key?"

"That'd be the captain, the exec or the CPO. It's a skeleton key, nothing fancy."

"Okay, good." I had the picks in my jacket pocket. "Guess what?" I said.

"What?" and the sailor managed a weak smile. I could see his broken teeth.

"You're going to give us the express guided tour. Let's go. No sudden moves. No noise, right?" The guy nodded. I pulled him to his feet.

"This way," he said.

He led us down a metal staircase to a dimly lit corridor. At the end of the corridor stood a metal door with a wheel lock. The sailor spun the wheel and pushed the door open. Another narrow staircase led into the bowels of the ship.

"How much farther?" I asked.

"Bottom of the stairs, end of the corridor and we're there," the guy answered.

"Let's go."

At the end of the corridor, the space widened out. I saw bars like any jail, similar to the holding cells we had in the city. I looked in.

"Whatever you guys are going to do, you better hurry up, okay?" The sailor looked agitated.

Eli and Jake had been trussed up to a reverse pulley that held them taut by a rope passed through a hook-up connected to the ceiling. If they sagged or got tired, the noose tightened. The more they slumped, the tighter it got until they'd strangle themselves. Cute.

"Hey." A sailor appeared at the far end of the corridor. He spotted us and before we could move, he yelled then disappeared.

"Better hurry up, Mo, for a lot of reasons," Birdie said.

"Mo," croaked Eli.

"Hang in there, Eli. We're going to get you out."

I took out the picks and began to fiddle with the lock. Birdie kept one eye on the corridor. The sailor paced back in forth in front of him.

I heard a burst and the pinging of metal as bullets ricocheted around us. The sailor went up on the balls of his feet.

"Sweet Jesus," he cried.

The air went out of him like a squeezed bulb. Birdie caught him as he slumped to the ground and fired both barrels of the 12-gauge down the corridor. He lay the sailor on the metal floor and reloaded.

"Make that double time," he said. Birdie let go of another blast to keep them honest.

"Almost there," I said.

I felt the last two tumblers click into place. The door swung open.

"Got it."

Jake's eyes bugged out of his face, his complexion puce. Eli had managed to hold himself up a bit better but he struggled. I cut Jake down and he flopped on the floor like a dying fish, grappling with the rope around his neck, coughing and wheezing. Eli managed to keep his feet. I helped him remove the rope.

"I'm glad to see you," he rasped and threw his arms around me. I pushed him back.

"Remind me to slug you when we're clear of this. I told you to get outta town and stay out."

He put his hands up in a defensive posture but managed a grin. "Okay. If we get clear, I'll let you slug me. C'mon, give me a hand with the old man." We reached down and hauled Jake to his feet.

"Good to see you, boychick. I knew you wouldn't leave us to rot in here." Jake coughed into his flabby chest.

"Yeah, yeah. Come on. We've got some distance to cover yet."

Birdie fired another deafening blast. We had two directions to go. Forward, toward the firing line or back through a door at the end of the corridor. Door number one. I took door number one. I turned the wheel and pushed it open. Birdie handed Eli one of his holstered .45's.

"Hey, what am I, chopped liver?" Jake said.

I sighed, looked to the heavens, then handed him the .38 in my waist band. "Try not to shoot one of us, okay?"

"Listen to him," Jake said. "Like I haven't been handling guns since you were in diapers."

"Cut the crap," Eli croaked. "Let's get the hell outta here."

I crouched and stepped through the door. A metal staircase led up. I motioned with the gun. Jake, then Eli stepped through. Birdie spun the wheel closed before following. I threaded my way up. A shot banged out. We hit the deck. The bullet ricocheted, pinging off the metal floor then up as it deflected near my chin off the metal banister.

"Sorry," Eli said. "I slipped."

"Might as well just invite the bastards over for a drink," Jake muttered.

"All right, all right," I groused.

We reached the top stair that opened up into a small platform with another door.

"You guys get on the other side."

Eli and Jake squeezed over. I noticed an acetylene tank propped up against the wall. I squeezed against the opposite side of the doorframe.

"Okay," I said. "Open it up."

Birdie rotated the wheel. He pulled the door open. A burst from an M60 greeted us. Bullets slammed off the walls. Eli and Jake went into a crouch. Birdie slammed it shut.

"So we know where some of them are," I said.

I opened up the knobs on the tank so the gas could leak out. "What are you doing?" Jake demanded.

"You'll see."

Birdie opened the door again. Another burst came our way. I chucked the tank into the corridor. Birdie blasted two rounds and slammed the door shut. Didn't take long. We heard a roar and a whoosh, then a kind of crumping sound. I felt some heat and the door buckled. We waited.

Two, three beats.

Cautiously, Birdie pulled the door toward him. The blast had twisted the frame. He gave it a good yank. It pulled away falling at his feet. We stayed low. A line of flame licked itself along the metal railing. Dark smudges marked the low ceiling and floor. Billows of smoke wafted in the air. I coughed into my sleeve.

At the far end, we found two guys out on their feet, slightly singed. The muzzles of their M60s had melted. I stepped over them and poked my head around the corner of the stairwell. More metal stairs led up. I could see the suffused light of a dawn beginning to break. I felt a shudder and some vibration.

"What's that?" Eli asked.

"The ship," I replied.

"What about it?"

"It's about to move, kid, that's what," Jake said.

"What were you saying about superstition?" Birdie asked.

"Okay, so maybe we forced his hand a little. Let's take a look."

I stood on the bottom step and looked up. I climbed the steps slowly, keeping the .45 ready and cocked.

Two steps from the top, a gun barrel, then a head appeared. The guy gave me a friendly grin. I put my hands up and gave him my best, resigned look. Before he could reply, Birdie grabbed his hand, jamming his big thumb behind the trigger of the M60. The gunsel went to pull and it wouldn't move. Birdie yanked him down where his chin met my knee. I grabbed the M60.

Jake pushed the guy down the stairs. The gunsel slithered to the bottom rolling over and over like a slinky.

Another guy looked in from the top of the stairwell. The 12-gauge roared and I saw his body lifted off its feet blown backwards. We surged up on to the deck, staying low. I sprayed the deck using the M60 for covering fire. My ears rang from the shotgun blast. The sound still echoed around the metal fittings down below or maybe it was just inside my head. I spotted Quan on the other side of the deck working the slide in his piece. We fanned out and took cover behind some wooden barrels. Birdie and I checked out the area, sweeping the deck, searching the high points for trouble. John's voice rang out. He'd gotten hold of a loud hailer.

"Mo. Birdie. Nice of you to drop in."

"Kind of you to have us," I called back.

"You're trapped, Mo. You'll never get off this ship," John blared then chuckled maniacally.

A couple of hands skirted the edge of the deck, untying the lines to cast off. I fired a burst in their direction. They dropped what they were doing and hit the floor. Quan let a burst go at the hawsers holding the ship in place. Birdie let loose a blast. Quan ducked behind a lifeboat.

"It's a stalemate, John," I called. "You won't get the ship untied, not with us stopping you. Let us go and you can take off. Sail into hell for all I care."

Just to convince him, I fired a burst in Quan's direction. He shrank back. I spotted a few heads bobbing up and down behind the foc'sle. I turned back to Birdie. "How many?" He held up two fingers.

John came back on the horn. "Generous of you, Mo."

"You're running out of time, John. The cops and the harbor patrol will be here any minute. Then you won't be going, anywhere."

A pause ensued. "I'm coming down," he squawked.

The door to the wheelhouse opened and John Fat Gai, jauntily dressed in a blue blazer, white slacks, a yellow cravat and a yachting cap made his way down to the deck. He lifted his arms and smiled. But I could see the cracks. Eyes unfocused. Unhinged expression.

He walked toward us, completely exposed. I went to stand up but Birdie put a big paw on my shoulder.

"It's okay," I said. "Cover me. He or Quan makes a move–blast'em."

"Boychick…"

"Shut up, Jake." I stepped out then tossed the M60 to the deck. I made certain to keep John in front of me, using him as cover. He did the same. I held the .45 down at my side. Fifteen feet separated us.

"Four means death, John. You know it and I know it. You're drowning in it."

"But it could be your death, Mo, not mine."

I smiled. "Don't think so. You have to believe in that mumbo jumbo and I don't. Today is your judgment day. You have debts that haven't been collected yet. Li said it. His spirit will haunt you forever, don't you remember?"

John pulled at the dragon pendant. His eyes flicked to the sky then down. "Perhaps I have underestimated you."

"You'll never last if you have to sit here all day. The authorities will be on you before then."

"Yes, you are probably right," he replied and chortled.

A bubble descended around us. I leaned in and whispered to him sotto voce, so the others couldn't hear. His expression didn't change but I saw movement behind his eyes. Some truth took hold of him. He answered me quietly.

I got distracted by sudden movement from above. Along the bridge and upper deck, the crew fanned out, fully armed with their weapons trained on us. All of us. They had the advantage and the angle. A guy I took to be the captain—Chinese—wearing similar clothes to those of John just dirtier and ragged—began to yammer. He spoke in a high-pitched screech.

"You are all surrounded. All of you will put your weapons down at once."

Quan appeared from his hidey-hole. He stood up, smirking and stepped into view still cradling his weapon. A burst from one of the seamen made him dance the cucaracha on the spot.

"I mean all of you," the captain yelled.

I holstered my .45. "Hey?" I called up but gestured for Birdie and the others to stay put.

"What do you want?" the captain replied.

"I understand this is Mr. Li's ship?" I asked almost innocently but shot John a grin.

"Yes," the captain replied. "That is correct."

"Mo," John said like a dog beginning to growl in its throat.

"Well, I'm sure it would interest you to know that Mr. Li is dead. Shot in the gut by John Fat Gai yesterday evening."

The captain switched his focus to John. Gun barrels swiveled in his direction. "Is this true?"

John Fat Gai shrugged. "I suppose I should take the credit when it is due."

Storm clouds gathered on the captain's face. He barked something in Mandarin. John Fat Gai's face froze, his body stiffened. Quan swiveled, bringing the M60 up aiming toward the bridge. A roar of double barrels lifted him off his feet. He smashed against the railing then eased to the deck and lay on his side folded up like a sparrow with a broken neck.

Birdie broke the smoking breech open and slid two shells home then snapped it shut. I noticed something now that the darkness had lifted. A line of metal barrels neatly placed around the perimeter of the lower deck. John hadn't moved. He remained standing, his posture loose and relaxed, an enigmatic smile on his face; beatific almost. I heard him humming under his breath. I turned to warn the others. I couldn't get the words out fast enough. The barrels exploded. The ship's deck buckled and lurched. I fell to my knees slamming my chin. I looked around blearily. Saw John wafting through a shimmery membrane of fire. He walked calmly to the gangplank and descended.

"Come on," I yelled.

Up on my feet shakily and pointed. Another round of explosions lit up the sky and the air around us. Threw us off-balance. I staggered up. Birdie turned and grabbed Jake. I pushed Eli in front of me. We stumbled aft and before Jake could utter a syllable, Birdie lifted him up and heaved him over the rail into the water, then jumped behind him.

"Jump," I yelled at Eli.

He hopped over the rail and dropped straight down. I let the momentum of my body carry me forward. I floated in space for a second, felt the impact of the water on the bottoms of my shoes and submerged for a few seconds before coming up spluttering.

"Swim for shore. Hurry."

We'd seen explosions but the ship must have been jammed with so much TNT it made the fireworks displays I'd seen as a kid on Canada Day look like a pathetic Roman candle. A gargantuan roar and whoosh enveloped us and hurled us toward the beach, the water spouting up like a huge geyser.

I glanced back and thought I saw John Fat Gai's slim form outlined in the phosphorescent hell he'd unleashed as he calmly stepped into a motorboat, cast off and sped away from the devil's cauldron. The upper level of the ship lay slathered in flames. Thick, toxic clouds of black smoke spiraled upward. More explosions echoed, one ignited the other in a chain. The ship's hull glistened darkly at the water line.

Jake flopped around in the water. "I can't swim. I can't swim."

I stroked toward him. He reached out to grab me in a chokehold. Panic flooded his eyes. I socked him hard in the jaw. Before he could slide under, I reached down, grabbed him under the chin and towed him to shore. I pulled his slack body on to the sand, let it roll over like a beached porpoise. Birdie sat in the sand watching the show. He'd removed his shoes and socks but still held on to the 12-gauge. Eli sat back on his haunches panting.

"You guys know how to show a fella a real good time," he gasped.

Birdie looked down at himself in disgust. "Another good suit ruined," he said.

I grinned at them. "It's good to be alive."

I reached into my jacket pocket and felt for the pack of Sweet Caps but they'd turned to mush.

By the time Callaway and Tobin showed, the ship had burnt down to the waterline, held upright by the metal hawsers tied to the pier.

"What took you?" I asked.

"We were delayed," he growled. Tobin just glared at me but said nothing. He sported a lovely shiner under his right eye. The big fish had swum away.

"By what?"

"You don't know?" Callaway asked. I looked at him blankly. I was wet and singed and tired. "The ferry terminal blew up. Two seriously hurt, three more missing and the ferries had to stop running. We commandeered some boats from the harbor patrol but by then the fireworks over here had already started."

I shook my head. "We were a little distracted."

Tobin couldn't stand it any longer. He pounded over. "I thought you said John Fat Gai wouldn't leave today because it's the fourth. That he was afraid he'd die."

"That's right," I replied, trying to stay calm. "He did die."

Tobin gaped at me. "What are you talking about?"

"A professional death."

"Huh?"

I sighed. "Think about it, Tobin. His house gone, warehouses gone, business gone—right now it's the closest we're going to get. Until next time. You've got the copy of the ledger and you and Callaway can roll up his network of dirty cops and politicians. That's not a bad deal, is it?"

He went to grab my shirtfront but I stepped back. "That's not good enough," he said.

"I don't care," I replied. "You've got most of what you wanted."

Two of Tobin's guys hauled Jake to his feet, spun him around and handcuffed him. They put leg shackles on him so he had to hobble over to an old Ford pick-up they'd managed to borrow.

Just before they shoved his head into the interior, Jake smirked over at me.

"See you later, boychick."

"Sure. I'll come visit you in the slam," I said and turned my back on him to bum a cigarette from one of the detectives working the scene. Eli came over to bum one too. He stared after Jake. I acted on my promise and decked him. He sat hard on his haunches, rubbed his jaw and nodded. I reached down. He hesitated then grabbed my hand. I pulled him up, stuck a fag in his gob and lit it for him.

49

Birdie and I had squeezed on to the sofa in Aida Turner's small living room. She poured tea. As usual, Birdie looked immaculate. Adele and Mrs. Turner took a look at my bruised face and the singed eyebrows but decided not to say anything.

"That poor family," Mrs. Turner said and handed each of us a cup. I tried not to rattle the cup against the saucer. "They are feeling such a burden of loss. And it is a heavy burden."

She referred to the Fosters. Adele sat opposite her aunt and averted my gaze.

"Yeah, it is tough, I suppose," I replied.

I didn't have a lot of sympathy for the Fosters but that was just me. We had apprised Aida Turner and her niece of the general sequence of events.

"I understand that feeling very well, Mr. Gold," Aida Turner continued. "Biscuit?" She offered up a plate.

"Thank you," I replied and chose a Peak Frean ginger snap. I'd always been a sucker for them.

Birdie smiled and shook his head. He slurped the tea draining the cup then set it down carefully.

"I can't believe it is all over," Aida Turner said. "It feels like a dream. I'm waiting for someone to wake me up."

"Auntie," Adele began then stopped.

"He still hasn't come around?" I asked.

Aida Turner shook her head. "Not yet. But I expect he will eventually. I know he's out there and he's safe. That's all I ever wanted. That reassurance. And I have you to thank for it."

"He's been living that life so long. I'm sure it's difficult to give it up," I replied.

"He needs to get his trust back," Birdie boomed. "Understand that the world isn't such a scary place. He's still afraid of what the white man can do, how much power he holds over folks. Henry's seen all kinds of crazy things happening, Chinese gangsters, dishonest police and the like, dead babies. He'll find a reason to come back, you'll see."

Aida Turner smiled. "I expect you are right, Mr. Birdwell. And that will take some time. Once my Henry knows it's safe, he will come back to me and we will go on as we did before." She sighed, imagining that version of paradise. Aida Turner set her cup down and reached into the pocket of her apron. "Now it's time to fulfill my debt, gentlemen." She drew out the roll of used bills and set them down on the table.

"Auntie," Adele said again.

"No, Adele," Aida Turner said. "These gentlemen have done what I asked them to do. And that is that."

Birdie and I had talked about this. Well, argued about it really. Until we came to a conclusion. A kind of solution.

"Thank you, Mrs. Turner. We're much obliged," I said. I pocketed the wad of used bills saved up over countless days and weeks. I imagined what she had to do to set it aside, what she had to sacrifice. But it was what she wanted in the end. "If there is anything else we can do for you..." I set my cup down and eyeing Birdie we both stood up.

"My heart is lighter than it has been for years. That is my reward," Aida Turner said.

"Goodbye then." I looked at Adele but she stared at the floor.

Birdie smiled and nodded then we took our leave.

We were at the gate when she called out. "Mr. Gold?" I turned and there were those magnificent ankles in full view.

"Yes?"

She hesitated and glanced at Birdie. He took the hint and sidled over to the Chevy that was parked half a block up. Adele came up to me.

"Yes?" I repeated.

She put her hand out and patted my lapel. "I, uh, I, think I misjudged you, Mr. Gold, er, Mo. Maybe I made a mistake, an error in judgment."

"You think so, Adele?"

"Yes. I'm sorry about that."

"And what about…?"

She swallowed hard. "That is over. Well and truly over. Another colossal mistake on my part, I'm afraid. Seems like I've been making a lot of mistakes lately." She smiled rather prettily. "I was wondering…"

"Yes?"

"I was wondering if, maybe we couldn't start again. Pretend that we've just met and see what happens. Would you be willing to do that, Mo? Try again?"

I looked down at her feet. She saw where I was looking and smiled faintly. My heart raced in spite of my head telling it not to.

"It seems like I misjudged you too, Adele. I mean, Ms. Rosewell." Her smile froze. "I want to wish you all the best. I hope all goes well with the trial. I know you'll have to testify on Lawson's behalf, I mean. If you see him, give him my regards. Goodbye." I touched her hand and it felt cold. About as cold as my heart.

If anything, the house looked more ramshackle than before, as if a stiff breeze would blow it over. The grey washing flapped on the sagging line and the threadbare lawn looked forlorn and abandoned. Nothing but sadness permeated Rochelle Dodson's property.

I stood at the gate as Birdie strode up to the front door. He knocked gently, concerned, I'm sure that if he put any more force into it, the whole house would come tumbling down. Rochelle Dodson answered tentatively, opening the door a crack. Then the door opened wider. I could see, from that distance, the bruising around her eyes. Two young children clung to her skirt, frightened of themselves and perhaps of the skyscraper of a man who stood on their threshold.

Yet I could hear his gentle tones as he told her what had happened. That Henry

was alive and well. That it was time for her to get a new life for her and her children. I saw Birdie press the worn bills into her hand. She shook her head and tried to push it back. Birdie closed both his hands over hers and spoke warmly but insistently. Rochelle Dodson cried. Fell to her knees and sobbed but I could also see they were tears of relief. In a mop-up operation, O'Rourke had been arrested as part of a gang that had been hijacking liquor shipments around the city. We'd put Callaway and the guys in robbery, particularly Dewey, on to Steve O'Rourke and they'd pulled him in. Caught him driving a truck full of cases to a warehouse down on the docks. Fortunately, Rance Callaway hadn't been with him. This time.

The money from Aida Turner would give her a fresh start. Birdie lifted Rochelle Dodson up, kissed her on the cheek, patted each of the children on the head and came back down the walk toward me. He looked happy and that was good enough for me.

Kernahan never did talk. After all the hubbub had died down, Callaway dragged himself back to the precinct. When he checked on the patrolman in the holding cell, he found vomit down the front of Kernahan's shirt, his meal tray upturned on the floor and a glazed, dead expression frozen on his face. Food poisoning apparently. Of the lethal variety.

50

I moped around the apartment, listening to the Jazz Hour on CBC radio keeping a bottle of Scotch company when the phone jangled.

"Yeah?"

"You might be interested in seeing this." Callaway.

"Oh yeah?"

"Yeah, I said so, didn't I?"

"Where are you?" He rattled off the address. "Give me half an hour."

"Right." He hung up.

I splashed some cold water on my face, pulled a clean shirt from the wardrobe and knotted my tie. Picking up my jacket, hat and .45, I was ready to go.

I lit a Sweet Cap, rolled down the window and fired the Chevy up. Still a warm evening—after midnight. Callaway was a dedicated guy, married to the job first then his wife. The address he gave me belonged to the Plaza Hotel. The top two floors laid out as apartments. I parked outside and took a ticket from the bellhop, told him where I was going and he practically saluted. Several patrol cars blocked the street with restless cops in them.

I went into the lobby and took the elevator up to the 18th floor. I could hear the activity as I trod down the hall. I knew the two bulls on the door and they nodded me in. The view opened up to a large living room with windows on two sides overlooking the city. It was a nice outlook. You could practically drink from the lake. A modern apartment–expensively furnished. Several cops searched the place. They didn't bother to look up when I came in. I heard the pop and saw the flash of a bulb coming from the bedroom. I went to the doorway and looked in. Callaway stood to one side while the photographer did his work.

"Make sure you get close-ups of everything. And I mean, everything," Callaway said. He glanced my way. "Hello Mo," he said casually. "Glad you could make it."

"Thanks for the invite, what have you got here?"

Callaway pointed to the victim. The photographer stepped aside and I saw a bloodied figure lying on the carpet. The carpet oozed blood. It foamed up through the fibres. The photographer tiptoed around the edges but I could hear the squish of his footsteps. A knife, looked like the bone handle of a kitchen knife, stuck out of the victim's chest. He wore silk pajamas. Of course. What else would you wear in a swanky joint like this?

"Got him right in the heart," Callaway said. "Remind you of anything?"

I edged closer taking in the dark, slicked back hair, the smooth, smug features.

"Troyer," I said.

His eyes had popped–his mouth frozen into an 'O'. "He looks surprised and it was one that wasn't particularly pleasant." I inhaled the rusty smell of blood. It permeated everything.

"No kidding," Callaway said. He beckoned me over. "I asked you a question," he said, quietly, almost in a whisper.

"Yeah, I heard you. Troyer let the killer in. Must have known who it was."

"Uh-huh."

"You're thinking, Alison Lawson?" Callaway nodded. "What about...?"

"Wasn't Lawson. He's being released on bail tomorrow morning. He's been in custody since his wife took it in the chest too."

I glanced down. “More than one wound. Seems that Harvey was stabbed multiple times just like Alison Lawson,” I said.

“That makes it personal,” Callaway said. “This give you any ideas?”

I shrugged. “Maybe.”

“You got any ideas I want to know about them. Right now, I gotta check if Harvey here stole from any of his clients or was fiddling his accounts as well as check into his known associates. I figured you’d want to see this because of the Lawson incident. There’s going to be a lot of heat on this one. The kid’s old man is a judge, for Christ sake. Why couldn’t he be a cabbie or a garbage man?”

“Just your lucky day I guess,” I said.

“Mason’s funeral is tomorrow,” Callaway said.

“And?”

“You thinking of going?”

I shook my head. “Hadn’t given it much thought.”

“I have to be there, of course.”

“Of course. He worked for you.”

“You’re old man’s going to be indicted by the feds. Racketeering, loan sharking, tax evasion, you name it. I think they’re even going to get him for jaywalking if they can. I don’t think he’ll be able to wriggle out of this one.”

“It’s what the old bastard deserves,” I said.

“You’re a hard case,” Callaway replied.

“You better believe it.”

I turned to go but stopped. “One more thing…”

“What?”

“Better hide your nephew until this blows over. He could be next.” I indicated the mess that stared back at us.

“Rance? I, uh, yeah not a bad idea at that,” Callaway admitted.

“Thought so.”

51

I lifted the heavy brass knocker and let it drop once. It hit the solid oak door with a resounding thud. Birdie and I stood on the veranda, hats in hand, shoes polished, trousers correctly creased. A bolt slid back, the door creaked open and the same bird-like maid eyed us with suspicion. She was about to slam the door in our faces when Birdie stuck his size 17 shoe against the frame.

I smiled as prettily as I could that early in the morning. "Tell her, it's us or the cops."

The maid froze. She looked down at Birdie's foot, then up at me. I gave her a wink. She harrumphed.

"Are you going to remove your foot or aren't you?" she snapped.

"Not until you let us in," Birdie said.

"Very well." The door swung back. We stepped inside the vestibule.

"Wait here," she ordered, after slamming the door closed and shooting the bolt.

The house remained hushed, like a mausoleum. I wondered where they kept the incinerators. The maid waddled off down the corridor and disappeared.

"As chirpy as ever," I said.

"Lives on the sunny side of the street," Birdie replied then chuckled.

She kept us cooling our heels for a good five minutes. Then, out of the gloom, she reappeared, the features still sharp, the eyes a piercing blue. The skin freckled parchment, lightly powdered. "This way," she said.

We followed her down the corridor to the same sitting room as before. The maid opened the door and stood back.

"Go on," she said. "Get in. It's what you wanted, isn't it?"

She sat upright on the settee looking so brittle I thought she'd crumble before our eyes. The Persian lay across her lap purring. She stroked its belly absently.

"Mrs. Sorenson," I said.

She looked up sharply. "Yes?"

"I think you know why we're here, Mrs. Sorenson."

"Do I?"

"Mind if we sit down?"

She started. "Yes, of course, where are my manners. Gone out the window I suppose, like everything else." She caught her breath and it came out in a stifled sob.

We each took a seat in the wingbacks opposite her. I settled myself.

"Look, Mrs. Sorenson, there's no point beating around the bush here. Like I told the maid, it's us or the cops. I think you're better off with us. Last night I came from Harvey Troyer's apartment…."

Her eyes clouded. "Harvey? What about him?"

"Well, the fact of the matter is that he's dead…."

There came a sharp intake of breath. She put a veined hand to her throat.

"How dreadful. I must call his parents at once." She made as if to rise.

"Just a second, Mrs. Sorenson. Harvey Troyer was killed in the same manner as Alison Lawson."

"What do you mean exactly?"

"It was a frenzied attack with a knife. The cops found the murder weapon. It was buried in Harvey's heart. There was a lot of blood. The carpet was swimming in it…"

Mrs. Sorenson shook her head. She'd gone so pale I thought she was going to pass out. "Both victims, Harvey and Alison opened the door to their killer. That means they knew whoever it was. There was no sign of forced entry and both of them were taken by surprise. The fact that the attack in each case involved multiple stab wounds with the final ones coming post-mortem, indicates that the killings weren't random. They were deliberate and they were personal. Someone was taking revenge."

"That is an interesting theory, Mr. Gold."

"No theory, Mrs. Sorenson. It's what happened and it wouldn't take much in a court of law to prove it, either."

"Prove what, exactly? Prove it how?"

One thing about the upper classes, their instinct for superiority re-asserted itself naturally. "Fingerprints. The same set on both of the murder weapons found at each scene. They just need to be matched to the right pair of hands."

I paused to let that sink in. I could see it had an effect. She waited for me to continue.

"Eight years ago, your daughter and Alison Foster were driven by Henry Turner to a club down by the waterfront called Blackstones."

"Blackstones?" she repeated.

"That's right," I said. "A club owned by a notorious Chinese gangster named John Fat Gai. John ran the club and had an interesting little business on the side."

Despite herself, she asked the question. "And what was that, pray tell?"

"In a word–blackmail. The club had rooms upstairs. John would lure young girls from prominent families to those rooms. The rooms were rigged with camera equipment. The girls were filmed high on opium having sex with men. Older men."

Mrs. Sorenson put a hand to her forehead. It was damp. From her sleeve she removed a lace handkerchief and patted her face.

"Now, you're straying into the realm of science fiction, Mr. Gold. An art form for which I have little use."

"Not science fiction, Mrs. Sorenson. More like horror. Hitchcock at his worst. Like I said, Allison Foster and your daughter were caught up in the shenanigans. This gave John Fat Gai the means to blackmail the families of those girls. Naturally, the families wouldn't tell anyone because they feared exposure. They would never go to the police, for instance."

"Yes," she replied vaguely. "I suppose that's true."

"John Fat Gai has been blackmailing your family for the past eight years, Mrs. Sorenson. He made you and the others pay and pay big."

"Where's your evidence, Mr. Gold? Otherwise, this is nothing but fantasy."

I slid my hand into my inside jacket pocket. It emerged with a metal film canister.

"Well, I expect a review of your financial records would be rather revealing but here's my hard evidence, Mrs. Sorenson. I retrieved it from John Fat Gai's office a few nights ago."

She moved fast, lunging for my hand.

"Give it to me. Give it to me at once. I must have it. I'll pay you. I'll pay you whatever you want."

Birdie intercepted her and gently moved her back to where she was. The cat had screeched then retreated into a corner folding itself into a large ball of white fluff.

"We don't want your money, Mrs. Sorenson."

"What do you want?"

"Just the truth, that's all. Simply the truth."

"What is that? I'm not sure I know anymore."

"Eight years ago, at Blackstones, Gayle and Alison were met by John Fat Gai's henchman, Quan, and hustled inside. Henry Turner stayed in the car. But then Henry became curious and worried. He decided to go inside and found a horrifying scene. There was Alison, your daughter, John Fat Gai and the corpse of a newborn infant. Something had happened to it…"

She shook her head back and forth, pressing her handkerchief to her mouth then her nostrils. "I think I'm going to be ill," she said. "Please call Effie for me…"

Birdie strode toward the door, flung it open and disappeared.

"It was your grandchild, wasn't it?" I said as gently as I could while mouthing such gut-wrenching words.

She nodded once.

Her body heaved with sobs and I thought she might break apart, shatter into pieces. The maid, Effie, rushed into the room and wrapped her arms around the stricken women, shushing her, stroking her to calm her down.

"Haven't you done enough," she snapped. "Can't you see what this has done to her?"

"It wasn't just that the baby died, though, was it? Something happened to it, to this helpless infant. That baby was strangled at birth…"

Mrs. Sorenson wailed. "She didn't know what she was doing. She was drugged and out of her head…please, please…"

"That's why Gayle had a nervous collapse. She murdered her own child."

"All right," Mrs. Sorenson said. "All right…yes…yes…yes…is that what you want to hear? Yes, she did it. She did it She did it…" and collapsed into a heaping, sobbing mess comforted by the elderly maid who glared at me with unrestrained hatred. That also surprised me. How the lower classes maintained such a strong bond of loyalty to their masters.

"What are you doing to my mama?"

I turned. Gayle, still dressed in her tutu and slippers, hair disheveled, eyes blazing, held a carving knife in her right hand and a broken doll in her left. Her child. She raised the knife as she advanced. The blade looked razor sharp and gleamed in the subdued light.

"You leave my mama alone. Leave her alone." She moved like a streak. I turned but stumbled over the coffee table. Gayle leapt into the air screaming like a banshee, brandishing the knife; I saw the point descend.

"Gayle! No! No!" her mother screamed.

A large hand caught Gayle's wrist and twisted the knife away. It skidded across the carpet toward the cat. It let out a growl then scooted out of the room like a shot. Birdie held the kicking, screaming hellion.

She tried to slash him with her nails but he held her off the floor where she was helpless. Her mother ran to her.

"Gayle honey…my darling…no…no…mommy's here….mommy's here. It will be all right. Come to me, my darling. Come to me…" she murmured.

Gradually, Gayle subsided. Birdie set her tentatively on the ground. Mrs. Sorenson folded her into her arms and walked her back to the couch where she and Effie stroked and whispered to her. Gayle buried her face in her mother's neck and sobbed.

Finally, Mrs. Sorenson looked at me. "What's going to happen now? What are you going to do, Mr. Gold?"

I looked at her feeling drained.

"We're not the police, Mrs. Sorenson. We don't have to do anything. Get her some help. Find a place for her where she'll be helped and where she can't harm anyone else. I'm sure you can get your physician to aid you. She's killed two people in the most savage manner but no jury would convict her. They'd see she was deranged but they could send her away to a prison hospital forever. I don't think you want that. These are, well, they aren't pleasant places, let's put it that way. You might want to get yourself a good lawyer just in case. The cops may come around asking questions. I suggest you take Gayle away before they find their way to your door, Mrs. Sorenson."

She stroked Gayle's hair. "Thank you," she whispered.

"Don't thank me. There's been enough suffering, don't you think? Maybe Gayle can heal some day. You never know."

Bringing it out into the open didn't make me feel any better. In some ways, it made me feel worse. Birdie and I rose.

"Goodbye Mrs. Sorenson and good luck."

Her head was bent over her daughter, softly crooning what sounded like a childhood lull-a-bye.

She stopped us in the cavernous hallway, her blue eyes piercing like cold rays of light. I shivered. Her uniform rumpled. Her face ashen.

"Those men. They destroyed her." We didn't move. "They didn't care if she was pregnant. They used her until they had their fill then threw her away like a piece of trash. She didn't know what she was doing. How could she?"

"I'm sorry."

Hatred infused her. "If I was 10 years younger, I'd kill them all myself for what they did to her, what they did to my baby. I'm glad they died." Tears rolled down her flaccid cheeks. "She was my baby. I cared for her. Looked after her since she was born. I'd kill them, I tell you. With no regrets. Look at her now. Look at her now." The elderly maid sank to the floor and sobbed for her own lost child.

We found our own way out. Stepping out of the gloom into the light, I took a deep breath. After the stale air we'd breathed, it felt good. The weight of the film canister pulled at my pocket. It wasn't just that though and this is something I didn't even tell Birdie.

Last night, after leaving Troyer's place, I went to Sully's gym. In the back, he kept a banged up projector for watching footage of old fights. Fights he'd been in and fighters he'd managed. I threaded the film into the machine, and watched what was on it. John had been clever, showing the girls in full view but never the men. There were a number of sequences with Alison Foster and Gayle Sorenson and also, a number of other girls I didn't recognize.

You could see an outline of the man, sometimes hear a few words. It didn't take much for me to know and it made my stomach lurch. Jake had been one of them. He'd been with Gayle. I didn't have any doubt whatever. My old man may have been the father of her doomed child. My little half-brother or sister murdered by a sick teenager who'd been drugged then assaulted by him. It felt like poison in my veins. I wanted to open myself up and let it all seep away.

For a second, I steadied myself on the rod iron railing.

"You okay?" Birdie asked.

I looked up into his concerned face. The face of a magnificent African prince.

"Yeah," I said. "I'm fine." I handed him the car keys. "You drive."

I fished out a Sweet Cap and lit it, drawing the smoke into my lungs and expelling it like pollution.

Later that night, I parked the Chevy outside Evelyn's apartment. I held a dozen roses in my left hand, a mickey of Scotch in my right. I struggled to open the door. I stood on the sidewalk and took a final glance at myself in the side view mirror. Tie adjusted, hair combed, face shaved. A taxi pulled up opposite. The fares emerged. I heard drunken laughter. A tall black man put his arm around Evelyn's shoulders as she helped him up the stairs to her door. She teetered on her heels. The short cocktail dress rode up her rump. I stepped back into the shadows. She fumbled with the key. He made a joke. She laughed again. The door opened and they stumbled inside. I crossed the street, mounted the steps then hesitated. Instead of pounding on the bell, I lay the roses across the threshold. I hefted the mickey of Scotch in my right hand. Company for the evening. I'd been a fool to take her for granted. A damned fool. I descended the stairs, crossed the street, got into the Chevy and drove home.

What had I whispered to John on the ship's deck? I told him that he'd been responsible for the deaths of many men but of all of them, only the soul of a murdered infant would haunt him for eternity. At first, he didn't respond. Then he said that Gayle had moved too fast for him to stop her. That it was regrettable. A moment later, he blew up the ship.

The next morning, I sat at my desk reading the Telly about the Argos latest calamity. I drank coffee from a paper cup. Half a Danish sat in its paper wrapper in front of me. Birdie leaned up against the credenza whistling under his breath swinging his polished shoe back and forth so that the toe scraped the floor. He had his bible out and leafed through it idly.

"Argos lost again," I said.

Birdie laughed. "Sure they did." He held up the bible. "They need some divine intervention."

The downstairs bell jangled. Another client climbed on up.

About the Author

W.L. Liberman believes in the power of storytelling but is not a fan of the often excruciating psychic pain required to bring stories to life. Truthfully, years of effort and of pure, unadulterated toil is demanded. Not to sugarcoat it, of course, writing is a serious endeavor. It is plain, hard work. If you've slogged away at construction work, at lumberjacking, delivery work, forest rangering, sandwich making, truck driving, house painting, among other things, as I have, writing is far and beyond more rigorous and exhausting. At the end of a long, often tedious, usually mind-cracking process, some individual you don't know pronounces judgment and that judgment is usually a resounding 'No'. This business of writing is about perseverance and stick-to-it-iveness. When you get knocked down and for most of us, this happens frequently, you take a moment to reflect, to self-pity, then get back at it. You need dogged determination and a thick skin to survive. And an alternate source of income.

W.L. Liberman is currently the author of eight novels, two graphic novels and a children's storybook. He is the founding editor and publisher of TEACH Magazine; www.teachmag.com, and has worked as a television producer and on-air commentator.

He holds an Honours BA from the University of Toronto in some subject or other and a Masters in Creative Writing from De Montfort University in the UK. He is married, currently lives in Toronto (although wishes to be elsewhere) and is father to three grown sons.

Manufactured by Amazon.ca
Bolton, ON